SEANAN McGUIRE

ONCE BROKEN FAITH

AN OCTOBER DAYE NOVEL

DAW BOOKS, INC.
DONALD A. WOLLHEIM, FOUNDER
375 Hudson Street, New York, NY 10014

ELIZABETH R. WOLLHEIM
SHEILA E. GILBERT
PUBLISHERS
www.dawbooks.com

Published by DAW Books, Inc.
375 Hudson Street, New York, NY 10014

First Printing, September 2016
1 2 3 4 5 6 7 8 9

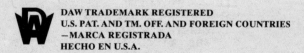

DAW Books presents the finest in urban fantasy from Seanan McGuire:

This book is for Margaret.

There are many books in the world, but this one is hers.

ACKNOWLEDGMENTS:

It's sometimes a little surprising for me to realize that we're ten books into this adventure, but here we are, and here we go, and we've traveled so far, and we have so far yet to go. Thank you for coming along with me. I promise I'll do things to make sure you get back safely.

A novel is never a solo undertaking, no matter how much it may feel like one. My thanks go to the Machete Squad, for their tireless attempts to make me better, and to the entire team at DAW, where they take excellent care of me. Thanks to the Agora, for hosting me, and to the staff of Disney's Old Key West resort, where chunks of this book were written. (Fun fact: the last book partially written at the Old Key West was *Late Eclipses*.)

Thank you Vixy, for continuing to be the star I steer by; Amy, for being ready to defend me at the crossroads; Brooke, for keeping me from destroying North America in a fit of pique; and Shawn, for cheering when I say I'm going to write the X-Men someday. Thanks to Alexis and Mary, for math and music, and to Randy, for grilled cheese and Target.

Sheila Gilbert remains the best of all possible editors, Diana Fox remains the best of all possible agents, and Chris McGrath remains the best of all possible cover artists. While we're on this track, my cats are the best of all possible cats. So are yours, if you have them. All hail the pit crew: Christopher Mangum, Tara O'Shea, and Kate Secor.

My soundtrack while writing *Once Broken Faith* consisted mostly of *After It All*, by Delta Rae, *1989*, by Taylor Swift, the soundtrack of *Hamilton*, endless live concert recordings of the Counting Crows, and all the Ludo a girl could hope to have (barring a new album). Any errors in this book are entirely my own. The errors that aren't here are the ones that all these people helped me fix.

It wouldn't be a party without you.

OCTOBER DAYE PRONUNCIATION GUIDE
THROUGH ONCE BROKEN FAITH

All pronunciations are given strictly phonetically. This only covers races explicitly named in the first nine books, omitting Undersea races not appearing or mentioned in book ten.

Afanc: *ah-fank*. Plural is "Afanc."
Annwn: *ah-noon*. No plural exists.
Bannick: *ban-nick*. Plural is "Bannicks."
Barghest: *bar-guy-st*. Plural is "Barghests."
Blodynbryd: *blow-din-brid*. Plural is "Blodynbryds."
Cait Sidhe: *kay-th shee*. Plural is "Cait Sidhe."
Candela: *can-dee-la*. Plural is "Candela."
Coblynau: *cob-lee-now*. Plural is "Coblynau."
Cu Sidhe: *coo shee*. Plural is "Cu Sidhe."
Daoine Sidhe: *doon-ya shee*. Plural is "Daoine Sidhe," diminutive is "Daoine."
Djinn: *jin*. Plural is "Djinn."
Dóchas Sidhe: *doe-sh-as shee*. Plural is "Dóchas Sidhe."
Ellyllon: *el-lee-lawn*. Plural is "Ellyllons."
Gean-Cannah: *gee-ann can-na*. Plural is "Gean-Cannah."

Glastig: *glass-tig*. Plural is "Glastigs."

Gwragen: *guh-war-a-gen*. Plural is "Gwragen."

Hamadryad: *ha-ma-dry-add*. Plural is "Hamadryads."

Hippocampus: *hip-po-cam-pus*. Plural is "Hippocampi."

Kelpie: *kel-pee*. Plural is "Kelpies."

Kitsune: *kit-soo-nay*. Plural is "Kitsune."

Lamia: *lay-me-a*. Plural is "Lamia."

The Luidaeg: *the lou-sha-k*. No plural exists.

Manticore: *man-tee-core*. Plural is "Manticores."

Merrow: *mare-oh*. Plural is "Merrow."

Naiad: *nigh-add*. Plural is "Naiads."

Nixie: *nix-ee*. Plural is "Nixen."

Peri: *pear-ee*. Plural is "Peri."

Piskie: *piss-key*. Plural is "Piskies."

Puca: *puh-ca*. Plural is "Pucas."

Roane: *row-n*. Plural is "Roane."

Satyr: *say-tur*. Plural is "Satyrs."

Selkie: *sell-key*. Plural is "Selkies."

Shyi Shuai: *shh-yee shh-why*. Plural is "Shyi Shuai."

Silene: *sigh-lean*. Plural is "Silene."

Sluagh Sidhe: *sloo-ah shee*. Plural is "Sluagh Sidhe."

Tuatha de Dannan: *tootha day danan.* Plural is "Tuatha de Dannan," diminutive is "Tuatha."

Tylwyth Teg: *till-with teeg*. Plural is "Tylwyth Teg," diminutive is "Tylwyth."

Urisk: *you-risk*. Plural is "Urisk."

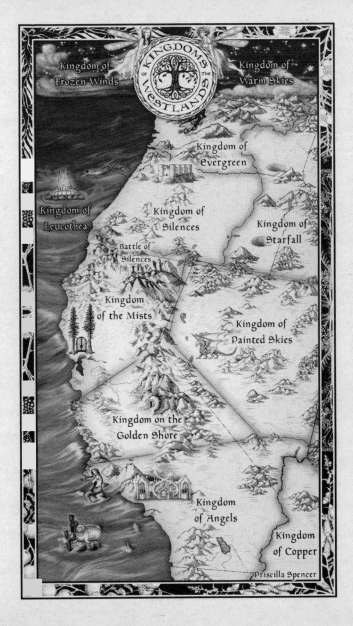

KINGDOMS OF THE WESTLANDS

Kingdom of Frozen Winds

Kingdom of Warm Skies

Kingdom of Evergreen

Kingdom of Leucothea

Kingdom of Silences

Kingdom of Starfall

Battle of Silences

Kingdom of the Mists

Kingdom of Painted Skies

Kingdom on the Golden Shore

Kingdom of Angels

Kingdom of Copper

Priscilla Spencer

ONE

June 5th, 2013

For trust not him that hath once broken faith.
—William Shakespeare, *King Henry VI, Part III*

QUENTIN AND RAJ were in the living room arguing about who got to pick the first movie of the night. Loudly. The walls and doors between us were thick enough to blunt their voices—mercifully—but I could still hear more than enough to know that I didn't want to get involved. I crossed my arms and leaned against the counter, casting a wry look at the kitchen door.

"All right," I said. "Somebody remind me again why we're doing this, and why I'm not drowning them both in the bathtub."

"Drowning Quentin would be an act of treason against the Westlands, and you'd probably be executed," said May. "Also, you'd miss him." She never took her eyes off the tray of cookies she was removing from the oven. My Fetch had been baking since she got out of bed. She hadn't slept much since she'd been elf-shot during our visit to the Kingdom of Silences—she got better, thanks to alchemical intervention—and that meant we had a *lot* of cookies. We didn't have anything near enough for the nightmare that was to come, but still. A *lot* of cookies.

The oncoming disaster didn't keep Jazz from snatching a cookie from the tray and retreating to the kitchen table, juggling her purloined treat from one hand to another the whole time. "Drowning Raj would be an act of treason against the Court of Dreaming Cats, you'd miss him, *and* Tybalt would look all sad and noble right before he put you through a wall."

"Actually, I think if Toby drowns Raj, she's just proving he was unfit to rule, which means it's not treason, it's natural selection. Sort of like you burning your mouth on that cookie is your punishment for stealing it. Tybalt would still probably be pissed, though." May began shifting the remaining cookies to the cooling rack. Jazz stuck her tongue out. May laughed.

I stayed where I was, avoiding the danger of molten chocolate chips, and grinned to myself. "Oh, right," I said. "I remember why I agreed to this." After months—after *years*—of chaos and life-threatening situations and people stabbing me for no good reason, we'd somehow managed to find a moment to breathe. That didn't just deserve to be enjoyed. It deserved to be celebrated, held up as proof that the world was a good place and didn't actually need to be destroyed in order for me to have a nap.

It used to be that I could have all the naps I wanted. Of course, back in those days, I had few friends, no prospects, and the life expectancy of a stray dog. These days, I have plenty of backup, and no time to sleep. As a knight errant and hero of the realm, any time something goes wrong, it's likely to become my problem. I'm the go-to girl for terrible adventures, whether I like it or not. Usually not. But things had been pretty calm since my allies and I returned home from overthrowing the puppet government of the Kingdom of Silences. Sure, we'd only been back for six weeks, but I'd take it. It was a hell of a lot better than nothing. I was safe and healthy, my chosen family was safe and healthy, and it was time to stop and smell the flowers.

Just not the roses. I have a bad track record with roses.

The argument in the living room was starting to get really heated. I was considering the wisdom of intervention when the doorbell rang. There was a moment of startled silence before both boys shouted, "I'LL GET IT!" in perfect unison. Then they started sniping at each other again. I pushed myself away from the counter.

"Let's see if I can answer the door before they finish deciding which one of them gets the honor," I said.

May snorted. "The future leadership of the Westlands, ladies and gentlemen."

I left the kitchen and walked down the hall, laughing all the way. Maybe most people don't have dueling princes in their houses, but this is my life, and I've had time to get used to it. I've even had time to learn to appreciate it. After all, the princes in question were my squire—Quentin Sollys, who will one day be the High King of the Westlands, the fae Kingdom that encompasses North America—and my fiancé's adopted nephew, Raj. Since I can't imagine the world without both those boys in it, I can put up with a little shouting.

My name is October Daye. My father was a human; my mother was, and is, a Firstborn daughter of Oberon, making her one of the more powerful people among the fae, and a definite pain in my still-mortal changeling ass. I was born and raised in San Francisco, which explains my willingness to stay in a city that's historically been full of people who insist on trying to kill me at the slightest provocation. Faeries are real. Magic is real. My tendency to greet dangerous situations by plunging in headfirst and seeing how long it takes to get myself covered head to toe in blood is also real.

I live an interesting life.

The front door was warded to the point of

redundancy. Had whoever was on the porch been human, the warnings about their identity would have reverberated through the house, giving the rest of us time to get any necessary illusions in place. May was the most human looking of our weird little band, and she'd be the one answering the door when the pizzas showed up. In the meantime, since the warnings hadn't sounded, I was able to unlock and open the door without messing around trying to spin a passable disguise.

My friend Stacy was on the porch with her middle daughter, Karen. At fourteen-going-on-fifteen, Karen no longer looked much like her mother; in fact, the resemblance seemed to decrease year on year. Her skin was milky pale, in contrast to Stacy's healthy peach, and her hair was the color of birch-bark, save for the tips, which looked like they'd been dipped in ink. Her ears were dully pointed, more like a bobcat's than a Daoine Sidhe's, and tufted with fluffy puffs of hair that followed the same black into white pattern as the hair on her head. She was clutching a pillow to her chest. In the interests of expedience, she was already wearing her pajamas, thin cotton patterned in colorful dinosaurs and flaming comets. She was also wearing a bra. That was still relatively new, and hence relatively unsettling. For me, Karen would always be the eleven-year-old I'd saved from Blind Michael's lands.

Stacy beamed. Karen glanced upward through the fringe of her hair, flashed a shy smile, and went back to looking at her feet.

"Do I smell cookies?" asked Stacy.

I laughed and leaned forward to steal a quick hug before ushering both of them inside. "May's been baking like a mad thing for hours. I think she's afraid we'll be stripped to the bone by a mob of wild teenagers if she doesn't generate enough unhealthy snacking material."

"Oh, she's right," said Stacy gravely. "I'm just glad you're the one hosting the slumber party for a change.

The last time Anthony played host, I wound up with an empty fridge and two broken windows."

"I don't understand why you always call them 'slumber parties,'" said Karen, glancing up again. "You're picking me up at dawn. That's *hours* before bedtime."

"Blame our terrible human upbringings, and enjoy the free cookies," I said. "Do I get a hug?"

Karen smiled, less shyly this time, and moved to hug me. "Hi, Auntie Birdie."

"Hey, puss," I said, and kissed the top of her head.

Fae kids are like human kids in many ways. They need love, approval, protection, and occasionally to be sent to their rooms to think about what they've done. That doesn't mean they *are* human kids. For one thing, fae kids tend to be nocturnal. Karen wasn't shining a light on bad parenting when she said dawn was hours before bedtime: she was making a statement of fact. Like most of her contemporaries, she probably went to bed around eight or nine in the morning, and then slept for the normal teenage ten to thirteen hours before getting up and starting her "day."

Karen's hair smelled of off-brand shampoo, which I dismissed as irrelevant, and of the cottonwood and quince signature of her magic. The notes had only been becoming really clear over the past few years. Her father, Mitch, was a halfblooded changeling—human mother, fae father—and her mother, Stacy, was a quarterblood, which meant Karen had started with less than the normal percentage of fae blood. It made sense that her magic was weak enough to have taken a long time to clarify. What didn't make sense was the fact that Karen was an oneiromancer, a dream-walker—one of the first to be seen in Faerie for centuries.

That's the thing about fae. We're always full of surprises. Karen tolerated my hug for a few seconds more before squirming away and asking, "Who's here?"

"You're the first to arrive," I said. The boys didn't

count. Quentin lived with me; Raj was at the house enough that he may as well live with me. "Quentin and Raj are in the living room. Stacy? You want a cup of coffee or something before you head home?"

"Can't," she said apologetically. "Jessica has therapy."

"Oh." I nodded. "All right. Well, give the family my love, and call if you need us to get Karen home."

"I will," said Stacy. She hugged me quick, and then she was gone, ghosting out the front door without another word.

Karen and I exchanged a look. Karen spoke first. "Mom's worried about Jess."

"Yeah," I said. "Is she getting any better?"

Karen shook her head. "No."

"Damn." I took a deep breath, trying to force my worries down. They didn't go easy. "Well, let's get you to the party, okay?"

"Don't be silly," said Karen serenely. "It's not a party until I arrive."

I laughed and pointed her down the hall. She trotted off, disappearing into the front room. A moment later the timbre of the ongoing argument shifted. I smiled. "A new challenger has arrived," I murmured, and walked back toward the kitchen.

Stacy Brown and I have been friends since we were younger than Karen was now, two frightened changelings clinging to each other in the mercurial landscape of the Summerlands. I don't know that I would have survived long enough to run away from home if it hadn't been for Stacy. Her happy ending had always been about family: finding someone who'd love her and help her raise a house full of changeling children. Karen was the third of five. An impressive achievement by human standards; a virtually unheard of achievement by fae ones. Which had just made things worse when Blind Michael decided to Ride through the Bay Area, snatching three of the Brown children in the process.

Andrew had been so young at the time that he seemed to have emerged mostly unscathed. He still had nightmares sometimes, but having an older sister who could walk in dreams meant he never felt like he was alone. Karen had returned from Blind Michael's lands quieter, more serious, and more aware of her powers. And Jessica . . .

In some ways, Jessica still hadn't made it home. She was terrified of the dark. She was even more afraid of any sort of wavering or flickering light. She wet the bed, she woke up screaming, and she refused to be in a room with me. Even though she knew intellectually that I'd saved her, part of her had associated me so absolutely with Blind Michael that she couldn't be near me. It was hard. I tried to understand, I really did, but . . . that didn't make it easy.

It was almost a relief to step into the kitchen and find myself looking at a glittering portal in the air. The smell of sycamore smoke and calla lilies had been lain over the top of the more ordinary chocolate chip cookies. I blinked. Then I grinned.

"Guess that potion wore off, huh?"

"Hi!" A girl's head popped around the edge of the portal, black-haired and copper-eyed and beaming. She looked pleased with herself. I couldn't blame her. "Oh, gosh, it really worked, didn't it? Dad! Dad, I opened a door to San Francisco!"

"What?" Etienne sounded equal parts bemused and concerned. He stepped into view, automatically centering himself on the portal. His expression turned nonplussed when he saw me. "Oh. Hello, October."

I didn't bother to muffle my grin, which was only getting wider. "Hi, Etienne. I see that everyone's powers are back to normal."

"Yes, the potion wore off as scheduled . . . I'm sorry about this. I thought we'd agreed that she would wait to open a gate to your home until *after* I had called to get your consent." He slanted a quick, irritated glance at Chelsea—but all the irritation in the world couldn't conceal his pride. He was still pretty new to the whole "father" gig, having only learned that he had a teenage daughter the year before. For most of that time, Chelsea's natural abilities had been suppressed by an alchemical tincture. Now it was gone, and she was showing her dad what she could do.

"Raj invited me," said Chelsea. "I haven't been to a slumber party in *years*."

"Chelsea?" As if the sound of his name had summoned him, Raj appeared behind me, standing straighter than normal, like he was trying to make himself look taller. His cheeks reddened at the sight of her, but his expression remained as imperiously calm as ever. "I see the homing stone I gave you has worked as intended. We have chips and dip in the front room."

"Come on, Dad, can I go through? Please? Pretty please? The gate looks stable, it's not going to snick me in half or anything, pleeeeease?" Chelsea turned fully to her father, expression pleading. Only the rolled-up sleeping bag under her arm spoiled the illusion of absolute need. Like Karen, she was wearing pajamas. Unlike Karen, her pajamas were patterned with spaceships and planets.

"It appears stable," said Etienne. "First, you must ask Sir Daye for permission. It is never appropriate to use a gate to enter a knight or noble's home without their consent."

Chelsea sighed, looking briefly like the teenage girl she was. Then she turned to me, and said, with perfect courtly grace, "Sir Daye, may I answer your invitation and cross the threshold from my halls into yours?"

It took everything I had to swallow my grin. May was less successful, but as she was out of Chelsea's line of sight, she probably wasn't trying as hard. "Yes, you may,"

I said. "Come on through. We're going to order the pizza in about half an hour."

"Yes!" Chelsea jumped straight through her transit gate, spinning on her toes to wave at Etienne and chirp, "Bye, Daddy! I'll see you in the morning!" She waved her hand, making a closing gesture, and the gate slammed shut before Etienne could get another word in.

"I don't know whether that was slick or rude," I said.

"It doesn't matter," said Raj, grabbing Chelsea's wrist and hauling her out of the kitchen without leaving her time to do more than wave to the rest of us. The argument in the front room changed timbre again only a few seconds later.

I looked at May. She grinned. I grinned back.

"Okay, this was a fantastic idea and we should do it every week," I said. As if on cue, there was a knock at the back door. I crossed the kitchen to answer it.

Dean Lorden—slightly older than the rest of our guests in chronological terms, slightly younger in terms of experience with the world outside the Undersea—was standing on my back porch, a backpack slung by one strap over his left shoulder. He was dressed in his usual Court clothes, which meant he looked a little old-fashioned, like he'd just stepped out of the 1920s and didn't understand the concept of "denim." He looked unsettled.

"Marcia drove you, huh?" I guessed.

"She says I need to get used to riding in cars if I want to live in the human world," he said, and stepped inside. He released the illusion making him look human as soon as he was over the threshold, adding a layer of eucalyptus and wet rock to the bizarre mix of magical scents already hanging in the air. His clothes remained the same; only his features shifted, becoming sharper and indefinably inhuman. He was a handsome kid, with his mother's sand-colored skin and his father's bronze hair, complete with a patina of verdigris highlights. His eyes were dark blue, like the sea at night, and his ears tapered to sharp points. He'd be a heartbreaker when he got a little older.

I was just hoping the heart he chose to start with wouldn't be Quentin's. Dean and my squire had been seeing each other for a few months. I wasn't sure yet whether "dating" was the word. Dean had grown up in the Undersea, and I had no idea what their formal courtships looked like; Quentin was a pureblooded scion of the Daoine Sidhe, destined to become High King of the Westlands. He'd dated once before, a human girl named Katie. It hadn't ended well. As long as he and Dean were being careful with each other, I was fine with their relationship, but the second I felt like someone was going to get hurt, I was going to . . .

Oak and ash, I didn't know what I was going to do. This was all outside my realm of experience, and I was as confused as everyone else.

May handed Dean a plate of cookies. "Take these to the front room," she said. "Everyone will be delighted to see you."

He smiled shyly. "Okay," he said. To me, he added, "You have a lovely home." Then he was gone, following the sound of shouting toward the rest of the party.

I walked over to one of the unoccupied kitchen chairs and collapsed into it. "Five," I said mournfully. "There are *five* teenagers in my house right now. Who thought this was a good idea? It can't have been me. I have more common sense than that."

"No, you don't," said May, setting a fresh-baked chocolate chip cookie down in front of me. "If you did, you wouldn't be you."

"I hate you all," I muttered, and reached for the cookie.

Someone knocked on the back door.

Slowly, we all turned toward the sound. Jazz spoke

first. "I thought everyone was here already," she said warily.

"And Tybalt doesn't knock," said May. "He just sort of shows up. Like the plague." ·

"Tybalt is busy at his court tonight," I said, standing. Being engaged to a King of Cats has come with its share of adjustments. Getting used to the idea that sometimes he wasn't going to be available, no matter how much I wanted him to be, had been one of the bigger ones. Raj was his chosen heir. Because of that, for Raj to have an official "night off"—as opposed to all the nights he spent unofficially hogging the remote and eating all my food— Tybalt needed to be with his people. It was going to get interesting when the time came to go out of town for our wedding. Raj was going to be *livid* if he didn't get to come, but I couldn't see any way the Cait Sidhe were going to go for that.

"Should I get your sword?" asked May, eyeing the door.

"It's in the car."

"Again?" She shifted her gaze to me, now admonishing. "A sword won't keep you safe if it's in the trunk of your car."

"True, but it won't be used to gut me in my own home, either." I pushed my shirt back enough to show her that I had my silver knife, and finished crossing the kitchen to the door. "Who is it?" I called.

"Um, Arden," was the reply. "Can I come in?"

I glanced over my shoulder at May, wide-eyed. She and Jazz were staring at me, looking about as baffled as I felt. I turned back to the door and unlocked it, pulling it open to reveal Arden Windermere, Queen in the Mists, regent of Northern California, standing on my back porch. She was wearing a black T-shirt with the Borderlands Books logo on the front, along with a pair of dark jeans and battered white tennis shoes. A human disguise blunted her features and removed the purple highlights from her hair, although her eyes remained mismatched, one brown, one gray trending into silver.

"Uh," I said.

She mustered a faint smile. "Yeah, I know," she said. "Can I come in?"

It abruptly hit me that I had the Queen at my back door, asking for my permission to enter. The Queen, who was Tuatha de Dannan, and hence fully capable of opening a portal into my kitchen and stepping through without so much as a by-your-leave. This was not a situation my etiquette classes had prepared me for. To be honest, it wasn't a situation I'd ever thought about. Maybe I should have.

"Sure," I said, and stepped aside.

Like Dean, Arden released her human disguise as soon as she was inside, filling the air with the scent of redwood sap and blackberry flowers. Her hair turned the color of ripe blackberries, while her eyes lost their mortal hues, becoming pyrite and mercury instead of brown and gray. Her ears were pointed like Dean's, but the shape of them marked her as Tuatha de Dannan as clearly as a sign would have. There was no mistaking her for anything but what she was.

She waited for me to shut the door before she said, "I'm here both as a courtesy, and to request a favor. Which would you like first? And where is your, ah, squire?"

Arden had learned Quentin's true identity at the same time I had: when he convinced her that being a princess wasn't the worst thing in the world, and that she owed it to her Kingdom to take the crown. That knowledge made her one of a small circle of people who'd been trusted with who he really was. May and Jazz knew, of course, and so did Raj. Dean might or might not; that was Quentin's choice to make. But I knew Chelsea and Karen didn't. Well. Karen might. She'd walked in his dreams, after all. "He's in the front room. Should I get him?"

"Oberon's eyes, no," she said, her own eyes widening in alarm. "He can't hear what I'm about to say."

I raised an eyebrow. "I know I'm a hero of *this* realm and all, but if you're here to plot sedition against the King of the Westlands, I want to be the first to say that it's probably not a good idea. Like, it's a really *bad* idea. I'm out of the king-breaking business. After getting stabbed in the heart the last time, I'm planning to stick with missing persons and the occasional murder for at least a year."

"I'm not plotting sedition," said Arden.

I started to relax.

"Much."

I stiffened again.

"Maybe this is me being out of touch with the modern realities of life in Faerie, but last time I checked, you couldn't be a little bit plotting sedition," said May. "It's like being a little bit pregnant. Sure, you think it'll be fine, but next thing you know, it's all diapers and daggers and who's your monarch."

Arden blinked slowly at her before turning back to me. "We've been waiting for High King Sollys to approve the use of Master Davies' elf-shot cure before we woke anyone else."

"I know," I said carefully. In this context, "anyone else" meant Madden, Arden's Cu Sidhe seneschal, and Nolan, her younger brother. "Because we're trying to avoid destabilizing the region. You know. More than we already have."

"He sent word at sundown that he won't approve use of the cure until there's been a proper conclave of local monarchs to discuss the matter. He'll be here next week."

"... Oh." Quentin's father was coming here? Quentin didn't know. Quentin *couldn't* know. He would have told me, even if he was trying not to. My squire was many things. Good at lying to me wasn't one of them. He'd managed to keep the truth about his parentage secret for as long as he had only because there had never been any reason for the subject to come up: his being Crown Prince wasn't going to impact me for years, if ever. His dad coming to town was something else entirely.

"I need you to come back to Muir Woods with me," said Arden. "Walther is already there, but he says he won't do anything without you."

"Anything like what?" I asked. I knew, really. There was only one thing she could want badly enough to risk pissing off the King of the entire continent. She had come to me effectively hat in hand, dressed like the mortal she'd been living as when we met, because she wanted this so badly. And she knew that she couldn't order me to help her do it.

"I need you to come back to Muir Woods with me," she repeated. "I need you to be there, so that Walther will wake up my brother and my best friend before the High King gets here, realizes he left a loophole in his orders, and makes it illegal."

I glanced to May and Jazz. They both nodded silently. I looked back to Arden and sighed.

"Let me get my coat."

TWO

ARDEN HAD COME IN through the back door, but as soon as I got back to the kitchen, it became clear that she wasn't planning to leave that way. She inscribed a wide arc in the air with her left hand. A portal opened in the air, accompanied by the sudden, sharp smell of blackberry flowers and redwood sap. Through it, I could see the entry hall of Arden's knowe in Muir Woods.

Right. "I'll be back soon," I said, shrugging my leather jacket on and tugging the collar into place. It was always chilly in Muir Woods. Call it a side effect of being close to the sea. "Remember to tip the pizza delivery guy, and try to avoid anything getting stuck to the ceiling."

"On it," said May, with a brief salute. "You crazy kids have fun now."

I didn't have time to respond before Arden was stepping through the portal, grabbing my right wrist and hauling me with her. The world shifted, performing the dizzying dip and wheel that always seemed to accompany point-to-point transportation, especially when it involved moving between the mortal world and the Summerlands. I pulled away from Arden, bending forward to put my hands on my knees and breathe away the dizziness.

"Come on," she said, making no effort to hide the urgency in her tone. "Get up, we have to hurry."

"And I have to breathe, so hang on." I pulled in a lungful of air. It went straight to my head, as Summerlands air often did. It was cleaner, purer than its mortal world equivalent: Faerie mostly skipped the industrial revolution, although we had our blacksmiths and tinkerers. Widespread air pollution just wasn't a thing in the Summerlands. Sometimes I wondered if that was the cause of my dizziness when I made the transition. My body was still too human to deal easily with the lack of toxins.

Arden stayed nearby, shifting her weight from foot to foot in a way more reminiscent of the teens currently invading my home than of a Queen in her own Kingdom. Then again, Arden didn't have much experience with Queenship, having been in the position for less than a year—ten months, at my last count. Prior to that, she'd been living a quiet mortal life, keeping her head down and concealing herself from the fae out of fear that she'd be assassinated or elf-shot by the imposter who was sitting on the throne that rightfully belonged to the Windermere line. Arden's father, King Gilad Windermere, had never married, choosing to hide his consort and heirs for their own safety. I guess he'd assumed that he'd have time to claim them publicly, when they were old enough to deal with the slings and arrows of royal life.

It hadn't worked out that way. He died, leaving them unprotected. Nolan had been elf-shot by the forces of the woman who was claiming to be Gilad's rightful heir. And Arden had gone into hiding, where she'd remained until I tracked her down and dragged her, kicking and screaming, back to her birthright. She didn't seem to be holding a grudge about that, but it was sort of hard to tell, given that since she'd taken the throne, she'd formally named me as a hero, sent me to act as a diplomatic attaché to a hostile neighboring Kingdom, and was now asking me to help her go against the wishes of the High King.

Okay, scratch that. She was *definitely* holding a grudge.

I took another breath, getting my balance back before I stood upright again. "Okay," I said, tugging my leather jacket straight to cover the last of my dizziness. "Where are we going?"

"This way." She spun on her heel and stalked deeper into the knowe, gesturing for me to follow.

The knowe in Muir Woods belonged to Arden's father before his death. Someone had sealed it after he died and she disappeared, keeping it from the clutches of the false Queen. Its continued existence had been our first real clue that Arden was still out there somewhere, waiting to be found. Without a member of the Windermere line to anchor it, it should have faded back into the Summerlands, becoming inaccessible from the mortal world. Instead, it had waited, patient as a faithful hound, certain that its master would return. Now, with her in full-time residence and her people working to open, restore, and decorate the place, it was slowly returning to the majesty it must have possessed before King Gilad's death.

Which was very inspirational and all, but knowes were living things that didn't have to play by the normal rules of linear space and sensible architecture. Every time I came to visit, the place seemed to have grown larger, and half the new rooms didn't make any sense in relation to the rooms around them. The entry hall was relatively static, for which I was grateful. Everything else was anybody's guess, and I've never been a fan of guessing games.

Arden led me down the entry hall to a narrow doorway and through that doorway to a winding stairway that seemed to stretch upward for the better part of forever. On the mortal side of the knowe, the whole vast estate was just a crude door in a redwood tree, surrounded by more on every side. Here in the Summerlands, the redwoods remained, although these were fae trees, never threatened by loggers or pollutants. Consequently, they'd grown even taller than the giants of the mortal California coast. They were interspersed with the equally tall spires of the castle battlements and towers. We were inside one of those towers; I realized that before we passed the first window and I saw the woolly red bark of the trees growing outside.

"Where are we going?" I asked.

"Patience," said Arden, and kept climbing.

Most of the responses I wanted to offer to that would have been inappropriate, especially considering that she was the Queen and I didn't want to be banished. Again. I bit my tongue and kept climbing, following the curve of the stairs up, up, up, until we came to a short landing. The stairs continued upward. Arden ignored them, opening the door on the landing and revealing a wooden walkway wending off into the trees. I inched close enough to see that we were at least fifty feet above the ground. The forest floor was a distant, far-off dream.

"Nope," I said, taking a step backward.

Arden turned to me, raising her eyebrows. "What?"

"I said, nope," I said. "Not going out there. No. Would I survive a fall from that height? Sure. I've done it before. I'd just lie there screaming while I waited for my bones to knit back together. No big deal, except for the part where no way in hell am I going out on that thing. That's what, three feet across and made of untreated redwood? In this fog? That's going to be as slippery as a Merrow's ass, and I'm not going to do it."

"I need you to come with me," said Arden. She seemed puzzled, like she couldn't understand why I wasn't jumping to obey.

"You're getting better at this whole 'monarch' thing, but no," I said. "I know my sense of balance, I know how often I get hurt, and I know it's not a good idea to tempt fate. I'm not going out there."

"Oh, for the love of Maeve," muttered Arden. She

took a step toward me. I braced myself for the inevitable attempt to haul me through the door. Instead, she waved a hand in the air before shoving me backward, through the portal that had opened behind me. I stumbled, caught off-guard—

—and emerged in the middle of the treetop walkway. As I'd feared, the wood was slick from the fog hanging around us, and my sneakers slipped slightly before I managed to catch my balance and go still. Standing dead center, there was only about a foot of wood to either side of me. It would be so easy to fall. So very, very easy to fall.

Arden stepped through the portal, which closed behind her, and looked at me. "There," she said. "They say the first step is the hardest, and so I've spared you that much. Now will you come *on*?"

I gaped at her. "Root and branch, you can't be serious right now." I waved one arm as much as I dared, trying to indicate the area around us without attracting the attention of gravity. "Bridge! Very long drop! If you can teleport me *here*, why can't you just teleport us to where Walther and your brother are waiting?"

"Because Master Davies says the potion he's brewed to counter the effects of elf-shot is delicate, and if we want it to have the best shot of working, we shouldn't do any magic in the room," said Arden. "No illusions, no gateways, nothing. I want them awake. That means we're not doing anything to endanger that."

"If you drop me off a bridge, I'm pretty sure Walther is going to be a little reluctant to wake up your brother!" I don't have a fear of heights. I have a healthy respect for heights. I really, really respected the fact that a fall from this height would hurt like hell, even if it probably wouldn't kill me. My particular bloodline came with accelerated healing, to the point that I'd survived being stabbed in the heart, and had probably drowned on at least two occasions. That didn't mean I didn't feel pain. If anything, it meant I felt pain *more*, since I could heal from my initial injuries before I finished receiving the next ones down the line.

"I'm not going to drop you off the bridge," said Arden. She was starting to look seriously annoyed. "Calm down and follow me. This is a perfectly safe walkway. No one's fallen since I took over."

"So people fell before you took over?"

She sighed. "My father had a lot of Cornish Pixies on his staff. They fell because they liked it. Look, you'll have to walk the same distance to get back to the stairs as you will to get to our destination. But if you turn and walk away from me, you'll have traveled that distance while also pissing off your regent. Do you really want to do that?"

"Dirty pool, Windermere," I said, narrowing my eyes.

"Madden is my best friend. Nolan is my brother. Those two, those two sleeping men, they are everything I have. You're the reason I had to give up my mortal life, remember? No more job at the bookstore, no more coffee with Jude and listening to Alan grumble about cleaning up after customers. I am not," she held out her hands, palms toward me, "running away from my responsibilities again. You said I got one shot at trying to quit, and I took it, and you were right. I can't do that again. But I have no one who *knows* me, October. Lowri is doing a fine job as my stand-in seneschal, but you know what she calls me?"

"Going to go with 'Your Highness,'" I said cautiously.

"Sometimes she gets informal and shortens it to 'Highness,'" said Arden. "I'm a crown to her, not a person. She doesn't know what I like to read, or care about how I made a living while I wasn't in charge. My time among the humans, it's like . . . it's like she thinks it's some weird kind of zoological expedition. I went out, I watched them, and then I came back home where I belonged. And she's the best of them! She's just about the only person who even bothers to pay attention to things like how uncomfortable I get when Court goes for more than six hours. I'm not threatening to run again, I'm *not*, but I don't know how long I can do this without someone around here who can call me on my bullshit."

"I'm calling you on your bullshit right now," I said. "I really don't want to plummet to my death today."

"You'll get better."

"I'm still not a fan of plummeting."

Arden sighed. "We're not friends, Toby. Maybe we can figure out a way we can be. Maybe we can't. You're always going to be the woman who hauled me back into this world."

"And barring death, dismemberment, or abdication, you're always going to be the queen," I said. "I get it."

"No, you don't," she said. "Do you have any idea what it's like to go from a life where things aren't perfect, but you're always surrounded by people who care about you, to being alone? Even when I'm surrounded, I'm *alone*."

I went cold. "I think I have a better idea than you know," I said.

In 1995, I was engaged to a human man named Cliff Marks. He and I had a two-year-old daughter. I was working as a private investigator, mostly taking on fae clients who wouldn't realize how little training I'd actually had. I had friends. I had a family. I had a future planned out, stretching ahead of us like a road to peace and prosperity. And I lost it all in a single moment, when Simon Torquill—my liege lord's brother, my mother's husband, and technically my stepfather—transformed me into a fish and left me in the Japanese Tea Gardens to be forgotten. He'd been trying to save my life. I'd remained there for fourteen years. Not long, by pureblood standards. Not even that long by changeling standards. But for humans like Cliff? For little girls like Gillian, who didn't even know she had fae heritage? It was forever. They had never taken me back.

Maybe the life I had now was better than the one I would've had if not for that day. There was no way of knowing, and honestly, it wasn't a question I liked to dwell on. I'd found a new family for myself, and I was happy. But before I was happy, I'd been very, very miserable.

"Then you should understand why I have to do this," said Arden. "I've been patient. I kept thinking he'd tell me to go ahead, that he'd say, you know, Master Davies is a citizen of the Mists who was traveling to Silences on official business, and if it was okay for him to wake up the citizens of Silences, he should be allowed to do the same at home before we start talking about bottling up and hiding his cure. But he didn't say that, and I can't wait any longer."

I took a deep breath. Held it. Let it out. "All right," I said finally. "Lead on."

As long as I kept my eyes on the back of Arden's head, I didn't have to think about how high up we were, or how close I was to falling every time I took a step. For all that she'd spent most of her life in the mortal world, she moved along the impossibly long walkway without hesitation or visible distress. Being a teleporter probably had something to do with that. If she fell, she could open a portal and land in her own bed, cushioned by feather pillows, entirely unbruised. I didn't have that sort of safety net.

We reached the next tower in surprisingly short order. Arden opened the door and held it while I stepped through. Moving past me, she offered a strained smile, said, "That wasn't so bad, now, was it?" and started up another stairway, identical to the one we'd left behind.

I swallowed my first response. Just to be safe, I also swallowed my second response, and followed her up the stairs. They terminated at a landing barely wider than one of the steps. She knocked.

"It's open!" called Walther.

Arden took a deep breath, squared her shoulders, and opened the door.

The tower room where Madden and Nolan slept couldn't have been farther from the basement King Rhys had used to store the elf-shot victims in Silences. It was round, airy, and circular, with wide windows set in the walls between the beds, open to allow the night air to flow through. Walther had apparently been serious about his "no magic" rule; there were no witch-lights or charmed lanterns. Instead, he'd set up several halogen camping lights around the edges of the room, creating the odd impression that we'd just stepped onto a film set. That was the only reason to light the place so unforgivingly.

There were eight beds arrayed like the spokes of a wheel. Only two were occupied, one by a burly man with white hair streaked in carnal red, the other by a man whose blackberry-dark locks and olive skin betrayed him as Arden's brother. Madden, who'd been asleep for less than two months, was wearing jeans and a T-shirt. This was still his time. Nolan had been asleep a lot longer. He was dressed like he was planning to roll out of bed and head for a *Great Gatsby*-themed party, down to his suspenders and polished shoes. He'd been elf-shot in the 1930s. His nap was nearly over. I still understood why Arden felt like she couldn't wait any longer, especially now that Madden had joined him. She needed her support system. I couldn't imagine going a hundred years without mine.

Walther was standing between the two beds, spinning a fine rosy liquid in a wine snifter like he was a sommelier and we were here to enjoy a pleasant dinner while surrounded by coma patients. He turned at the sound of the door opening, and looked relieved at the sight of me. That was a fun change. "Toby," he said. "I was afraid you weren't going to come."

"Why, because this might technically be an act of

treason against the High King, and hence a good way to wind up locked in gaol for the next, oh, twenty years?" I shrugged like it was no big thing as I strolled into the room and sat down on one of the empty beds. It wasn't as soft as it had looked from a distance, more like a bier than a bower. I blinked. "Wow. Orthopedic?"

"It wouldn't do to have your sleepers wake up in need of a chiropractor," said Walther, with a tight smile. I smiled back, trying to look sympathetic and encouraging at the same time. He was in a tough spot. If he refused Arden—who was, after all, the Queen of the Kingdom he was currently living in—he could wind up banished. Not the end of the world, but he'd been working for a while to get tenure at UC Berkeley, and a change of address would mean starting all over again. If he didn't refuse her, he could be pissing off the man in charge of the entire continent. No wonder he'd wanted me present. I was his security blanket.

Walther was originally from the Kingdom of Silences to the north, overlapping the human state of Oregon. His aunt and uncle were the rightful rulers of the place, and he'd been raised, along with his sister Marlis, under the expectation that he'd eventually become one of their court alchemists. Only there'd been a war, and his family had lost the throne for a hundred years. During that time, Walther had fled to avoid elf-shot or enslavement— the two fates that befell the rest of his family—and had eventually become a chemistry teacher. The work suited him. He would probably never have gone back to Silences if I hadn't dragged him.

Good thing: going back to Silences had resulted in his family regaining their place. Better thing: we'd come away with a functional cure for elf-shot, the purebloods' weapon of choice when it came to waging war. Little enchanted arrows that could put a person to sleep for a century. Problem: having a cure changed everything. We'd barely managed to get home before the edict had come from the High King, asking us to keep the cure secret while he decided what to do next. And now he was coming here, which was a whole new problem.

Arden cleared her throat. "The beds were designed by a Coblynau crafter who knew what would be best for our sleepers," she said. "Now let's wake those sleepers *up*."

"Before High King Sollys gets here and says absolutely not, don't do it," I said.

She shot me a sharp look. I shook my head.

"I came when you asked me to. That means I'm going to be in just as much trouble as you are. More, it means I'm supporting you in this. If he asks, 'Did Queen Windermere wake her brother after I told her not to?' I'll tell him the truth, but I'll also tell him you had a good reason to do what you did. That doesn't mean I'm going to pretend you had permission." I turned to Walther. "You have a queen and a hero, which is another word for 'scapegoat,' telling you to go ahead and wake them up. So go ahead. Wake them up."

"You're also the only person I know who's been elf-shot twice and can still give orders," said Walther. He gave his rose-colored liquid one more swirl and turned to Arden. His posture shifted with his attention, becoming formal and serious. Arden hadn't been kidding about the way people behaved when they were talking to royalty. "Who would you like me to wake first, Highness?"

"My seneschal," she said, without hesitation. "Madden will want to know what happened, and Nolan is going to need a lot more catching up."

Walther nodded, and moved to Madden's bedside, bending to press the lip of his wine snifter against the other man's lips. He placed his free hand under Madden's head, bringing it a few inches up from the pillow, so that gravity would be working on his side. I wanted to ask how he could be sure that Madden wouldn't choke, but I held my tongue. Walther had already managed to wake me, May, and his entire sleeping family. He knew what he was doing.

After a moment, he pulled the snifter away and stepped back, letting Madden's head return to the pillow. I risked a glance at Arden. She had folded her hands and pressed them beneath her chin, eyes wide and solemn as a child's as she watched.

Seconds ticked by, and everything was silence and the growing scent of roses. I shivered. Elf-shot had been created by Eira Rosynhwyr, the Firstborn of the Daoine Sidhe, and the countercharm was made using roses that matched the precise smell of her magic. Eira and I have . . . calling it "a history" seems too simple, but I don't know how else to describe a relationship defined by her lying to me and me being so eager for approval that I'd never seen the signs. She's dangerous. She's terrifying. She's asleep, thanks to her own elf-shot, which once would have meant she was out of the way for a hundred years. Now, with Walther's cure in play, there's no telling when she'll wake up. So no, I do not care for the scent of roses.

Madden sighed. It would have been unremarkable, but he'd been elf-shot, and people sleeping under an enchantment don't sigh. Arden clasped her hands tighter. He yawned. And then, like it was the most ordinary thing in the world, he opened his eyes.

"That's not the sky," he said, sounding puzzled. "I was outside a second ago. Why isn't that the sky?" He sat up, frowning at Walther. His eyes flashed wolfish gold. "Do I know you?"

"Madden!" Arden dropped her hands and flung herself at him, slinging her arms around his neck.

Madden caught her easily, taking his attention from Walther in order to frown at his friend and liege as she buried her face against his shoulder. "Ardy? What's wrong? Why do I feel like I missed something?"

"That's an excellent question," said a semi-familiar voice. My heart sank.

It kept sinking as I turned to see High King Aethlin Sollys standing in the doorway. He was wearing a charcoal-gray tailored suit that would have looked perfectly appropriate on a San Francisco street corner. His tie was wine-red and snowy white: the colors of the Westlands. He wasn't wearing a human disguise, allowing the points of his ears and the burnished bronze color of his hair to show. His eyes were sunrise red, and narrowed as he watched Arden and Madden's embrace.

"Why," he said, echoing Madden's words, "do I feel like I've missed something?"

THREE

ARDEN SCRAMBLED TO EXTRICATE herself from Madden's embrace, wiping the tears from her cheeks with quick, almost shamed swipes of her hand. She positioned herself so that her body blocked Walther and Madden from the High King. It was a noble gesture. It was also a futile one—she was a slender girl, and Madden alone could have made two of her; there was no way she could shield them from Aethlin's regard—but the fact that she was willing to try made me feel a little better about the situation. A little. Not nearly enough, especially since she wasn't shielding *me*.

"Your herald said we should expect you next week, Your Highness," said Arden. Her voice was thick with tears and worry. "I apologize that I was not prepared for your arrival."

"Really? It looks to me as though you were taking advantage of every moment you believed you had before I got here," said High King Sollys. He raised an eyebrow, looking briefly so much like his son that it hurt. This man, tall and regal and terrifying, was Quentin's future. This was his *birthright*. No matter how much I enjoyed having him with me, I was only ever going to be a way station on his path to the throne.

If that was dismaying for me as his knight, how did it feel for Dean as his boyfriend? Had they even talked about it? Dating is hard for the children of the nobility. Maybe that's why they have formal courtships. Putting all those layers of formality and obligation in the way of casual dating made things easier on the heart.

Arden bit her lip, and didn't move. "Please. I didn't mean to defy you. I just . . ."

"Madden was elf-shot by an agent of Silences as part of the declaration of war against the Mists," I said. High King Sollys looked at me. I forced myself to remain casually seated on the bed, resting the bulk of my weight on my hands. Every etiquette lesson I'd ever been given was screaming for me to stand, but that was exactly why I couldn't do it. If I kept things informal, maybe he'd do the same. "Everyone else who was elf-shot during the failed attempt at a coup has been woken up. He would've been, too, if we hadn't been so quick about telling you what was going on. It was fair."

"Sir Daye," said High King Sollys. "Of course you're involved. I'm not sure whether you know this, but 'fair' and royal decrees are rarely acquainted with one another."

"Maybe they should be," I said. "He's awake now. What are you going to do, ram another arrow into his arm to punish Arden for disobeying you? Maybe it's just me, but that seems kind of extreme, especially since the only thing he ever did wrong was stand by the woman who rightfully inherited the throne in the Mists, instead of supporting the woman who should never have been confirmed as our Queen."

It was a small but calculated dig. Aethlin flinched as it hit home. When the 1906 earthquake had left King Gilad dead and Arden and her brother in hiding,

Evening Winterrose had been right there to present a
"lost heir" who could take the throne and stabilize the
region. The High King had been dealing with a lot of
things when all that went down. By the time he got to
the Mists, it had basically been a done deal, and he'd
confirmed a pretender. Arden's life among the humans,
beneficial as it may have been for her in some ways,
was entirely his doing. I wasn't going to let him forget
that.

"I asked you not to act before I arrived," he said,
looking back to Arden. "As it seems you woke your seneschal while I was being ushered into your halls, you've
done as I asked. I'll be more precise in my requests from
now on. No one else is to be awoken until we have discussed the proper use and distribution of the elf-shot
cure. Do I make myself clear?"

"Yes, sire," said Arden. She glanced at her sleeping
brother, mouth twisting, before she returned her attention to the High King. "You are very generous."

"And you're in a difficult position, Queen Windermere. If I seem generous, it's because, as Sir Daye says, I
understand that your current lack of experience with our
politics is partially on me. You're learning as you go. I
won't punish you this time. Or perhaps your punishment
will be hosting this conclave. As for you, Sir Daye . . ."
High King Sollys turned to me.

I offered him my best, brightest smile. "I should get
ice cream and a pony as my reward for preventing another war."

"You should be commended for your role in preventing the war between the Mists and Silences; we'll speak
of that later," he said. "Unlike Queen Windermere, you
do not have the excuse of ignorance to shield you from
your own actions. You knew what I intended by my instructions, and you allowed it anyway."

"She's Queen, I'm not," I said. "I don't 'allow' Arden

to do anything. I just try really hard to minimize its impact on the people around me."

Arden wasn't saying anything in my defense. I couldn't blame her for that. If she spoke, she might attract the High King's attention again, and worse, he might decide to censure Walther or Madden, neither of whom was at fault here.

"Still, you can't be allowed to flaunt my decrees just because you don't feel like arguing with your regent," he said. The corner of his mouth was turning upward, like he was fighting a smile. Somehow, that didn't make me feel any better. "I'm afraid I must order you to attend the conclave, as you need to understand what your actions could have done. Bring your squire. I'm sure it will be educational for him."

I resisted the urge to glare. This wasn't about punishing me: this was about getting Quentin to the conclave without blowing his cover. Never mind that anyone who looked at my squire next to the High King was likely to start asking questions about Quentin's blind fosterage. There was no way a responsible regent could pass up this kind of learning opportunity for a king-to-be.

"I'll clear my calendar," I said, standing and bowing deeply. "So this has been fun and everything, but I'm supposed to be hosting a slumber party for a bunch of teenagers right now, and I'd like to get back to it before they burn my house down. May I be excused?"

"Certainly," said High King Sollys, with a broad wink. He turned to Arden. "I'm assuming you brought Sir Daye here?"

"Yes, sire," she said. She scribed a wide arch in the air with one hand. Apparently the injunction against magic was no longer in effect if she wasn't getting ready to wake her brother. A portal appeared at the center of the room, showing a lovely view of my back yard. It was a good call. The yard was sheltered from mortal eyes, which meant I wouldn't need to embarrass myself by fumbling with my clumsy illusions in front of the High King, and since it wasn't inside, she didn't need to worry about freaking out any of my guests.

"Sir Daye?" said Aethlin, looking back to me. "I believe your road home is open." .

"I see that," I said. "Mind if I take Walther with me? May's making cookies. He loves her cookies."

"You may take the alchemist," said the High King.

Walther put his wine snifter down on the nearest table and all but bounded to my side, clearly as eager to be out of there as I was. I reached for his hand, ready to pull him through with me, and paused as High King Sollys cleared his throat.

"The alchemist—Master Walther Davies, is it not?" He paused long enough for Walther to nod before he continued, "Master Davies will also be required to attend the coming conclave, as it's his work that will be under discussion. You will make yourself available to us, yes?"

"Yes, sire," said Walther, with a quick bow. His voice was tight, and I knew he was thinking about his class schedule, what he could move or pawn off on grad students without endangering his students. Teaching chemistry might seem mundane compared to, oh, being a knight errant of a fae kingdom, but he took it very seriously. That was part of what made him so good at his job, and such a skilled alchemist.

"Good," said the High King. "You are both excused."

He was turning back to Arden as I yanked Walther through the portal, which slammed closed behind us. She was probably going to get a lecture, and I was fine with that. She'd disrupted my evening and caused me to be compelled to attend a political event. She deserved to be yelled at a little.

The night air was warm and scented with my neighbors' honeysuckle, which was blooming so violently that it seemed likely to rip down the trellis where it grew. I let go of Walther's hand, coughing as I inhaled a great lungful of smoggy mortal air.

"I appreciate the save," he said, pulling his glasses out of his pocket and putting them on. They were nonprescription, intended to blunt the unnatural blue of his eyes. The color bled through his human disguises, making him seem inhuman no matter how hard he tried. "I had no idea how I was going to get out of that room."

"I sort of figured," I said. "Do we need to give you a ride home? May and Jazz don't know that I'm back yet. I could probably sneak away."

"I have my own transportation." Walther reached into his coat and pulled out a bundle of yarrow twigs, holding them up with a wry smile. "It's a nice offer, but I'd like some time to think about what just happened."

"Sure," I said. "Come by any time, and I guess I'll see you at the conclave, whenever that is."

He nodded. "See you there." Then he positioned the bundle of twigs so that it was basically under his butt, kicked off from the ground, and flew away.

Sometimes life in Faerie is deeply, deeply weird. I unlocked the back door and let myself inside.

The kitchen was a disaster zone. Empty pizza boxes were piled on the counter, someone had spilled nacho cheese on the table, and May was in the process of mixing a batch of Rice Krispie treats, if the smell of hot marshmallow was anything to go by. She blinked when she saw me. I blinked back.

"I was gone for less than an hour," I said. "How did you make this big of a mess? And where's Jazz?"

"At the store; we ran out of ice cream," said May. "As for 'how did we make this big of a mess,' there are five — count them, *five* — teenagers in the other room who were told that for tonight, they got to be normal. Not in charge of anything, not afraid of anything, not learning how to exist in a strange new world, just normal. So they tore through the kitchen like a buzz saw, made nachos when they realized that we'd foolishly failed to order enough pizza for an army, and now they're in the living room watching Disney movies."

Her voice rose a bit on the last two words, breaking like she was struggling not to laugh. My eyes widened. "Oh, sweet Maeve, you're not serious."

"I am." She nodded solemnly. "I am serious. They are enjoying the animated stylings of the Walt Disney Corporation. Dean has never seen a cartoon before."

"He had Internet in the Undersea."

"Sure, but he lacked the cultural context to tell him why he should want to waste his time watching movies about things that weren't real." May glanced to the kitchen door as she lost her battle against her grin. It spread across her face like she was in the process of becoming a Cheshire cat, until it seemed like she was nothing but the smile. "That poor, unfortunate soul."

"Yeah, his mother's going to kill us." I walked over and stole a finger-scoop of Rice Krispie treat.

Dean's mother, Dianda Lorden, was the Duchess of Saltmist, the neighboring Undersea demesne. She was also a Merrow, which meant that in human terms, she was a mermaid—just like humans would lump me, Arden, and Walther all under the banner of "elf," if they knew that we existed. Dianda was amiably violent, as seemed to be the norm among Undersea nobles. She was either going to find us showing her son *The Little Mermaid* hysterically funny or incredibly offensive and, sadly, I didn't know which way she was likely to go.

"What happened with Arden?" May sounded concerned. I couldn't blame her.

"Good job waiting to ask that until I'd been home for five minutes," I said. I took a breath. "Remember how she said the High King was coming next week, so she needed to wake Madden and her brother up now if she wanted to be certain she'd be able to give them the cure?"

May nodded. "It was less than an hour ago, so yes."

"She woke Madden up. That was all we had time for before the High King walked in."

May audibly gasped. "He's already here?"

"Yeah," I said grimly. "He's not going to punish her for waking Madden, but he's forbidden her to wake Nolan. As for me, my punishment for helping her go against his wishes is attending the conclave—*with* Quentin. I'm guessing he was planning to convince-slash-command me to do that anyway, since this is the sort of thing Quentin really ought to see. Doesn't mean I'm thrilled. What's the dress code for a conclave?"

"Since you're unlanded and attending as a witness and observer, you should be fine with whatever you'd normally wear to a court function," said May. "Bring your knife, but be prepared to surrender it at the door."

"Wouldn't it be better not to bring a weapon if they're just going to take it away from me?"

"Not really." May resumed stirring her Rice Krispie mixture. The marshmallow had begun to set. The treats resisted her machinations. "By bringing a weapon, you show that you're willing to defend the conclave. By giving it up, you show that you trust your hosts to protect you, and your fellow attendees not to need stabbing. It's a show of good faith. It also means that if day one goes really well—or really poorly—they might let you keep your knife on day two, because you'll have earned the right to go armed."

"Pureblood hospitality gives me a headache," I grumbled, snatching another piece of gooey cereal.

May shot me a sympathetic look. "It's designed to be learned over the course of decades and refined over the course of centuries. It's not your fault that you don't take to it naturally."

"I wish you could go instead of me."

"I'll probably go in addition to you," said May. I blinked at her. She shrugged, beginning to spoon her cereal mixture into a serving dish. "Apart from the fact that I was one of the people elf-shot in Silences, I have a long, long memory. None of the people whose lives I consumed had been elf-shot themselves, but some of them had lost friends and loved ones that way. One man, his wife was elf-shot and still decades away from waking when we came for him. He died with her name on his lips, and I put his face on to finish it. Elf-shot is supposed to be merciful, but I'm pretty sure it's not. I want to see how this goes."

"Oh."

May was my Fetch: a night-haunt who had consumed the blood of the living and transformed into a duplicate of that person when the time came to play death omen. She'd expected her long, long life to end when she became my mirror, and she'd done it anyway, because the night-haunts lived vicariously through the people whose corpses they ate, and the last person she'd consumed had been a girl named Dare. Like me, Dare had been trained as a street thug by Devin, a modern day Fagin crossed with Peter Pan. Unlike me, she'd never been able to escape the gravity of his attention. Dare died thinking I was her hero, and that thought had been enough to influence the night-haunt who took on the bulk of her personality. She had chosen to die a second time, all for the sake of warning me that my own life was coming to an end.

Under normal circumstances, May would have appeared, I would have died, and she would have vanished, dissolving into mist and the smell of rain. Instead, my mother, Amandine, had intervened, changing the balance of my blood for the first time in my adult life. Somehow, that had cleansed the elf-shot that was killing me from my body, and transformed me just enough to break the tether tying May's existence to my own. She was something unique now, a Fetch with nothing to bind her. And while the bulk of her memories were taken from either me or Dare, sometimes she'd say things to remind me that she was so much older.

I sighed. Speaking of things that were older . . . "Do you have everything under control down here? I think I need to give the Luidaeg a call, let her know what's happening, and tell her the High King is in town." She might already know. She was often surprisingly well-informed—or not so surprisingly, given that she was the sea-witch, Firstborn daughter of Maeve, and fully capable of grilling the local pixie population for news. Still, she'd appreciate hearing it from me, and it was always good to avoid getting on her bad side.

"Go, go," said May, making a shooing gesture with her free hand. "I can control the ravening hordes for a while longer. I think they're enjoying the lack of adult supervision."

"You're the best," I said, and grabbed one more chunk of Rice Krispie treat before leaving the kitchen and heading up the stairs to my room.

San Francisco is one of the most expensive cities in the world, and getting worse as the tech boom moves more and more multimillion-dollar human companies into the business district. Jazz owns a secondhand shop in Berkeley. May works there occasionally, when Jazz needs the help, and spends the rest of her time doing whatever strikes her fancy. My PI work brings in a reasonable amount, although very few nobles ever think to pay me for knight errantry. Quentin mostly eats whatever appears in the fridge and spends his time learning how to be a better ruler. So how is it that we're able to afford a two-story Victorian near Dolores Park, in a rapidly gentrifying neighborhood?

Simple: my liege, Duke Sylvester Torquill, has been in the Bay Area for centuries, and owns enough land in San Francisco to make the snootiest of human tech millionaires sit up and salivate. We live rent-free, and the foundation he'd established to handle mortal upkeep of his properties paid the taxes. It's a sweet setup. It would be even sweeter if I didn't feel so guilty about it. Sylvester and I were ... not estranged, exactly, but not exactly speaking to each other, either.

He's my liege. He's supposed to be straight with me. He's supposed to be the person I could trust no matter what. And he'd destroyed that in the name of keeping a promise he'd made to my mother before I'd even been born. He hadn't lied to me according to pureblood standards, which were often more fixated on the letter of the law than on anything else, but as far I was concerned, a lie of omission was still a lie. He'd withheld a lot of information from me—information that could have helped me understand my past and protect my future—and he'd done it because he cared more about his word to Amandine than about his word to me. Maybe I have trust issues. I think I've earned them. That doesn't change the fact that Sylvester, who I had trusted with everything, had still been willing to betray me.

No matter how I currently felt about Sylvester, I loved our house. It was *home*. I'd been trying to find my way home for a long, long time.

My cats, Cagney and Lacey, and my resident rose goblin, Spike, were curled on the bed when I stepped into my room. Of the three of them, only Lacey bothered to open an eye, although she didn't move. They had clearly fled before the onslaught of teenage invaders, and had no interest in doing anything that could bring them back into the line of fire. I smiled at them as I closed the bedroom door.

"It's okay, guys," I said. "Nobody's going to follow you up here."

Lacey closed her eye.

Pulling out my phone, I sat on the edge of the bed and dialed a long string of numbers, tracing a spiral pattern from one to five and then back out again. The smell of cut-grass and copper rose around me as my magic responded to the intent in my gesture. I lifted the phone to my ear, listening to the silence.

"To market, to market, to buy a fat hen," I chanted. "We'll cook it and then we'll be hungry again, which is why I really appreciate the easy availability of KFC in the modern world."

The magic gathered and broke around me, and the silence was replaced by the soft, distant sound of waves lapping against the shore of some tropical lagoon. I leaned back on the bed and waited.

There was a click, and suddenly a woman's voice was in my ear, snarling, "Who is this, and why am I not juggling your internal organs right now?"

"Hi, Luidaeg; it's Toby," I said. "Got a moment?"

"Toby!" Her tone shifted, becoming warm—even welcoming. We hadn't always been friends, but our relationship was, at this point, built on a foundation of mutual respect and saving each other's asses. That was enough to buy me a positive reception. "Quentin's sleepover party is tonight, isn't it? Why did you call it that, anyway? It's not like they're going to sleep."

"Human teenagers don't usually sleep during these parties either," I said. "It's an excuse for them to hang out in their pajamas, eat lots of junk food, and not have to worry about going outside. Call it an artifact of my weird upbringing and let it go."

"Right," she said. "If I ever needed more proof that you were Dad's descendant, you filling your home with those kids would do it. That's heroism of the stupid kind. Please tell me you're not calling because you want me to come over and help you deal with them. I'd just turn them all into axolotls until the sun came up."

"Peaceful, but probably stressful," I said. The Luidaeg can't lie. That meant she *could* turn both my resident and visiting teenagers into axolotls. I wasn't even sure what those were, but I was pretty sure I didn't like the idea. "That's not why I'm calling."

"No? What impossible quest are you planning to embark on now?"

"I'm skipping the impossible quest in favor of attending the High King's conclave to discuss what's going to happen with the elf-shot cure." I explained the situation in quick, terse sentences, leaving nothing out, but not embroidering either. The Luidaeg didn't like it when people danced around the point. I guess a few millennia of listening to lies, bullshit, and pointlessly florid pureblood etiquette had eroded her patience.

When I was done, she said, "Well."

"Yes."

"That's a thing."

"Yes."

"A thing which is actually happening."

"Probably."

"You realize I'll be showing up to watch the fireworks, right?"

I sat up a little straighter. "What?"

The Luidaeg sighed. "Much as I hate my sister—and trust me, *no one* hates my sister like I do—she's still Firstborn. Elf-shot was her gift to our father, to curry favor with him when she was out of his good graces. I applaud unmaking it. I think this is a good thing. But that doesn't mean I can sit by while the work of one of the First is unmade, and not at least come for the sake of witnessing the process. I won't speak on her behalf. I won't try to suppress this cure. I'm still going to come, and watch, and see."

The Luidaeg was the eldest among the Firstborn. Almost everyone I'd ever met was afraid of her, and with good reason: she was terrifying when she wanted to be. Having her at the conclave would make a lot of people very uncomfortable. That alone would make the proceedings more entertaining, at least for me. But if the Luidaeg was planning to show up . . .

"Should we be worried about other Firstborn deciding they need to come sit in the audience?"

She was quiet for a moment before she said, "Acacia might. She's been getting out more, and I know that some of Blind Michael's Riders have been elf-shot and locked away by people who didn't see any other means of protecting their children. She could come just to see if she'll be able to free the last of her husband's victims. Your mother isn't likely to show up, if that's what you're worried about. Amandine never considered herself Firstborn, and she doesn't care enough about the work of her elder siblings."

"I don't know if I'm worried about seeing Mom so much as I just really, really don't want to."

"If she does decide to come, that'll give me the opportunity to drag her away by the ear and ask what the fuck she thinks she's doing. It'll be okay, Toby. This isn't an army marching on the Mists. This isn't a case you have to solve. It's just a bunch of nobles coming to puff their chests out at each other and try to look important. Do what I do. Bring popcorn."

I smiled. Maybe it was weird to be reassured by the words of a woman who could remember the rise and fall of almost every mortal civilization, but my life has never been particularly normal. "Okay," I said. "See you there."

"Yup," she said, and hung up.

I lowered my phone, looking at it thoughtfully for a moment before I stood. The kids probably didn't want my company, but May might, and there were Rice Krispie treats. It was time to focus on the ordinary, for as long as the world allowed.

FOUR

BY SEVEN IN THE MORNING all the kids except for Quentin and Raj had been collected by their guardians. They slunk home with sugar-glazed expressions and doggie bags of leftovers. Etienne was going to learn a lot about nacho cheese over the course of the next day or so. I sort of wished I could be there for that. Quentin and Raj, meanwhile, had retreated to Quentin's room for an *actual* slumber party, meaning they were *actually* going to sleep. Raj's tendency to sleep in feline form meant they could both fit in a single bed, which was nice. One trip to the Mattress Outlet with the family had been enough to hold me for a decade—or until the mattresses needed replacing, whichever came first.

Please let it be the decade.

I turned out the last of the lights and drew the last of the curtains before retreating to my room. The house was blissfully quiet. The air smelled like fresh-baked cookies, a combination of burnt sugar and chocolate that would linger for hours yet. Jazz had gone to bed shortly after one o'clock in the morning, pleading the fact that she was diurnal. May had gone to join her at dawn.

Now it was my turn. I shut my bedroom door and

started toward the bed, unbuttoning my jeans as I walked. It was rare for me to be the only person awake in the house. I reveled in the feeling.

The smell of pennyroyal and musk cut through the scent of cookies, telling me that I wasn't alone after all. That was all the warning I got before Tybalt's hands grasped my waist, turning me to face him. I saw him smile, and then he was pulling me close and kissing me so fiercely that it was like we hadn't seen each other in weeks. It had only been hours, but I wasn't complaining. I slid my hands up his chest and linked them behind his neck, not hesitating as I kissed him back. A purr reverberated through his body, vibrating my skin and reinforcing the feeling that this, just this, was proof that I was finally home.

If someone had told me right after I stumbled out of the pond that I'd eventually fall in love again, I might have believed them. After all, the heart is a hardy organ: it heals, it moves on. If that same someone had added "with the asshole King of Cats," I would have laughed until I threw up, and then probably started punching people. Tybalt wasn't my friend back then, much less a potential lover. He was a bastard and a bully who took too much joy in tormenting me for me to even consider the possibility that one day I'd start keeping company with him.

It's funny what time can do. Bit by bit, I'd come to realize that Tybalt's barbs were less about cruelty and more about keeping me at arm's length, where I couldn't hurt him—something I'd never imagined I could do until I was doing it. We'd traded a few kisses almost accidentally, and then, with no real fanfare or warning, we'd been in love. Me, the changeling street rat, and him, the handsome Cait Sidhe monarch. Maybe it shouldn't have worked, but it did, and it had become one of the rocks I put my trust in. The sun rose; the tide turned; Tybalt loved me.

He slid his hands down to cup my ass, pulling my feet off the floor. I responded by kicking my feet up and wrapping my legs around his waist, making it easier for him to carry me to the bed. There was an aggravated yowl as one of the cats protested. I didn't look to see which one it was. I was distracted by Tybalt's hand in my hair and Tybalt's lips on my throat, and then I didn't pay attention to anything but him for a little while. Who could blame me?

One major advantage to living in the Victorian, rather than my old two-bedroom apartment: much thicker walls, and much less chance of someone wandering in to see what all the fuss was about.

Afterward, naked and sweaty and pleasantly loose in that way that followed strenuous exercise, I stretched and rested my head against Tybalt's chest, closing my eyes. He was purring again. I couldn't think of a more comforting sound.

"I take it you missed me, little fish," he said, playing his fingers through my tangled hair.

"Excuse me?" I rolled over, opening my eyes and squinting at him. "Who jumped who here? I ask not because I'm complaining, but because I think it's important we keep the sequence of events as clear as possible."

He chuckled. "Ah, but you see, had you not missed me, you wouldn't have responded so ardently to what could have been merely a simple hello. I kiss you quite often. Most of the time, you're capable of kissing me back without dislodging your undergarments in the process."

"You waited until I was taking my pants off!"

"An accident of timing." He waved a hand, dismissing my protest. "There's no need to be ashamed. Were I fortunate enough to be engaged to me, I would take every opportunity to get me to bed."

"You are such a cat sometimes." I yawned, snuggling down and closing my eyes again. "Did you have a good night at Court?"

"I did. Nothing of much interest happened, which is always the ideal; better a night where my people are free to make their own entertainment than a night where I must race from place to place, extinguishing fires and praying we'll live to see the morning. Alazne is finally able to hold her human form for more than an hour at a time. Opal and Gabriel are very proud, and hope you'll be able to come and visit soon."

"I'd like that."

"And you? Was your night a welter of teenage vexations and not enough quiet? I saw the kitchen when I first got home. The fridge appears to have been attacked by wild beasts."

I couldn't suppress the thrill that went through me when Tybalt referred to reaching the house as getting home. Eyes still closed, I said, "Oh, the kids were great. They showed Dean *The Little Mermaid*. I'm expecting Dianda to call it a declaration of war and slaughter us all in our sleep. Arden came by, dragged me back to Muir Woods, and used me to get Walther to go ahead and wake Madden up before the High King got here. Only just before—he's in the Mists now, he's holding a conclave next week to discuss how they're going to distribute the elf-shot cure, and—oh yeah, right—I'm expected to attend. Are you going to be there? I know it's going to involve the neighboring Kings and Queens, but I'm not sure what involvement the Cait Sidhe would have with something like this."

Tybalt was silent. Seconds stretched out like taffy until I opened my eyes, disturbed by the sudden weight of the air. I rolled over and sat up in the same motion, gathering the sheets up around my collarbone as I turned to look at him.

He was worth looking at, under any circumstances. Most fae are either beautiful by human standards or completely alien and inhuman, covered in leaves or feathers or spines. Tybalt managed to straddle the line between the two. His face was lovely; his body was better. But his pupils were cat-slit narrow, against irises the banded color of malachite, and there were black tabby stripes in the brown of his hair. When he was distracted or distressed, as he was now, more stripes appeared on his skin. They were visible as I faced him, curving up the sides of his ribs and wrapping around his arms.

"Tybalt?" I said.

"If the conclave is to be held next week, it's reasonable that no invitation has yet been sent to us; perhaps one was always intended and perhaps not. Now that I'm aware a conclave is to occur at all, I must attend, or take it as an insult from a Court that has often been far too willing to dismiss us," he said. He sat up, reaching out to cup the curve of my cheek with his hand. "I love you. You know that, yes?"

I blinked. "Okay, now you're worrying me. Of course I know that you love me."

"Good." He leaned in and kissed me, sweet and slow. Only the tension in his hand betrayed the fact that all was not well, that this wasn't just some sweet gesture motivated by affection. Something was really wrong.

Because of that, I was already braced when he pulled back and said, "I have to go."

"Why?" The question came out harsher than I'd intended. I didn't try to take it back or temper it. I knew I had to share him with his Court, but Oberon's teeth, I'd already done that today. He was supposed to be with me for at least a night before he left again.

"Because my Court will need to be told that so many monarchs of the Divided are coming to our territory; because you are a daughter of the Divided Courts, and until I know whether they intend to shun us or curry our favor, I mustn't seem to have already been pacified. I must seem aloof. Because I need to prepare myself to walk among Kings and Queens who stand too much on ceremony as their equal." His smile was brief and wry. "I *am* their equal, of course; I am a King. But they'll look for any excuse to say that I'm less than they are."

I caught his meaning. I didn't want to. Shoulders going tight, I asked, "Excuses like arriving next to a knight who swears to the throne of the Mists? One who might have 'pacified' you?"

He didn't answer me. He didn't need to.

Irritation flared in my chest, hot and toxic as bile. I swallowed it down as best I could. "You should go, then."

"I'll make it up to you." He slid from the bed, grabbed his clothes, and was gone. He didn't bother getting dressed first. Cait Sidhe are even more casual about nudity than the rest of Faerie. Cats are technically naked under their fur, after all. Combine that with the whole "grooming with their tongues" thing, and body shyness just isn't an option.

I stared at the place where he'd been, inhaling the mixed scents of pennyroyal and musk. Then I groaned and flopped backward into the pillows, closing my eyes. We were going to make this work. We were *going* to make this work. The fact that he was the monarch of an independent Court and I was tied inextricably to the Divided Courts wasn't going to change the fact that we loved each other—and as long as we could keep loving each other, we could find a way through this. We could do it. I was a hero, after all. What was a hero, if not someone who went up against impossible odds, and won?

Sleep claimed me while I was worrying the problem over and over in my head, like a dog with a bone. I fell into tangled, confusing dreams, and found myself looking for Karen in every corner. She could guide the things I dreamed about. Normally, it was nice to have some privacy in my own dreams, but after the day I'd had, being able to say "hey, kiddo, wanna go to the imaginary carnival and eat cotton candy until the sun goes down?" would have been a nice change.

A knock at my bedroom door pulled me back to

consciousness at — I checked the clock — a little after two in the afternoon. I sat up, blinking and groggy, clutching the sheet around my chest like it would somehow transform into a nightgown if I wished hard enough. The blackout curtains over my windows kept the light from getting in. So where was the light coming from?

"Toby?"

Oh. The bedroom door was open. I turned to blink blearily in that direction. Jazz, fully dressed and looking far too alert, with the feathered band that held her fae nature tied in her hair, was standing there, grimacing apologetically.

"Huh?" I said.

"You need to get up now."

I blinked at her again before pointing at the clock. "Nuh-*uh*."

"The High King and High Queen are here," said Jazz. "In the dining room. With May. Drinking lemonade and eating the last of the Rice Krispie treats. *Please* will you get up now? I'm really not equipped to deal with this."

The words "High King and High Queen" acted like an electric shock to the part of my brain that had been trying to drag me back to sleep. I stiffened. "They're where?"

"In the dining room. Are you up?"

"I'm up," I confirmed. I paused. "Is Quentin?"

Jazz shook her head. "They, um, asked us to let him sleep."

Great. So this wasn't a social visit: it was a job evaluation. "I'll be right down."

"Good. Hurry." Jazz shut the door, leaving me alone in my darkened bedroom.

Most fae are nocturnal, which means we have excellent night vision. I got up and got dressed without turning on the lights, retrieving yesterday's jeans from the floor and digging a charcoal gray tank top out of my drawer. Most of my wardrobe is designed not to show the blood. That sort of thing was an occupational hazard for me, and I didn't enjoy shopping, which meant that darker colors were better.

I didn't have time for a shower, but I had time to run a brush through my hair and take a quick, critical look at myself in the mirror. There were dark circles under my eyes from the lack of sleep. Well, that was the High King's fault. He could deal with it.

Voices drifted from the dining room when I was halfway down the stairs. They were talking quietly, presumably so as not to wake Quentin. I could have told them not to bother. He was a teenage boy. He didn't wake up for anything short of a small explosion, and even then, he was just as likely to decide that I could take care of things, roll over, and go back to sleep.

Then I came around the corner at the bottom of the stairs, and the dining room appeared before me, and I stopped worrying about little things like that. I had much bigger problems.

High King Aethlin Sollys was settled in what was normally my seat, a tumbler of lemonade in front of him. To his left sat a woman with hair the color of molten silver and eyes like chips of blue topaz. They were both wearing human clothes—him a button-down shirt, her a Toronto Furies jersey—and neither was wearing a human disguise. I blinked, schooling my expression. They weren't wearing cosmetic illusions, either, and the left side of the High Queen's face was covered in small, pitted scars, like the aftermath of a bad case of acne. She was pureblooded Daoine Sidhe. Daoine Sidhe don't *get* acne.

Almost as if she'd read my mind, Maida smiled, shrugged, and said, "Fae may be immune to most human skin conditions, but it turns out we're not immune to smallpox."

"Oh," I said. There didn't seem to be another good response. May, who was sitting on the other side of the table, gave me a pointed look. Right. I couldn't stand here silently forever. "So, um, to what do we owe this not at all terrifying honor?"

"Well, as you may have noticed, we were in the neighborhood," said Aethlin. He chuckled at his own joke. May mustered a sickly smile.

Maida sighed and planted her elbow in her husband's ribs. He made an exaggerated "oof" noise. Rolling her eyes, she looked to me, and said, "We wanted to come and see where Quentin is living, and talk to you a bit, as his parents, rather than as the High Monarchs of the Westlands. Do you think you can try to make that separation? For me?"

She sounded so earnest—and more importantly, so sincere—that I took a deep breath and said, "I'll try. But you have to promise not to charge me with treason or something if I complain about the way he never wants to do the dishes."

"He's going to be High King someday," said Aethlin. "He'll never have to do the dishes."

He'd said something similar the first time we met, during their visit to the Mists to confirm Arden as Queen. Believe it or not, I was much more relaxed with them now. "Which makes it all the more important that he do the dishes *now*, while he can still learn something from it," I said. "Plus I'm really bad at doing the dishes, and why do I have a squire if not to make him do menial household chores?"

"Dishes build character," said Maida. "Is he happy? Healthy? Is he eating his vegetables and making friends and having a *normal* life?"

I paused, looking between the two of them before I settled on Maida and said, "I'm guessing you're the one who married into the royal family, huh?"

She smiled. "Is it that obvious?"

"Pretty sure he," I gestured to Aethlin, "has never done the dishes voluntarily in his life, so yeah, it's that obvious."

"I was a Baron's daughter in the Kingdom of Endless Skies," she said. Kansas, in other words: a Kingdom so broad and so flat that in the end, they'd had to go with "we have no mountains" as a name. "No household to speak of, and my father didn't want me treated differently by his staff, so he let most of them go after I was born. I did dishes. Also milked cows and fed chickens and learned how to wash my own clothes. It's part of why I was willing to agree to the proposal that Quentin be put into a blind fosterage. It was important to me that he understand the people he would eventually be ruling from the bottom up, and not just from the top down."

The other part of her agreement had been, of course, the fact that the request was coming from Eira Rosynhwyr, the Daoine Sidhe Firstborn, whose every wish was her descendants' command. If Maida didn't want to bring that up, I wasn't going to do it either. I still paused. No household, no staff, and those scars on her face . . . "Forgive me if I'm overstepping my bounds right now, although you *did* promise not to have me arrested for treason, so there's that, but . . . um . . ." I stopped, realizing I had no idea how to address the High Queen without taking us back toward the overly formal.

"Maida," she prompted. "You can use my name when I'm talking to you as the mother of your squire. If anything, in this social context, I should be the one using your title."

"Please don't," I said. "All right, um, Maida, forgive me if this is a delicate question, but I've never heard of a pureblood catching smallpox. It's usually a human disease. Was your mother human, by any chance?"

She smiled radiantly. "Oh, I told you we'd found a good knight for Quentin, didn't I?" she asked, glancing at her husband. "She's smart, and she makes him do the dishes. Our son is in excellent hands."

"Yes, dear," said the High King. I swallowed a laugh.

Under the circumstances, it could have been miscon-strued, and I was still trying to dodge that whole "trea-son" thing.

Maida looked back to me. "Yes," she said. "She was a local girl. Father had purchased her from one of the other nobles, who had snatched her to be a nursemaid for his children."

"Ah." I nodded. Using humans as nannies and wet nurses is an old fae tradition that thankfully never man-aged to get much traction on the West Coast. Grab a human girl and make her take care of your kids during those messy, inconvenient parts of childhood, then dump her fae-struck and confused back into the mortal world. Fairy ointment is used to keep the kidnapped women connected to the fae world. Wipe it from their eyes be-fore they're sent home and they'll have no way of ex-plaining what happened to them. It's cruel. It is, in every sense of the world, inhumane. But then, everything the purebloods do is inhumane, because they were never hu-man to begin with.

"It wasn't like that," she said. "He bought her so he could set her free. He didn't think it was right to keep slaves. And she refused to leave. She'd been in the Sum-merlands for fifty years by that point; everything she'd ever known was dead and gone, and she was still young because of the spells she'd been under. She was happy not to be beholden to a cruel master. She didn't want to go and live among the humans. So she took over running his household, and eventually they fell in love, and I came along. I was his first child. He made me his heir."

"I thought changelings couldn't inherit," I said.

"They can't," said Maida. "Father didn't care. He was going to do right by me. He fired half his staff when he realized my mother was pregnant, and he fired the rest after I was born. I grew up surrounded by the people he thought of as family, and none of them ever cared that I was a mortal child. But then the pox came." She touched the side of her face, looking briefly self-conscious. "Mother died. I lived, but barely. Father became withdrawn and quiet. He'd found the love of his life, and while he'd always known that he'd outlive her, he'd been expecting more time. So much more time."

"I was a United States Senator when all this happened," said Aethlin. May and I looked at him blankly. He chuckled. "It was part of my training to be King. I had to wander the whole continent, meet all sorts of people—Quentin will be expected to do the same, once he becomes a knight errant."

"Right," I said. Because he was going to be High King someday. He couldn't learn the whole country if he stayed in California forever. We were many things, but we were not absolutely representative of the people he would be expected to rule.

Aethlin continued: "Part of my duties involved calling on every noble with a holding large enough to offer me hospitality. I'd already visited the King of Endless Skies, and both Duchies; there were no Counties at the time, so I came to a Barony, and met the most beautiful girl I had ever seen."

"I had pox scars on my face and chicken shit in my hair," said Maida.

"You hit me with a broom," said Aethlin. "No one had ever hit me with a broom before."

"You scared my chickens," said Maida.

I looked between them slowly, finally focusing on Maida's hair. It was pure silver, with no hints of tarnish. Changelings could inherit a lot of things from their fae parents, but signs of mortality always showed through. I knew Quentin had no human blood. His mother didn't appear to either. "You have a hope chest," I said, looking back to Aethlin.

He nodded. "I do. Well, I do now. It belonged to my parents, back when I brought Maida home to meet them."

"They told me the cost of marrying their son would be my humanity, and I was glad to pay it," she said. "The human world held nothing for me, and the fae world was promising me everything I could have ever wanted. My father came to the wedding. He still holds his Barony. He says my mother would be proud of what I've become, and I believe him."

"It's not every human woman's daughter who can become Queen of a continent," I agreed. "Does Quentin know?"

"No." Maida looked regretful. "He was too young to understand when we sent him on fosterage. He knows I was ill when I was younger. He doesn't know with what, or that it was a disease that purebloods rarely, if ever, suffer from."

"But he wasn't too young to have been picking up the wrong attitudes about changelings from the ruffians at Court," said Aethlin. "He needs to rule everyone with fae blood, no matter how thin, and he needs to do it fairly. We couldn't tell him where his mother had come from, but we could send him out into the world and hope that he would learn the right lessons."

"Because telling him would make it look like human blood was something to be ashamed of and concealed," I said.

Maida nodded. "We don't tell many people about my origins, because there are people who would take it as a reason to question my authority. I'm not ashamed. I'm not going to weaken myself in the eyes of my vassals, either."

"No, I understand," I said.

"Sometimes I don't," said Maida. "I heard what you did for the changelings of Silences. Thank you. Truly."

I managed not to flinch at the forbidden thanks, although it was a near thing. Faerie has some pretty strong prohibitions against saying "thank you." It implies fealty and debt, two things the fae prefer to avoid. Having the

High Queen thank me wasn't just awkward and weird, it was alarming.

May shared my sentiments. She was struggling not to stare. Suddenly, the reason Jazz wasn't here made perfect sense. I wouldn't have been here either, if I'd had any way of avoiding it.

"It needed to be done," I said. "There were almost fifty of them in the knowe." Fifty in the knowe, and another dozen in the local Court of Cats. All of them had been offered the same choice: I would shift their blood, if they wanted me to, carrying them either all the way fae or all the way human. For the ones who'd already been exposed to goblin fruit, turning human would have been a death sentence, but I'd offered it all the same, because they had the right to choose.

Some had chosen to stay as they were. None of them had chosen to be human. And the rest . . . I had burned the humanity out of them, allowing them to rise pure-blooded and immortal. It had been painful for everyone involved. I still felt like I'd done the right thing. Portland's King of Cats, a pleasant, silver-haired man named Jolgeir, had kissed my cheeks after I pulled the humanity out of his daughters, promising to give me anything I ever wanted, for the rest of my life, as thanks for what I'd done for him.

"It needed to be done, but you did it," said Maida. "We have a hope chest and no way to make the same offer without making people feel like they should be ashamed of where they came from. Things are changing. A lot of that change is starting here, in the Mists. That's why we're so glad to have you teaching our son."

"But we still miss him," said Aethlin. "Please, is he happy? We've missed so much. Tell us about him."

"He *is* happy," I said, and finally sat down. "Healthy, too, and he's even started applying himself in his lessons. He and Raj are still pretty much joined at the hip. We hosted a slumber party last night . . ."

Once I started talking about Quentin, it was surprisingly easy to keep going. I was still talking when he came stumbling down the stairs, Raj in cat-form slung over his shoulder like a hand towel. Then there was shouting and hugging and all the joys of a boy enjoying a too-rare reunion with his parents, and for a moment—just a moment—everything felt like it was going to be okay.

FIVE

MUIR WOODS WAS WRAPPED in fog, transformed by the marine weather into a phantom forest, as much legend as reality. I pulled into the parking lot, squinting at seemingly empty spaces as I looked for a safe place to stow my car. At least I didn't have to deal with tourists for a change. The mortal side of the park was closed due to unsafe weather conditions, all of which had been conjured by our helpful local Leshy and Merrow. Even Dianda had gotten into the act, whipping up the kind of waves that normally appeared only in the bad CGI disaster movies Quentin was so fond of. The storm had been raging for three days, clearing out the humans and leaving the place open for the rest of us.

A few park rangers and members of the Coast Guard had probably noticed that rain was falling everywhere but on Muir Woods, which remained silent and dry, or as dry as anything could be when completely fogged in. They would have chalked it up to California's often eccentric weather patterns. When you live in a state where it can be raining on one side of the street and eighty degrees and sunny on the other side, you learn to cope.

Coping was something I could have used some help

with. In the week since I'd woken up to find the High King and Queen in my dining room, I had crammed so much etiquette into my brain that my skull throbbed, protesting the weight of seemingly useless knowledge. It was sadly necessary. I might be the only changeling at this conclave. If I wasn't, I'd still be a knight surrounded by Dukes and Countesses, Queens and Marquises, and every other part of the titled alphabet. I needed to be on my best behavior, or I was going to have a lot to answer for.

Most of the parking spaces were already filled by vehicles under don't-look-here spells, or invisibility charms, or the more blatant holes of absolute nothingness, not even mist, which looked like someone had taken a pair of scissors to the air. I drove past them, finally stopping and peering at the farthest, darkest corner of the lot. It looked empty, but . . .

I elbowed Quentin. "Hey. Is there a car there?" As a Daoine Sidhe, he was better with illusions—both casting and detecting—than I was.

"What?" He looked up. I pointed. He followed my finger, squinted, and said, "No, it's empty. Except for that big pile of dog poop. Humans don't clean up after their pets as well as they should."

"Neither do fae," I said, pulling forward. "Sylvester's Afanc crapped all over the walking path the last time I was at Shadowed Hills. I had to throw those shoes away."

"Oh, yeah." Quentin quieted again as I finished parking. He'd been quiet for the entire drive, not even objecting when I turned the radio to the local oldies station. Normally he would have argued with me about that, but not today.

I killed the engine and turned in my seat to look at him. "All right, spill," I said. "Before we get to the knowe and have to deal with every petty noble Arden could scrape out of a crevice, you're going to tell me what's wrong."

"I look like my parents." Quentin didn't look at me as he spoke. His attention remained focused on his hands. "I have my dad's hair, and my mom's eyes, and her jaw. How are these people not going to know who I am? I might as well be wearing a sign."

"Oh. I thought you were worried about something major." I tried to keep my tone light, even informal. It was still a real concern. As the Crown Prince of the Westlands, Quentin would one day be the regent of every single person we were about to go observe. That made him something to be courted and cosseted. More, it made him a target. Take out the primary heir to the throne and maybe they'd get lucky: maybe his little sister wouldn't have been prepared for her birthright, and they could enjoy a few years of relative freedom from supervision when she took the throne. Of course, that assumed Aethlin and Maida would be stepping down any time soon, which didn't seem to be their plan, but things could change. Assassinating heirs was a good way to kick-start the process.

I was also worried about the local nobles realizing Quentin could be useful to them and trying to take him away from me. He was my squire and semi-adopted little brother, and I wasn't going to let him go without a fight. Not even if the people who were trying to remove him from my care were his parents. Not unless they had a damn good reason for doing it.

Quentin gave me a sidelong look. "This *is* something major."

"I know. That's why it's not something you need to be worried about right now." I indicated him with a sweep of my hand. "Look at you. The secret son of a pureblood noble line. If this were a human fantasy novel, of *course* you would be a prince in disguise. Nothing else makes sense. But this is real life, and more, this is pureblood politics. Anyone who looks at you and thinks 'gosh, he looks a lot like the High King' is going to follow the thought with 'but he's squired to a changeling, which gives him no political advantage, and could actually hurt him when the time comes to take the throne; there's no way High King Sollys would be that bone-numbingly stupid. I guess he's a distant cousin or something.' Maybe you'll find yourself in a funny *Prince-and-the-Pauper* situation, where you have to try to hide the fact that you don't have a convenient identical double, but nobody's going to finger you for the prince. It just doesn't make sense. And they're used to you! They see you all the time. You're furniture to them. Annoying furniture with bad taste in friends."

"Do you really think so?" he asked, starting to look hopeful.

"Kiddo, I know so. If you're really worried, eat a plate of salad with your fingers or something. Your absolute lack of table manners and social graces will convince anyone who happens to be watching that you *can't* be the Crown Prince."

Quentin looked horrified. Even years of exposure to me hadn't been enough to cancel out his early socialization, which said he needed to be poised and polite at all times, or at least whenever he was in front of people who never saw him five minutes after he rolled out of bed. He was an ordinary teenage boy when we were alone, but put him in front of someone with a title and he was Martha Stewart reborn with pointy ears.

I was still laughing as we climbed out of the car and into the cool evening air. I wasn't wearing a human disguise: I didn't need one. Between the storms and the warding spells, no humans were going to come within a mile of Muir Woods tonight, unless they were being compelled by some outside force. I was wearing a nice pseudo-medieval blouse that May had dug out of the back of my closet in my mother's tower; it was black spider-silk and red samite, and while I felt like I was in danger of having my clothes wear me, rather than me wearing my clothes, May had insisted. Instead of jeans, I had black spider-silk pants that clung like they were made of Saran Wrap. I wasn't sure I was comfortable with that. I wasn't sure I was comfortable with any of this. Just to gild the lily, my jewelry was tarnished silver and garnets, and all of it was real, estate sale stuff Jazz had found in the back of her store. No amount of dispelling my illusions would change a thing about my clothes.

Spider-silk is expensive. I was wearing the equivalent of more money than most changelings would see in their lifetimes. It made me seriously uncomfortable—although there was something to be said for the amusement factor of standing me next to Quentin. He was the pureblood, but he was wearing blue linen trousers, a white peasant shirt, and a vest in the pale shade of daffodil favored in Shadowed Hills. His attire was a quiet reminder of who technically held his fosterage, even as mine was a reminder that I was my mother's daughter, and bleeding around me would be unwise.

I would have felt better if May and Jazz had *been* there, rather than dressing me up like a giant Barbie and throwing me to the wolves. May was concerned that her whole "I'm a Fetch, howdy" routine might cause problems with some of the visiting nobles, and wasn't planning to come to the conclave until night two, when everyone would presumably be too preoccupied sniping at each other to notice that she wasn't supposed to exist. It was logical. It was sensible. It still left me feeling like I didn't have as much backup as I really, really wanted to have.

Quentin looked at me gloomily across the roof of the car. "I'm glad you think this is funny."

"Somebody should," I said. "Come on. Let's go embarrass ourselves in front of the nobility."

He snorted, but said nothing as he followed me out of the parking lot.

The stretch of land known as Muir Woods is one of the last remaining semi-virgin redwood forests in California. The giant evergreens used to cover the entire coast, towering over anyone who stood before them. These days, they're tourist attractions and the vegetative equivalent of zoo animals, hemmed in by cities and protected by laws that do too little and started doing it too late. Mist swirled around the trunks of the ancient trees as we walked into their shadow, following the trails human rangers had cut through the underbrush. Some fae would have no need for those little wooden paths. Tybalt could have stalked across the forest floor and never disturbed a leaf. Grianne, a Candela in Sylvester's service, could have walked across the surface of the ponds without a ripple. Sadly, some of us were more limited, and some of us were very grateful to the parks service for their help.

Pixies appeared in the trees as we climbed the hill toward the entry to Arden's knowe. Some of them flew down to perform loops around us, leaving trails of glittering pixie-sweat in the air as they passed. I smiled. The pixies were no more than four inches tall—most were closer to three—and came in every color of the rainbow. They were some of the smallest members of Faerie. The health of the local pixie colonies was a good indicator of the health of the realm. Judging by the looks of this group, the Mists were thriving under Arden's rule.

Lowri was in full armor, standing beside the open doors to the knowe, with a Cornish Pixie in matching attire standing on the other side. Lowri was Arden's Captain of the Guard, and had served as temporary seneschal while Madden was asleep. Presumably, Madden had his job back now. I tensed. If she held a grudge about my helping Arden wake Madden up so early . . .

"Sir Daye," said Lowri, smiling brightly. Her Welsh accent broadened her consonants and flattened her vowels, adding a lilt to her words. "And Quentin. You're looking awfully formal today, young master."

"It's a conclave," said Quentin. He looked at his feet, shoulders tense. I elbowed him. If he didn't want to blow our cover, he needed to stop acting like we were going to be caught at any moment. Lowri knew him as my squire, and a minor noble at best. She wasn't going to figure out that things were any different just because we were here.

"It is, and you're properly early," said Lowri. Her smile faded as she turned back to me, replaced by grave concern. "You . . . *do* understand the company you're to be keeping these next few nights? There are some who won't like that you're allowed inside, much less permitted to have a voice in the proceedings."

"I'm not here to have a voice," I said. "I'm here because the High King of the Westlands wants me to be, and because I had something to do with the whole 'let's cure elf-shot' thing succeeding in the first place. Which reminds me. You were sworn to the Yates family before Rhys took Silences. Are you going to go back when all this is done?"

Lowri gave a quick, decisive shake of her head. "No," she said. "I loved my lieges when I served them, but that part of my life is over, and my oaths are sworn to Queen Windermere in the Mists. I wish the Kingdom of Silences well. Their recovery will be performed without me."

"Good," I said. "I'd miss you. Quentin, come on. We need to check in." He hurried to dog my heels as I walked through the open doors into the long redwood entry hall. Carved panels on the walls around us showed stylized scenes from the history of the Mists, including Arden's crowning and a figure who looked suspiciously like Walther pressing a bowl to the lips of a man who looked like Madden. More and more, I was coming to suspect that the knowe did its own carving. Fae craftsmen were good, but I didn't see how the best of them could have finished that panel and put it in place among the others in only three days.

A new doorway opened off the end of the hall,

revealing a secondary hall that curved away from the receiving room where Arden normally held Court. We walked down it. Voices drifted back to meet us, until we stepped into a gallery as grand as any theater. I stopped dead.

"Whoa," I said.

Quentin didn't say anything. He just blinked, his thoughts apparently mirroring my own.

The room we were now in had two stories—there was an actual balcony section, which wasn't something I'd ever expected to see in something that *wasn't* a theater. There was a stage at the far end of the room, flanked by gray velvet curtains, like someone was trying to use stagecraft to create an impression of the mist across the Bay. I couldn't be sure how many people the space would seat, but I was guessing somewhere between a hundred and fifty and two hundred, depending on how deep that balcony was.

Arden was on the stage conjuring balls of witch-light and tossing them up to join the others that were already bobbing among the rafters. With each ball, the light in the room got a little brighter, twilight melting into day. She looked toward the sound of my voice and smiled, although it didn't remove the lines of strain around her eyes. "The bookstore used to host a lot of author events," she said. She didn't seem to be raising her voice, but it carried, clean and clear, to the back of the gallery. There must have been amplification charms on the stage. Neat trick.

Arden continued her thought as we walked toward her: "Usually, we just had to move a couple of shelves and set up folding chairs, but it could still get pretty intense. Genre authors can attract some weird crowds. So I'm trying to think of this as if it were that. We're hosting like, Stephen King and J.K. Rowling at the same time, and the weirdoes are going to ride, ride, ride."

"I thought I heard voices while we were in the hall," I said, looking around. "Who else is here?"

"I am," chirped Madden, sticking his head out of the wings. This place really *was* a little theater. Tybalt might try to move in and stage a new Shakespeare production every Thursday. "Hi, Toby. Hi, Quentin. Ever cater a banquet for royalty?"

"Can't say as I have," I said. Peanut butter and tuna sandwiches slapped together for Quentin and Raj at two o'clock in the morning probably didn't count.

"Well, don't. It's awful. Just awful." He vanished again.

I turned to Arden. "We're here. Where do you want us?"

"My Court is going to be sitting over there," she said, indicating the seats curving around the left side of the stage. "I was planning on putting anyone unaffiliated but with good reason to be heard on the other side."

It was clear she wanted me to decide where we belonged. I knew what she was hoping for, but I still smiled as I said, "Okay, cool," and led Quentin to the unaffiliated seats.

Arden did a good job of hiding her disappointment. Her face only fell a little. It was the best I could do. My fealty has been sworn to Duke Sylvester Torquill since I was young. Even though he's Arden's vassal, that doesn't make me hers. He would have to release me formally for that to happen, and he's not going to do that unless I ask him to.

Quentin's fealty ultimately lies with the Westlands, but while he's my squire, he's also considered sworn to Sylvester, at least until the day when I declare him a knight in his own right. When that happens, Quentin's obligations to Sylvester will dissolve, allowing him to go out into the world for his knight errantry. During that time, he'll answer only to the High King—and his knight. Up until the day he takes the throne, he'll be expected to answer to me.

No pressure or anything.

Quentin and I took our seats. Madden reappeared a few minutes later, waving before heading to his place on the other side of the stage. As if that were a cue of some sort, other members of Arden's court began appearing and settling themselves nearby. Walther entered through a side door and moved toward us, pointing to the seat on the other side of me.

"Is this seat taken?" he asked.

"Please. Spare me the anxiety of wondering who might come and claim it," I said.

"Excellent." He looked profoundly relieved as he sank into the cushion. "Marlis just called to let me know she's in the queue outside with our parents, Aunt Siwan, and Uncle Holger. They'll be entering when the heralds announce them. She wanted to know if I was going to sit with her."

Walther's Aunt Siwan was better known as the rightful Queen of Silences. Holger was her King and consort, and Walther's parents were the court alchemists. Marlis was still seneschal, as far as I knew; she'd served under the pretender King, Rhys, and knew the modern shape of the Kingdom better than anyone else in her family. In a human monarchy, she would probably have been executed as a traitor, or at the very least imprisoned for life. Oberon's Law changes things, and so does magic. Rhys had been using loyalty potions to compel her obedience. She couldn't be held responsible for that.

Arden walked onto the stage, followed by a group of courtiers. They set out four thrones. One was silver, patterned with graven redwood branches and blackberry vines. One was golden, patterned with yarrow branches and rose briars. The other two were bronze, patterned with maple leaves and heather flowers. Arden, Queen Siwan, and the High King and Queen. Which made sense. The ownership of the cure was split between Silences and the Mists, and the High King and Queen were here to oversee the proceedings. Of course, those would be the four who sat at the head of the room.

Humans would probably have insisted on giving the

High King and Queen golden thrones, focusing on the value of the metal. Because this was Faerie, the division was determined by the colors of their Kingdoms, and how well the metals suited them. Arden had silver, for fog; Queen Siwan had gold, for yarrow; and the High King and Queen had bronze, presumably for King Aethlin's hair.

The doors opened, and people began entering. Normal people, people who'd heard a conclave was happening and had come to witness the largest gathering of Kings and Queens that they were ever likely to see. I had to wonder whether this was a ploy on Arden's part to keep the cure from being suppressed; after all, it was harder to bury something people knew about. Or maybe it was just the natural result of gathering this much royalty in one place. Even if each of the Kings and Queens traveled with a minimal staff, they'd still fill the gallery without trying. That would also explain the number of faces I didn't recognize.

There were no other changelings in the first wave of arrivals. That was no real surprise.

The crowd settled quickly, filling the balcony and the back of the room. When the last of them was seated, Arden's herald took up a position next to the rear door. "Her Royal Highness, by right of blood, the Queen in the Mists, Arden Windermere," he announced.

Arden, who was already on the stage, bowed her head to the audience and walked regally to the throne marked for her use. She sat. The people applauded. So did I. It seemed like the only appropriate response.

The applause died down. The herald spoke again. "His Grace, by right of appointment, Duke Sylvester Torquill of Shadowed Hills, and his consort, Her Grace, by right of marriage, Duchess Luna Torquill of Shadowed Hills."

"Oh, sweet Oberon's ass, they're going to tell us how *every single person* got their throne, aren't they?" I whispered, before flinching and waiting for the reaction from the crowd. There wasn't one. The amplification charms apparently didn't cover our part of the gallery. Thank the rose and the branch for that.

Quentin smirked and said nothing.

Sylvester and Luna appeared at the back of the gallery, followed by Etienne. They made their way to the middle rows of seats, well ahead of Arden's courtiers and the commoners who'd come just to watch, but leaving plenty of room in the front for the higher-ranking nobility. It was the first time I'd seen Sylvester since before I'd gone to Silences to play diplomat. He glanced my way. I didn't smile. I didn't look away either. We were going to have to find our peace sooner or later. Honestly, I wanted it to be sooner. He was my liege. I was planning to get married. He shouldn't be excluded from being part of that.

The list of mid-ranked nobility—important enough to announce, unimportant enough that I'd never heard of most of them—went on and on. Li Qin was announced as interim Duchess of Dreamer's Glass, which probably pleased her. April O'Leary was announced as the Countess of Tamed Lightning, unable to attend due to duties at home, to be represented at the conclave by her seneschal, Elliot. It was a smart move. April was weird even for Faerie, and sending her to something like this would probably result in her finding a way to baffle and offend all the Kings and Queens at once. Wiring a Dryad into a computer system has that sort of effect.

Finally, the heralds ran out of Dukes and Counts and Barons and Earls. After a brief pause for consultation, the announcements resumed. "Her Royal Highness, by right of blood, Queen Siwan Yates of Silences, and her consort, His Royal Highness, by right of marriage, King Holger Yates of Silences."

Walther's aunt and uncle entered through the rear door and proceeded down the aisle. Marlis was close behind them, almost as if she were guarding them against possible attack. She glanced our way and offered a quick, genial nod as they neared the stage. Walther, who was less constrained by propriety, grinned and waved. I split the difference with a smile and a nod.

Queen Siwan kissed her husband on the cheek before mounting the stairs to the stage. Marlis stepped into the front row of seats, gesturing for King Holger to follow her. As he did, he turned, bringing the left side of his body into view. I stopped smiling and sat up straighter. The last time I'd seen him, he'd been missing the lower half of his left arm. Now, it was present and accounted for, supported by a sling, but as much flesh and blood as the rest of him.

I'd left a portion of my blood in Silences. Queen Siwan had explained her intent to try to work it into a regenerative potion. Looked like she'd succeeded. The ramifications of *that* were … well. I just hoped they wouldn't be leading to another conclave. I might heal fast, but there was no way I was going to agree to becoming a pharmacy for the rest of Faerie.

"Their Majesties, by right of equal ascension, King and Queen upon the Golden Shore, Theron and Chrysanthe."

A pair of Ceryneian Hinds—Golden Hinds—made their way down the aisle, heads high, hooves tapping on the carpeted floor. Like all of their kind, they were elegant and lithe from the waist up, looking more like Tylwyth Teg than anything else, and golden-furred, bipedal deer from the waist down. They wore tunics belted with woven gold-and-silver wire, but left their legs bare. Their ears were long, curving, and lightly furred. Chrysanthe's hair fell to her waist, white-gold and curly enough to have some bounce, despite its weight. Theron had antlers, small but distinct, growing from his forehead. His crown had clearly been designed to accommodate them, and echoed the forms in hers. They walked, together, to settle in the front row.

"Golden Shore," Quentin murmured, trying to sound

like he was doing a casual review, when we both knew it was for my benefit. "Kingdom directly to the South, mostly agrarian, few political aspirations."

I knew the basics about my neighbors, but I didn't tell him to stop. He might tell me something I didn't already know, and I was so far out of my depth that anything would help.

"His Royal Highness, by right of conquest, King Antonio Robinson of Angels."

Antonio didn't enter through the doors, although the doors opened: instead, he appeared at the center of the aisle, already halfway to the stage. He was a tall, striking man, with skin the color of slate and hair the color of ashes. Two Merry Dancers appeared with him, globes of floating light that turned and twisted around his body. It was rare for a Candela to aspire to a throne, much less fight to take it. King Robinson was an anomaly in many ways. Still, the people dutifully applauded as he made his way to his seat.

So it went, on and on, as the monarchs of the neighboring kingdoms made their appearances. It looked like Aethlin's invitation had gone out to the entire West Coast—that, or the West Coast monarchs were the only ones who'd felt comfortable leaving their Kingdoms for the duration of this meeting, which made a certain measure of sense. The people who were most likely to stage an invasion were always your immediate neighbors, since they were the ones who knew how nice your apple trees were, or how much parking you had. If all your neighbors were in the room, there was no one left to invade you. That was pureblood logic for you.

The herald named their Kingdoms, places I'd never seen and wasn't sure I ever would, and I translated them as best I could into mortal landmarks. The Kingdom of Evergreen was Washington and part of Vancouver, ignoring the America-Canada border in favor of drawing its own. The Kingdom of Prisms was farther up the coast, encompassing Alaska, but they hadn't sent a representative. Either they didn't care what we decided, or that whole "we might get invaded" problem was a real concern for them. Painted Sands was Nevada, represented by a Crown Princess and two Dukes. Highmountain was Colorado, represented by their Daoine Sidhe monarchs. They were accompanied by a single silent, downcast handmaiden—a Barrow Wight, from the looks of her. Interesting. Copper was Arizona, and their Centaur King took up half an aisle. The delegation that had traveled the farthest to sit in this room and listen to everyone fighting was from Starfall, in Idaho. They hadn't brought their monarch, but were a small group of interested nobles, no doubt hoping to curry favor by bringing home news of what transpired here.

Starfall was the last land Kingdom to be announced and seated. There was a brief pause as the heralds checked their notes, and the introductions continued:

"Representing the Undersea Kingdom of Leucothea, Her Grace, by right of blood, Duchess Dianda Lorden of Saltmist, and her consort, by right of marriage, Duke Patrick Lorden of Saltmist."

Dianda and Patrick entered through the rear door. The conclave was likely to go on for quite some time, and while Dianda preferred to deal with land fae on her own two feet, assuming—probably correctly—that most would view anything else as weakness, pride didn't make her foolish. She was in fins and scales, seated in her wheelchair with her flukes defiantly exposed, like she was daring anyone to say a word about her presence. Patrick was pushing her, a mild expression on his face. He was probably the reason the King of Leucothea had assigned Dianda to be his representative; as the only Undersea noble I knew of who was married to someone who'd grown up on the land, her husband was an invaluable resource for explaining what the hell it was that everyone around her was talking about.

Arden had thoughtfully reserved a wheelchair accessible seat for Dianda in the front row. One more helpful consequence of having a queen who'd been socialized in the human world: she understood the need for proper disability access, rather than trusting in magic to work it all out.

The herald continued. "Representing the Oversky Kingdom of Frozen Winds, His Grace, by right of conquest, Duke Islay of Staggered Clouds."

Duke Islay was a thin man with shadows in his eyes and hair like a storm cloud. He floated down the aisle, his feet pointed down at the carpet, and settled in an open seat with no immediate neighbors. I couldn't blame him for that. If he'd settled next to me, I would probably have moved. The Sluagh Sidhe are as much a part of Faerie as anyone else, but they're damn creepy, and I've always been glad that they belonged to the Oversky.

"They should be just about done," murmured Quentin. "I can't think of anyone else they would have invited."

"Invited, maybe not, but showing up, definitely," I whispered back, just as the herald began to speak again.

"His Majesty, by right of conquest, King Tybalt of the Court of Dreaming Cats."

The room went quiet. People twisted in their seats to watch as Tybalt walked down the aisle toward the front row. Raj followed him. So did several cat-form Cait Sidhe, their tails up and their whiskers forward, trotting at his heels like this was the most normal thing in the world.

There was always something regal about Tybalt: he'd been a King longer than I'd been alive, and graceful arrogance comes easily to the feline. I'd seen him in his element before, among the cats who were his subjects, but I had never seen him in a place like this. He was dressed in brown, with dark leather trousers, boots a few shades darker, and a tan silk shirt. His vest was the same color as his boots. The stripes in his hair and the points of his teeth as he smiled at the gathered nobility marked him clearly as one of the Cait Sidhe, and hence "lesser" in the eyes of many members of the Divided Courts.

Raj was wearing blue jeans and a Delta Rae T-shirt. He looked exactly as disrespectful as everyone around him expected him to be. I had to suppress a smile at that. They were playing to the expectations of their audience. It was glorious.

It was frightening. By allowing Tybalt to be announced as a King—and hence equal to every other monarch at this conclave—Arden had shown how much respect she had for the Court of Cats. That was good. That was the right thing to do. And it just might have made things infinitely more complex, where my relationship was concerned.

"Their Majesties, by right of blood and ascension, High King Aethlin Sollys and High Queen Maida Sollys, of the Westlands."

Everyone stood, even Tybalt, who had barely had time to sit. Dianda was the only one who remained where she was, although she placed her hands upon her shoulders, fingers pointing toward the back wall, as a sign of respect. It showed that she was neither armed nor making a fist. Among the Undersea, there wasn't much more of an honor.

Maida and Aethlin came gliding down the center aisle, their steps so smooth and measured that they might as well have been floating. I wondered how much time they'd spent practicing entrances like this one, smoothing away their rough edges and rendering them brief but potent expressions of effortless grace. I decided to stop thinking about it, and just be grateful that there was no circumstance, however unlikely, that could put me in their place.

They joined Arden on the stage. She remained standing until both of them were seated. Then, after bowing deeply to each of them in turn, she settled in her throne.

"Welcome," she began. "This conclave—"

The doors at the back of the room slammed open. Everyone turned, eyes wide, to stare at the figure standing there.

She wasn't tall, or thin, or gloriously beautiful. She didn't need to be any of those things to catch our eyes and hold them, silencing the room. Her skin held the ghosts of old acne scars. Her hair was thick, black, and curly, falling loose down her back. Her dress cascaded down her body and broke into white foam at the hem, a slice of the tide captured eternally in the process of flowing out. It was clear as water, but showed nothing of the skin beneath it. Her eyes were green as driftglass, filled with the deep and silent shadows of the sea. They betrayed nothing. They revealed nothing.

The Luidaeg stepped over the threshold into the room, and said, "As eldest of Maeve's children, I claim the right to witness. To observe. And to speak, should the need come upon me. Would any deny me this right?"

No one said a word.

"Good." She took another step forward, moving off to the side as she was followed into the room by another figure. A teenage girl with bone-white hair, looking profoundly uncertain and uncomfortable in her gown of white spider-silk. I gasped. I couldn't stop myself.

It was Karen.

SIX

"THIS IS KAREN BROWN, and she is under my protection," said the Luidaeg. She sounded strained, like the words she was using weren't the ones she would have chosen. That worried me, almost as much as the sight of Karen standing there, small and scared and alone. "Any who would harm her will need to first pass through me."

All right. Maybe not totally alone.

The Luidaeg put a hand on Karen's shoulder. "It's all right, honey," she said, and while the charms amplifying the room carried her words clean and clear to the rest of us, her voice was gentler than it had been before. "Just tell everyone why you're here, and then we can sit down until it's time for us to talk."

"Are . . . are you sure?" asked Karen. Her voice was barely a whisper. It was the loudest thing I'd ever heard.

"I promise."

Karen bit her lip. Then she turned to face the gallery full of nobles and monarchs, and said, "I'm an oneiromancer. I walk in dreams. I can speak to the sleeping. I'm here because I've been commanded to come by Eira Rosynhwyr, Firstborn daughter of Titania, who created elf-shot, and wishes to have a voice in its fate. I'm . . . I'm really sorry. I know I'm not supposed to be here, but I couldn't tell her no. She said I'd never sleep peacefully again."

"I'm going to kill her," I said. I wasn't sure how loudly I was speaking. I didn't actually care. "I'm going to get Acacia to open a Rose Road, and I'm going to go back to where we left Evening sleeping, and I'm going to kill her."

The Luidaeg looked amused. She shouldn't have been able to hear me, but she had. Maybe I shouldn't have been surprised. "Always the hero," she said. "Come along, Karen." She took my niece's hand and walked the length of the silent gallery with her, until they came to the row where I was seated. Karen moved to sit on Quentin's other side. He took her hand and squeezed. It was a brotherly gesture, comforting. Her eyes filled with tears, and she dropped her head to his shoulder. The Luidaeg met my eyes and nodded once as she settled next to Karen. She wasn't happy about this either. But then, when was she happy about anything involving her sister?

The silence in the gallery was profound. I turned back to the stage. All four of the seated monarchs were staring at us. Siwan looked confused. The High King and Queen looked stunned. Arden looked more resigned. This was the sort of thing she'd been dealing with since the start of her reign. She might not be the most accomplished Queen in the Westlands, but she was well on her way to becoming the most unflappable.

I grimaced, spreading my hands and mouthing, "Sorry." Arden shook herself, snapping out of her surprise, and turned to the rest of the room.

"As you can see, this conclave is of great importance, and will shape the future of our people in a way that cannot be overstated. Everyone will be heard, although the final decision lies with the High King and High Queen of our fair land. For those of you who've come because you were summoned, but do not fully understand what is to be discussed, I ask you to be patient, and listen. Master Davies?" Arden beckoned Walther. "Please come, and explain."

"Yes, Your Highness." Walther rose, knees only knocking a little, and stepped onto the stage. There was a small "X" on the far right corner, marking the place where guest speakers should go for their presentations. He took his position, took a deep breath, and began telling the room how he'd been able to alchemically create a cure for elf-shot.

I knew this story—I'd been there when it was unfolding—and so I took the opportunity to look around the gallery, trying to size up the participants in this little production. Some of them were familiar to me, Sylvester and Li Qin and Dianda and the rest. Most were strangers, which made it hard for me to judge how opinions were going to go. Sylvester and Luna would want the cure distributed freely: they'd be thinking of their daughter, asleep on her bier of roses, who could wake up so much sooner than a century from now if she had the opportunity. Li Qin would probably also support the cure. She had no one under elf-shot—the people who'd served under her wife, January O'Leary, had been murdered, not put to sleep—but she knew what it was like to lose someone she cared about. Dianda, I didn't know which way she'd go. The rest of our guests from the Divided Courts . . . I didn't know which way they'd go, either.

Golden Shore was a mostly changeling Kingdom. Theron and Chrysanthe would probably be in favor. Highmountain was a very traditional Kingdom. Verona and Kabos could go either way, but would most likely support whatever gave the purebloods the most power. And so it went, the math of control, down through all the gathered monarchs, nobles, and silent observers.

The door at the back of the room opened and someone slipped through, taking a seat at the back. Elizabeth

Ryan, the head of our local Selkie colony. She sat straight and uncomfortable, holding her purse in her lap like she was afraid it would be stolen. It wasn't that odd to see her here. If anything, it was odd that she hadn't arrived earlier. Elf-shot was fatal to Selkies, because of the human bodies under their fae-touched skins. If anyone would want the stuff gone, it was her.

Walther finished explaining the alchemical processes and principles behind his cure. Reaching up to remove his glasses, he tucked them into his pocket, and asked, "Are there any questions?"

King Antonio of Angels stood before anyone else could react, his Merry Dancers spinning a pirouette in the air around his head. "How are we to trust that this cure works, and is not simply a bid by the alliance of Mists and Silences to poison our people?" He asked the question mildly enough that it didn't sound like an accusation, which was a neat trick. He must have spent a lot of time practicing.

"We know it works because it's been used, while we were trying to retake my family's throne and didn't have time to request permission from the High King." Walther frowned. "I was worried about that, but he forgave us for our indiscretion, once we explained the situation, and he realized that there'd been some major injustices perpetrated against our people."

High Queen Maida cleared her throat. "Please, Master Davies, stay on the path of alchemy, and not the path of politics. Your aunt's claim to the throne of Silences is not under debate here, and does not need to be defended."

"My apologies," said Walther. He paused for a moment, clearly buying time, before returning his attention to King Antonio. "We know it works because those who've used it have been moving amongst us for months now, with no ill-effects."

"You say this, counting the Queen and King of

Silences among their number, but—and forgive me for my indelicacy—it is well understood that the Tylwyth Teg are sensitive to alchemical workings. What works for one of that bloodline will not necessarily work for another, and you do not produce another," said King Antonio. "Are you hiding something?"

"This is making my head hurt," I muttered.

Walther kept his temper remarkably well. "Your Highness, I am an alchemist in a room filled with royalty," he said. "It would not be in my best interests to hide anything right now. Not if I want to be allowed to leave here a free man."

On the stage, Arden glanced at me. That was all: just a glance, a flicker of her eyes. I knew what it meant. It took everything I had to suppress my sigh as I stood, turned to the High King, and asked, "May I have permission to join Master Davies?"

"Of course you may," said High King Aethlin.

All eyes were on me as I climbed the steps. Some were sympathetic, understanding, even concerned. More were confused verging into hostile. Why was I, a changeling, allowed to speak, much less stand upon a stage that contained the great powers of our region?

Tybalt's eyes were cool and unreadable, as they'd been in the days and years before the first time he told me that he loved me. I tried not to let myself be hurt by that as I took up my position next to Walther.

"My name is October Daye, Knight of Lost Words, sworn in service to Duke Sylvester Torquill of Shadowed Hills, hero of the realm. I'm also a changeling," I said. My voice didn't shake. I was pretty proud of that. "While in Silences, I was elf-shot, and fell into an enchanted sleep. Because elf-shot is fatal to those of us with mortal blood, my body began to die. The alchemical tincture Walther Davies created was able to both wake me and cleanse the elf-shot from my system sufficiently that I did not, in fact, pass away."

King Antonio switched his attention to me. I read no malice in his expression. Then again, he was a King. That meant he was probably a pretty good liar, even for one of the fae. "Why should we believe this claim?"

Sylvester moved like he was going to stand. I made a quick motion with my hand, hoping he'd understand that I was waving him off. Luna gave me a hard look as he settled back in his seat. I did my best to ignore them both, focusing instead on the greater threat: King Antonio, who didn't know me and had no reason to trust me. I had too many allies who didn't let my human blood call my words into question. I needed to remember that it didn't work that way for everyone in Faerie.

"The High King is Daoine Sidhe," I said. "I'm willing to let him ride my blood, if that will reassure you."

"Better plan: I can do it," said the Luidaeg. She rose. King Antonio shrank back. I might be used to people trusting me, but I was also used to dealing with the First-born. That, too, was not common in Faerie.

Smirking, the Luidaeg climbed the stairs and came to stand beside me on the stage. Walther—who, like most people, viewed avoiding the Firstborn as a good, reliable life choice that was unlikely to get him brutally murdered—shifted to the side, cheeks coloring red even as the rest of his face got paler. Poor guy really hadn't signed up for this when he'd agreed to help me out.

"Does anyone here question my ability to read the blood of a changeling, or the integrity of my word?" the Luidaeg asked, in a voice as mild as milk and laced with sugary sweetness. She was at her most dangerous when she was talking like that, if only because there was the potential that someone might *forget*. Forget that she was the oldest of us, the most dangerous of us; the one who could slaughter everyone around her without any real effort.

No one spoke.

"That's good. Especially since I can only tell the truth,

so anyone who calls me a liar is out to lose a head." She turned to High King Aethlin. "I grant you no power over me, child of a child thrice-removed of my father, but I grant that you have power over this gathering. If I sample her blood and tell you its secrets, will that be acceptable to you, and hence, to your vassals?"

Sometimes pureblood protocol makes me want to scream and tear my hair out. I forced myself to remain silent and still, waiting for the High King's verdict.

"It will, but only if Sir Daye consents," said the High King. "I will not command any among my subjects to tithe their blood or body to the sea witch without their understanding what it means for them."

"Oh, Toby's given me her blood before, haven't you, Toby?" The Luidaeg smiled at me. Her teeth, which had seemed so blunt and human only a few moments before, were sharp as knives. That sort of swift, mercurial change was almost reassuring, coming from her. If she was changing, she was still herself. No masks. No lies. Just the ever-shifting, ever-faithless sea given demihuman form and a siren's subtle grace.

"Not normally for something like this," I said. I looked past her to the High King and nodded. "I consent. There's no point in having this meeting if we can't all agree that the cure works."

"We could always shoot someone and see if they can be awakened," said Antonio. There was an edge to his voice that hadn't been there before. Apparently, he didn't like being interrupted by a changeling and one of the Firstborn—someone below him and someone so far above him that he might as well have been mortal himself. I could see where that might be jarring, but I didn't feel too bad for him. This was all part of the business of being King.

Tybalt still wasn't saying or doing anything. That stung. Every other time I'd been questioned in his presence, he'd been there to rise and take my side. Even before we'd been officially together, he'd been willing to stand up for me before the pretender Queen. Now he was silent, not speaking, not raising a hand to challenge a man who'd challenged my honor. I'd always known he was a King, and that sometimes he'd need to do things that put his people ahead of me. But this . . . this sort of silence stung, even if it was necessary. I'd never realized how much silence could *hurt*.

"No, we can't," I said flatly, focusing on Antonio and trying not to let my frustration with Tybalt color my tone. "Elf-shot is a poison. Maybe it's one we can counter now, if this conclave finds in favor of distributing the cure, but it's still poisonous, and it still hurts. No one needs to suffer that when we have another way."

Antonio raised both eyebrows. "I'm sorry, little miss. I was unaware that you were a queen in your own right. Tell me, what demesne do you claim, that you can contradict my words so forcefully, and with so little hesitation? What fiefdom is yours by blood, or conquest, or appointment?"

Dianda made a gagging motion. Oddly, that helped. It broke the back of my anger, allowing me to take a deep breath and look to Arden for the support Tybalt couldn't give me.

"She is no queen, as well you know, but she speaks from a position of authority that none of us have," said Arden coolly. "If you like, we can elf-shoot you, and awaken you, and let you testify as to your experience. In fact, I would have to insist. Sir Daye is sworn to one of my most trusted vassals, and by questioning her, you question me. The only way to avoid that becoming dire insult would be to allow honor to cause you to feel the poison for yourself."

King Antonio stood perfectly still for a moment, weighing his options. Finally, he said, "I yield to the sea witch and her interpretation of the changeling's blood," and sat.

"Now that *that's* over," said the Luidaeg. She turned back to me, holding out her hand. "Arm."

I grimaced as I laid my forearm across her palm. "Please try not to open an artery. I don't want to have this whole stage bathed in blood."

"You have so little faith in me," she said, and bent forward, and bit down.

Her teeth were as sharp as they'd appeared. That didn't make it hurt any less. The smell of my blood filled the air, mixing with the bitter-cold sea-smell of her magic, which stung like salt when it touched my skin. She drank deeply, and the feel of her pulling the blood from my veins was disorienting enough to make me close my eyes for a moment, centering myself.

I opened them when she pulled away. The wound in my forearm was already healing, leaving only a smear of blood and saliva behind. I wiped it away with my free hand, then scrubbed my palm against the leg of my pants.

The Luidaeg, eyes now black from side to side like the depths of an angry sea, turned to the gallery, and said, "I, the Luidaeg, sea witch and undying daughter of Maeve, tell you that the woman beside me, Sir October Christine Daye of Shadowed Hills, was elf-shot twice, and lived each time through the intervention of outside forces. The first shot was delivered by an assassin's bow, and was countered by the magic of my sister, who changed the blood in Sir Daye's body such as to sunder her from her own death. The second shot was delivered by the hand of the deposed King Rhys of Silences, and was countered by a tincture brewed by Master Walther Davies, alchemist. In both cases, the elf-shot was true: her sleep, and death, should have followed. It did not. The cure works."

"So it is said," said High King Aethlin. "Let it be accepted within these chambers that the cure works."

Some of the people in the gallery muttered, but no one objected. That was a relief.

"You may be excused, Sir Daye," said the High King.

I turned to him, bowed, and walked back to my seat as quickly as I dared. The Luidaeg followed me, leaving Walther to face the ensuing inquisition alone.

It felt like everyone in the room had a question for him. What was in the tincture? How was it made? Could *anyone* make it, assuming it wasn't banned as a result of this conclave? Was he holding anything back? Had there been earlier versions that hadn't worked? How had he tested them? How had he been sure that using the cure wouldn't kill us, and result in a violation of the Law? It went on and on, and frankly, I wasn't listening. I was too busy sinking into my seat, rubbing the place on my arm where the ghosts of the Luidaeg's teeth still lingered, continuing to try and get a feel for the room.

Most of these people had previously been only names on paper to me, if that. The monarchs of Golden Shore, for example. Their Kingdom is known for being a safe haven for changelings, as long as those changelings are willing to work. Everyone works in Golden Shore. It's an agrarian community, responsible for providing most of the noble houses on the West Coast with fae produce and livestock. Yes, there are fae cows, called Crodh Sith by people who want to be pretentious about it, and their milk and butter are supposed to be some of the finest in this world or any other. Golden apples, silver grapes, sheep with fleece finer than silk . . . if you want any of those things, you get them from Golden Shore. Golden Hinds are rare, as they breed even more slowly than most fae and don't like to live in human cities. Seeing a married couple was fascinating.

Both of them were frowning as Walther spoke, and their questions were sharp-edged, like they were trying to trip him up. I didn't get the feeling they were on the side of distributing the cure. I just couldn't figure out *why*.

King Antonio, on the other hand, was definitely opposed to distributing the cure, and I knew *exactly* why.

Angels has a reputation as a place where you could do what you wanted without fear of noble intervention, because the nobility of Angels don't care. As long as they can party the nights away, the riff-raff in the streets doesn't matter to them. Elf-shot was the monarchy's primary method of enforcing the few rules they did have. I'd always thought it was sort of like Shakespeare's Verona: gleefully lawless, with brawls breaking out every time two warring factions tripped over each other in the grocery store. Take away elf-shot as a threat and a pacifying tool, and Antonio and his court might actually start needing to *work*.

Queen Siwan of Silences was obviously in favor of distributing the cure, for a lot of reasons. Walther was her nephew. Even if he was currently residing in and serving the Mists, having him be the one to discover a way to break one of the oldest enchantments in our world reflected well on his family and the Kingdom that they held. Aspiring alchemists from all over the world would want to go and train in Silences, the Kingdom that had created the finest alchemist of our age. Also, I was pretty sure the Yates family had already used the cure to wake everyone in their Kingdom, and that would be easier to explain if the cure didn't wind up illegal.

It was hard to say which side of the argument Dianda came down on. She was glaring at the stage with such intensity that it was almost surprising when no one burst spontaneously into flames. Patrick looked thoughtful. Patrick usually looks thoughtful. Patrick is the leavening influence that keeps Dianda from killing us all because she's bored, or hungry, or doesn't like the way someone's looking at her. I'm very fond of Patrick.

High Queen Maida leaned over and murmured something to her husband who, in turn, leaned over and murmured something to Arden. She nodded, rising gracefully from her throne and clasping her hands together as a signal for silence. The room quieted.

"We're agreed, then, that this is no small topic: whatever we decide will change the course of Faerie for however long remains before Oberon returns to us. In light of this, no decisions will be made rashly, or without consideration of all perspectives. Many of you have traveled far to be here. The hospitality of my home is open to you for the duration of this conclave, plus the traditional three days, should you wish to remain and enjoy the courtesies of my Kingdom when our business here is done. For now, we'll stop to enjoy a meal, and to consider what we have heard so far. The conclave will resume after we have all eaten."

She waited for Siwan to rise and join her before the pair turned and walked off the stage, followed by the High King and High Queen. I stayed where I was. If I could avoid being trampled by royalty, that would be swell.

I wasn't the only one: basically everyone in my row was holding still, as if that would somehow keep them from being noticed by the outgoing kings and queens. Having the Luidaeg with us probably helped a lot, since no one wanted to poke the Firstborn if they could help it.

Sylvester cast a look in our direction as he walked up the aisle, like he wanted to come over and speak to me, but didn't quite have the nerve. I turned my face to the side, not waving him over, and eventually, he just left.

Tybalt didn't look at us at all.

Politics were politics, and I could worry about them later. For now, I had bigger things to focus on. Twisting in my seat, I leaned forward until I could see Karen. "Honey, are you okay?"

Her face crumpled, like she'd been holding herself together by the thinnest of lines. "Auntie Birdie!" she wailed, flinging herself across Quentin to get to me. She wound up mostly in my lap, arms around my neck, legs slung over his lap. Quentin looked nonplussed but didn't say anything. He knew she wasn't trying to invade his personal space, no matter how much she was succeeding.

"Oh, *honey*." I put my arms around her and held her as tightly as I could, feeling the warm wetness of her tears against my neck. She was crying too hard to talk. I stroked her back with one hand, turning to look at the Luidaeg.

"Karen appeared on my doorstep at sundown," she said. "I was already planning to come to this shit-storm circus, so she's lucky she didn't miss me. Said my scumbag sister had appeared in her dreams and threatened her family if she didn't come and represent her interests."

There was a lot of "she" and "her" in that sentence, but I followed it well enough, especially because I knew where the Luidaeg's restrictions were. She couldn't say Eira's name, or any of her aliases. For her, Evening Winterrose was a pronoun and a problem, a looming disaster that had already killed her once and wouldn't hesitate to do it again.

I also knew that whatever Evening had said to threaten Karen, she could follow through on those threats. We'd learned that Karen was an oneiromancer after she was taken captive by Blind Michael, who had been a Firstborn son of Oberon and Maeve, and hence the Luidaeg's younger brother. He'd stolen Karen while she was sleeping, leaving her body behind while he prisoned her dreaming form in a glass ball. If one of the Firstborn could hurt her that way, I had no doubt that another Firstborn—especially one as powerful as Evening—could do the same.

"You know, I was worried when we started working on this cure," I said bitterly. "I thought 'well, hell, we just got Evening out of the way for a hundred years, and now we have to worry about somebody waking her up like the villain from a bad slasher movie.' Only now even elf-shot can't keep her from hurting my family. Why didn't we kill her, again?"

"Because if you were in violation of Oberon's Law,

you'd be imprisoned or executed, and either way, you wouldn't be able to finish my training," said Quentin. His voice shook. He was as unhappy as I was about this; he just didn't know what to do about it. It didn't help that Evening was his Firstborn. Everything he was told him he should obey and honor her, not side against her. Carefully, he reached over and patted Karen's shoulder. "Hey. It'll be okay. Toby's not going to let her hurt you."

Sometimes I was so proud of that kid that it hurt. I stroked Karen's hair with one hand, and asked, "Anybody got any bright ideas about how to keep Evening from using Karen as her catspaw forever once she gets woken up?"

"What?" Karen pulled back, letting me see her tear-streaked face. Her eyes were wide, glossy, and filled with tears. "What do you mean?"

I frowned at her, confused. "I meant that after the cure is approved, and Evening is woken up, what's going to make her leave you alone?"

"She didn't send me here because she wants the cure to be used, Auntie Birdie," said Karen. "She sent me here because she wants it to be buried."

I stared at her. So did Quentin. The Luidaeg, who had presumably heard this before, sighed and pushed herself to her feet.

"Okay, kids," she said. "Let's go eat."

Karen climbed out of my lap. Walther, Quentin, and I stood, and together, the five of us walked toward the door. When we were halfway there, Karen took my hand. I didn't pull away.

SEVEN

MOST OF THE LOCAL NOBLES had loaned Arden members of their household for the duration of the conclave, making up for the shortcomings in staffing at the kingdom level. Arden was still getting established, and had a lot of hiring to do before she'd be operating at full capacity. Besides, this guaranteed those nobles a steady source of gossip, even if they weren't attending the conclave themselves.

It also meant that when we stepped into the ballroom, Karen and I were no longer the only changelings in the place. The fact that we were the only changelings not holding serving trays wasn't exactly reassuring, but that's life in Faerie. Sometimes the reminders that we'll always be a feudal society are impossible to ignore.

Tables were set up around the room. There were no assigned seats, but people tended to stick to what they knew. One table was on a raised dais, reserved for the leaders of the conclave. It held Arden, the High King and High Queen, Queen Siwan of Silences . . . and Tybalt. I stopped dead when I saw him sitting there, talking with High King Sollys, an expression of deep solemnity on his face.

The Luidaeg touched my elbow. "Muir Woods is technically within the bounds of the Court of Dreaming Cats," she murmured, voice low enough that she probably wouldn't be overheard. "That gives your kitty-boy equal claim to the land, if he wanted to get cranky about it. By attending this conclave, he said, 'Hey, treat me as an equal,' and so they are. I bet he's on the stage when we resume. They just didn't know he was coming in time to avoid putting him in the audience when he first showed up."

Tybalt knew Arden. He could have told her he was coming. The fact that he hadn't could only have been intentional, a move designed to put her off her guard. It might have been a reaction to her failure to invite him in the first place: I didn't know. I didn't know a lot of things, including what sort of game he was playing here, and since I couldn't ask him, it was difficult to keep the pit in my stomach from opening even wider than it had before.

The Luidaeg gave me a sympathetic look. "Never forget that he's from a different Court. You can love him—I know you do—and he can love you, but there are places where your differences will always win out. Maybe it's good that this is happening now, while you still have the distance to see them." She reached over and carefully untangled my fingers from Karen's. "You, come with me. We need to do a circuit of the room, so everyone here remembers you're under my protection."

Karen bit her lip and nodded, only looking back once as the Luidaeg led her away.

Walther, Quentin, and I stood silent for a moment, taking in the room. Whoever was in charge of the decorating—probably Lowri, given how recently Madden had been woken—had pulled out all the stops. Redwood boughs draped with fog-colored ribbons formed great arcs across the ceiling, heavy with the glittering shapes of pixies and fireflies. The floor was hidden by a warm, conjured mist that smelled of blackberries and the

sea. Everywhere I looked there were servers in the colors
of the Kingdom, moving through the crowd with trays of
drinks and small canapés. Most people were seated by
this point, and the servers were bringing them baskets of
fragrant bread and larger glasses of sparkling wine.

The only table not being attended by one or more
servers in Arden's livery had been claimed by the King
and Queen of Highmountain. They sat alone while their
Barrow Wight handmaid rushed back and forth, bringing
them trays of delicacies, carting away their empty glasses,
and trying to avoid colliding with any of the servers.

"Paranoid about poison?" I guessed.

"Or they're just jerks," said Walther. "Not uncommon,
as it turns out."

"I can take you to your table, if you want."

All three of us turned. Madden was behind us, golden
eyes glowing in the diffuse light, dressed in the colors of
the Kingdom. He'd never looked so much like a seneschal. Mostly, I was just glad to see him awake and moving around.

"That would be nice," I said. "I'm not quite sure what
the pecking order here is supposed to be, apart from 'everyone is more important than you.'"

"Nah, not everyone," he said. "Some people are less
important. But, mostly, you're right. Come with me." He
started across the room toward one of the tables that still
had open seats. One of the people already seated there
had hair the color of fox fur, russet red and inhuman.

Sylvester.

For a brief moment, I considered turning and running
for the door. My fiancé was ignoring me, my niece was
being tormented by a woman who should have been incapable of hurting us until she woke up, and now I was
being seated with my semi-estranged liege? There wasn't
enough "no, thank you" in the world. In the end, I
couldn't do it. Walther needed me here. The High King
had ordered me to be here. *Karen* needed me to be here.

I squared my shoulders, straightened as much as I could, and allowed Madden to lead us to the table.

There were seats for ten. The five occupied seats were held by Sylvester, Luna, Li Qin, Elliott, and Elizabeth Ryan, who had somehow convinced the servers to give her a large glass of whiskey instead of the sparkling wine that everyone else was drinking. She barely glanced up as we approached the table.

Sylvester, on the other hand, rose and offered me his hands. "October," he said. There was no mistaking the delight, or the relief, in his voice. "I was hoping you'd come sit with us."

No matter how angry with him I was, he was my liege, and the man who'd been the closest thing I had to a father for most of my life. I slipped my hands over his, letting him close his fingers around mine, and said, "I guess this is where Arden wanted us. Hi, Sylvester. Hello, Luna."

Luna Torquill, Duchess of Shadowed Hills, and formerly a friend, did not reply. She turned her face to the side, showing me the tapered point of one white-skinned ear. Her hair was pale pink at the roots, tapering to red-black at the end, and had been partially braided to form a crown around her head, while the bulk of it fell, loose and unencumbered, down her back. She was beautiful. There was no denying that. But she wasn't the woman who'd known me as a child, or the one who used to comfort me. That version of Luna had died when her own daughter poisoned her, forcing her to abandon her stolen Kitsune skin in order to survive.

"I met your sister," I said, partially out of spite, partially out of sheer stubbornness. I wanted her to *see* me. I wanted her to acknowledge that we had a history, and she couldn't just cut me out of her life because she didn't want me anymore. "Ceres, I mean, in case you have other sisters. She's living in Silences these days. She said she was glad to hear that you were doing well."

"I'm not doing well," said Luna. "My daughter yet sleeps, for all that you changed her blood. When your mother changed your own, you woke. The same for your own child. You've kept my Rayseline from me. So no, October, I have nothing to say to you."

"Luna," said Sylvester, in a chiding tone.

Luna said nothing.

"I think I know why that is, actually," said Walther. I turned to look at him. So did Sylvester. Walther flushed red, and continued, "When I'm mixing a potion, a lot of it is about intent, telling the spell what I want it to do."

"All magic is like that," I said finally, pulling my hands out of Sylvester's and sitting down. He held on to me for a few seconds longer than I wanted him to, resisting my efforts to remove myself. In the end, however, he had to let me go. Anything else would have been rude.

"Sure, but that's the point," said Walther. He sat. So did Quentin. As if by magic, servers appeared to set goblets and bread in front of the three of us. "When your mother changed you, she wanted you to wake up. When you changed your daughter, you made her mortal, and you knew she needed to wake up or she was going to die. So you both brought intent to what you were doing. You removed the elf-shot as part of removing the parts of the blood that weren't needed anymore."

"Oh," I said quietly. That was all. I didn't dare say anything else: I was too afraid that he was right.

Rayseline Torquill was Sylvester and Luna's only child. She had been born the daughter of a Daoine Sidhe and a Blodynbryd, something that would have been impossible if Luna hadn't been wearing a skin stolen from a dying Kitsune, making herself part-mammal for as long as she had it. Faerie genetics don't follow rules so much as they obey vague suggestions, at least when they feel like it. Rayseline had been born with biology that was forever in the process of tearing itself apart, and eventually, she'd snapped under the strain, trying to murder her parents and claim their lands as her own. She'd killed my lover—her ex-husband—Connor O'Dell when he'd jumped in front of the arrow intended for my daughter. Sadly, his sacrifice hadn't been enough to keep Gillian from being hurt. It had just been enough to make me lose them both, him to death, her to the human world.

Raysel had also been elf-shot on that day, and her mother had asked me to soothe her pain. I'd done the best I could, slipping into Rayseline's sleeping mind the way I had once slipped into Gillian's—the way my mother had slipped into mine—and asking what she wanted to be. When I'd finished, she was purely Daoine Sidhe, more prepared to control her magic and her mind . . . and she'd still been asleep, because I hadn't wanted her awake.

Luna must have known that from the start. It explained a lot. And it didn't make things any better between us. I wasn't sure anything could.

Li Qin smiled at me across the table. She was a short, lovely woman of Chinese descent, with eyes almost as black as her hair, and an air of serenity that came from knowing she was in control of her own luck. Literally: her breed of fae, the Shyi Shuai, manipulated probability in a way that could lead to remarkable good fortune and equally remarkable backlash. I sometimes suspected, although I'd never asked her, that one of those backlashes had influenced Li's widowing. Her wife, January O'Leary, had been Sylvester's niece, and she'd died when I wasn't fast enough to save her.

Sometimes I wondered why Sylvester *wanted* to make peace with me. I wasn't good for his family.

"How have you been, October?" asked Li. "You haven't been to visit in a while."

"Busy," I said. "Preventing a war. Deposing a king. Keeping Walther alive while he figured out how to unmake elf-shot. You know, nothing big, but it all took up a lot of time."

"We miss you," said Elliot. "April sends her regards."

Quentin perked up. He liked April. She was always happy to fix his phone when he broke it, which was surprisingly often. "How is she?"

"Doing well," said Elliot. "She's really grown into her role. Although she still acts as the company intercom most of the time."

"Naturally," I said. April was Li and January's adopted daughter. As the world's only cyber-Dryad, she was half electricity, and lived in the County wireless when she didn't have a reason to be physical. Again, fae genetics are weird. "I'm sort of relieved that she's not here."

"Believe me, so am I," said Elliot. "She's a wonderful regent, but she doesn't do diplomacy well."

I had to laugh at that. Diplomacy was not and would never be one of my strong suits, and somehow it kept turning into my job. Elliot answered my laughter with a lopsided smile, eyes twinkling above the bushy tangle of his beard.

Elizabeth finally looked up from her glass, eyes hazy with her omnipresent inebriation. I'd never seen her without a drink in her hand. Sometimes I wondered whether she rolled out of bed and straight into her cups. "Could you please keep the noise down?" she asked. "I intend to get righteously drunk before they bring the first course around, and you're slowing me down."

"Hi to you, too, Liz," I said.

"Hello, October." She sighed, and took a swig before setting her glass aside. "We've been waiting for you."

"I know." According to the Luidaeg, the bargain she'd struck with the Selkies after their ancestors killed her children was coming to an end. I was going to play a part in whatever that meant. I just didn't know what that part was, or when it was going to be necessary.

"But until that grand day comes, you're all going to play nicely, or I'm going to pull your fucking spines out through your nostrils," said the Luidaeg, stepping up behind me. I twisted to look at her. Karen was sticking close by her side, and while my niece looked shaken, she didn't seem any more traumatized than she'd been when they walked away. That was a nice change.

The Luidaeg's eyes, however, were only for Elizabeth. "Hello, Liz," she said. "I wasn't sure I'd see you here."

"However much I may dislike my position, I'm still leader of our colony, and that means things like this are important," said Elizabeth, making no effort to conceal the bitterness in her tone. She lifted her glass in a mocking half-salute. "Hello, Annie-my-love. Broken any young girls' hearts recently?"

"No, but I haven't spent much time trying. Maybe I've lost my touch." The Luidaeg took one of our table's two remaining seats, leaving the place between her and me open for Karen. "When are they going to feed us?"

I blinked. "Uh. Shouldn't you be at the high table? Please don't claim insult on the Queen. My nerves can't take it right now."

"Please, that bullshit? No. I gave my seat to your kitty-boy. He needed it more than I did, and he's making them even twitchier than I would." The Luidaeg smirked before looking to Karen. Her expression softened. "Sit down, honey. It's okay."

Karen sat, and again as if by magic—maybe actually by magic; this was Faerie, after all—more servers appeared, this time carrying platters of food. There'd been no survey asking what we wanted to eat, and yet almost everyone seemed to receive a different meal, one suited to their tastes. The Luidaeg got a bowl of fish chowder. Elizabeth got a piece of baked salmon surrounded by potatoes carved into rosebuds. Luna got a salad made entirely of edible roses.

I got a bowl of spaghetti with meat sauce, covered in parmesan cheese. Quentin and Karen got the same thing, only twice as large, accounting for their teenage metabolisms. I chose to see this as a sign that I was rubbing off on them, rather than a comment about how immature my taste in food was. It wasn't easy, but like I've always said, if you can't lie to yourself, who can you lie to?

The food was excellent. I expected nothing less from Arden's kitchen. And, for a while, everything was quiet. That's the nice thing about formal dinners: they give people an excuse to cut the small talk and pretend that things aren't as awkward as they inevitably are.

Naturally, it couldn't last. King Antonio of Silences shoved his chair back from the table, sending it clattering to the ground. Dianda, who was sitting across from him, calmly put her fork down and looked at him with all the flat blankness of a snake getting ready to strike at its prey.

The room went silent. I stole a glance at the high table. Everyone there was looking toward the disturbance, but none of them had moved yet. I couldn't decide whether that was a good sign or a bad one, and so I turned my attention back to the standing king.

"How *dare* you," Antonio snarled, eyes fixed on Dianda. "This is an insult and an outrage, and one I should have expected from a perverted daughter of the sea." His Merry Dancers swirled around him, mirroring his supposed fury.

Dianda raised an eyebrow before pushing her wheelchair back from the table and standing. She made the transition from mermaid to woman look effortless, even though I knew from experience that it was nothing of the sort. "All I said, *sir*, was that there was no reason to restrict regency of our greater demesnes to those of unmixed blood. My son is my heir. The fact that his father is Daoine Sidhe is no reason to deny him his birthright."

"You should never have married outside your own kind if you wanted your bloodline to endure," he snapped. "The very idea—"

"Oberon passed no laws against inheritance by

children of mixed blood, unless you consider a ruling made by one of his descendants to carry backward through the family tree," said Dianda, her tone icy. "As I seem to recall, the ruling in question said only that *changelings* could not inherit their family lands or titles. Nothing about fully fae children." She seemed unbothered by the fact that the entire room was staring at her. The Undersea was still largely alien to me, but I knew enough to know that they solved their disputes in a much more violent, visceral way than most of the Divided Courts.

Her comment seemed to have been enough to enflame a few more tempers—just what we needed. Chrysanthe, the Queen of Golden Shore, stood, hooves clattering against the marble floor, and braced her hands on her own table as she demanded, "Why do we still abide by such an outdated, archaic ruling? Changelings have as much of a right to their inheritance as anyone!"

That was the final straw. The room was suddenly full of shouting nobility, all with their own ideas and opinions about what was to be done. Most were against the idea of changelings inheriting; about half were against the idea of mixed-bloods inheriting; all of them were against the idea of somehow being overlooked in the fracas. Liz started drinking faster, holding her tongue. Quentin and Karen sat frozen to either side of me, too stunned to eat.

Right. "I don't think this is the part we're needed for," I said, standing and offering each of them a hand. "How about you come with me, and we'll see if we can't get out of here before someone starts throwing punches?"

"Okay," said Karen gratefully, taking my hand in hers. Quentin didn't take my hand, but he did stand. Given that he was eighteen now—almost an adult by human standards, even if he was still a baby to the fae—that was all I'd been expecting.

Sylvester started to stand. The Luidaeg looked at him, narrow-eyed and silent, and he sat back down. I'd have to thank her for that later.

If anyone else noticed the three of us making our quick, quiet escape, they didn't say anything. I didn't know the layout of the knowe as well as I would have liked, but I knew knowes in general, and I knew there were always multiple ways out of a room. In the end, all we had to do was follow the servants to find our way to a narrow door in the corner near the balcony windows, half-hidden by tapestries. We slipped through. The door closed behind us, and we were in a quiet, well-lit hallway, with no shouting nobles or risk of flying food.

Quentin looked at me. "Next time, can we be out of town when something like this happens? Like, in another Kingdom or something?"

"Next time, I will take you to Disneyland," I said. "Karen, you okay?"

"Sure." She laughed unsteadily. "That was sort of like being in someone else's nightmare, only no one was naked, and there were no lobsters on the walls."

"Come on, you two," I said. "Let's see if we can find the kitchen and get a replacement dinner."

We walked along the silent hall, Karen still holding my hand, Quentin following slightly behind us, like he was guarding the rear. It would have been nice, if not for the omnipresent fear that we'd be found and dragged back to the banquet hall. I was pretty sure Arden was letting the nobles shout themselves into exhaustion. Her years working retail at the bookstore must have taught her a few things about crowd control.

The hall ended in a redwood door carved with moths. We stopped, looking at each other, before I shrugged and pushed the door open, revealing a small balcony. Three tables were set up there. One held three plates of spaghetti and meatballs, a large basket of bread, and a pitcher of what looked like sparkling lemonade. Raj was already seated in one of the chairs, slurping down spaghetti like it was about to be made illegal.

The second table had no occupants, but held a wide assortment of desserts. The third had a large tea tower covered in sandwiches, scones, and small, savory pastries. All three of us stopped again, this time blinking at the scene in front of us.

"As it turns out, no one takes offense when a King of Cats declares the anger of the Divided Courts to be misaimed and leaves until they can stop acting like children," purred a voice behind me. "Or perhaps they *do* take offense, and simply don't bother to say anything, as I'm not worthy of being scolded by my betters. Regardless, the kitchen staff sends their regards, and hopes you'll enjoy your meal."

I dropped Karen's hand as I turned. Tybalt was behind me. He offered a small, almost shy smile, revealing the pointed tip of one incisor.

"Did you miss me?" he asked.

I punched him in the arm.

Tybalt raised his eyebrows. "I see." He looked past me to Quentin. "Did she miss me?"

"I'm pretty sure she's going to murder you," he said. "I'm pretty sure I'm going to help."

"Ah." Tybalt sighed as he returned his attention to my face. "I told you I couldn't arrive with you. I told you I had to stand as a King, and not as an accessory to one of their own."

"Funny," I said. "You didn't tell me you weren't going to speak to me for a *week* beforehand. I figured you'd have to ignore me once we got here, but before? I understand politics, I do, but ash and oak, Tybalt, that was a little much to drop on a girl without some kind of warning." I punched him again, not as hard this time. My anger was fading, replaced by relief.

To his credit, he bore my unhappiness with a small

nod and a mild, "You're right. I shouldn't have done that. But there aren't really precedents for this sort of event. Most Kings of Cats will never have the opportunity to remind the High King of their domain of their existence, much less do so in such a plain and evident fashion."

"That reminds me," I said. "Where's Shade?" Shade was the Queen of Cats who had dominion over the Berkeley area. I'd only met her once, and she'd remained in her feline form for the entire time, but she'd seemed nice enough.

"She'll be joining us tomorrow, after my nephew has gone home," said Tybalt, offering me his arm. "Since my domain corresponds to the seat of Arden's Kingdom, we knew that only I would be welcome at the high table, and it was important I be seated there, to make the point that my Court is an equal partner in this discussion. Shall we sit?"

"We shall," I said, taking his arm. Quentin and Karen, looking relieved, made for the table where Raj was waiting. I grinned as I watched them go. "It was good of you to make sure the kids got a second dinner."

"I knew as soon as that man," Tybalt's nose wrinkled, "started shouting about mixed-bloods and inheritance that you'd be making your escape sooner rather than later, and further, I knew there was no way you'd go without your charges. Honestly, I'm just relieved you managed to escape without bringing your entire table along." He took his arm away from mine in order to pull my chair out.

I settled into it, flashing him a quick smile. Tybalt smiled back, his own relief painted clearly across his features. His position had been as bad as mine was, maybe worse: I had to worry about my fiancé rejecting me, but he had to worry about the political status of his entire race. What he did here, he did for all Cait Sidhe, not just for the Court of Dreaming Cats. Maybe he could have handled things better—absolutely he could have handled things better—but I couldn't blame him for a few small missteps. Just like always, we were standing on uncharted ground.

"How did you arrange all this?" I asked.

He settled into the chair across from mine, picking up the pitcher and pouring us each a glass of dark, faintly fizzing liquid that smelled of blackcurrants and roses. "As I said, the kitchen staff sends their regards. You're well liked in this court, although I couldn't for the life of me say why, insufferable creature that you are."

"I thought you liked me insufferable," I said, reaching for my glass.

Tybalt put his hand over mine and smiled. There was nothing but fondness in his eyes.

"My dearest October, I *adore* you insufferable," he said.

I laughed, and for the first time since this conclave had been announced, I started to feel like things were going to be all right.

EIGHT

WE SPENT AN HOUR or so out on the balcony, eating slowly, enjoying the night air. I was enjoying the absence of the nobility—well, except for Tybalt, Raj, and Quentin, which really meant that I was enjoying the absence of *annoying* nobility—even more. The teenagers finished their spaghetti and made a raid on our tea tower, taking half the scones back to their table. I threw a wadded-up napkin at them, and they laughed, and everything was perfect.

That alone should have told me it couldn't last. The air rippled and Sir Grianne of Shadowed Hills was suddenly sitting on the balcony rail. Her Merry Dancers spun in the air around her. Like King Antonio, she was sketched in shades of gray. Unlike him, her skin was ash and her hair was granite, striated in bands of dark and light. Also unlike him, she was wearing simple livery: a tunic in the blue and gold of Shadowed Hills and a sash around her waist in the silver and purple of Arden's household.

"Grianne," I said. "I didn't know you were here."

She lifted one shoulder in a shrug, like my ignorance was none of her concern. "On loan," she said.

Candela tend to be short-spoken, preferring to

communicate through pulses of light and the motion of their Merry Dancers, the glowing orbs that accompanied them everywhere from birth onward. Grianne exemplified her race. I waited several seconds, and no further details were offered.

Right. "Did you need something?" I asked.

"The conclave is resuming," she said, her voice thin and reedy as the wind through the trees. "Your presence is requested by the High King."

"I guess that's our cue." I stood. Quentin and Karen did the same. I started to turn toward Tybalt, but stopped as the smell of pennyroyal and musk tickled my nose, carried to me by the light midnight wind. He was already gone. So was Raj. It made sense: they hadn't left the gallery with us, so they couldn't exactly return with us without making the declaration of allegiance that Tybalt had been trying so hard to avoid. I understood the necessity, but it still bothered me.

Quentin put a hand on my shoulder. I didn't have to look down when I turned to meet his eyes. That bothered me, too, but in a different way. He was growing up. He wasn't going to need me much longer. He already didn't need me in the way he had, once, when he'd been trying to muddle his way through puberty and I'd been the one who was willing to restock the fridge and let him crash on my couch. Everything was changing, and I wasn't sure I liked it.

"Come on," I said. "Let's go sit through more political screaming."

There was a flash of greenish-white light as Grianne toppled backward off the railing and was gone. Sometimes I feel like we hang out with too many teleporters.

It didn't take long to walk back to the dining room where we'd been served our first, abandoned dinner. It was empty. The tables had been cleaned, and the lights were turned down low, presumably so no one would get confused and try to come here for the conclave. There was a strange sound as we stepped through the door, like the distant rustle of skeleton leaves, or the beating of a thousand autumn leaf wings on the wind. My heart dropped into my stomach. I knew that sound. It stopped almost instantly, but it was too late. I'd already heard it.

I stopped and spread my arms, keeping Quentin and Karen from moving forward. They were good kids. Better yet, they had both known me long enough that when I indicated that I needed them to stay where they were, they froze immediately.

"What is it?" asked Quentin.

"That sound," I said. "Did you hear it? When we first came in."

"Dead leaves," he said. "The whole place is decorated in redwoods. There's going to be some settling, especially when there's no one talking to cover it up."

"Redwoods don't have leaves, you doof," said Karen. "They're evergreens."

"Just stay here, both of you." I stepped forward, wishing I'd been allowed to bring my knife; wishing I wasn't walking, unarmed, into a large, empty dining hall where I'd heard—or thought that I'd heard—the beating of the night-haunts' wings. It hadn't been loud enough to have placed them in this room. They were approaching. But why?

Something crunched underfoot. I glanced down to be sure that it was neither glass nor bone, and saw that I'd stepped on what looked like the shell of some large egg. Nothing to worry about, then. I resumed my forward progress, and stopped again as something else crunched. This time, I knelt and picked up a piece of what I'd stepped on.

It was thin, curved, and brittle as an old snail's shell, colored like carnival glass and patterned with thin whorls and swirls, as distinctive as a fingerprint. I frowned, trying to figure out where I had seen this before, and why it looked so familiar.

The answer came to me on the beating of the night-haunts' wings, still distant, still impossible to ignore. I was holding the shell of a broken Merry Dancer.

I was holding proof that King Antonio Robertson of Angels was dead.

"Stay where you are, kids," I said, staring at the broken shell in my hand. "Quentin, I know you've been working on illumination spells. Can you throw me a globe of witch-light please?" Casting a spell inside Arden's knowe might be enough to get her attention, or at least the attention of a member of her staff. That wouldn't be a bad thing. This wasn't the sort of situation that I could handle on my own.

"Okay," said Quentin. He murmured something incomprehensible. The scent of heather and steel washed over the room and a globe of light appeared above me. It looked distressingly like one of Antonio's Merry Dancers, before they had been broken, save for the fact that it didn't dance or weave; it just hung there, casting a cool white light over everything below it.

Thin, glittering shards littered the floor, like someone had smashed a giant Christmas ornament. The point of impact was somewhere ahead of me. I started gingerly forward, careful to avoid as many of the shards as possible. I didn't want to destroy the evidence before I'd had a chance to really look at it. Quentin's ball of witch-light caught on the shards, making them easier to see.

After five steps, I found King Antonio.

He was sprawled in a way that mostly hid his body under one of the dining tables; if not for the shards of Merry Dancer scattered everywhere, it would have been easy to write him off as a shadow cast by the intersection of curtain and wall. With Quentin's mage-light to brighten the scene, and the curved shell in my hand, it was impossible for me to pretend he was anything but what he was. A corpse.

The night-haunts hadn't arrived yet. We'd interrupted

them before they could descend and devour the evidence. That was a good thing, in a way; it's easier to examine a body when there actually *is* one. I knelt, looking carefully at what had once been King Antonio Robinson of Angels. It wasn't hard to guess what killed him. Purebloods can be difficult to kill, but on the whole, a rosewood spike through the chest will stop virtually any of us where we stand. His eyes were open, staring in silent horror at the table above him.

"Huh," I said.

On the other side of the room, Karen gasped. It was a squeak of a sound, barely worthy of the name, but it was enough to warn me. I went still, just before the tip of a sword was laid against the back of my neck.

Please be Lowri, I thought, and said, "Hi. Who's about to decapitate me?"

"October, why are you kneeling over the body of a dead king?" Lowri sounded more puzzled than angry. That wasn't going to last. "What have you done?"

"Nothing. May I stand?"

"Keep your hands where I can see them, and make no sudden moves. I won't kill you, but I'd hate to remove your arms."

I believed her when she said that. Lowri was reasonably fond of me, even if we weren't friends. Plus cutting my arms off would really contaminate the scene. Still, I moved carefully as I straightened, the piece of broken Merry Dancer in my right hand, and turned to face the head of Arden's guard.

Lowri had traded her customary and ceremonial spear for a proper sword, one which was too close to me for comfort. There were two more guards behind her. I knew neither of them by name. Quentin and Karen were still on the far side of the room, near the door we had entered through. That made me feel a little better. They could duck out if things got bad. Quentin was good enough at navigating the back halls of most knowes that

I had faith in his ability to keep them safe, and Tybalt would come to find them, eventually. I trusted him to do that.

"What did you *do*?" asked Lowri, modifying her question only slightly. Her eyes went to the piece of Merry Dancer in my hand.

Holding it probably made me look guilty, but dropping it was out of the question. It would shatter, and I didn't know whether that was disrespectful to the Candela, or whether it would be dishonoring his memory. All I could do was hold the empty shell of what he'd been, and hope that I'd be able to talk my way out of the situation.

"I left the dining room when people started shouting," I said, as calmly as I could. "I took my niece and squire with me, because they're my responsibility, and as long as that's the case, I won't leave them in a room full of angry nobles." Quentin officially had no title until he left my custodianship. Karen was a changeling whose parents didn't even serve a noble house. My taking them with me wasn't just logical, it was practically required. To do anything else would have been to fail in my duties.

"That doesn't explain why we've found you here, standing over the body of a dead king," said Lowri.

The scent of blackberry flowers and redwood bark teased my nostrils. I relaxed slightly. "We had dinner on the balcony at the end of the adjoining servant's hall," I said. "The kitchen staff should be able to confirm that we were fed out there. After we were finished, Sir Grianne of Shadowed Hills came to tell us the conclave was resuming. Since we were on the balcony, we had to come through here to get back to the gallery. Upon entering, I heard a strange noise, and went to investigate. That's pretty much everything that happened. You found *me* right after I found him."

"Found who?" asked Arden.

I turned. Somehow, I didn't think Lowri was going to stab me for turning toward my queen. "Your Highness,"

I said, dropping to one knee. I can be irreverent and resistant to many of the finer points of pureblood etiquette, but some forms can't be ignored. Reporting the death of a noble is among them. "When the Root and Branch were young, when the Rose still grew unplucked upon the tree; when all our lands were new and green and we danced without care, then, we were immortal. Then, we lived forever."

I hadn't said those words in years—not since I'd told the false Queen of the Mists that Evening Winterrose was dead. My head was bowed. I couldn't see the look on Arden's face. I was pretty sure I didn't want to. "We left those lands for the world where time dwells, dancing, that we might see the passage of the sun and the growing of the world. Here we may die, and here we can fall, and here His Highness Antonio Robinson, King of the demesne of Angels, has stopped his dancing."

He'd stopped his dancing so completely that his body was on the floor not three feet away, motionless, waiting for the night-haunts to come and claim him. As I lifted my head, it was difficult to focus on Arden, and not on the dead body.

She had come alone. That made sense. High King Aethlin and High Queen Maida were probably doing their best to keep the rest of the conclave from getting angry over the apparent disrespect of the missing attendees. Me being late was only to be expected. A king not showing up when he was supposed to? That was the sort of thing that could spark a coup.

She had also changed her dress, swapping it for a cream sheath trimmed in iridescent white-and-silver feathers. She looked more like someone getting ready to present at the Oscars than a queen in charge of a large conclave, but maybe that was part of the point. This was her Kingdom, but as long as Aethlin and Maida were here, she wasn't the heavy hand of authority. She could afford to look a little softer, and allow people to think of her as one of the good guys, rather than one of the ones they should be afraid of.

"What are you saying?" she asked.

Belatedly, I realized she might never have *heard* the traditional form for announcing the death of a pure-blood noble. "I'm saying King Antonio Robinson has been murdered." I held up the fragment of Merry Dancer I was still holding. "I found this on the floor. They broke when they fell, and they fell when he was killed." A Candela's Merry Dancers were born alongside them, and lived as long as they did.

Her eyes went to the shell, and then darted toward the shadows under the table. She had to see the way the shadows pooled, gathering around the body. That didn't mean she had to admit it. Her gaze shifted back to me.

"Who did this?"

At least she wasn't making accusations. That was a nice change. "I don't know," I said. "But the night-haunts haven't arrived. There's still time to examine the body, if we can keep this room sealed for long enough for me to do it. Send in the Luidaeg, if you're worried people will say I killed him and am trying to get official dispensation to cover it up."

Arden blinked. "Why the Luidaeg?"

"Because she's Firstborn, which means Oberon's Law doesn't apply to her unless she kills another of the First-born," I said. Oberon might not have meant for his Law to be interpreted that way, but since none of us had the magical strength to challenge one of the First, his intentions on the point didn't really matter. They could kill with impunity, and sometimes did. Even the Luidaeg was a killer under the right circumstances, if the stories were to be believed. And the stories usually were. "She could have broken King Antonio's neck in the middle of the conclave, and no one would have been able to do a damn thing about it. That means she probably didn't do it, and has nothing to hide. She's the only person here that I know for sure didn't do it, aside from me, Quentin, Karen, Raj, and Tybalt. And she can't lie—physically *can't*—which means no one can say she's lying to cover up my part in the murder."

"How do you know they didn't do it?"

"They were with me. Tybalt is the one who arranged the meal on the balcony."

"It could have been a means of misdirecting your attention," said Lowri. "Every killer needs an alibi."

I turned to frown at her. "Tybalt is a cat and sometimes he's a jerk, but he's also a king. He wouldn't commit a murder at a conclave. Not when it could hurt his people."

As if the repeated mentions of his name had summoned him, Tybalt stepped out of the shadows in the nearest corner of the room, nostrils flaring as he scented blood. Finally, his gaze settled on me. "I can't leave you alone for a moment, can I?" he asked wearily.

"What are you doing here?" I countered.

"The nobles are growing restless," he said. "Queen Windermere left to find their missing colleague, and I have been dispatched to find Queen Windermere. I would take offense, had I not so dearly wished to escape that room. Raj wished to escape as well; I have no doubt he's halfway home by now. And I find you standing over a dead body. Some things, it seems, are incapable of changing." He finally allowed himself to look directly at the shape under the table, and wrinkled his nose. "King Robinson. How predictable. If anyone was going to get themselves murdered to guarantee they would remain the center of attention, it would be him."

"You don't sound upset," said Arden. For the first time, I heard the quaver in her voice, and realized she wasn't calm, no matter how she might seem: she was frozen, gripped by the sort of shock I hadn't been able to feel for years.

"Oh, oak and ash," I said. "Is this your first dead body?"

To my surprise, Arden laughed. It was a low, bitter sound, viscous and cloying. "No," she said. "That was my mother, when I found her with her throat slit in this very knowe. But it's my first in over a century, and it's a goddamn *King* dead under *my fucking roof*, so you'll forgive me if I'm a little on edge!"

"My apologies, Your Highness," said Tybalt, moving to stand next to me. He wasn't as close as he normally was—he was still holding himself that little bit apart, on ceremony, reminding the world of his dignity—but he was *there*, close enough for me to smell the faint pennyroyal warmth of his magic. That helped more than I could say. "When one spends as much time in October's company as I have, one grows more accustomed to the dead than is perhaps ideal. I'm sorry I can't be distressed over the death of a petty man who invited assassination with his every act and word. I wish I could. It would make the pleas of my innocence easier to accept."

"This is awful." Arden shoved her hair back from her forehead, dislodging several feathers. On cue, pixies appeared from somewhere in the folds of her skirt and began restyling her hair, chiming angrily. Arden ignored them. "How can he be dead? He was under the hospitality of my house, for Titania's sake!"

Her switching between mortal and fae profanity was starting to become jarring. "We can fix this," I said. "We can find out who killed him. We can keep this from getting any worse than it's already going to be. Just get me the Luidaeg."

"Why, so you can cover up another murder?" The voice was unfamiliar. I turned. There, in the doorway of the room, stood Kabos and Verona, the King and Queen of Highmountain. Kabos looked furious. Verona looked like she was about to be sick.

Kabos left his wife behind as he advanced on me, expression filled with surprising anger. I resisted the urge to fall back, away from the accusation in his eyes. Mortals often have trouble standing up to purebloods. Old survival instincts and the memory of a time when a human fighting with the fae always ended badly keep humanity from crossing certain lines. The more fae I've become, the easier it's become for me to stand my ground. Still, a part of me knew that I should be terrified. The distance between me and Tybalt seemed suddenly very great.

"How could you?" demanded Kabos. He was close enough that I could see the silver specks in his eyes, like someone had attacked him with a bucket of glitter.

The image was surreal enough to let me shake off the stillness that had fallen over me, and say, "I didn't do anything. I found the body. That's all. You've never even *met* me. How is it that you're first in line to accuse me?"

"We drew numbers back in the gallery," said Tybalt mildly, earning himself a poisonous look from Verona and a confused blink from Kabos.

The distraction only lasted for a moment. Kabos' gaze swung back to me as he said, "You're a changeling. Your presence here is an honor you should be laboring with every instant to earn, to prove that you deserve the things you've been given. Things that might have been better given to someone more deserving—someone who would truly appreciate them."

I blinked slowly, trying to reconcile the corpse on the floor with the sudden lecture about my place in the political structure of Faerie. I couldn't do it. I could do a *lot* of things, but that? That was a thing I couldn't do. It was too nonsensical. "The hell is wrong with you?" I demanded. "Did someone walk around hitting you every time you made sense when you were a kid, and when that worked they decided to give you a crown? A man is dead. I'm going to focus on that, rather than focusing on whether or not I'm somehow letting down the side."

Kabos looked startled. All things considered, I was willing to bet it had been a long time since anyone had talked to him like that.

If Kabos had been stunned into silence, his wife sadly hadn't. Verona stepped up next to him, eyes narrowed, shoulders tight. I knew righteous fury when I saw it. I didn't have *time* for it—not unless we wanted every royal in the place to find their way, one by one, to the dining hall and the corpse of King Antonio—but it was still pretty impressive.

"You do not have the rank, the standing, or quite frankly, the breeding to speak to my husband in that manner," she said. "You will apologize immediately."

"Nope," I said. "But thanks for playing." She recoiled at the word "thanks." I hadn't used the direct, forbidden form. I'd come close enough to be rude. That was good. That was what I'd been shooting for. "Also, if it's breeding you're looking for, yeah, my dad was human. He was a good man, and I'm proud to be his daughter. My mother, on the other hand, was Firstborn. So unless you call the First of your race Mommy or Daddy, I think my breeding is better than yours."

Verona glared. I gazed coolly back. And the sound of someone slowly clapping filtered into the silence between us, causing us both to turn and look at Tybalt.

"Brava," he said. "Encore. Or, perhaps, consider this: instead of an encore, we could move on to the meat of the matter, and consult with the dead man as to what happened to him?"

I didn't know whether I wanted to kiss or kill Tybalt. I settled for rolling my eyes, looking at Arden, and asking, "Well? Are you going to let me deal with this?"

"I don't think we have any choice," she said. Turning to Kabos and Verona, she bowed shallowly, and said, "If you'll come with me back to the gallery, I will inform the others as to what has happened. Sir Daye has volunteered to endure the supervision of the sea witch as she attempts to determine the cause of King Robinson's demise. This should be enough to satisfy even the most traditional among us."

"And I will stay to watch her until the sea witch comes," said Tybalt. It was a nice move. If anyone said he couldn't, they'd be questioning his standing as a king, and he would be within his rights to claim insult against them. I had no idea what that would look like when it was a King of Cats claiming insult against a monarch who wasn't even in their own demesne, but I had no doubt that it would derail the conclave for longer than anyone wanted. Dead body or not, everyone else still needed to conduct their business and get back home before anyone decided that their thrones had been abandoned.

There are days when I am very, very glad that I will never be a queen.

Kabos and Verona glared at me in unison before they turned to Arden. "Highmountain has been insulted on this day, and we will not forget it," said Kabos. The phrasing was deliberate: he wasn't claiming personal insult, which was sort of the pureblood equivalent of saying "make it up to me, or you're going to be sorry," but he was making sure Arden knew it was time to start sucking up.

Arden, for her part, clearly understood the situation. She inclined her head and said, "We will find a way to repair the friendship between our peoples. Lowri, please remain here and offer Sir Daye any assistance she needs while she is under the eye of King Tybalt."

"Yes, Your Highness," said Lowri.

"Good." Arden turned and walked for the door, leaving Kabos and Verona with no choice but to follow, if they didn't want to look like they were slighting her authority. In short order, I was alone again—except for my fiancé, Lowri and the other two guards, my squire, my niece, and—oh, right—the dead body.

"I did not sign up for this," I muttered, and knelt, looking critically at King Antonio's corpse. It was always jarring to see a dead pureblood. The night-haunts would come for him as soon as we left his body alone.

"What are you doing?" asked Lowri suspiciously.

"Nothing, yet," I said. "Once the Luidaeg gets here, I'm going to ride his blood, see if he saw his killer. That could wrap this up in a nice little bow and let me get home before the sun comes up. But until then, if you could back up and permit me to work, that would be swell." I was annoyed and I was taking it out on her, maybe unfairly, maybe not.

Then again, she *had* basically accused me of murder. Although . . .

"Why did you come in here?" I looked over my shoulder, assessing Lowri's stance and expression. Quentin and Karen were still in the far corner of the room, having gone unnoticed during the chaos. Good. This was going to be educational enough without them getting dragged into the conversation. "I mean, Arden came looking for the missing members of her conclave, and the monarchs of Highmountain came looking for Arden, but why did *you* come in here?"

"Note how easily I am cut from her narrative," said Tybalt, with pointed mildness. He sounded like a sarcastic accountant. It worked surprisingly well for him. "I am injured. I am slain."

"You're going to be, if you don't shut up and let Lowri answer."

He snorted his amusement.

Lowri hesitated before she said, "One of the servers claimed to have heard a strange noise from the dining hall. We went to investigate. When there are this many strangers in the knowe, anything that seems out of place must be investigated. I thought we'd find a scullery maid stealing silver, or a group of changelings scavenging for leftover food. Instead, we found you, standing over the dead body of a king."

"And I'm the one who's deposed two monarchs, so naturally, the first question is not 'did you see anyone else when you came in here,' but 'what did you do.'" I resisted the urge to groan. It wouldn't do me any good. It certainly wouldn't make Lowri more inclined to keep talking to me. "There's so much wrong with what you just said that I'm having trouble figuring out where to begin." Maybe she was going to stop talking to me anyway. "Did anyone bother to hang on to the server who said that they'd heard something strange? I'd like to talk to them."

There's a very strict hierarchy among the servant classes in most knowes. Courtiers—people like heralds, pages, even ladies' maids and butlers—hold themselves apart from guards and security staff. Seneschals tend to come from the guard, which pisses everybody else in the hierarchy off, since it's like promoting your bouncer to general manager of the bar rather than elevating the assistant manager. Kitchen staff rarely communicate with the rest of the household staff when they can help it, and everybody has a tendency to ignore servers, sculleries, and other "menial" positions. It's a way of continuing to feel like the sort of jobs the human world phased out years ago still matter, and it creates communication gaps that made me want to scream.

Lowri's cheeks colored. "No," she admitted. "There's to be an hour of drinks and small confections after this phase of the conclave, and all the servers were needed in the kitchen. We let him go."

"So I'll be going to the kitchen next, to see if I can find our only possible witness. Got it." Sometimes I wonder how I got my job, given how bad I am at some of the basic tasks that it entails. And then I spend five minutes in the company of purebloods, and I'm reminded that no matter how inept I sometimes feel, I am worlds and miles ahead of most of the people around me. "Quentin, Karen, can you two start collecting the bits of King Antonio's Merry Dancers? They're sort of everywhere."

"And what am I to do?" asked Tybalt.

I turned to look at him. He was still wearing a mask of cool unconcern, but that was exactly what it was—a mask. I could see the worry in his eyes. He was shaken by all of this, the dead body, the thinly veiled accusations from people we normally regarded as our allies. No matter how much time we spent together, parts of my world would always be as alien to him as parts of his were to me. That was oddly comforting, and gave me the strength I needed to do what had to be done.

"You?" I rose from my crouch, glancing down to be sure that I wasn't about to crush any more fragments of Merry Dancer as I moved to put my hands on his shoulders. "You're going to go back to the conclave. You're going to do what you came here for, and remind those petty, squabbling jerks that you're a King. Oberon himself said you were their equal. When they try to ignore that, they're going against the father of us all. So you don't let them ignore it."

His mask slipped, revealing relief and confusion behind it. "Don't you need me here?"

"Need? No. I have Quentin. I have Karen, at least until the Luidaeg comes. I can handle anything this dead body can throw at me. Want? Always. But as you've reminded me already, we can't always put desires above duty."

Tybalt's mouth twisted. "I can't help feeling as though this is a punishment for neglecting you over these last few days. I wasn't there when you needed me to be, and so now I am to be sent away, like a second son who can never inherit the estate."

"I'm not an estate. Even if I were, you would already have inherited me and oh, oak and ash, I'm sure that sort of thing sounds super-romantic in your weird pureblood brain but right now, you need to go. You need to go be a King." I leaned up and kissed him, just a quick peck. "I'm in the Queen's knowe. I have my squire, and I'm about to have the supervision and wisdom of the most terrifying woman I've ever met. I promise you, I'll be fine without you for a short period of time. Besides, it'll give you time to miss me more, so that you'll remember never to pull this crap again."

"Beware of women, children," said Tybalt, turning on Quentin and Karen with the poise and exaggerated dignity of a professor offering wisdom to the young. "This is how they will treat with your tender hearts."

"I'm too young to date," said Karen.

"I'm sort of seeing someone, and I'm pretty sure Toby's about to punch you," said Quentin.

I punched Tybalt in the arm. He was laughing as he slipped into the shadows and was gone.

Lowri and the other guards were surprisingly silent through all of this. I turned to look at them. They were all staring at the door, wary as mice watching the approach of a cat. Ah. I turned further, to the object of their attentions, and offered a taut smile.

"Luidaeg," I said. "Good. Now we can get started."

"I suppose that's true," she agreed. She was still wearing her gown of crashing seawater and the tide, but the blackness had bled out of her eyes, leaving them green as driftglass, devoid of shadows. She turned those green, green eyes on Lowri and the others, quirked an eyebrow upward, and asked, "Well? Are you going to stand there staring at me like a bunch of old owls, or are you going to go do your jobs? I should warn you that if you elect for the 'owls' option, I can have you in feathers like *that*." She snapped her fingers. Lowri flinched.

"Call if you need us," she said, and all but ran for the door, with her people following close behind her.

The Luidaeg waited until they were gone before she turned to me. "What happened?" she asked.

"The same thing that always happens," I said. "We were having a perfectly nice evening until it got ruined by a corpse."

Her smile was full of teeth. "Oh, good," she said. "I was worried that it was something serious."

NINE

KING ROBINSON'S MAGIC SMELLED of walnut shells and Spanish moss. Its ghost lingered in his blood, like spices dusted over the coppery brightness of the blood itself. I sat on the floor next to his body, knowing the Luidaeg was there to pull me back into myself if I sank too far into the blood memory. More importantly, I knew that Quentin and Karen were watching, and would see it if I lost control. Karen will never be a blood-worker. Her heritage, tangled and strange as it is, doesn't include any of Oberon's lines. But Quentin would need to do these things when he became High King, and I refused to be the reason he was afraid of his own magic.

I raised my fingers to my mouth. I tasted the blood. The memory closed around me like a glove, and the world went away.

How dare they act as though this is a simple vote, something to be decided in an afternoon. How dare they pretend this is "diplomacy," when it's clear where the High King's loyalties lie. He's meant to be so far above us as to serve as an objective party, a judge, jury, and when need be, executioner. How does this stripling queen have such a strong grip upon his ear, when no one knew she existed before she was crowned? Something is wrong. Something is out of true. And I am, by Oberon, going to find out what it is, and put a stop to it before this madness goes any further.

His thoughts were cold but not cruel. From his perspective, something had gone horribly wrong in the Mists, something symbolized by the way the High King dealt with Arden. I didn't get the impression that he'd been an evil man. Set in his ways, maybe, and more interested in the good of his Kingdom than anything else— but really, what monarch *wasn't* going to put the needs of their own people ahead of the rest of the world? That was practically the job description. I swallowed hard, forcing more of his blood into my system, letting the memories pull me down.

I have stepped away from the noise and nonsense of the dining room to be alone with my thoughts. There are no lights in this part of the knowe. I do not need them. Candela have better night vision than most, and my Merry Dancers spin around me, comforting companions. They pulse with their understanding of my unhappiness. They would soothe me, if they could. How lonely other fae must be, in their strange, singular lives!

A noise behind me, like metal being torn. I stop and turn, suddenly dizzy, as if I am out of breath, even though I am breathing normally. Perhaps the meal is ending; perhaps we are about to return to the pointless pretense of diplomacy. I walk back to the dining room.

It is empty. Where has everyone gone? The curtains are drawn.

That tearing-metal sound repeats. I turn, and there is pain, pain like I have never felt. I am falling. I am falling, I am dying, and even death holds no mercy, for I am still alive when the first of my Merry Dancers hits the ground, and I feel it when she shatters—

Gasping, I ripped myself free of his memories before they could drag me down to the actual moment of his death. I hadn't been weak enough to kill that easily in a while; riding someone else's blood to the end was still dangerous. Some rules were never intended to be broken. Not by me. Maybe by my mother, but she's First-born, and I'm not. I'll never be as strong as she is.

Then the Luidaeg was there, placing a hand between my shoulder blades and holding me up, keeping me from falling over. "What did you see?"

"Nothing." I closed my eyes. My own body felt strange, too small, too female, and too alone. There should have been Merry Dancers swirling around me, their lives connected to my own on a level too deep to explain with words. The feeling would pass. That didn't mean I enjoyed it. This wasn't the first time I'd felt out of synch with myself after riding the blood, but it had never been this strong. "He didn't see the person who killed him, or detect their magic. He heard a weird sound, fol-lowed it back to the dining room, and someone he didn't get a decent look at stabbed him."

"So it didn't work?" Quentin sounded disappointed. He also sounded scared. He'd been with me for long enough to understand that sometimes, when the first, safest method of getting information failed, we had to keep going. We had to find another way.

He was right to be concerned. There was always an-other way, and it was rarely a good idea. "It worked," I said, opening my eyes and turning toward the sound of his voice. He and Karen had been busy; the table next to them was covered in shining shards of Merry Dancer. Seeing them that way hurt my heart. That, too, would fade; I wouldn't be mourning for Christmas ornaments forever.

But someone should have been. I gripped the Lui-daeg's arm as I levered myself to my feet. The feeling of strangeness was already fading, replaced by the more usual absolute faith in my own body, which was familiar and comfortable and *home*.

"He couldn't tell me anything because he didn't see

anything worth telling," I continued, wiping the blood off my hand and onto my trousers. Black is forgiving in more ways than one. "At the same time, we're going to have company soon, and maybe he can tell me something I can't intuit from his blood."

Quentin's eyes went wide. Karen looked confused. And the Luidaeg sighed.

"You *really* want to talk to them again?" she asked. "I'm pretty sure they weren't kidding when they threatened to eat you. They're not big jokesters."

"I saved May's life. That has to earn me a little tolerance."

"It's already earned you a little tolerance. They didn't eat you the last time they saw you."

"No, they didn't, because their leader had something he wanted me to do. I've done it. They'll talk to me."

The Luidaeg threw up her hands and turned her eyes toward the ceiling. "Dad's bones, you people never learn. Fine. Do you want me to call them? Maybe they'll be less hostile if I'm the one who calls."

"Um, excuse me?" Karen's voice shook. We all looked at her. She bit her lip, worrying it between her teeth before she asked, "Who are you talking about?"

Oh. "Quentin, maybe you should take Karen back out to the balcony," I said quietly. "She doesn't need to see this."

"That doesn't answer my question," said Karen.

"October still believes children can be sheltered," said the Luidaeg. There was no blame in her tone: she was stating a fact, something plain and simple and immutable. "She forgets to ask herself whether they *should*. More, she forgets that everyone is a child to someone. Compared to me, you're all infants."

I sighed. "Okay. Point taken. We're talking about the night-haunts, Karen. They're going to come for King Antonio's body, which means they'll know what he knew, and maybe we can get some answers."

"I hate it when you summon the night-haunts," said Quentin.

"But I'm not summoning them," I said. "I'm just going to be here when they show up. Totally different."

Quentin did not look like he thought this was totally different. Quentin looked at me like this was the worst idea in a long string of bad ideas, stretching back to "hey, I think I might like to be born." He didn't say anything. He didn't need to. The kid has some of the most expressive eyebrows I've ever seen. I glanced to the Luidaeg, looking for support.

What I found was vague amusement, and a shrug so expansive that her hand hit the side of my arm. "You're the hero of the realm here, Toby. I'm just the sea witch. You're supposed to leave me slumbering in my watery cavern until you need a handy deus ex machina."

Karen was looking back and forth between us, increasingly agitated. It had only ever been a matter of time before the dam broke. "What's *wrong* with you?" she demanded. "There's a man . . . he's *dead*, Aunt Birdie! He's right there, and he's *dead*, and you're making *jokes*! How can you do that? It's mean, and it's petty, and it's . . . it's not fair." She sounded petulant as only the young ever could.

I missed being that upset by the cruelty of the world. I just couldn't seem to work up the anger anymore. "You're right, pumpkin: it's not fair," I said, walking over to put an arm around her shoulder. I kept my still blood-sticky hand behind my back. She knew it was there, but that didn't mean she should be forced to look at it. "Nothing about the world is ever fair. You know that. We joke because we're not happy either. King Robinson was a jerk, but he didn't deserve to die, and we can't bring him back. So we try to make ourselves feel better when we can, because we know the world isn't going to suddenly turn kind. That sort of thing would take more magic than there is in the whole world."

"He was a pureblood," said Karen. The quiet puzzlement in her voice broke my heart to hear. She was so young. The Luidaeg was right that I never asked myself whether children should be protected: I knew the answer. They should be protected for as long as they could be, for as long as our shoulders could bear the weight of the world, because innocence was so fragile, and so easily destroyed. Karen had lost most of hers when Blind Michael had taken her captive. As for what remained . . .

There was so much more of it than I'd ever suspected. And it was so very, very fragile.

"I know," I said. "Purebloods aren't supposed to die. When they do, all we can do is try to make sure that justice is done. We're going to figure out who killed him. I promise."

It was a foolish promise to make. I'd made worse, and I could hear, distantly, the beating of paper-thin wings against the wind. The night-haunts were coming.

Quentin heard it, too. "Do you want us to go wait somewhere else?" he asked.

Karen was an oneiromancer. She could see the night-haunts any time she wanted to, just by visiting my dreams, or May's. It might be better for her to see them in the flesh, not colored by whatever nightmare they were flying through.

"No," I said. "Stay." I turned toward the open balcony door. So did the others.

We waited as the air grew hazy with fragile, half-seen wings, and the night-haunts streamed into the room. The flock moved like smoke, buffeted by an unseen wind. The frailer, more faded night-haunts stuck to the middle, where they could be protected by the bodies of their more solid kindred. The night-haunts around the edges of the flock were doll-sized replicas of Faerie's dead, wearing heartbreakingly familiar faces and forms, turned alien and strange by the tattered wings that grew from their backs, by the emotions hanging frozen in their eyes.

The flock circled the room twice, wings buzzing, searching for danger. None of us said anything. We simply waited to see what the night-haunts would do. Karen shivered against me but didn't pull away. Finally, the night-haunts landed on one of the long banquet tables, the shadowy central figures clustering together while the others shielded them with wing and body. One night-haunt—slightly taller than some of the others, with eyes as purple as wildflowers, and the face of a decadent, black-hearted Peter Pan—stepped forward, eyes fixed on the Luidaeg.

"Auntie," said the night-haunt, and his voice was the voice of Devin, my old mentor and first lover, and hearing it was like sandpaper on my soul. I had seen this night-haunt every time I'd faced the flock since Devin's death, and it never stopped hurting. "Why do you come between us and our prey? The flock must feed. We've lost two to the wind in the last year."

"Father did you no favors when he bound you," said the Luidaeg. "Hello, Egil."

He bowed, only half mockingly. "It's been a long time."

"Indeed, it has."

I still said nothing. It was easy to forget that the night-haunts had lives aside from the ones they stole from Faerie's dead. Sometimes they seemed to forget, too. But they were purebloods, even when they wore changeling faces: their mother had been one of the Luidaeg's sisters, and they had been born predators, intended to devour fae flesh, which would never rot under normal circumstances. Without the night-haunts, we would never have been able to hide our existence from the human world. It was just that at first, they'd preferred the taste of the living. They'd been a scourge upon our kind, eternally hungry, fast and fierce and unstoppable . . . until Oberon changed them, binding them to eat only the dead. Without the lives they took from the blood we left behind, they had nothing. They would fade, and fade, until they became the only purebloods in Faerie who could die of natural causes.

Fae died rarely. The night-haunts were always there.

The night-haunt with Devin's face—Egil—was joined by another, this one shorter, stockier, and wearing the face of my dead Selkie lover, Connor O'Dell. I didn't know this night-haunt's true name. I wasn't sure it would have helped if I had. He turned to face me, sadness and longing in his eyes. The night-haunts got more than just form from the blood. They got memory, emotion, even personality, to a certain degree. Connor had died to save my daughter. He'd died loving me. And now he was a night-haunt, and I was in love with another man.

"Hi, Toby," he said.

"Hi," I replied, keeping my arm around Karen. That didn't feel like enough, and so I continued, "I kept my promise. I stopped the goblin fruit."

Egil laughed. He sounded so much like Devin that I shivered. "You did, and you knocked down a monarchy to do it. Oh, October, I wish I'd understood what a glorious disaster you were when I was alive. I would have used you to undermine the world, and laughed while it was burning."

"I can't tell whether that was meant to be a compliment or not," I said. "Either way, I did what I promised, and now I need a favor."

Both night-haunts blinked at me. So did several others, some of whom had faces I recognized. Others were foreign to me. Death was rare in Faerie, but not so rare that I was present every time it happened. Thank Maeve for that. If I'd been the sole cause of death in Faerie, High King Sollys would have locked me up and thrown away the key.

"We told you once that we would eat you if you kept summoning us," said Egil. "What makes you think that's changed?"

"Well, first, I didn't summon you. The body under the table did. Second, I did you a favor. You don't want there to be any chance I could claim you were in my debt, do you?"

Egil narrowed his eyes. "I take back what I said. You're too destructive to be trusted. What do you want from us?"

"I want something that should be pretty easy to give, all things considered. I want you to feed on the dead king, and then let me talk to whoever gets his memories. I need to know if there's anything he saw that I wouldn't know how to interpret when I saw it in his blood."

There was a momentary silence, broken only by the endless dead-leaf rustle of the night-haunts opening and closing their wings. Finally, almost cautiously, the night-haunt with Connor's face said, "If you leave this room, we won't be here when you come back. We won't wait for you."

"I know."

"You'll have to watch us feed."

"I know that, too." I glanced to Quentin and Karen. "The others can leave if they need to, but I'm going to stay. I need answers."

"I want to see," said Quentin, which seemed brave but ill-thought-out to me. I didn't say anything. He was going to command a continent someday. The night-haunts who patrolled North America would be subjects of his, as much as anyone else was. Maybe it would make a difference if they felt they were allowed to speak to the High King. They certainly didn't feel that way now.

"If Quentin's staying, so am I." Karen's voice shook. I turned to frown at her.

"Sweetheart, are you sure?"

She looked at me with cool, bleach-blue eyes, and nodded. "I can handle anything he can handle. Maybe more. He doesn't spend his days walking through other peoples' nightmares."

I wanted to tell her she didn't have to be strong for me, that I'd love her no matter what. I wanted to remind her that Quentin was older than she was, and that she didn't have to compete with him. I did neither of those things. Karen was a changeling. I knew what that meant. She was going to spend her whole life trying to prove she was as good as the purebloods around her, and now that more and more people knew about her oneiromancy, she was going to be fighting to be sure they understood she wasn't there to be controlled. If she wanted to be her own person, she would have to be stronger, better, and capable of standing up to more than anyone around her, or they'd use her blood against her. Every time.

No one in this room would try to do that to her, but that didn't matter. If you wanted to be steel, you had to be steel every day of your life, until it came naturally; until you no longer had to beat yourself bloody trying to achieve it.

"All right," I said, and turned back to the night-haunts. "You can go ahead and feed."

"Ah, milady grants permission!" Egil sketched a mocking bow, his wings rattling like plastic bags rolling down a gutter. Then he straightened, smile fading, and turned to speak to the flock.

The language he used wasn't English, or Welsh, or anything else I recognized, but it suited the strange accent that sometimes crept into May's words, the one she only had when she was reaching past the memories she'd received from me and Dare. It was an old language, I knew that much, sweet and fluid and filled with vowel sounds that more modern languages had tucked away as too hard on the ear.

The Luidaeg stepped up next to me. "We had our own language once," she murmured, in English. "Mother spoke it, when she talked to the children who spent less time around humanity. But it was *easier* to use the words the mortals had. They were lords of language in those days, spreading across the world and naming everything they saw as quick as a blink. We've never been fond of doing labor that we didn't have to do for ourselves. My tatterdemalion nieces and nephews may be the only native speakers of Faerie left in the world."

"Can you understand them?" asked Quentin.

"No." She shook her head, a sweet, bitter smile on her lips. "Words you don't use fall away and are forgotten. I can't even speak it in my dreams." Looking to Karen, she smiled less ruefully, and added, "Don't try to check that. You won't like what you find in my head."

"I don't like what I find in your sister's head," said Karen.

"That's because her sister is a murderous, psychopathic bitch, and you shouldn't spend any time in her brain that can be avoided," I said. "If evil is contagious, your mother will kill me."

Karen snorted.

The night-haunts stopped speaking.

I turned to see the flock rise, moving like smoke across the water, and descend on the body of King Antonio Robertson. The more solid night-haunts, the ones whose bodies were firm and whose faces were clear, formed an outer ring around the body. The next tier was slightly less solid. They seemed to waver, but I could pick out individual features, like the curve of an ear or the color of an eye. It would have been possible to describe those night-haunts to an artist and get something a family member might be able to identify. And at the center . . .

At the center were the night-haunts who looked like shadows, so faded that their bodies seemed to have no weight or substance. They were the idea of fae, the concept of solidity, and they couldn't stay as they were forever; the first stiff wind would rip them into nothingness. Then even those parted, easing a ghost toward the body. The night-haunt they'd chosen to eat first seemed to flicker with every step it took, barely holding itself together. The flock guided it to the skin of King Robinson's neck.

The shadowy night-haunt stopped. The only sound was the rustle of a hundred wings, and my own breath, which seemed impossibly loud in my own ears. The shadowy night-haunt sniffed the air. And then it opened its mouth, revealing teeth that would have been better suited to some deep-sea horror, and sank them into the dead King's neck.

That was the signal for the rest of the flock to move, swarming over the body like so many leaf-winged piranha. I fought the urge to clap my hand over Karen's eyes. I fought the urge to clap my hand over *my* eyes. They ate like beasts, ripping and tearing at the flesh in front of them, moving with such furious hunger that they left nothing behind. When blood was spilled, they were right there, lapping it up, even lifting it out of the fabric of the carpet and stuffing it into their mouths. When they hit bone, they just kept right on eating, chewing down until there was nothing for them to consume but dust and shadow.

The flock pulsed, beating like a heart, and was still. The weaker night-haunts seemed stronger now, thicker and more distinct, even if they still had no coherent faces. The night-haunts like Egil, like the one who wore Connor's face, had been the last to eat; they looked no different. Most of their sustenance was coming from the lives they had already consumed, and would be for years, if I was correct in my understanding of how they were able to survive on scraps as rare as the dead of Faerie.

The flock parted. King Antonio Robinson, now reduced to the height of a Barbie and accented with autumn-leaf wings, walked to the front. He looked . . . lost. There was no other word for the confusion on his face, or the way his eyes darted from side to side, seeking some explanation. Finally, he settled them on me.

"The changeling knight," he said, a slight sneer in his voice. I couldn't be offended. Maybe if he'd been alive, I would have been, but now . . . I couldn't blame a dead man for his prejudices. It felt somehow unfair. "I . . . am I dead?"

"He'll be disoriented for a time," said Egil, his tone so much like Devin's. Devin had been a bad man, in so many ways, but he'd always taken care of the ones who needed him. Even if he hurt us, he kept us safe from the rest of the world. "Ask your questions. After you do, we'll be gone."

"Okay," I said, and focused on the night-haunt with Antonio's face. "You're a night-haunt now. You'll start remembering that soon, if eating a life is anything like riding the blood. But yes, you died. I'm sorry. You have stopped your dancing."

"Where are my girls?" He turned to look to either side of himself, searching the air. "Why can't I find my girls?"

My heart sank. Antonio had been Candela. The night-haunts hadn't taken *everything* for a change; not everything had been food to them. "Merry Dancers don't transition that way, I guess. I'm sorry. They broke when you died."

"Ah." His eyes closed. He made no effort to conceal his pain. I was almost grateful for that. If he could hurt that badly over a pair of dancing lights, he truly *was* King Antonio, if only until the first rush of blood memories began to fade.

He opened his eyes again, and looked at me. "Why are you speaking to me, changeling knight? I was above you when I lived, and am below you now that I do not. Shouldn't you shun me, refuse to acknowledge the reality of me, leave me for ballad and for bone?"

"There's a phrasing I haven't heard in years," murmured the Luidaeg.

I ignored her. It was a specialized skill, and one I had

better control of than most. "I rode your blood before the night-haunts came," I said. "I didn't see what killed you. I thought you might have picked up on something I wouldn't realize was important." I had been a voyeur in his life. He had *lived* it. "Please, can you tell me what happened?"

Antonio looked at me for a moment before he said, "You'll need to do something for me."

Of course a pureblood king who couldn't think of me as his equal would have demands, apart from the natural "avenge me." I should have known. "What do you want?"

"My wife has never been my queen. I wanted her to have safety and the freedom to move through the world as she liked. She never desired the pleasures of a throne. I want you to go to her. I want you to tell her, 'you are a widow now.' I want you to tell her that our son will rule in my stead. He's young, yet. Too young for such a burden. My seneschal will help him. My seneschal will probably also try to assassinate him." He smirked, looking more at ease now that he was talking about backstabbing and betrayal. "My boy is quick and clever. He'll learn. He'll adapt. And he'll be a better king than I ever was."

"Where can I find her?" I asked.

He gave me the address: a street in Anaheim, far from the bustle and decay of Hollywood, close to Disneyland. Arden's parents had had a similar arrangement, with her mother raising her and her brother in the shadows of her father's court, never admitting that they were his heirs, for fear they would be harmed. I had to wonder how many hidden princes and princesses we had scattered around the Westlands, tucked away by parents who'd learned the hard way that accepting a crown was a good way to limit your life expectancy.

When this was over, I was going to have a long talk with High King Sollys about the way the nobility took care of their children.

"I'll find her," I said. "Now please. What do you re-member?"

"I was angry. That woman from the water — a Merrow, married to a Daoine Sidhe. Can you imagine? Their children must be so confused." He shook his head, disgust written across his features. "She said her eldest son was a Count upon the land, and that one day her youngest would be a Duke beneath the waves. As if that were something to be proud of. When they tear themselves apart trying to be one thing or another, they'll drown the world."

"I was there when you started yelling at Dianda," I said, voice carefully neutral. "Where did you go after that?"

"Just down the hall. I wanted to clear my head. I wasn't gone for long — minutes, only — I planned to come back, make my apologies, even if I didn't mean them, and maintain my standing within the conclave. But when I returned to the dining hall, there was no one there. It was like I'd been gone for hours."

The sound. "I heard something, when I rode your blood."

"My wife doesn't believe in using magic to preserve food."

The statement was odd enough that for a moment, I didn't know what to say. "Um, okay," I offered finally.

Antonio looked at me like I was beneath contempt. "It would be a waste of her skills. She uses a mortal invention instead. Tin foil. Have you heard of it?"

I bit my lip to keep from laughing as I nodded. "Yes. I've encountered the stuff."

"There's this *sound* when she tears off a sheet . . . I heard it. From this room. And then the shadows jumped."

Wait. "What?"

"My Merry Dancers were never still, and their light meant the shadows were never solid. They didn't have the opportunity to freeze." He looked at the shadows around him, expression growing grim. "The world flickered like a candle. I never knew how much I would miss it until it was over."

"I'm sorry," I said. "But what do you mean, the shadows jumped? Did they actually come for you?" I hadn't noticed anything like that. I had been hoping Antonio could reveal some motive or facet of the situation that his blood hadn't given me, but moving shadows seemed a bit big for me to have missed.

"No, you stupid girl," he said. "They *shifted*, as if my Merry Dancers had been moved. Which is quite impossible."

But it wasn't impossible for something else to have moved. "I heard the sound twice when I rode your blood," I said. "Once here, once in the hall. Does that match with what you remember?"

The night-haunt who had been King Antonio nodded.

"One last question, and then you can go," I said. "Do you know anyone who might have wanted you dead?"

His laughter surprised me. "Oh, you simple changeling creature," he said. "I was a king, and a good one. Everyone wanted me dead."

Egil took his arm. "We must away," he said. He snapped his wings open, launching himself upward, into the air. Antonio was pulled along, and other night-haunts moved to support him, holding him in the air until the instincts of his new body took hold, and his wings began to work. Silently, those of us who were still among the living watched the dead flying away, until only the night-haunt with Connor's face remained.

"October," he said.

I turned to him. I didn't say anything. I didn't know what to say. I still felt guilty when I saw him, as if his death had been entirely my fault, and not the result of his own actions. I was grateful for those actions—I always would be—but I hadn't asked him to die for my daughter. He had chosen to do that entirely on his own.

"Egil won't thank you for stopping the goblin fruit. His memories of being Devin are too strong, and he blames you for letting the stuff into his streets in the first place, after he died. I've talked to the changelings who died because they got hooked, and they wanted me to tell you that they're grateful, and they don't share his anger. The flock is not your friend. The flock will never be your friend, not until you join us, and fly with us, and belong to us. But the flock isn't your enemy, either." He paused. Then he smiled, that old, familiar smile, the one that used to greet me when I woke up. My heart clenched. I loved Tybalt more than I would have believed possible, but that didn't mean I didn't miss Connor. He'd been my friend before he was my lover. I don't think I'll ever get used to losing friends.

"I'll see you soon," said the night-haunt with Connor's face, and launched himself into the air, and left me alone with the living.

TEN

WHEN THE NIGHT-HAUNTS TAKE a body from the mortal world, they leave a mannequin behind, one that mimics the mortal disguise of the deceased. Those mannequins rot, bloat, and decay, just like a human corpse. There's no need for that sort of subterfuge in the Summerlands. All the night-haunts had left of King Antonio were a few scraps of clothing and the shattered husks of his Merry Dancers, which were already dissolving into sand.

"What would have happened if Toby hadn't found the body?" asked Quentin, after a long silence. "Would the night-haunts just have *come*, and not left anything to let us know that somebody was actually dead?"

"Historically, if there was no one to witness the feeding, they would leave dried leaves and rose petals, lovelies-bleeding and sprigs of marigold," said the Luidaeg. "It's a very specific bouquet. Anyone who found it right after someone had gone missing would know what it meant. I'm surprised you don't."

"We haven't reached 'mysterious deaths' in my lessons," said Quentin uncomfortably.

"Also, I didn't know the answer to that," I said. "Mom never taught me. Neither did Etienne."

"Deaths in Faerie are rare enough that they probably thought you'd never need to know." The Luidaeg snorted. "They never did understand you very well."

"I guess not." I turned to Karen. "You okay?"

She was pale, even for her, but she wasn't shaking, and her eyes were clear. "I didn't know it was like that," she said. "How long will that night-haunt look like him?"

"A year for every year he lived," said the Luidaeg. "Anything more would be unfair; anything less would kill them all, and we'd be right back where we started. You'll have two lives, when your time comes. The one you lead among the living, and the one you lead among the dead."

"Wow," I said. "If that's meant to be reassuring, you need to redefine how you think about the word. Any ideas on that whole 'I heard tearing metal and then the shadows moved' thing?"

"Not yet," said the Luidaeg. She put a hand on Karen's shoulder. "You ready to go back to the conclave, kiddo?"

Karen looked startled. "What? Why would we go back? Isn't it over now?"

"If you think a murder is enough to disrupt a collection of kings and queens, it's a good thing you'll never be asked to be a part of the monarchy," said the Luidaeg. "If anything, this is going to make them more determined to come to a consensus. Their honor has been threatened. How dare the world intrude?"

"Yes," I said softly. "How dare it."

We left the dissolving fragments of Merry Dancer where they were. I didn't have anything to carry them in, and I didn't know what the protocols were for handling something that was, in its way, evidence of the existence of Faerie. Maybe once they'd finished dissolving, the sand would be returned to Antonio's widow, or maybe it would just be scattered to the wind. Either way, that was something to worry about later. Now, I had bigger problems.

I saw the Luidaeg palm one of the larger shards, slipping it into the endlessly cascading waves of her gown. I didn't say anything. If the sea witch had a use for a piece of Merry Dancer, I didn't want to know what it was, and I've learned to trust her over the years. I've also learned that sometimes, I have to be able to put my life in her hands—and that's usually easier for me when I have no idea what she's planning to do.

The hall outside the dining room seemed almost obscenely bright after spending so much time in darkness. Arden's staff had been through, lowering the lights and hanging wreaths of black roses and blood-orange poppies below the windows as a gesture of respect for the departed. The air smelled too sweet, like they were trying frantically to stave off any hints of death.

Quentin walked beside me, his shoulders squared, his chin lifted, and his eyes fixed on the door to the gallery like he was being led to his execution. I understood the feeling. Karen and the Luidaeg trailed behind us, and somehow it seemed less like we were being followed and more like we were their appointed heralds, leading the way and attracting any dangers onto ourselves. Which nicely summed up the relationship between the monarchs of Faerie and its heroes, all things considered.

Lowri and another guard stood to either side of the gallery door. She nodded when she saw us, acknowledging our presence, but she didn't say anything. She just stepped aside, and the doors swung open, allowing us to enter.

We were at the back of the gallery—naturally— forcing us to walk down the long aisle past the gathered nobles and vassals who'd come to participate. The room went silent as we moved toward our seats. Walther was already there, looking about as uncomfortable as I felt.

No one spoke until Quentin, Karen, and the Luidaeg were settled. I was sinking into my own seat when High King Sollys said, "Sir Daye, if you would come before us."

Well, crap. "Of course, Your Highness," I said, and straightened, heading for the stage.

I couldn't resist glancing at the audience as I climbed the stairs. Tybalt was back in his seat, and while his lips were pressed into a neutral expression, I could read the worry in his eyes. That made me feel better. At least I wasn't the only one who was miserable and scared. Maybe that was cruel of me. Honestly, it didn't change anything, and so I didn't feel the need to care.

"If you would tell the conclave what you have learned, we would be most grateful," said High King Sollys. His voice was level. If he was upset about the death of one of his vassals, he wasn't letting it show. I couldn't decide whether that was impressive or chilling.

And it wasn't like it mattered. "Of course, Your Highness," I said. Stopping at my mark, I turned to face the audience. "You have been informed that King Antonio Robertson of Angels has stopped his dancing. I remained behind, along with the Luidaeg, better known to many as the sea witch, to ride his blood and determine what had happened."

"Why do we trust you?" demanded a voice from the back of the gallery. It was unfamiliar. I squinted in its direction.

"Well, for one thing, you can see my face," I said. "Who are you?"

"Duke Michel of Starfall," said the voice. Its owner stood, revealing himself as a slim, green-haired Daoine Sidhe whose tabard appeared to have been made by stitching together hundreds of tiny malachite disks. Pureblood women don't have a monopoly on clothes made of ridiculous materials.

I swallowed several comments to exactly that effect. Instead, I said, as calmly as I could, "I was under the supervision of the Luidaeg at all times. If you wish to challenge my honor, I'll be happy to meet with you and discuss whether or not I should be insulted. If you wish to challenge *her* honor, that's between the two of you. But I don't recommend it."

Duke Michel opened his mouth to answer. Then he stopped, eyes going to a point off to the side, and paled. I had no doubt that the Luidaeg was doing something horrible with her teeth. She was fond of that sort of thing.

"I appreciate the clarification," he said, and sat. The other nobles from Starfall closed around him, rustling and murmuring behind their hands.

I glanced to Arden. She nodded marginally. I turned back to the gallery.

"I rode King Robinson's blood, not because I'm a changeling, but because I'm a knight errant and hero of the realm; it's my duty to investigate such matters. I was unable to identify his killer. He never saw them clearly." There were other issues—the shadows jumping, that torn metal sound—but I didn't want to reveal them like this. I would chase them down. I would find my answers. I would do it without a dozen nobles tripping over themselves trying to beat me to the prize, to prove they were better than the changeling who thought she could act like a real girl. "Because his body was still present, we decided to wait for the night-haunts to arrive."

A murmur ran through the crowd, disbelieving, even angry. No one saw the night-haunts. No one questioned them. That's what I'd thought, once upon a time, before I realized that sometimes doing what no one does is the right way to get what I needed. My whole career has been based around doing what no one does.

The Luidaeg stood, the hem of her gown splashing against the floor as she turned to glare at the room. The gallery went quiet again.

"Once the night-haunts arrived, I questioned them

about King Robinson's death," I said. "They couldn't give me any useful information, although I was able to determine, between the blood and the night-haunts, that King Robinson has an heir who'll need to be informed of his father's death, and protected until he can assume the throne."

"When this conclave is over, I will travel with you to Angels to confirm this," said High King Sollys.

"Great," I said, feeling briefly light-headed with relief. "I'll take the kids to Disneyland. Well. Then. Right now, I'm going to return to the dining hall, and—"

"No," said High Queen Sollys.

I blinked. "I'm sorry?"

"We need you here," she said. "You were present for the creation of this 'cure,' and your testimony may be required."

Yelling at Arden got me in trouble. Yelling at Maida would probably get me arrested. I swallowed my anger, forcing my voice to stay steady as I said, "I'm not asking you to delay or cancel the remainder of this conclave. But a man is dead, and I need to find out who killed him. I can't do that sitting here."

"We have faith in you," said High King Sollys. "You'll remain with the conclave until we stop for the day."

Of course I would. Of course the purebloods, angry at the taint of death and consumed by their own pride, would refuse to let me leave. Of course they'd risk more lives to show they weren't afraid. Of course. Why would I have thought, even for a second, that this would go any differently? Keeping my voice tightly controlled, I asked the only question I had left: "May I sit?"

"You may," said the High King.

I bowed, angling my body so that the gesture was directed half to the figures on the stage, half to the gallery, and fled to my seat. The Luidaeg's eyes had gone black from side to side, and it was like looking at the deepest part of an unforgiving sea. Her lips were closed, but they seemed malformed somehow, like she was holding back too many teeth. Then she smiled at me, the color bleeding back into her eyes and the flesh of her mouth smoothing into something that looked almost human, if you didn't know better.

"Good job not fucking it up too badly," she whispered.

I didn't say anything, although I rolled my eyes toward the ceiling to make sure she knew how frustrated I was. We had a dead man. We might be sharing this room with a killer. And now I got to sit and listen as a bunch of nobles argued about whether or not we could counteract a spell that had been designed by a woman who enjoyed watching changelings die. This wasn't just foolishness. This was willful pigheadedness, and I didn't want any part of it.

"Who will speak?" asked Arden.

Theron and Chrysanthe, the monarchs of Golden Shores, stood. "We will speak," they said, in eerie, practiced unison. I struggled not to grimace. A glance to the side showed that Quentin was doing the same. Creepy monarchs doing their best impression of the twins from *The Shining* weren't exactly a favorite of either of us.

"Then speak," said Arden. She managed to make it sound like she was conveying a great and precious favor upon them. I wondered if she knew how much of a queen she was becoming. Maybe more importantly, I wondered if she would forgive me when she realized.

Chrysanthe and Theron exchanged a look, silent but laden with meaning. Chrysanthe was the one who took a quarter-step forward, enough to make it clear that she'd speak for both of them. "I was born daughter of the King and Queen upon the Golden Shore, and I married for love before I was tasked with the throne. When my time to ascend came, I bore my crown as an equal to my husband's, that we might balance each other in our regency."

Several other monarchs nodded. This was apparently important. It was uncommon, I knew that much: most demesnes were more like Shadowed Hills, where Sylvester and Luna were both in charge, but Sylvester was generally accepted as *more* in charge than she was, since he would keep his title if they got divorced. The arrangement Theron and Chrysanthe had meant even if they separated, took new lovers, and remarried, they'd still be King and Queen together, and would have to agree on their heir. It was a complicated way to do things, and it either signaled true love or a genuine desire for balance. Or the sort of delusion that *looks* like true love.

"Your Highnesses, Golden Shore is a rarity among the Westlands: we are a changeling Kingdom. Those purebloods who choose to remain among our population know well that they are considered no better than their changeling cousins. No worse, either. Equality has long been our goal, and we have, for the most part, achieved it."

"First among farmers," said a voice from somewhere in the gallery. Snickering followed.

Color rose in Chrysanthe's cheeks, tinting them an odd shade of rose-gold. Golden Hinds even bled gilded. "Yes, we are a farming community. The agrarian arts are as important as any other—or have you forgotten who provides your fairy fruits? Your pomegranates full and fine, as the poets say? We grow wine-pears and silver grapes in mortal soil, and make them taste as rich as anything grown in Faerie. Without us, you'd all be shopping at Whole Foods and trying to make sense of the tasteless blobs that humans insist count as 'tomatoes.' We *feed* you. Perhaps ours is a bad hand to bite."

The snickers subsided. No one looked particularly annoyed. This was the way purebloods did things: with snide comments and little jabs, to make sure no one forgot their place.

"The last kingdom census of Golden Shore showed

that fully two-thirds of our subjects were changelings, and that is why we stand before you today, and ask you not to approve the distribution of this so-called 'cure.'" Chrysanthe bowed. "Your attention is most gratifyingly received."

"Wait, *what*?" My voice rang out through the gallery. Chrysanthe froze in the act of sitting, turning to stare at me. She looked less offended than simply surprised.

That wasn't true of everyone. Some of the nobles who were now looking in my direction seemed frankly offended by the fact that a changeling had opened her mouth. I considered sinking into my seat and trying to disappear, but as no one was commanding me to shut up, I decided to push my luck. I stood.

"Why would having so many changelings in your community make you decide *against* the cure?" I asked. "Most of us don't have a hundred years to lose."

Chrysanthe straightened, standing again, and looked at me with almost sympathetic eyes. "How far back in your family line is your human ancestor?" she asked. There was kindness in her voice. That was surprising. "A grandparent? A great-grandparent? You may not understand the challenges faced by those who are more mortal."

"My father," I said, somehow managing not to wince. I was used to living in the Mists, where everyone sort of understood the circumstances of my birth, and had grown accustomed to watching the mortality bleed out of me, one drop at a time. Faerie always demanded payment for the sort of things I did. All too often, what it wanted was my heritage.

"What?" Chrysanthe looked confused. Then her eyes narrowed. "I would appreciate it, Queen Windermere, if you'd keep your vassals from making jokes during what should be a serious discussion."

"She isn't making a joke, I assure you," said Arden. "She's Amandine's daughter."

Mom has a reputation for being the best blood-worker in Faerie. Maybe it's unfair—I bet Eira could have given her a run for her money, if she were, you know, *awake*—but as she's one of the only Firstborn still walking around and doing things, it's not unearned. Mom being Firstborn isn't common knowledge outside of the Mists. Quickly, I said, "My mother changed the balance of my blood to protect me, and I had access to a hope chest for a short time. I promise you, my father was human. I haven't given up this much of my mortality out of shame or pride, but for the sake of Faerie, and to protect the ones I care for."

"I . . . see," said Chrysanthe, looking faintly bemused. "The choices you have made aren't available to most of our subjects. Hope chests are rare to the point of becoming legend, and Amandine doesn't come to visit very often. The blood they are given by their parents is the blood they will carry all the days of their lives."

"I know," I said. "That's why I'm confused."

Chrysanthe blinked slowly. "You really don't understand, do you? You are aware of what elf-shot does to those with mortal blood?"

"As you were told earlier, I've been elf-shot twice," I said, fighting to keep the chill from my voice. "I nearly died both times. So yeah, I have some idea." The image of my daughter struggling to breathe flashed unbidden through my mind. Gillian had been too human from the beginning. The elf-shot would have claimed her if I hadn't changed her blood. To save her, I had been forced to lose her forever. How dare this pureblood queen look at me like I didn't understand what elf-shot could cost? I knew better than anyone.

Elf-shot could cost the world.

"Right now, with no cure, when purebloods go to war, we have to weigh the chance of putting our people to sleep for a hundred years against the desire to end the conflict quickly and cleanly," she said. "We have to decide between real arrows and elf-shot, because it *is* a decision. Oberon's Law allows for deaths in war, but most of us don't want to kill each other, even when a conflict must turn violent."

A general murmur of agreement swept through the room. I didn't believe it—most of the purebloods I'd known were perfectly happy to kill each other, as long as they felt like they could get away with it—but I didn't say anything.

"Give the world a cure, and there's no decision," said Chrysanthe. "Most purebloods would have the elf-shot notched before they knew whether there was a changeling in the room, because under the Law, *changelings don't count*. If they kill a few mongrels in the process of subduing an enemy force, who cares? They can always wake up the people who matter. They can fill the air with arrows, and suffer no losses at all."

I stared at her, mouth suddenly dry. What she was saying made a terrible, brutal sort of sense. I'd been looking at the cure for elf-shot as if it would somehow remove elf-shot from the equation completely: like the purebloods would willingly set aside one of their greatest weapons because the game had changed. They wouldn't. They were never going to give it up. They were just going to change the way that they used it.

Faerie was never going to be safe for changelings. The fact that I persisted in believing it someday, somehow could be was just another sort of madness.

Chrysanthe shook her head. "The cure is too dangerous. It would take a weapon used judiciously and turn it into a weapon to be used without hesitation or thought. The Kingdom on the Golden Shore will not support its distribution, and we hope those of you with compassion in your hearts will see as we do." She remained standing for a few seconds longer, clearly waiting for someone to speak. When no one did, she offered a shallow bow to the stage, and sat.

"We appreciate your candor," said Maida. There was a thin note of strain in her voice. Like me, she hadn't considered what the cure might mean for the changelings of the Westlands; she'd seen it as a salve, and not a new form of poison. I wondered whether anyone who didn't know her origins would hear that unhappiness, or whether it only seemed clear to me because of what I'd already learned. "Who will speak?"

"I will speak," said Sylvester. I stiffened as my liege stood, standing as straight and proud as he had on the day when he first came through the wall of my room and offered me the Changeling's Choice. That was the real problem with being surrounded by immortals: my childhood heroes still looked exactly the same. The only one changing was me.

"Then speak," said Maida.

Sylvester inclined his head in gracious acknowledgment. "I was granted regency over the Duchy of Shadowed Hills as a reward for my service to the Kingdom of the Westlands, and for my service before coming here, when I dwelt in the Kingdom of Londinium. I have been a hero of the realm for centuries, called upon to serve as Faerie required. By any measure, I have paid my dues as a member of our glorious society of the undying, and while I have no aspirations to be a king in my own right, I have as much a place in our world as any who wears the crown."

His words were smooth, evenly cadenced: he was drawing on some obscure point of pureblood etiquette to make his point, reminding the others of the days when crowns were passed with more regularity. Kingdoms used to be smaller, and more prone to randomly invading each other. The situation with King Rhys and his puppet government in Silences had been unusual for the modern world. There was a time, though, when that was just as common a means of taking a throne as inheritance.

Then again, considering what had happened to King Antonio, maybe things hadn't changed that much after all.

"We see and acknowledge your place," said High King Aethlin.

"My wife, Luna, is the daughter of two of the First-born," said Sylvester. "Her father was the monster we called 'Blind Michael.' Her mother, Acacia, yet lives, and is known as the Mother of the Trees."

There was barely time to register the tension in the Luidaeg's shoulders before she was on her feet, eyes narrowed and mouth twisted. "You can't use your wife's parentage to support your claims of status and call my brother 'monster' in the same breath," she said. "That right is not yours."

To his credit—his small, self-destructive credit—Sylvester met her eyes without flinching. "My apologies, sea witch, and believe me when I say I have no desire to incur your wrath, but . . . your brother *was* a monster."

"That doesn't mean you have the right to call him that," the Luidaeg spat back.

A murmur ran through the crowd, and a few people shifted in their seats, putting themselves a little further from Sylvester and the smiting that was presumably about to happen. I didn't move. Neither did Quentin. Sylvester was Daoine Sidhe. That made him a child of Titania's bloodline, and meant the Luidaeg couldn't raise a hand against him, no matter how much she wanted to. The bindings Evening had placed upon her were too strong. For the first time, I was grateful for that. Sylvester and I might not currently be on the best of terms, but that didn't mean I wanted him reduced to a fine red mist.

There was a long pause before Sylvester offered her a shallow bow. "I meant neither offense nor to claim status that was not mine by right," he said. "I merely wish to be sure my situation is known and understood before I make my plea."

The Luidaeg said nothing. She just stood there and looked at him. I was close enough to see the white lines beginning to thread through her irises like creeping fog. Nothing good ever came of the Luidaeg's eyes changing. Quickly, before I thought better, I reached over and put a hand on her arm. She glanced at me, eyes going wide, startled, and—thankfully—back to driftglass green as she snapped back into the moment.

"Please," I said softly, and managed not to scowl when the spells on the stage caught my voice and projected it to the entire room. "Can we just let him finish? Please. For me."

"Does the changeling run this conclave?" asked a voice—Duke Michel from Starfall again. I should probably have expected him to be on my case after he'd been told to basically sit down and shut up.

What I wasn't expecting was for Sylvester to whirl before anyone else had a chance to speak, and say, in a low, grating tone, "You have insulted the honor of my household, sir. I will see you on the dueling grounds at dawn."

Duke Michel stared. I stared. For one shining, bizarre moment, we were united. Then Michel turned to the stage, and the moment was over.

"I've insulted no one," he said. "Duke Torquill insults *me* by claiming insult when none was offered. I simply asked a question."

"A question you had already asked, if in a different form, that you posed without permission to a knight sworn into his service," said High King Sollys. He sounded almost bored, like this sort of disruption was to be expected, but was still beneath his notice. "How was that not an insult? You continually call the honor of a member of his household into question, and now he wants recompense. His claim is supported. The insult is valid."

Duke Michel looked stunned. Sylvester looked smug. I gave serious thought to how much trouble I'd get in if

I started knocking people's heads together. I couldn't tell whether Michel was so prejudiced that he didn't realize what he was doing, or whether this was a calculated means of keeping the attention of the conclave focused on the wrong thing: me. The elf-shot cure was what mattered here, not my honor.

"Sir Daye is a hero of the realm and a valued part of my court," said Sylvester, tone turning deceptively mild. "Defending her honor is only a fraction of what I, as her liege, owe to her. Bring your second, Michel. Bring your sword. And prepare to learn the error of your ways."

"Now that this has been settled, please, Duke Torquill, if you would continue in your petition for understanding?" Maida settled deeper into her throne, posture reflecting disinterest that I had absolute faith she didn't feel. No one could slouch that insouciantly without intent.

"My apologies, Your Highness," said Sylvester, switching his attention back to the stage and offering the High Queen a quick bow. He was bowing so often that he was starting to look like one of those ballpark bobblehead dolls. "I have given my wife's pedigree so that you'll understand what we have faced, what we have endured, and what we have risen above."

The Luidaeg, who had been standing throughout the discussion, sank back into her seat. Her eyes were clear and green and filled with shadows.

"My sister, September, is dead. My brother, Simon, lies elf-shot and sleeping, and will stand trial for his crimes against me when he wakes—crimes which, once, would have carried the penalty of elf-shot." Sylvester's mouth twisted like he was trying to smile. If he had, it wouldn't have been a gentle expression. "Who knows what the penalty for kidnapping and treason will be now? My only child and heir, Rayseline, also lies sleeping. They'll wake within a few years of each other if allowed to slumber out their spans. How is that fair, I ask you? When my brother the criminal and my daughter his victim must sleep through the same number of years, must miss the same portion of their lives? My counterparts from the Golden Shore make a true and valid point—that we endanger the weakest among us if we distribute this cure but do not also ask that the use of elf-shot be reduced. So why not take that additional step? Restrict the use of elf-shot to the field of war and to the punishment of those who must make reparation for what they have done."

"I would speak," said Dianda.

Several heads turned in her direction, Sylvester's included. He looked briefly bemused. Then he bowed again, and said, "I yield the floor."

"Then speak," said Arden.

Dianda rose from her wheelchair, fins and scales melting into legs as her gown, previously bundled around her waist, fell to cover her to the ankle. It was a striking, elegant movement, and I wondered how often she'd practiced it before she'd managed to get it right.

"I'm here to represent the Undersea," she said. Her voice was level, calm; regal. She sounded like the reigning monarch she was, and it was more than a little jarring. Dianda was meant to be punching people and gleefully threatening everyone in range, not standing there giving her credentials. "We do things differently below the waves, as some of you may know. We've never stooped to the use of elf-shot. A sleeping prisoner must be housed, kept safe, protected; better to keep them awake and allow them to understand what they've done to earn their punishment. I have two questions for you, nobles of the land. First, if the Undersea can do without elf-shot, without a weapon that turns napping into imprisonment, why can't you? And second . . . are you not regents? Are you not the rulers of your lands? How is it that this cure can't be used as an opportunity to ban elf-shot entirely? Oberon's Law allows for death on the battlefield. If you feel a war is so warranted that it can't be avoided, carry real arrows. Pay for your convictions."

"That's easy for you to say," snarled the King of Highmountain, jumping to his feet without being recognized or granted permission to speak. "The humans and their ilk aren't banging on your door, stripping away your protections by the hour. We can't *afford* to let our people die on the battlefield."

"Tell that to the coral reefs, to the whales on the brink of extinction," said Dianda. "Tell that to the dead and dying places in the sea. The humans live alongside you. They shit on us."

"If you can't afford the deaths you'd risk, perhaps you can't afford to go to war," said Patrick mildly. He didn't rise. Technically, Dianda was the one with authority to speak here: he was just the consort. Still, no one cut him off as he continued, in that deceptively mild tone, "I was raised in the Westlands; I moved to the Undersea after I was married. It was a bit of a culture shock, going from a world where elf-shot allowed us to cut each other down while pretending our hands remained clean to one where every battle was paid for in blood, but I came to see the sense of it. When the Undersea goes to war, the seas bleed. It's much less casual."

"May I speak?"

I stiffened. The voice belonged to Tybalt.

Dianda glanced in his direction, looking only faintly annoyed. She didn't like many land-dwellers, and as a mermaid, she didn't think much of cats. But she and Tybalt were reasonably well acquainted, and she liked me; this might have been one of the only times when our association put him in *better* social shape, not worse. "I yield," she said.

"Then speak," said Aethlin.

Tybalt rose, fluid and elegant, as Dianda sat. "The Cait Sidhe have never used elf-shot," he said. "I've heard the Divided Courts refer to us as brutes and barbarians— I'm sure no one in this room would ever speak of the

Court of Cats in such terms, of course, but I must speak as truly as you do, and I *have* heard these things—but to us, the helplessness elf-shot enforces upon its victims has always seemed the more barbarous thing. As the Duchess Lorden says, you must store them, protect them, shield them, and do it all for a century's time, and for what? So you can say you are not killers? We go to war to kill. Admit that, and let the cure be shared."

He sat. Arden rose.

"We have much to consider, and the night grows old," she said. "Your rooms have been prepared. My guards will stand watch alongside your own, to prevent tragedy striking us a second time. If you have any needs, please, relay them to my staff, and they will be met. For now, we are grateful for your presence, and we say good morning to you."

The members of the audience began to rise and head for the exit. I stayed where I was, watching them go, studying their posture and expressions as well as I could without staring. Some of them looked annoyed; others looked frightened, or pleased, or even amused. No one was so obviously murderous that I felt like I could point a finger and say: "there, that's the one who did it."

Duke Michel of Starfall attempted to approach the stage, and was stopped by two of Arden's guards, who moved smoothly from the wings to stand in front of him. The spells that shared everyone's words with the room must have been dispelled or put on hold by Arden's farewell, because I couldn't hear what he said, only see his frustration as he wasn't allowed to get any closer to the people in charge. The rest of the delegation from his kingdom was leaving. Finally, frustrated, he turned and went after them.

Of the four people seated on the stage, only Siwan rose and left with the rest. Arden's guards closed the door after the last of the audience was out. Arden herself held her position for a count of five, shoulders locked, chin up, the picture of a queen. Then she collapsed onto her throne, curling her knees against her chest and putting her hands over her face. "I need a drink," she said, voice muffled by her hands. "And then I'm going to need a drink for my drink, so the first one doesn't get lonely. Fuck it, just give me the bottle and walk away."

"I think you're doing very well," said Maida, sounding amused. Her gaze went to me. She sobered, amusement fading. "Sir Daye. Would you come here, please?"

I'd been waiting for this summons. That didn't mean I was happy to hear it. I stood, brushing off my pants like that could take the smell of blood away, and walked toward the stage. Quentin followed. Technically, he hadn't been invited, but as my squire, the lack of an explicit "come alone" meant he was allowed to accompany me anywhere I went. He was supposed to be learning by watching what I did. Hard to do that from a distance, no matter how much I might sometimes wish otherwise.

Maida's gaze flicked to Quentin. She wanted him here less than I did. I could understand that. She didn't tell him to go. I could understand that, too, and I was grateful. Being his mother gave her no authority over him when he was acting as my squire. Being High Queen gave her plenty of authority—it just wouldn't have been appropriate for her to exercise it.

"Did you tell the assembly everything you knew of King Robinson's death?" she asked.

"Mostly," I said.

Aethlin raised an eyebrow. "It's amazing how you can find a response other than 'yes' or 'no' to a question that shouldn't be that complicated."

"Nothing about this is uncomplicated," I replied. "I told the assembly everything in broad strokes; I left out the details. King Robinson didn't smell the magic of whoever attacked him, but he heard a sound like tin foil being ripped, and he felt a small amount of disorientation. I'm wondering if we have a teleporter playing silly games."

"Tuatha de Dannan don't make a sound when we open portals," said Arden.

"No, and he didn't feel cold or shortness of breath, which means he wasn't pulled through the Shadow Roads," I said. "That rules out the Cait Sidhe. I'm pretty sure he'd have noticed if it had been another Candela messing with him. How many types of teleporter are there in Faerie? Roughly?"

"No one knows," said the Luidaeg. I glanced over my shoulder. She was still seated, slumped in her chair like the bored teenager she sometimes resembled. Her apparent age was as fluid as the rest of her. It was jarring how young she could look. "If all the descendant races were still out there, it would be dozens. But some of them have died out. Some have been slaughtered. I haven't seen an actual Aarnivalkea in centuries. They were never that common to begin with. I think the Lampads are still around. Maybe. It's hard to say."

"Did no one ever think to keep track?"

The Luidaeg lifted her head and looked at me. Her face was young, but her eyes . . . those were very, very old. "We kept track of our own children, October. We did the best we could. Look how well that turned out for me."

There was a momentary, uncomfortable silence. The Luidaeg wasn't widely associated with a single descendant race, because most of her children and grandchildren were dead, killed by merlins who'd been armed by her sister. The Roane were on the verge of extinction. The Luidaeg, in her grief, had been holding herself apart from them for centuries.

Maybe keeping track wasn't that easy after all.

I turned back to the waiting monarchs, all three of whom looked concerned, in that "I am in a room with an unhappy Firstborn" way, but none of whom looked like they *understood*. The Luidaeg's status as mother of the Roane wasn't commonly known. For the first time, it occurred to me that Quentin would be carrying an awful lot of secrets when he took the crown. Whether that would make him a better king was yet to be determined.

"So there are options for who could have been messing with him, if that was even what was happening," I said. "How do you want me to proceed?"

"We have a king-killer among us," said High King Aethlin gravely. "You're known as a king-breaker. If we don't want people to assume that you've escalated—which we don't—you'll need to find out who did this, and avenge King Robinson."

"I already got that far on my own," I said. My own voice was flat. This wasn't what I'd been hoping would happen. "I can't look for a killer and attend every minute of this conclave. I need three things from you."

"You may ask."

"I need permission to leave this room whenever I need to. I may not even enter it unless the evidence leads me here. I can leave Quentin to observe, if you like; he's my squire, he'll tell me everything that happens." And that would nicely deal with both the issue of making sure the future High King understood what had been decided, and with my discomfort at the idea of stalking a killer through a half-familiar knowe with my teenage squire.

"Um, what?" Quentin gave me a sidelong look. "Backup? You're supposed to have it, or Tybalt looks at me like I've done something really wrong, and I hate that."

"Don't look at me," said the Luidaeg. "Unless another one of my siblings shows up, I'm staying and witnessing this whole shit show."

"Lowri," I said. "Or Madden. Either of them has Arden's trust, which means they can't be questioned without questioning the queen. Or I can call May and have her come stand between me and whatever's out there." Having a completely indestructible roommate was occasionally useful.

"Can't do that," said the Luidaeg, almost lazily. "A Fetch shows up now, all these people lose their shit. Never invite a death omen to a murder party."

May was *not* going to be happy to learn that she'd just been disinvited by the Luidaeg. I pressed on, saying, "I'll figure something out. I'll be careful. But I need your support in this."

"That was the first thing," said Aethlin. "You said there were three."

"Yeah," I said. "The second is that I need to be able to remove people from the conclave to talk to them, with your authority, so no one can say, 'No, I don't talk to changelings.' There's a good chance our killer is here for the conclave. Before anyone takes offense, I'm also going to need to talk to the staff, and see whether anyone moved here from Angels, since our other option is that somebody with a grudge saw an opportunity and took it."

"You don't think that's what happened, though, do you?" asked Maida.

I shook my head. "No, because if Arden had anyone on staff who could do what King Robinson described, I think I'd know about it. I could be wrong, which is why I still want to talk to them, but . . . it feels wrong. If I could ask for blood—"

"No." Aethlin's voice was hard as he cut me off.

I blinked at him. "But blood can't lie. We'd know."

"And I would be the High King who'd betrayed all his subjects by requiring them to bleed for someone who did not hold their oaths. Blood can be used for more than just divination. It can be used to bind, to compel loyalty. I won't order them to bleed for you."

I knew all too well how blood could be used to compel loyalty. That was Evening's entire modus operandi. I still stared at him, fumbling for another way. "What if . . . what if they bled for you? You're Daoine Sidhe."

"My blood magic is not as strong as it could be," Aethlin admitted. "I would exhaust myself while learning nothing useful. No blood. Not until you have cause to demand it."

Well, this was just swell. "Got it."

"What was the third thing?" asked Maida.

"I sort of have a bad track record with kings and queens and accusing them of things and them getting pissed at me," I said. "I need you to tell everyone here that they can't leave until we find the killer, and make sure they know that I'm doing this because it's my job, not because I think it's fun to harass the monarchy."

"But you *do* think it's fun to harass the monarchy," said Quentin.

I wrinkled my nose at him. "That's not the point."

"Sir Daye," said High King Aethlin, pulling my attention back to him. "Can you find the person who did this?"

"I don't know," I said. "But I can sure as hell try."

"Then you will have everything you've requested, and may the root and the branch grace us with the answers that we need," he said.

I nodded but didn't speak. I was going to have to solve another murder.

Goody.

ELEVEN

I SAT ON THE FLOOR of the quarters I was sharing with Quentin, my back to the door and my head in my hands. People were shouting in the hall outside. The process of telling the kings and queens that neither they nor their retinues would be allowed to leave the knowe until we found King Robinson's killer was in full swing, and people were *pissed*. No one likes having their freedom restricted. As it turns out, fae monarchs like it even less than most. There would be privacy spells cast eventually, allowing everyone to have a little peace and quiet while they were in their rooms, but that was going to take time.

At least Raj had already gotten out of here. At least May was at the house, and could feed the cats.

At least.

"They sure can yell," said Quentin.

"Don't speak poorly of your peers," I said.

He didn't say anything. I lifted my head and he was grimacing at me. "Don't call them my peers," he said. "It's weird."

"But it's true," I said, and dropped my head again. "Any one of them would be happy to tell you that you have more in common with them than I do, being a pureblood and all. And that's before they know that you're ... you know." Until the privacy spells came down, I wasn't going to call him a prince. That was a risk too big for me to take. "To most of these people, I'm no better than a dog."

"Arden's seneschal *is* a dog half the time." Quentin walked across the room and sat next to me, settling with his back against the door. "I don't think being a dog is so bad. Dogs are loyal. And fun to be with. And won't call you names, or get mad at you for things you can't help, like who your parents are."

"You are a weird kid."

"Whose fault is that?" I could almost hear him smiling. If I looked up, I knew he'd be looking at me, one corner of his mouth curved in lopsided amusement. He'd been with me long enough that I probably knew the man he was becoming—the man who was sitting beside me— better than his mother did.

There was something sad about that. Blind fosterage keeps the children of the nobility safe, and when the choice is that or what King Gilad had done, failing to acknowledge his children out of fear of losing them, I could almost understand. It was still a terrible loss. Childhood is precious whether or not you live forever. Quentin and his parents would have centuries to be adults together. They should have been allowed to see him being a child.

The smell of pennyroyal drifted into the room. I raised my head. Tybalt was standing half in shadow by the far wall. The interplay of light and darkness cast stripes across his skin, making him look like the tabby pattern of his feline form had somehow managed to carry over to his fae self. He met my eyes. Relief flooded his expression, and he took a step forward, leaving stripes and shadows behind.

"October," he said. "It took long enough to make my way here that I began to fear I'd waited too long, and you would already be off on your fool's errand, clawing your way down the walls of the world. I assume you're partially responsible for the restrictions placed upon our movement?"

"I told the High King and Queen that we needed to lock down the knowe," I said, and tensed, waiting for him to get mad. If the rest of the nobility was pissed about being confined to Muir Woods, a King of Cats might explode.

"Good," he said, continuing across the room toward me. "As it happens, no amount of 'please stay put' can sever cat from shadows. I've already walked the Shadow Roads to my own Court to inform Raj that I am under a quaintly optimistic form of house arrest and he is not to return tomorrow. I'll remain here with the rest of you until this is over. Shade will not be attending, as we do not wish to leave *all* the cats of the Bay Area without firm supervision."

"I like the phrase 'quaintly optimistic,'" I said.

Tybalt smirked. "Yes, well. If I've already broken the wall, gone out, done my business, and come back, who's to say your large assortment of overly entitled rabble won't do the same? I'm sure some of them were looking forward to a lovely afternoon of tourism before the conclave resumed."

"Riding cable cars, looking at sea lions," I said.

"Maybe punching them, if we're talking about Dianda," said Quentin.

"Now, now," tutted Tybalt. He sat down on my free side, closer than Quentin, so I could feel the reassuringly solid warmth of him. I inched closer still, resting my head against his shoulder. "The Duchess Lorden no doubt has an excess of sea lions, which she can use for pugilistic exercises whenever she feels the need."

"How are they going to keep her from drying out?" asked Quentin. "She's, you know. A fish when she sleeps."

I grimaced. "Please don't use the 'f' word. She's a mer-maid. That's different."

"She'll still dry out if she doesn't sleep in a lake or something."

"That's easy," I said, relieved to have a question I could answer. "One of the guest rooms has a private 're-clining pool' in it, according to Madden. They've put Di-anda and Patrick there. She'll just sleep in the water."

Quentin looked dubious. "That doesn't sound very comfortable."

"Especially not for the poor, bipedal Duke." Tybalt pressed a kiss to the crown of my head. "I am deeply grateful that you do not transform into anything un-pleasant when you sleep."

"If you two are going to start talking about your sex life, I'm going to go help Queen Windermere's staff make the beds," said Quentin. I lifted my cheek from Tybalt's shoulder and smiled at my squire.

"You know I wouldn't do that to you," I said. "I want you to voluntarily show up for the wedding."

Quentin laughed, and was starting to reply when someone rapped on the door. His laughter died, taking his smile along with it. Tybalt and I both twisted to look at the door, like it would somehow reveal the identity of whoever was on the other side.

It didn't. "Who is it?" I called.

"Sylvester. Please, may I come in?"

I exchanged a startled look with Quentin as I picked myself up from the floor, Tybalt a reassuring presence behind me. As my liege, Sylvester could technically order me to open the door, now that he knew for sure that I was in here. The fact that he hadn't done so probably meant he was here because he wanted to try rebuilding some of the bridges between us. That was a good thing. That was an important thing. That was a thing I'd been meaning to force myself to do for months, ever since the last time I'd been at Shadowed Hills. And it was absolutely not the sort of thing I wanted to deal with when I was getting ready to go out looking for a murderer.

I'd paused too long. Sylvester sighed, and said, "I promise you, October, I'm not here to make you have a conversation you're not ready for. This is about Antonio's death."

"Just a second," I said. Turning to Tybalt, I asked, "Can you please go walk the halls? Watch for anyone acting suspicious. See if anything looks out of place. Talk to the bats in the attic, if you have to. Just . . . do my job while I deal with my liege, okay?"

"For you, the world," he said, and kissed me, quick and glancing, before turning to stride across the room, moving toward the shadow he'd used to enter.

I didn't wait to watch him disappear. I just straightened my shirt, ran my hands through my hair, and turned back to the door. Quentin stood, moving to fall in behind me in the squire's position as I opened the door for Duke Sylvester Torquill of Shadowed Hills, my liege, substitute father figure, and technically, step-uncle.

Faerie gets confusing sometimes.

For his part, Sylvester looked . . . relieved. The emotion in his face was more complicated than that, seeming composed of equal parts exhaustion, worry, and pleasure, but relief was the end result. Fae don't age, but there were shadows in his honey-colored eyes that hadn't been there the last time we'd been face-to-face, and his russet-red hair was less carefully combed than it should have been. All these were small things, things I'd been able to miss from a distance. With him right in front of me, I couldn't ignore them.

"October," he said, and smiled.

For a moment—a single, heartbreaking moment—I wanted nothing more than to throw myself into his arms and let the familiar dogwood and daffodils scent of his magic surround me. He'd been my mentor, my teacher, and my surrogate parent for almost as long as I could remember. Compared to that, our estrangement seemed to be of little consequence, something so recent and pointless that I wanted to throw it aside. I just couldn't.

He'd lied to me. He'd kept secrets that had caused me and the people around me to suffer. He'd done it because of promises he'd made to my mother, and while I could respect his desire to keep his word, I couldn't forgive the fact that he'd hurt me in the process. Some prices were too high to pay. "Sylvester," I said, moving to the side. "Please, come in."

His smile died as he realized that an open door was not the same thing as forgiveness. "Of course," he said, and stepped past me, allowing me to close the door. Before I could ask, he said, "Luna is in our quarters, resting. Queen Windermere was kind enough to provide a room with a door which opens on the garden, considering Luna's special circumstances."

Luna was a Blodynbryd, a rose who walked like a woman. I nodded. "It was smart of you not to bring her along. I'm not sure she's in the mood to talk to me. Ever again."

"I know." He didn't make apologies. He didn't try to justify his wife's behavior. He just looked at me, and I was struck again by how *tired* he seemed.

The longer I looked at him, the worse I felt about our estrangement. This needed to end. I took a deep breath, and asked, "All right: why are you here? I don't think it's because you want to find out whether Tybalt still wants to strangle you. Which, by the way, he does."

"Congratulations on the occasion of your engagement," said Sylvester. "Given our current circumstances, I know you won't accept this offer, but should you like, you would be more than welcome to hold your wedding at Shadowed Hills. I would be delighted — no, I would be *honored* — to witness your marriage."

"It seems like everyone in the Mists wants to choose my wedding venue for me," I said.

"If Toby had her way, she'd be getting married at the city hall," said Quentin.

"Nothing wrong with a good civil ceremony," I said. "Sylvester, not that it's not nice to see you and everything, but why are you here?"

"Because I wish to offer assistance," he said. "Grianne is willing to help you look for King Antonio's killer. You know her well enough to know that she'd be a valuable ally, and I would feel better knowing you had someone with you who could remove you from the situation quickly, should it turn hazardous."

I frowned, tilting my head as I asked, "What makes this situation any different from all the other dangerous situations I've walked into? If there's something you're not telling me, that's really a habit that you should get out of. Now, if possible."

Sylvester was silent for a long moment before he sighed, and said, "Normally, you have Tybalt with you. It's no secret that he and I aren't friends—"

"He tried to kill you. He *used* to respect you, you know. I'd never seen him bow to a noble of the Divided Courts before he bowed to you. You've pretty much spoiled that."

"It seems I'm even more adept than my brother at spoiling things, and he slumbers for his sins," said Sylvester. There was a profound weariness to his tone. "Regardless of your lover's hatred of me—hatred I do not contest having earned, believe me—I trust him to keep you safe and well. If I can't fight beside you, he is who I'd choose for the position. But he can't hold that position and sit the conclave at the same time, and with the doors sealed to keep us on the inside, I assume he can't summon any additional monarchs of the Cait Sidhe to free him from his duties."

"No, he can't, or at least he won't," I admitted. "You're sure you want to loan me Grianne?"

"I would rather loan you Etienne. Unfortunately, the doors are locked, and he's not inside." Sylvester shrugged. "We work with what we have."

"You taught me that." I took a step back, looking around the room Arden had assigned to me and Quentin as I tried to buy a little time.

It was less fancy than the guest quarters in Silences, thank Maeve, with redwood flooring and walls papered in an art deco blackberry pattern. The sliding door to our balcony was stained glass, worked in a riot of blackberry blossoms and bright California poppies in shades ranging from honey to wildfire. Blackout curtains hung to either side, ready to be drawn when we needed to block the morning sun. As in Silences, Quentin had a smaller secondary chamber, barely big enough for a single narrow bed. That was standard housing for knights with squires. We'd earned bigger beds and actual wardrobes for our clothing. They were still proving themselves, at least supposedly. As far as I was concerned, Quentin had proven himself several dozen times over—but until he had his knighthood, this was how it was going to be.

"I like Grianne," I said finally, turning back to Sylvester. "She's always been good to me, and she doesn't talk much. But right now, I can't accept personal staff from a noble who hasn't been cleared of the murder of King Antonio Robinson. Not without opening a *lot* of doors that I'd like to keep closed for as long as possible."

Sylvester looked stunned. "But I'm your *liege*."

"Yeah, and that makes it all the more important that I don't appear to be favoring you, since I've been ordered to investigate by the High King, and he's going to be watching for signs that I can't handle this," I said. "If I question everyone but you while I'm running around with Grianne as my backup, and I don't find the murderer, what does that look like? Because to me, it looks like I knowingly harbored a killer while I was pointing the finger at everyone else to keep them from noticing that no one was asking you anything."

Sylvester's expression deepened, going from simple surprise to something bleak and bone-deep. It was like he'd realized, in that instant, how broken things were between us.

Faerie has always been a feudal society. Kings and Queens, Dukes and Duchesses, all the way down to the loyal courtiers and Knights, who do as they're told and protect the honor of the households that they serve. As long as Sylvester was my liege, he was supposed to have my absolute loyalty, unquestioning and unchanging, no matter what he did to me. I was supposed to be, quite literally, his dog, incapable of biting the hand that fed me. And maybe once I had been. Once, I'd been so happy to serve him that it had been physically painful. But times had changed, and no matter how much either of us wished it, they weren't going to change back.

"You must question me, then," he said finally. "I won't ask if you believe I could do this, because I don't want to hear your answer, but you must question me, and I will answer you honestly. I'd offer you my blood, if I thought that would help you to judge the honesty of my words." He paused then, looking at me expectantly.

I shook my head. "No. No blood, not yet. High King Sollys can't order every monarch in the Westlands to bleed for me, and that means I can't use blood evidence as the thing that proves my case. I already know you didn't do it." I was almost relieved that Aethlin had given me such an easy out. If I rode Sylvester's blood, if I saw things from his side, it would be almost impossible for me to keep being angry at him the way part of me still wanted to be—the way I needed to be, unless I was ready to forgive. And I wasn't. Not yet. Maybe that was small and petty and *mortal* of me, or maybe it was the most fae thing I'd ever done. For a society of immortals, they sure did enjoy holding a grudge.

Sylvester nodded, looking disappointed but not surprised. "Then how will you determine my innocence?"

I shrugged. "I don't know. I was thinking I'd, you know, ask you some questions and see how you answered them. Like who were you sitting with after I left the dining hall?"

"Luna, Li Qin, Elliot, Grianne, and a Baroness from Helen's Hand." I must have looked blank, because he added, "Small, independent Barony from the territory between Silences and Evergreen. They have no neighbors for miles. Pleasant woman. Hamadryad. You don't meet many of them with titles to their names. So to speak."

Hamadryads were similar to Dryads, as the names implied, but they weren't bound to their trees in the same way. They also had a tendency to use whistles, sighs, and hand gestures as names, which worked well for them, and meant the rest of us referred to them as "hey, you." I nodded. "I'll confirm that with them. Why did the Baroness come down? Hamadryads tend to take multi-decade naps *without* elf-shot."

"True, but they can't bond with their home trees while sleeping, and elf-shot rarely waits for them to gown themselves in green," said Sylvester. "They'd prefer to sleep when they choose, and not be enchanted into it."

"Fair," I said. "What did you talk about at dinner?"

He raised an eyebrow. "What does this have to do with anything?"

"Humor me."

"Ah." He sighed. "Li Qin's adjustment to being Duchess, however temporarily, of Dreamer's Glass. April's progress as Countess of Tamed Lightning. The two have been discussing bringing Tamed Lightning back into Dreamer's Glass, once Li Qin's appointment becomes permanent. April cannot produce heirs, and having a second layer of protection would do them some good. Elliot and the Hamadryad discussed the best techniques for cleaning untreated wood floors without damaging them. Luna said little, and complained about the food."

"When the argument between Antonio and Dianda began, what did you do?"

"We continued to eat our meals." He frowned at my expression. "Don't look so judgmental, October, it doesn't suit you. A monarch—a *King*—wanted to brawl with a woman whose rank equals my own, who currently stands as chosen representative of another King. It wasn't my place to interfere, and if it wasn't mine, it wasn't Li Qin's either."

"Purebloods," I said, resisting the urge to grab and shake him. "I'll never understand purebloods. So you just sat there while they yelled at each other? What happened after that?"

"They settled their differences and resumed speaking more quietly. You may wish to speak to Duchess Lorden about what they discussed after the yelling ceased. We enjoyed dessert as a group, and were shown to our quarters to freshen up before the conclave resumed. I was accompanied to my quarters by Luna and Grianne. Elliot and Li Qin are down the hall from us. I'm not sure where the Baroness is housed."

"Probably in one of the trees outside the knowe," said Quentin. Sylvester jumped, looking at my squire like he'd forgotten we weren't alone. I turned more slowly, giving Quentin a curious look. Quentin shrugged. "Hamadryads like to sleep in trees a lot more than they like to sleep in beds. Unless she brought a tree with her from Helen's Hand, that's where she'll be."

"She'll still have a room for her things and her staff, assuming she brought any," I said, and turned back to Sylvester. "I'll be honest: I know you didn't kill King Antonio. It's not your style. But I do genuinely appreciate you being willing to answer my questions. I'll come to you if I have more."

"My offer of aid remains open," he said. He paused before adding, "You look well, October. I miss you very much, and hope you will be able to come home soon."

"I miss you, too," I said. I didn't comment on his assumption that Shadowed Hills was home for me, now or ever. Let him have that much. No matter how mad at him I was right now, I had loved him for most of my life, and he had always deserved it.

Sylvester opened the door to let himself out, revealing Patrick Lorden hurrying toward us, face pale and sweat standing out on his temples, like he couldn't decide whether he should collapse or have a panic attack. Sylvester froze. So did Patrick. For a split-second, so did I.

Then I shoved my way past Sylvester, crossing the threshold into the hall, until I was close enough to see the hazy, unfocused look in Patrick's eyes.

"Patrick?" I asked.

His gaze snapped to my face, becoming clear. Then he grabbed my arms. He'd never done that before. His grip was surprisingly strong, and I had a moment to be glad any bruises would fade before Tybalt had a chance to see them.

Then Patrick spoke. "Dianda," he said. "It's . . . you have to . . . please. You *have* to."

"Have to what, Patrick? Is Dianda all right?" *Please don't let her be dead,* I thought desperately. She was my friend. She was my ally. More importantly than either of those things, she was the representative of the local Undersea. If she was dead, war might become inevitable.

He shook his head, letting me go. "No," he said. "Please."

"Please?"

"Come with me." He turned and started down the hall. He hadn't gone more than a few steps when he broke into a run. I ran after him, and from the sound of things, Quentin and Sylvester ran after me. I might have been angry at that, under other circumstances: I might have stopped and told Sylvester to go back to his quarters and let me do my job, to remember that he was the retired hero and I was the woman Patrick had come to find. I didn't slow down. I needed all the help I could get, and neither my pride nor my preference was going to change that. So we ran.

The room Arden had set aside for Patrick and Dianda was a floor down from mine—something that would have seemed odd, considering I was on the ground floor, if it weren't for the often alien nature of knowes. Knowes viewed geometry as a plaything, and were happy to rearrange it to suit their own needs, or the needs of their inhabitants. I'd have to ask Patrick how they'd dealt with Dianda's wheelchair, after all this was cleared up and I knew she was all right. For now, I just ran, and the others ran with me, until the open door to the Lordens' chambers came into view.

Dianda wasn't visible, but as I got closer, I saw the pond in the center of the room, larger than the average hot tub and recessed into the floor, surrounded by a ring of red brick that seemed less decorative and more a matter of making the area around the water less slippery. Water weeds rooted to the sides, drifting lazily and almost concealing the woman curled on the bottom, her fins spread in jewel-toned array, her eyes closed. She wasn't moving. She wasn't moving at all.

The arrow protruding from her left shoulder may have had something to do with that.

I skidded to a stop just before I hit the brick demarcation between room and pondside. The water was clear and cool and so much like the ponds in the Japanese Tea Gardens that my stomach did an unhappy flip before contracting into a tight ball of dread. No matter how far removed I was from my own time in the water, it was always going to be terrible for me.

"We need her out of the water," I said, and my voice sounded distant and thin, like it was being ripped away by some unfelt wind. "Sylvester?"

"Of course." My liege pushed past me and plunged into the pond, heedless of what that would do to his clothes.

I lifted my eyes, not wanting to watch him wrangle Dianda's motionless body out of the weeds, and found Patrick standing on the other side of the pond, his own eyes fixed bleakly on the water. "Patrick," I said. "What happened?"

"I don't . . . I . . ." He looked up. He looked so *lost*, like this was one of those situations he'd never even allowed himself to consider, out of fear that thinking it might somehow make it true. "We met here. For the first time, I mean, back when Gilad was King and she was about to become Duchess of Saltmist. We ran away from this fancy banquet in her honor and ate cake in the kitchen. I thought it would be nice, romantic, even, if I brought her some cake, since we're here again. So I left her alone. I left her alone for ten minutes. No more."

And when he'd returned, she had been lying elf-shot at the bottom of the pond. I glanced around the room, finding the plate of cake where it had fallen a few feet from the door. That explained the faint scent of chocolate in the air—it was possible we were dealing with someone whose magic smelled of chocolate, of course, but that was unlikely enough that I didn't need to focus on it. Not until we'd run through all other options.

I looked back to Patrick. "Can she drown?"

It wasn't as odd a question as it seemed. Of Patrick and Dianda's two sons, only the younger had inherited his mother's ability to breathe water. Dean could drown, despite being a mermaid's son. To my great relief, Patrick shook his head and said, "Not in her natural form. I think . . . I think if she'd been on legs and been pushed into the water, it might be different, but she was relaxing when I left to get the cake. That's why she didn't go with me. She didn't want to put her feet back on."

There was a splash, followed by a wet, meaty smacking sound. I turned back to the water. Sylvester had hauled Dianda out, her tail hitting against the bricks as he dragged her to dry ground. I grabbed her flukes, lifting them before too much damage could be done to the delicate scales marking the transition between flesh and fin. Dianda wasn't going to thank us if she woke to find her tail damaged.

"Is there a bed?" I asked, hoisting my portion of unconscious mermaid. Quentin moved to support her midsection, and between the three of us, we were able to lift her with relative ease, keeping Patrick from needing to get involved. There were a lot of things I was happy to ask him to do. Carrying his elf-shot wife wasn't on the list.

"Yes," he said. "This way." White-faced and shaking, he turned and led us across the room to a latticework door. It was more like a screen than anything else: he pushed it aside to reveal a covered balcony, open to the night air on three sides, with a large canopied bed at the center. The bedposts were carved into blackberry vines rich with fruit, and the bedclothes were the rich purple and fragile lilac of the berries and flowers that normally accompanied the vines.

"Sometimes I really admire Arden's commitment to her theme," I commented, as we carried Dianda over to the bed. There was a shrill note to my voice, like part of me knew I was whistling past the graveyard, and still couldn't stop. Dianda was my *friend*. Maybe more importantly . . . this really looked like a declaration of war.

We slid her onto the mattress. Patrick leaned over to brush her wet hair away from her face, grimacing. He didn't say anything, but I knew a small part of what he was thinking. When Merrow transformed from fin to flesh, they magically became dry at the same time. He'd probably never seen her with a pillow under her head and water in her hair. In that moment, she could have been dead.

As if he'd read my mind, he said, "Di loves pillows. She sleeps with me in the bed as often as she can, just because she enjoys having something under her head that isn't a mossy rock. Linens don't do so well when you submerge them."

"Sandbags?" suggested Quentin.

Patrick flashed him a surprised look. Then he smiled, the expression tinged with worry and sorrow. "Those work, too. I . . ." His gaze went to the arrow protruding from Dianda's shoulder. "Should we be taking this out of her?"

"Not yet," I said. "She can't get *more* elf-shot than she already is, and if we leave it there, we don't have to worry that she'll start bleeding. Quentin, I have a job for you."

My squire straightened. "What is it?"

"Go find Arden. Don't be seen."

He nodded, catching my meaning immediately, and turned to head out of the room at a brisk pace. Sylvester and Patrick both looked at me, the one quizzical, the other alarmed.

"How much time has he spent in this knowe?" asked Sylvester.

"Is it safe for him to go off alone?" asked Patrick.

"Quentin was a courtier at Shadowed Hills before becoming my squire," I said, picking up Dianda's left wrist and studying her webbed hand. Her fingertips were scraped, ever so slightly. She must have been clinging to the pool's edge when she was shot, and fallen backward into the water as the elf-shot took effect. "He knows how to navigate servants' halls. If there's anyone who can get through this place without attracting any attention to himself, it's Quentin."

"Can we wake her up?" asked Patrick.

The longing in his voice was so nakedly pure that I froze, allowing several seconds to tick past before I looked up, met his eyes, and said softly, "You know I can't answer that."

"We have a cure. It's here, in this knowe. No one knows she's been shot. Please, can't we just ... wake her?"

"No," said Sylvester. We both turned to him. He looked at Patrick as he said, "Someone knows she's been shot: whoever shot her. There are landlocked kingdoms represented at this conclave, people for whom the threat of the Undersea means nothing, because the Undersea could never touch them. Any one of them could have decided to make their point by targeting someone who couldn't deliver direct retribution—the Law never forbids elf-shot, just cautions that there will always be consequences. Wake her, and whoever shot her can stand before the conclave and announce that the Mists intends to use the cure, no matter what decision is reached."

"We're talking about my *wife*, dammit," snapped Patrick. "This isn't one of your idealistic stories about chivalry and heroes. This is my *wife*. Do you think I give a damn about politics?"

"You never have before," said Sylvester. "Simon despaired of you ever making anything of yourself."

Patrick's expression turned to ice. "Never say his name to me again," he said. His voice was, if anything, colder than his eyes. "I was more of a brother to him than you ever attempted to be. Do what you like, but be aware that we're not—will never be—friends."

"Believe me, I've known that for a very long time," said Sylvester. He turned to me, and said, "I'm reasonably sure Duke Lorden would be happier if I left. Will you be safe with him? Is there anything I can do for you?"

"If you see Madden, ask him to come here." Madden worked for the Queen. Assuming he wasn't involved wasn't just allowed, it was practically required. But as a Cu Sidhe, he had an unbeatable sense of smell, and might be able to tell me who'd been in this room.

Sylvester nodded. "I will."

"Great. Don't get shot." I turned my back on my liege, effectively dismissing him, and focused on Patrick. "We can take the arrow out when Quentin gets back with Arden. That gives us enough warm bodies that we should be able to stop the bleeding long enough to call for a medic. I don't want to volunteer to ride Dianda's blood— I don't know what the elf-shot would do to me, and I'm sure there are things she doesn't want me to know—but there may be another way, if we wait a few hours." Once Karen was asleep, she could enter Dianda's sleeping mind and ask if she'd seen the shooter. It was a clunky solution, one which relied on a teenage oneiromancer being able to reliably repeat what she learned from a comatose mermaid, but it was better than Dianda kicking my teeth in after she'd decided that I knew too much.

"We have to wake her up," said Patrick. "If we don't . . . Peter isn't ready to be Duke. I *can't* be Duke. I've only ever been ducal consort because there was never any question of my taking over if something happened to her. The Undersea won't submit to rule by an air-breather. They have standards. If Dianda sleeps for a hundred years, the entire political shape of Saltmist changes. And by the standards of the culture that shaped her, Dianda is a pacifist."

I stared at him. I couldn't help myself. Dianda was a good friend and a better ally, but her solution to almost every problem was blunt-force trauma. "Oh," I said. "Crap."

"Yes." He looked toward the door and then back to me. "Sylvester is gone. You can ask, if you like. I saw the expression on your face when I started ripping into him."

"Um, yeah. You two were . . . friends?"

"Only if the lobster is a friend to the tuna—which is

to say, we moved in *very* different circles," said Patrick. "Sylvester was a Duke and a settled man when I met him. Dedicated to his wife, to his people, and to the idea that his brother was a fainting flower who needed to be protected. As I said before, I was more brother to Simon than he could ever have been."

Something about the way he said that . . . "So you're another of the people who didn't think I needed to know that Simon was married to my mother."

"I'll be honest: I never cared much for Amandine, who always seemed to view the world as an amusement staged just for her. August was a sweet girl, but after she disappeared, your mother stopped caring about anything, including her husband. The Simon I knew died a long time ago. The man he became . . . I could see the bones of my friend in him. That was all. Nothing more, and sadly, nothing less."

I wanted to yell at him, to make sure he understood that I was done with people keeping secrets from me. I didn't say anything. His wife was asleep, maybe for a hundred years, and his world was crumbling. The best thing I could do for him—for both of them—was to be quiet, and wait for help to come, and do whatever was required of me. We had a cure. We had a chance. All we had to do now was convince the world to let us use it.

TWELVE

PATRICK AND ARDEN WERE having a discussion, which really meant they were shouting at each other. If I'd taken that tone with a Queen, even one who was reasonably fond of me, I would've been waiting for the hammer to drop. Either Patrick didn't care, or he was confident that his status as a citizen of the Undersea would protect him from anything Arden wanted to do. So he yelled, and she yelled back for the sake of making herself heard, and I stood next to the pond, feeling awkward and trying to find something that could help us. Quentin stood nearby, watching me, ready to do whatever I asked of him. I appreciated that.

I would have appreciated a break in the shouting even more, but you can't always get what you want in this world, or any other.

My two big investigative advantages were blood and magic. The untainted blood from Dianda's injury would have been scant enough to hold only a few memories, but since those memories would probably have included the face of the person who'd put the arrow in her shoulder, that would have been enough for me. Unfortunately, the shot had knocked her into the pond, and the water had carried any traces of blood away. Even if I'd been willing to drink what was effectively someone else's bathwater, I wasn't my mother; the blood would have been too diluted to be of any use. I'd just get a mouthful of dead skin and whatever nasty things were coexisting with those water weeds.

The blood from her wound wasn't safe. It was tainted by the elf-shot. Even if I wanted to invade her privacy that way, I couldn't do it without risking an unplanned nap.

Magic was a better target. Everyone in Faerie has a unique magical signature, and almost everyone can smell a fresh spell or casting. Historically, I've vastly underestimated how sensitive my own nose is to that sort of thing: magic is a function of the blood, I'm Dóchas Sidhe, and I can detect traces most people wouldn't even realize were there. Arden hadn't gated herself into the room, preferring to accompany Quentin on foot, so I didn't need to worry about her blackberry and redwood signature overwriting something more subtle.

I didn't need to worry about any of us overwriting anything. No matter how hard I focused, closing my eyes and pacing around the room, I found no unfamiliar magical traces. There were hints of amber and water lilies around the pool; Dianda's magic, which rose when she transformed. She must have been on two legs when she got into the water, before putting her fins back on to relax.

I was on my third circuit of the room when I stopped, sniffing the air, and opened my eyes. There was a trace of something unfamiliar, something I'd never detected before. It wasn't Dianda or Arden, but they weren't the only people in the room. Turning on my heel, I strode back toward the sleeping area, where the shouting showed no signs of stopping any time soon.

Patrick and Arden didn't seem to notice me there, continuing to argue too fast and too loud for me to get more than a general impression of anger on his part and frustration on hers. Finally, when it became clear that they weren't going to stop any time soon, I stuck two fingers in my mouth and whistled. The sound was high, shrill, and amplified by the shape of the balcony, making it impossible to ignore. Patrick and Arden froze before turning to look at me.

"Sir Daye?" said Arden, a warning note in her voice. Apparently, I wasn't supposed to whistle at the Queen.

Whatever. I focused on Patrick. "I need you to gather your magic."

He blinked. "What?"

"I'm trying to figure out whether Dianda's attacker used magic to get into the room. I've found a signature I don't recognize, but it's too faded for me to pick out the elements. If you could gather your magic so I can eliminate it as belonging to our suspect, that would be a huge help." I crossed my arms and looked at him expectantly.

"Ah," said Patrick. He raised a hand, palm turned toward the ceiling, cleared his throat, and recited calmly, "Red sky at morning, sailors take warning. Red sky at night, sailors delight." The smell of wood and flowers rose around him, briefly unfamiliar, before the part of my mind that was an inexplicable encyclopedia of magical scents kicked in and identified them.

"Cranberry blossoms and . . . some sort of flower, some sort of small white flower with five petals that grows close to the ground," I said. "It's your magic near the door."

"Yes, and the white flower is 'mayflower,'" he said, dropping his hand and letting the magic dispel. "Dianda was having trouble with the stairs. I cast an illusion over both of us, to keep anyone from seeing and judging her based on her difficulty walking—she's a mermaid, she's allowed to have trouble staying on her feet for long—and let it go once we got inside."

I paused. "Before she was shot, you mean. You released your spell *before* she was shot."

"I certainly didn't stand around waiting for my wife to be elf-shot before I dropped a simple don't-look-here spell, if that's what you're asking," he said, a dangerously irritated note creeping into his voice.

"That's not what I mean," I said, shaking my head. "The person who shot her didn't leave any magical traces in the room. They could have been under a don't-look-here, but it would have broken when they opened the door. They can't have teleported in, or they'd have filled the room with their magic. But if I can still pick up *your* magic, from before she was shot, I should have been able to pick up *theirs*. Dianda saw the person who shot her."

"Which means all we need to do is wake her up and she can tell us," said Patrick, turning back to Arden.

"We can't do that," she said. "You know we can't do that. My own brother is still asleep, because until the High King judges this cure acceptable, we can't use it."

"She's asleep," I said. "Honestly, until we know who did this and why, maybe that's for the best." Patrick turned a stunned, furious look on me. I raised my hands, palms out, as if to ward him off. "Hey, I *like* Dianda, and I don't want her to spend the next hundred years napping, okay? But she's not calm, and she could start hitting people who don't deserve it. This way, we can find out what happened, and why, and wake her up when we have the right people all gift-wrapped for her punching pleasure."

Arden was staring at me. "That's . . . that's not how the fae judicial system works," she said.

"Oh, please," I replied. "We don't *have* a judicial system. We have one law, which we break constantly, and everything else is arbitrary punishments handed down by whoever's higher-ranked in the nobility than the person who did something wrong. If High King Aethlin says someone's punishment is getting punched in the face over and over by an angry mermaid, that's as valid as anything else he might want to hand down. Now. If you two are done shouting at each other, we need to move her. This room is completely indefensible."

"I can have her taken to the room where my brother is sleeping, if that would be acceptable to Duke Lorden," said Arden.

"It would be," said Patrick. "Will you let me help you find the people who harmed my wife?"

"Maybe," I said. "If I need you. First, though, I'm going to need that arrow." I gestured toward the shaft that protruded from Dianda's shoulder. It was fletched in undyed brown feathers that looked like they'd come from some sort of bird of prey. That might help me track down where the shooter had come from, assuming they'd gathered feathers from a native bird. Of course, with my luck, they'd be red-tailed hawk feathers, and I'd learn nothing.

The elf-shot itself, on the other hand . . . thanks to the timing of the lockdown, Walther was in here with us. And I knew he had his kit. We could figure out who'd brewed the tincture, and go from there.

"I thought we needed to leave the arrow where it was," said Patrick.

"Only until we had help," I said. "If there's too much blood or anything like that, Arden can open a portal and get her straight to the doctor. You do have a doctor, right, Arden?"

"I haven't needed one yet," she said uncomfortably.

I resisted the urge to groan. "Okay," I said. "Sylvester Torquill is here. He has an Ellyllon on his staff—Jin— who's one of the best healers I've ever worked with. If we can get permission from the High King to open the conclave long enough to invite someone else in, either Sir Etienne can gate her over, or Arden can open a portal to Shadowed Hills and bring her through."

"I'll speak to the High King, and to Duke Torquill, as soon as we have Duchess Lorden appropriately settled," said Arden.

"Good. Sylvester will want to be asked. He'd do it if I

asked, but it would be a favor to me, not a service to the crown. I think the latter is more important right now." I glanced at Dianda. She looked so peaceful, sleeping like that. It was really too bad she was going to wake up furious. "Nolan's still in that awful tower room?"

"One way in, one way out," said Arden. "There's nowhere safer."

"I'll get Tybalt to bring me up to get the arrow," I said. "For right now, I'm going to trust the two of you to take care of things."

Patrick's eyes widened. "Where are you going?"

"Remember I mentioned that there might be a way for me to find out what Dianda had seen without riding her blood? I need to go find out if it's available to me." Assuming Karen was still awake. Assuming she was willing.

Assuming a lot of things.

"We'll be in the tower room," said Arden. "As before, all the resources of my knowe are open to you."

"Which is a good thing, because I think I'm going to need them." I offered the pair—technically, the trio—a quick, shallow bow. "Open roads."

"Kind tides," said Patrick reflexively. Arden didn't say anything, only nodded. I turned quickly, before the shouting could start again, and walked back out to the main room, where Quentin was waiting.

"Come on," I said, waving for him to follow me. He was well-trained, and had been with me a long time: he followed without question or complaint.

Better yet, he waited until we were in the hallway before he asked, "Where are we going?"

"You have Karen's phone number, right? You two text."

"Not as much as I text with some other people, but sure," he said, frowning at my non-answer. "What about it?"

"Text her and ask where in the knowe her room is. I need to ask her for a favor, and I'd rather do it face-to-face."

Quentin gave me a sidelong look. "Are you going to ask her to take you into Dianda's dreams so you can find out who shot her?"

"Either it's a really obvious plan, or you've been with me for too long," I said.

"Or both." Quentin produced his phone from inside his shirt, swiping words across the screen as we walked toward the stairs. "It's a good plan. Why didn't you just, you know, do the blood thing?"

"Dianda will still have elf-shot in her system, and I've never tried riding the blood of someone who's been poisoned so recently," I said. "So apart from the concern I'd see things she didn't want me to see, since I'd be going in without consent, we might have issues with secondary exposure. I'd rather not spend another week having seizures." I was still mortal enough for elf-shot to be deadly. My body, however, didn't like the idea of dying, and would fight anything that tried to kill me. When I was elf-shot and unconscious, that meant the balance of my blood started shifting without my conscious command, pushing me farther and farther away from human.

I wasn't ready to give up my humanity yet. It was thin and frayed, and yes, I'd come to terms with the fact that the life I'd chosen meant that eventually, I was probably going to have to lose it, but it was *mine*. It was all I had left of my father, who had died lonely and believing that his only daughter was gone forever. Things were never really pretty when Faerie and the human world intersected. We just liked to pretend they were.

"Karen says she's up, and that her room is near a weird fountain thing," said Quentin. He squinted at his screen. "There's a fountain inside the knowe?"

"Apparently." I didn't spend enough time in Muir Woods to know where everything was. There was a way around that. I stopped walking, looking up at the ceiling, and said, "Hi. You remember me, right? I was here when we got the prisoners out of you. I was here when Arden reopened you. I'm the one who found her. Can you help us find the fountain? I need to talk to my niece."

Quentin gave me a sidelong look but didn't say anything. He'd seen me pull this sort of trick before.

Knowes are flexible in a way human homes could never be, capable of expanding themselves and rearranging their interiors when the urge strikes. Knowes are *alive*. I'd always suspected that, but I'd confirmed it a few years prior, when the knowe at Tamed Lightning had changed to help me. This was nowhere near as urgent, but a little help would still go a long way.

A section of the wall in front of us—redwood, carved in flowers and dragonflies and even a few fat banana slugs, down near the floor—swung open like a door, welcoming us into the hidden stairwell on the other side. Quentin stared at it.

"I am never, ever going to be comfortable with the way you do that," he said.

"You don't need to be comfortable, you just need to come with me," I said, and stepped through the impromptu door, into the gloom on the other side. Quentin followed, and the door swung shut behind us.

Fae eyes are better suited to seeing in the dark than human ones, which makes sense, since fae are largely nocturnal. Even so, we need a *little* light to be able to see where we're going, and with the door shut, the darkness on the stairs was absolute. I was opening my mouth to ask Quentin to call a ball of witch-light when something glimmered to life near the top of the wall. Lights. Tiny pinprick lights, coming on one at a time, until the carved redwood sky was bright with stars. I could even recognize constellations, although none of them were mortal. This was a reproduction of a Summerlands sky. Half a dozen moons were represented, their lights filtered through thinly sliced gemstones, so that they glowed cherry, or orange, or creamy gold.

"Wow," said Quentin. "Do you think . . . did the

knowe make this for you?" He sounded almost awed, and more than a little unnerved. He had been born to the nobility, and the idea that the knowes would listen to a changeling when they might not listen to a King was probably disconcerting.

I wanted to tell him the knowes would listen to him, too, when he needed them to, because he treated them with respect; because he'd been with me for so long that he had started believing that they were living things, which was all they seemed to want, at least so far as I could see. This wasn't the time. "I think this stairwell was always here, but might have gone somewhere else in the knowe," I said. "It's easier with a place like this, where no one really remembers how things are supposed to fit together. It makes it easier for the knowe to decide what it wants to be without attracting attention to the fact that it's been changing."

"These are really beautiful carvings," said Quentin. "I hope the stairs stay where they are, so people can see them."

Was it my imagination, or did the stars in the wall glitter marginally brighter? "That would be cool," I agreed, and kept walking.

The stairs ended at a door which, when opened, led us out into a cobblestone courtyard. I glanced upward. The sky was hemmed by the towering trunks of the great redwoods surrounding and growing throughout the knowe. It was twilight—it was always twilight in the Summerlands—but the sky was light around the edges, signaling the coming of morning in the human world. The trees were impossibly, gloriously large. Bridges and tower rooms circled their trunks like strange mushrooms. "It's like the damn Ewok village," I muttered.

"What?" said Quentin.

I gave him a sidelong look. "Okay, add the original *Star Wars* trilogy to the long list of things you still need to experience. How do you spend so much time on the Internet without knowing about *Star Wars*?"

"Raj likes romantic comedies, and April likes movies where everything explodes. Dean is still catching up."

"Chelsea had spaceships all over the walls in her old room. Ask her what an Ewok is." Aside from the door we'd come through, there were five others, radiating off the central courtyard like the petals of a flower. That shape was mirrored by the fountain, which had a carved blackberry flower supported by stylized figures at its center. "Text Karen. Have her open the door."

Quentin blinked at me. "Why?"

"Because I don't want to go banging on doors and waking up nobles who have good reason not to want to talk to me right now," I said. "I'm going to have to make them talk to me sooner or later, so it's better not to burn what little good will I have."

"Oh." Quentin bent his head back over his phone.

A door on the other side of the courtyard opened, and Karen appeared. She'd traded her fancy dress for jeans and a gray sweatshirt, and she looked so young and small that it made my heart hurt. Her oldest sister, Cassandra, was the image of their mother, but Karen was the image of no one but herself, a pale dream of a girl, bleached like bone in the desert. I took a step forward. Her gaze snapped to me, and then she was running, arms already outstretched, eyes wide and bright and terrified. I braced myself for impact. If this was hard on me, an adult who had been in worse situations, what was it like for her? She was just a child, sharing quarters with one of Faerie's greatest monsters, unable to go home.

Guiltily, I realized I hadn't called Stacy to tell her what was going on. I didn't even know if the Luidaeg had bothered to tell Karen's mother before she'd carried her away, off to become part of a story that was bigger than anything a changeling girl from Colma should have been pulled into. Then Karen was throwing herself into my arms, and I didn't have time to worry about what Stacy was thinking right now. All I could do was hold my honorary niece tight, and let her press her face against my shoulder, and wait for her to stop shaking.

When I raised my head, the Luidaeg was standing in the open doorway to the room the two of them were sharing. She nodded politely. I returned the gesture.

"Quentin said you needed me," said Karen, finally pulling back far enough that she could tilt her chin up and look at my face. "What's going on?"

"Come here," I said. I disentangled myself from her arms and led her to the edge of the fountain, where I sat, pulling her down beside me. Quentin followed at a slight distance, and remained standing, almost like he was keeping watch. That was good. It meant I could focus on Karen and not worry about an ambush as I said, "Dianda—you remember Dianda, the Merrow Duchess from Saltmist— has been elf-shot, and I need to find out who did it. The arrow went into the front of her shoulder. I think she saw the shooter before she lost consciousness."

"You want me to take you into her dreams." The statement was soft, resigned, and not questioning in the least. "You know dreams aren't like linear reality, right? When I come into yours, you're almost always the one who decides where we are, unless I'm forcing your dreamscape to show us something specific. You'd be going into whatever a mermaid dreams about."

Which probably meant water. Lots of water, surrounding me, encompassing me, until I was back in the pond where I'd lost fourteen years of my life. I took a shaky breath and nodded. "I know. But riding her blood isn't safe with the elf-shot in her system, and Arden won't let us wake her, since someone knows she's been elf-shot. It sends a bad political message if the allies of the Mists can be woken up when we're refusing to share the cure with anyone else."

"It's still dangerous," said Karen. She bit her lip, worrying it between her teeth before she let it go, and said, "But I'll do it for you. You'll just need to go to sleep."

"Will you be able to sleep?"

She smiled a little. "It's sort of part of the power. I can make myself go to sleep by thinking that I want it to happen. I can't always wake myself up quite so well. I'm still learning, and there's no one to teach me."

The idea of sleeping in the middle of a crisis wasn't appealing, especially since I wasn't sure that Dianda's condition had anything to do with King Antonio's murder. And yet it was the only thing I could do that would bring me closer to an answer, and keep Patrick from pulling the knowe down around our ears. "All right," I said. "How will you know when I'm asleep?"

"She'll know because you're going to come and sleep where I can keep an eye on you, dumbass," said the Luidaeg. I looked up. She had crossed the courtyard, and was now standing on the other side of the fountain. The spray didn't touch her as it fell. Like Karen, she had changed her clothes, trading her tidal gown for a pair of overalls and a white blouse that looked like it had been stolen from the late seventies.

"Um, what?" I said.

"You, Karen, our room, now," said the Luidaeg. "I can put you under, no problem. Quentin can go do whatever weird-ass errands you're not going to be doing while you're asleep. He's your squire. It's his job."

"She's right," said Quentin. "You have to start trusting me sometime."

"I do trust you," I said. "I just don't trust anyone else. A man's been murdered, remember? That sort of makes me, the nontrusting one, more correct than you, the overly trusting one."

"All I'm going to do is go up to the tower and ask Walther about the elf-shot," protested Quentin. "I can do that on my own. I'll stick to the servants' halls, and if I get stuck, I'll ask the knowe where I'm supposed to be. You can't be the only one who knows how that trick works. I'll be fine."

"If you get yourself killed, I'm telling your parents," I said.

Quentin smiled. "If I get myself killed, I'll tell my parents myself."

"You would," I said, and resisted the urge to ruffle his hair. He was getting too old for that. He was getting too old for a lot of things—like letting me protect him.

Oh, who was I kidding? He'd been *born* too old to let me protect him. He'd just been willing to pretend for a while. As I watched him walk back to the door we'd arrived through, I couldn't shake the feeling that pretending time was over, and he was finally prepared to face the world for what it really was. Dark, complicated, and unforgiving. He glanced back once, offering me a quick, encouraging smile. Then he was gone, slipping through the door, back into that narrow stairwell full of stars, and I was alone in the courtyard with a frightened little girl and a woman who'd seen the death of empires.

I turned to look at the Luidaeg. Her lips were twisted in a small moue of understanding; her eyes were kind. "It's never easy when they grow up on you," she said. "Believe me, I'm an expert on people growing up and leaving you behind. But he's a good kid. You've trained him well. So have I, if you count destroying his ability to feel healthy fear as 'training' him. He'll be fine."

"I hope so." I stood. "You said you could knock me out. Can you guarantee I'll wake up again without sleeping a full eight hours? I have work to do."

"You can't storm around the knowe waking kings and queens at your leisure."

"Watch me."

The Luidaeg snorted. "Spoken like a true changeling. These are people who don't like to be inconvenienced. They'll be furious if you drag them out of bed in the middle of the day."

"Ask me if I care." I spread my arms, not looking away from her face. "A man is dead. A woman has been elf-shot. I don't know if the two are connected. I don't know how they could not be. I don't have a fingerprint kit or a clue. I didn't get to go talk to the servers because I got dragged back to the conclave. If interviewing Dianda gets me something I can use, that's what I have to do—and if I'm willing to disrupt her *dreams* to ask my questions, why wouldn't I interrupt someone else's way less enchanted sleep? They can always nap on the way back to their own damn Kingdoms."

"When you decide it's time to make enemies, you don't fuck around," said the Luidaeg. "I've always respected that about you. Karen? You sure you're all right with this?"

There was something in her tone that I recognized, and it stung: she was talking to Karen the way I'd always spoken to Quentin, to Raj, to the flock of teenagers that fell into and out of my life like so many lost puppies looking for a home. She was checking to make sure Karen felt safe and protected. *I* was Karen's aunt. *I* should have been the one she turned to. But I wasn't. Faerie's greatest monster was.

I was never going to get used to the idea of being jealous of the Luidaeg.

Karen bit her lip and nodded. "I am," she said. "Auntie Birdie needs me, and what's the point of me having this weird power if I don't use it to help the people I care about? It's already ruining my life. I may as well get some good out of it."

"Good girl," said the Luidaeg, and touched Karen's hair with an almost proprietary hand. Then she turned, walking back toward the open door to their shared chambers. "Come on, both of you. I don't have all day."

Karen and I exchanged a glance before we both stood. She slipped her hand into mine, her fingers cool against my skin, and we trailed across the courtyard, following the sea witch to whatever fate awaited us.

Arden had apparently been assigning suites based on

status and how dangerous it would be to piss the occupants off. The Luidaeg was the most frightening person currently in the Bay Area, and so she got the nicest chambers. The door from the courtyard led into a beautifully decorated room larger than my old apartment, with redwood floors and walls papered in velvety paper patterned with tangled blackberry briars. The furniture was elegant and rustic, all plain, varnish-stained wood and comfortable looking cushions. One entire wall was made of stained glass panels, all of them set to slide open, if the occupants desired, and reveal the good green world outside.

"Whoa," I said. "And I thought Quentin and I had a nice room."

"Ask your kitty-boy to show you where he's supposedly sleeping; the monarchs get the *really* good spots," said the Luidaeg, walking onward. "Come on. The kitchen's this way."

"Wait—you mean you have an actual kitchen?" The idea that *every* large suite would have its own kitchen seemed improbable in the extreme, both logistically and because it would have put an awful lot of royal poison tasters out of work. When you lived in a feudal society mostly controlled by functional immortals, losing your job was a big deal.

"Yup." The Luidaeg looked over her shoulder and smirked at me. "I'm reasonably sure this is where the parents of the current monarch are supposed to stay when they come to visit. 'See Mom, see Dad, I still respect you, even if I *really* don't want to give back the throne.' We're in here because no one wants to tell me I can't fix my own dinner if I feel like it, but they want me near the communal food sources even less."

"Gotcha," I said. In the normal course of things, assuming fewer murders, Kings and Queens were made when their parents got tired of being in charge and stepped aside in favor of a younger generation. It happened more often than most people would think. Yes, purebloods enjoyed having power, but after a few centuries of not being able to travel or take a weekend off, finding something else to do started to seem extremely attractive. And there was always the option to wander away for a century or two, come back, claim the throne was still yours by right, and lead a dandy war against your own kid. Fae parents weren't always as attached to their adult children as my human upbringing told me they ought to be. I guess when you were a thousand years old, your eight-hundred-year-old kid looked less like your baby, and more like the competition.

The kitchen matched the front room for elegance and simplicity: all redwood and polished California quartz, with an old-fashioned stove and an actual icebox instead of a refrigerator. "I hope Arden can convince her staff to modernize this place," said the Luidaeg, going to the sink and turning on the water. "Faerie has embraced the idea of indoor plumbing and using small quantities of ice, rather than turning entire towers into eternally frozen storage boxes for our vegetables. It's not unreasonable to want a microwave."

"Ice is modern?" asked Karen blankly.

"Honey, when you've lived as long as I have, *everything* is modern. The idea of being a teenager is modern. In my day, you'd have already been declared an adult, thrown out of your parents' house, and left to fend for yourself." She opened a drawer. Empty. She scowled at it, closed it, and opened it again. This time it rattled as the small jars filled with herbs and oddly-colored liquids knocked against each other. She began pulling them out and lining them up on the counter. "This idea that Faerie should always be a twisted mirror of the human medieval age is proof that sometimes, people don't like change. I love cable. The Internet is amazing. Not having my ice cream melt is amazing. Hell, *having* ice cream is amazing. There was a time where you either found a Snow Fairy or you waited until November—and even that's a new word, as we measure such things. Anyone who says the past was perfect is a liar and wasn't there. Everything that thinks can aspire, and everything that aspires wants something better than what they've left behind them. Get me a bowl."

It took me a second to realize her last comment had been aimed at me. I started opening cupboards, finally finding the one that held the dishes. As befitted the setting, they were made of carnival glass, brightly colored and sturdier than they looked. Thank Maeve. If they had been as fragile as they should have been, I would have broken them just by opening the cupboard.

The Luidaeg took the bowl I offered her without comment, beginning to open jars and dump their contents into it. The smell of rosemary and honey tickled my nostrils.

That reminded me. "How come I can name smells I've never smelled before?"

"You're going to have to be more specific than that, weirdo," said the Luidaeg, adding a sharp-smelling lichen to the bowl.

"Patrick Lorden. His magic smells like cranberry blossoms and mayflower. I've never smelled either of those things before, but I knew what they were as soon as I smelled them clearly. Why?"

"Because magic lives in blood, and that means your magic is abnormally sensitive to the magic of others," said the Luidaeg. "If you've ever heard the name of a smell or a sensation, your magic will dig it out of the wet mess you call a brain and serve the word up to you on a silver platter. If you haven't, you'll keep getting details until someone tells you what to call it. I have no idea what Dad was thinking when he made you people. We didn't need bloodhounds with an attitude, we already had the Cu Sidhe." She waved her hand over the bowl. The smell of sea foam filled the air, accompanied with a biting overlay of salt that made the back of my throat ache.

The liquid in the bowl turned black, and then red, and finally a clear gold, like the finest honey in the world. The Luidaeg held it out to me.

"Drink this," she said.

I took the bowl and brought it to my lips. Whether or not it was wise to drink a potion prepared by the sea witch didn't matter: she and I had passed that point a long time ago.

The potion tasted like apple cider, with just a hint of rosehip tea.

I was asleep before I hit the floor.

THIRTEEN

I SAT UP WITH A GASP, looking frantically around me. I was in my room in Amandine's tower, lying atop the covers on my narrow bed, the ridges of the blankets digging into my butt and thighs as I put more weight on them than I'd possessed when I slept here on a regular basis. My clothes were gone, replaced not by finery or court gear, but by my favorite pair of jeans from when I was a teenager, the denim worn so soft that it was like wearing air, and a T-shirt advertising a 1994 Shakespeare in the Park production of *The Tempest*.

"Hi, Auntie Birdie."

I turned. Karen was sitting in the reading nook, wearing her white dress. I didn't know whether that was her choice, as the oneiromancer, or mine, as the one who'd presumably started this dream; I decided it was better not to ask. "Hi, pumpkin," I said. "Are we asleep?"

"The Luidaeg made me help her carry you to the bed," she said, and wrinkled her nose. "I don't know why she couldn't have knocked you out there instead of in the kitchen, but she thought it was funny when you fell on the floor."

"That, right there, is your answer." I slid off the bed.

As always when I was dreaming in concert with Karen, the motion felt real. Even when I knew I was asleep, even when the ceiling melted or the floor turned into butterflies, it felt absolutely right, like this was the way the world was always supposed to work. "When you've been alive as long as she has, you take your humor where you can get it. Do you need to do anything before you can take us to Dianda?"

"Yes. No. It's . . . complicated right now." Karen stood, and was suddenly standing in front of me, without visibly crossing the space between us. Lowering her voice, she said, "You can't mention any of *her* things, or even think about her too hard, or she might find us. She's always asleep. She's always watching."

I frowned, bemused. "Who are you—"

Karen's eyes widened in panic. I stopped talking. Everything was suddenly clear.

Evening. Karen was attending the conclave as Evening's representative; Evening, who had been elf-shot, Evening, who could access Karen through her dreams. Evening, who might be listening to us even now.

"Okay," I said. "I won't think about her, or any of her things."

"You will," said Karen, sounding resigned. "You would have even if I hadn't said anything. But at least now you were warned, I guess. Take my hands and hold your breath."

This time, there was no need for me to ask why. We were going into the dreams of a mermaid, and there was no reason to assume Dianda would be dreaming of dry land. She was born to the sea. Everything else was inconsequential. I slid my hands into Karen's and breathed in deep.

No sooner had I filled my lungs with as much dream-air as they could hold than the water appeared around our feet, quickly rising to mid-calf. I shuddered, swallowing the urge to panic. Panic would do me no good. This wasn't real. This was a dream—a terrible, cruel, necessary dream—and all the wetness in the world couldn't send me back into the dark at the bottom of the pond. The water kept getting higher, cold and smelling of salt, cupping my thighs and then my hips like the hands of a lover.

Karen smiled encouragingly. "It's okay," she said. "It'll be okay. It's just a dream."

She didn't say it couldn't hurt me. If anyone would know that for a lie, it was her. Dreams can do damage even when they're not dreamt in the company of an oneiromancer. And then the water closed over my head and the light slipped away, leaving us floating in the dark. The current pulled Karen's hands from mine. I flailed, grasping wildly for her, only to realize that my arms were withering, becoming fins, stubby and useless for anything but moving through the watery deep. The salt stung the gills that opened in my neck. Koi were freshwater fish. I had been condemned to the pond; never to the sea. Never to the sea.

As with all dreams that Karen walked through, this one felt absolutely, inalienably real. I was a fish again, scaled and sleek and helpless, trapped beneath the crushing weight of the water. I swam, panicked, looking for the surface, for the air, for anything that would keep the next step of Simon's spell from taking hold and changing me completely. When he'd originally transformed me into a koi and abandoned me to my prisoning pond, the spell had changed my mind along with my body. I don't really remember anything about the fourteen years he stole from me. I spent those years as a *fish*. Fish don't want, or wonder, or dream about going back to their families. Fish just exist, trapped in a moment that never ends.

Someone grabbed me. I thrashed harder, trying to pull away. The hands tightened, lifting me until one of my frantically searching eyes was level with Dianda

Lorden's face. She looked different, viewed underwater through a fish's eyes. She was always beautiful, but here, like this, she was transcendent. There were glittering specks on her skin, places where microscopic scales caught and threw back the light. Her hair floated around her head like a corona, each strand seeking and finding its perfect place. She peered at me, dubiousness and confusion written plainly on her face.

"Toby?" she said. The fact that we were underwater didn't seem to be interfering with her ability to speak. That was a good thing, I supposed, although I wasn't sure how I could hear her. Did fish even *have* ears? "Stop messing around and turn yourself into something useful already." She let me go.

I hung in the water in front of her, not swimming away, trying to figure out how to do what she wanted. This wasn't my dream anymore. I didn't dream myself wet and scaled and . . . wait. That wasn't true. Sometimes I dreamed myself all of those things, because bad dreams could happen to anybody. Sometimes the pond was inescapable. So this *was* my dream, on some level.

I'd joined Dianda in the ocean in the real world once, courtesy of a transformation spell designed by the Luidaeg. It had turned me into a Merrow in every way that counted, including the ability to go from my natural bipedal shape into something a little more Disney-esque. There had been a particular sideways way of thinking necessary to trigger the transformation, like stretching a muscle that was less a reality than it was an idea. I couldn't close my eyes—fish didn't have eyelids—but I let my vision go as unfocused as biology allowed, and reached into myself for that stretching feeling.

There was a pop, like my entire body had been replaced by rapidly bursting bubbles, and I expanded, instantly and painlessly, into the Merrow form the Luidaeg had spun for me. My legs were still missing, replaced by a great sweep of calico scales and ending in a set of powerful flukes, but I had *hands*, I had *arms*, I was the next best thing to myself again. Even my tacky Shakespeare shirt was back. I did a somersault in the water, resisting the urge to whoop.

When I stopped flipping, Dianda was looking at me flatly, arms folded over her chest. Her hair was longer than I was used to, I realized, cut to conceal her gills, and her top was an elaborate confection of pearls and watered blue silk that shimmered in the light filtering through the water. She caught me staring, and said, "This is how I looked when I met Patrick. I was dreaming of our first date when the whole place flooded and you showed up. You *are* Toby, aren't you? Because I swear, if I'm just dreaming about your pasty face when I could be dreaming of my husband, I'm going to murder you when we both wake up."

"I'm really me," I said. My words, like hers, carried clearly through the water. "My niece is an oneiromancer, remember? She brought me into your dreams because I needed to talk to you. Do you have time to talk to me?"

"Time?" Dianda chuckled bitterly. "I have nothing *but* time. And really, I should thank you for interrupting. None of my dreams ever get to the good stuff. They get close enough that I start to think maybe taking a long nap won't be the worst thing ever, and then bam, they break up and turn into something else. I don't normally dream like that. Something's wrong."

"Yes," I agreed. The elf-shot spell was originally just supposed to knock people out, but it had been around for centuries, and there were lots of different variations. Some of them included a slow poison, one that would kill the sleeper long before their enchanted slumber came to an end. Others had been tooled to condemn the victim to a hundred years of nightmares. What Dianda was describing wasn't quite that bad, but was possibly

even crueler, in its own strange way. A hundred years of
unfulfillment, of stories that never reached their natural
endings . . . that would be enough to make anyone suffer.

"So what did you want to talk about?" Dianda did a
lazy loop-de-loop, flukes trailing like a veil in front of her
face before she resumed her formerly upright position.
"It's not like I have any appointments to get to."

I frowned. "I thought you'd be more upset."

She shrugged. "I'm livid. So mad I can't even think
about it without losing my temper. But there's nothing I
can *do*. Either Arden will let them wake me up, or she
won't. If she does, I go home to my husband and son. If
she doesn't . . ." For a moment, her bravado cracked, and
I saw how frightened she was. "Dean is a landed Count
with a knowe of his own, because of you. Patrick and
Peter can go to him, and he'll take care of them. He's a
good boy. He'll protect his family until I wake up and can
fight to reclaim my demesne from whoever seizes it in
my absence."

"Peter's a Merrow, like you," I said. "He could claim
your place when he gets older."

"Please. You know better than that. No matter how
often I claim him as my heir, Peter's a mixed-blood, just
like his brother. It doesn't matter how Merrow he looks.
The Undersea will eat him alive and spit out his bones. I
knew when I married Patrick that if we had children, I
would have to be absolutely ruthless in order to protect
them. I forgot that ruthlessness is a fulltime commitment. I dropped my guard. Now we're all paying the
price."

"About that." I swept my arms through the water, sta-
bilizing myself. There was a flash of light off to one side,
and I glanced in that direction long enough to see Karen,
now equipped with a white-scaled, black-fluked mermaid tail, swimming delighted loops through Dianda's
dream ocean. Kids are kids, no matter what kind of
magic they have. I looked back to Dianda. "You were

facing the door when you were shot. Did you see the person who shot you?"

"See them? Reef and bone, I was about to get out of the water and strangle them when they put that damn arrow in my arm," said Dianda. "It was that Daoine Sidhe with the green hair. What's his name, Michel. From Starfall. I don't even know where that *is*."

"Idaho," I said automatically. "It's inland. Very inland. I don't think they even have any big lakes. There was no way you would have met him before this. Did you, I don't know, drown one of his relatives? Insult his clothes? Anything that might have made him think putting you to sleep for a hundred years would be a good idea?"

"The only Daoine Sidhe I've ever threatened to drown was my husband," said Dianda. "He likes it when I get threatening."

"Please don't finish that thought," I said. "You're *sure* this man had no reason to hold a grudge against you."

"On Maeve's bones, Toby, if I've done something to wrong him or his family, I don't know about it. We had a fight at dinner, but that's all," said Dianda. "I was waiting for Patrick to come back and suddenly there was this green-haired bastard in my room. I felt the arrow hit my shoulder, and then everything went away. I didn't really understand what had happened to me until you appeared." She glanced away, off into the watery blue.

Karen's lucid dreaming effect. It was hitting Dianda also, turning a series of unpleasant, unfulfilling dreams into a prison. It took everything I had not to wince as I realized what I'd inadvertently done to her. "We'll be leaving soon," I said. "I'm pretty sure you'll go back to normal dreams once we're gone. And we're working on getting Arden to let us wake you up."

"She won't. Not until the High King says she's allowed to use your precious cure that way—and if he doesn't, I guess I'm spending the next century or so napping at Dean's place. He's a good boy. He'll take good care of me."

"It's not going to come to that."

Dianda shrugged. "If it does, it does. Patrick and I have dealt with every obstacle Faerie has thrown at us this far. What's one more? Goldengreen is as good a crypt as anything e—"

She stopped mid-word as Karen flung herself between us, gills flared and eyes wide in her paler than usual face. "Aunt Birdie, *you promised*," she wailed, and then a giant, unseen hand was grabbing the bottom of my tail and yanking me downward.

Through the bubbles that rose up to curtain my face, I could see Dianda and Karen similarly descending. In the moment, I had bigger concerns, like the fact that I couldn't breathe anymore: we were moving so fast that my gills were finding no oxygen in the water around me, and I was choking. I was surrounded by water, and I was going to drown.

Keeping the panic from rising up and overwhelming me took everything I had. *This is just a dream,* I thought fiercely. *This is just a dream; you can't die here. You're going to wake up.* But was that true? There might not be a horror movie monster with knives on his hands waiting to steal my soul, but having Karen in the dream meant it felt just as real as the waking world. Could we die if we died while she was dreaming with us?

The thought had time to form before there was one last, convulsive yank, and we were falling through dry air, suddenly devoid of oxygen. I took a greedy breath, coughing as the last of the water in my gills was knocked loose. Then Dianda screamed, high and shrill and uncharacteristically terrified. I turned toward the sound, and realized we weren't falling through a void: we were falling toward the ground. A vast meadow filled with rose briars had appeared beneath us, thorns reaching up as if to welcome us home.

"Auntie Birdie!" shouted Karen. I didn't turn, just flung my hand out in her direction, while I reached for Dianda with the other hand. Mermaids were designed to be aerodynamic, but not to land safely on solid ground. If she fell without us . . .

Her fingers strained toward mine. I leaned, clasping my hand around her wrist just as I felt Karen grab hold of me—and with Karen's touch, gravity seemed to lose most of its urgency. We drifted, like strange, finny feathers, down to one of the few clear spots in that field of briars. Where we promptly collapsed in a heap, since none of us was exactly equipped to stand up.

"Oh, for Oberon's sake," snapped Dianda, squeezing my hand hard enough to hurt. "Focus and shift." There was no scent of amber and water lilies as she changed forms, her top extending into an elegant, old-fashioned gown when the magic took hold. This was a dream. Normal rules did not apply.

But some things still worked. I reached deep, looking for the tension that would give me back my legs. I knew it was there, however hard it might be to find; all I had to do was remember the feeling of the change. Everything tingled, and then I was standing, pulling Karen to her newly-recovered feet. My jeans and sneakers were dry, unlike my shirt and hair. I felt like I'd been overenthusiastically bobbing for apples.

Karen was back in her white dress, and looked like she was scared out of her mind. "I can't wake up," she whispered, clinging to my arms. "You promised, and now she knows we're here, and she's not going to let me wake *up*."

"Who knows—oh." I stopped myself, realization sinking in. "Of course." Karen had cautioned me not to think about Evening if I could avoid it; not to think about the things Evening considered to be her own. Evening was the Firstborn of the Daoine Sidhe. Patrick and Michel were both Daoine Sidhe; by the old rules of Faerie, they both belonged to her. Maybe that wouldn't have been enough, but Goldengreen had been her demesne once, before she faked her own death and left the knowe standing empty. Invoking it by name had been the last straw.

I should have warned Dianda.

The air around me tasted like roses. I peeled Karen's hands away from my arms and turned, shielding her with my body as much as I could. As I'd feared and expected, Evening was standing in the field behind me, head cocked to the side, a smile painted on her lips. She was wearing a dress of rose petals in red and pink and sunset orange, arranged into a gradient and stitched together with tiny loops of silver wire. Flashes of snow-white skin showed through the gaps, pale enough that I would have called her a corpse if she hadn't been moving, and breathing, and looking at me.

"That took you less time than I had expected," she said. "Well *done*, October."

"Leave my niece alone," I said.

Her smile faded. "I thought I taught you better than that," she said, shaking her head slowly. "You were meant to know how to respect your betters, not flap your tongue like a bird's wings and think it would help you fly away."

I blinked. "Wow. Did you level up in 'pretentious' after we shot you, or are you going with the whole 'dream logic' bullshit? Karen is *mine*. Her mother is my best friend, and I'm her honorary aunt. That means hands off. She's not going to help you wake up."

Evening actually laughed. "You have no idea what you're talking about. Karen—such a bland name; there's no majesty in it, no mystery. It means 'pure,' you know. Such irony, when you consider where she comes from. But none of that matters, because your little Karen isn't yours to claim, and she isn't here to help me wake up. She's here to make sure you people don't destroy my greatest creation in the name of 'playing fair.'"

"Uh, not to be pushy or anything, but who is this

lady?" asked Dianda. She stepped up next to me, adding her body to the screen blocking Karen from Evening's view. I'd never been more grateful to her. "She looks like she could use some sun, and maybe a good kick in the teeth."

"Dianda Lorden, may I present Evening Winterrose, better known in some circles as Eira Rosynhwyr, the Firstborn of the Daoine Sidhe, and the woman who locked the wards at Goldengreen." I gestured grandly toward Evening. "I'd call her names, but none of them would be suitable for mixed company."

"Wait—that's Evening Winterrose?" Dianda shook her head. "It can't be. Evening's dead, and she never looked that much like a waterlogged corpse. She was pale. She wasn't bloodless."

"I may have played down a few aspects of my appearance when I walked among my inferiors," said Evening. "Hello, Dianda. Still the little Merrow slut who thought mixing her bloodline with my own would somehow make her worthy of a throne. How *is* dear Patrick? Is he tired of you yet? I expected better of him than I got. Marrying a mermaid and running off to sea . . . such a disappointment."

"I take it back," said Dianda. "That's Evening."

"Unfortunately," I said. "Why are you harassing my niece, Evening? Why don't you want this cure getting out?"

"There you go, assuming she's yours again," said Evening. She looked at me tolerantly, like a mother facing a recalcitrant child. "What's a hundred years to me? It's inconvenient, and I would rather be awake, but not if that wakefulness comes with the unmaking of my greatest creation. A hundred years is nothing. Long enough for your alchemist to find another calling, and for you to get yourself killed when one of your 'adventures' goes awry. I'll wake to a world that still respects my strength, and I'll carry on like nothing had ever changed. You can't win. I already have."

"If a hundred years is nothing to you, if you can just wait me out, why did you come back in the first place?" It was something I'd been wondering since the moment I'd first seen her again, back from the dead and never really on my side. Maybe now, in this dreamscape, she would actually tell me.

Evening cocked her head to the side. "You don't know, do you?" This time her smile was slow and poisonous. "Oh, this is going to be beautiful. You're stumbling from goalpost to goalpost, triggering all manner of dangerous things, and you have no idea. I came back because you opened certain doors and put certain pieces back on the board, and I wanted them. Maybe I can't have everything I want right now, but I'm not sorry I tried. I'm only sorry you survived."

"Leave my niece alone."

"Or you'll do what? Have me elf-shot and abandoned on one of Maeve's ancient Roads? Please. Unless you're willing to kill me, and have all my descendants know that you, October Daye, daughter of Amandine the Liar, murdered the mother of the Daoine Sidhe, there's nothing else you can do. Go pick yourself a rose, little girl. That's always worked out so *well* for your family."

I narrowed my eyes before doing the worst thing I could think of, and turning my back on her. "Honey, can you wake us up?" I asked, focusing on Karen.

"Don't ignore me," snapped Evening. "You have no right to ignore me."

"I told you before that I can't," whispered Karen. "Not if she doesn't want me to. She's . . . she's stronger than I am."

"Not here she's not," I said. "This is *your* dream, Karen, not hers. Maybe she can pull you in, but she can't make you stay. Believe me, and get us out of here."

She bit her lip as she looked at my face, searching for some sign that I was wrong. Then she seized my hands. "We're going to wake up."

"That's right." I looked to Dianda. "You should snap back to your own dream as soon as we're gone." I wasn't sure of that—I wasn't sure of anything where this magic was concerned—but it seemed likely, and if dream logic held sway here, Dianda would probably do whatever she thought she was supposed to do.

"If I don't, I'll just need to find something to hit," said Dianda mildly. "The lady who locked the wards at Goldengreen and kept me away from my son when he needed me should make a great target."

The wisdom of punching one of the Firstborn was questionable. But again, this was a dream. "Just don't get hurt before we can wake you up."

"I won't," said Dianda. Her face twisted into something feral and terrifying. "Make sure that Michel boy is still breathing when I get back. I want to have a talk with him."

He wasn't going to enjoy hearing whatever she had to say, but that didn't matter, because the field of roses was going hazy around the edges, until the only solid thing remaining was Karen's hand holding fast to mine. Someone played a fiddle tune, far on the edge of my hearing, and the air smelled like ashes. Evening shouted, a wordless cry of fury as she realized we weren't going to look at her again. And the dreamscape dissolved around us.

FOURTEEN

I OPENED MY EYES.
The bed beneath me was so soft that it was like sprawling on a cloud, and the bedroom was a sea of rainbows, thanks to the stained glass panels covering the walls. I sat up, moving from a beam of green light to a beam of red. The motion dislodged Karen's arm, which had been slung loosely across my chest like she'd been hoping to keep hold of me in the dream world by keeping hold of me in the real one. Her breathing was smooth and level, and she didn't look distressed. That didn't necessarily mean anything. Not everyone wears their nightmares on the outside.

"Oh, good; you're awake," said the Luidaeg. I turned. She was standing in the doorway, a carnival glass bowl tucked into the crook of her arm. She had a wooden spoon in the opposite hand, and was vigorously stirring the bowl's contents. "Before you start yelling at me, the spell I hit you with was designed to keep you under until you decided to wake up, not a moment longer. So I didn't knock you out until afternoon on purpose."

I stared at her for a moment, uncomprehending. Then I gasped and slid out of the bed, staggering slightly as my legs protested the speed of my getting up. "What time is it?"

"Almost four."

The whole conclave would be starting to stir. It wasn't safe. "Where's Quentin? He was supposed to go talk to Walther. He must be worried sick by now—"

"Nope," said the Luidaeg. "He found your pet alchemist, the elf-shot is being analyzed, and there was nothing else he could do to help, so he came back here, after finding your kitty-boy and telling him what was going on. Smart kid. I would have hated to kill your betrothed when he busted in here and accused me of attacking you. We made it through the day with no injuries and no nonconsensual enchantments. Quentin's asleep on the couch in the front room. I guarantee I can have him up in five minutes. Maybe less."

"Please don't stab my squire." I scrubbed at my face with one hand, trying to clear the last of the cobwebs away. Karen was still sleeping. I didn't know whether or not I should be concerned about that. "He functions best unstabbed. So do I, if you were wondering."

"I'm not going to stab Quentin without an excellent reason," said the Luidaeg. "I *like* Quentin. People I like are at the back of the line for stabbing."

"All right, if you're not planning to stab him, how are you going to get him up?"

The Luidaeg hefted her bowl. "I'm making pancakes." With that, she stepped back out of the room, leaving me alone with Karen. I turned to look at my niece.

Sleep had stripped away her defenses, rendering her small and fragile. Her hair covered half her face like sea foam covering the beach, one inky tip resting across her lips. More than ever, it struck me how little she looked like her parents. That, combined with her unlikely, inexplicable magical gifts, made her seem like a changeling in the mortal sense—a child who shouldn't have been where she was, who belonged to different parents, in a different world.

None of that mattered. Her parents loved her. Her brothers and sisters loved her. *I* loved her, and if she'd grown up somewhere else, with people who were better equipped to understand her oddities, she wouldn't have been my niece.

Leaning over, I brushed her hair away from her face and let my fingers rest against her cheek. She made a small, grumpy noise, stretched, and opened her eyes, blinking blearily before she smiled at me.

"Hey, Auntie Birdie," she said. "We did it. We got out of Dianda's dreams."

"We did," I agreed solemnly. I paused. "Karen . . . can Evening invade *any* dream you're walking through?"

Her face crumpled like a discarded sheet of paper, her eyes going shuttered and shifty. "She found me when I was visiting Anthony. He's been having trouble with math, so sometimes I go into his dreams and tutor him. Math can be fun, if the world changes to make it easier to understand. We were doing fractions with dinosaurs and continents when this *woman* was just there, and she said Anthony had to go because the adults were talking now, and she pulled me out of his dream and into hers. I couldn't get away! I tried and I tried, and she followed me. I know so many tricks, when I'm in dreams. I know so much more than I knew when B . . . when Blind Michael took me. And it didn't matter."

"She's Firstborn," I said softly. "It's natural that she'd be stronger than you. There's no shame in being beaten by someone who's that much stronger."

"But no one's supposed to be stronger than me when I'm dreaming," she said, with all the petulance and resentment of a teenage girl whose one true stronghold has been invaded. "I want her to stop. She doesn't want the elf-shot to be fixed, but I do. I want her awake. I want her out of my mind."

I put my arms around her, and for a moment, I didn't say anything. I wanted the elf-shot cure to be distributed, despite what Theron and Chrysanthe had said about people getting careless around changelings. They were insulated, living in a community where changelings were the majority, where they were respected and prized and considered valuable. For the rest of us, a cure for elf-shot wasn't going to make that big of a difference, because people were already careless with changelings. And I wanted the sleepers awake. I wanted Raysel to have the chance to learn what it was like to live with a body that wasn't ripping itself apart. I wanted Dianda to threaten and laugh and love her family. I wanted a lot of things, and I wanted them as soon as possible. But I'd never wanted to wake Evening Winterrose, the woman I'd once considered my friend—the woman who'd cost me everything.

Karen must have heard the conflict in my silence, because she tilted her head back, meeting my eyes, and said, "No matter what we do, we can't all win. This isn't the kind of game that works like that."

"Maybe," I said. "But we can sure as hell try. Come on, sweetie. The Luidaeg's making pancakes. Not everyone can say that the sea witch made them breakfast."

That actually earned me a giggle—oh, small mercies— as Karen slid out of the bed and followed me from the bedroom to the front of the suite. Quentin was on the couch as promised, his head pillowed on one arm and his knees drawn up against his chest. He looked like a discarded marionette, and I had never felt the weight of my duty to him more. He was my responsibility, and I was going to take care of him if it killed me.

From the kitchen came the hiss of batter hitting a griddle, followed by the hot flour and butter smell of pancakes cooking. Quentin sat up, eyes still closed. "I'm awake," he announced.

"Good," I said. "Tell me what you know."

He cracked one eye open. Then he opened the other, and said, "You're awake and you're not pancakes."

"Those are both true and things that you know, but it's not good enough," I said. "What did Walther say?"

"The elf-shot that put Dianda to sleep was about as close to generic as you can get. No hidden poisons, and the only add-on is something that will frustrate her dreams without turning them into nightmares. She'll sleep for a hundred years and wake up feeling rested and probably super-pissed." Quentin shrugged. "He said the cure would counter the elf-shot—no problem—if he was allowed to use it, but since he's not, she's just going to nap."

"We'll see about that," I said. "Dianda was able to tell us who elf-shot her."

"Oh," said Quentin. "Wow. What are we going to do about it?"

"We're not going to do anything," I said. "I'm going to go talk to the High King." I barely caught myself in time to keep from saying "your father."

Quentin saw my correction in the way my eyes tightened. He grimaced. "Karen knows," he said. "She knew before you did."

I blinked. "What?"

"I walk in dreams," said Karen. "Um. Not to be creepy or anything, but if I've visited you while you were dreaming, you probably don't have that many secrets from me. I try not to visit people I don't know. It seems rude. And I always let people know that I'm there."

"Not actually reducing the creepy factor by that much, but I appreciate the warning," I said, feeling the tips of my ears turn red. Some of the dreams I'd had about Tybalt before we'd finally managed to make our relationship more formal had been, well, inappropriate for teenage girls. Some of the dreams I'd had *since* then made those look positively tame. I had never really considered this aspect of Karen's dream-walking before.

I also hadn't considered what it meant to have Quentin forming all his friendships and allegiances here on the West Coast, rather than back home in Toronto. When the time came for him to become High King, was he going to try to carry half the kids I considered mine to take care of away with him? Was he going to try to take *me*? And if he did, would I be able to tell him "no"?

"What about Dianda's injuries?" I asked, to distract myself from the question.

"Their Majesties approved Queen Windermere's request to have Duke Torquill summon Jin from Shadowed Hills," said Quentin. "Jin was able to heal the wound left by the arrow."

"Good," I said, once I had finished working my way through the chain of monarchs in the sentence. Jin was here. That was one worry off my long and growing list.

The smell of bacon joined the smell of pancakes. Both teens lit up, beaming at the air behind me. I turned. There was Tybalt, a smile on his face and a tray in his hands, laden with bacon, cinnamon rolls, and various sliced fruits.

"Breakfast is to be an informal affair, eaten largely in private rooms and not forcing any of us to deal with one another before absolutely necessary," he said. "I thought you might like food. The, ah, fruit may be a little frozen. I tried to move quickly."

"You brought breakfast through the Shadow Roads," I said. "I can't decide if that was romantic or really, really stupid."

"Always elect for the blessed 'both,'" said Tybalt.

"Both it is, then," I said, and reached for a cinnamon roll. The outside was cool to the touch and the frosting had iced over, but I could still feel the warmth inside the pastry. He really had moved quickly. "How did you sleep?"

"Poorly and alone, but you're forgiven, as you had things to do," said Tybalt. "I thought perhaps the lady sea witch would be less inclined to transform me into something unpleasant if I brought her bacon. Not that I think *you* would be so easily bribed," he added, attention shifting to Karen, "but in case you had considered it, I note that there are chocolate croissants buried beneath these more pedestrian pastries."

Karen giggled. I rolled my eyes.

"Stop flattering my niece and put down the tray," I said. "We need to go see the High King."

Tybalt raised an eyebrow. "Am I nothing but a taxi service to you?"

"No," I said. "Danny, who actually has his license, is a taxi service. You're more like a transporter from *Star Trek*. Me and you to beam up, Scotty."

He looked at me blankly. Karen covered her mouth with one hand. Quentin started to snicker.

"Sometimes I wonder if you've ever actually encountered the English language," Tybalt said, putting the tray gingerly down on the nearest flat surface. Quentin and Karen fell upon it, moving with the speed and efficiency known only to hungry teenagers and the occasional swarm of locusts. Then they took off for the kitchen, carting their ill-gotten gains with them.

"I'll tell the Luidaeg you're leaving!" called Quentin, before ducking through the door and out of sight.

Tybalt shook his head. "I think that's the first time I can remember when he didn't demand to come with you on the dangerous errand."

"I don't think he wants to spend too much time around his folks; there's always a chance someone would notice the family resemblance," I said. "Besides, breakfast is available. He's a black hole with legs. He'll catch up with us later, after he's eaten three pounds of bacon and so many pancakes that the thought makes me feel sort of sick. Now come on. We really, really need to get to the High King."

"Without a change of clothing?" Tybalt gestured to my outfit. "Not that I have any issues with your attire—you look lovely, as always, and even more lovely now that you're rumpled—but there's something to be said for not appearing before the ruler of this fair land in the trousers you wore yesterday."

"He knows I was working all day, and I'll change before the conclave," I said. "This is important."

Tybalt paused to search my face. I knew what he was looking for—signs of strain, of worry, that I needed something other than a quick, private transit to another part of the knowe—and so I didn't look away. I met his eyes instead, letting him see everything he wanted. For once, thanks to the Luidaeg's little sleep potion, I wasn't absolutely exhausted. I'd even eaten two bites of a cinnamon roll. For me, that was the next best thing to "in fighting trim."

But more importantly—most importantly—I knew what needed to be done. I needed to be able to tell King Antonio's son that I'd caught the people who killed his daddy. I needed to wake my friend. I had to keep moving, and I needed Tybalt to help me do that.

Finally, he sighed, and looped one arm around my waist. "Take a breath," he said, and stepped backward, pulling me with him, into the shadows.

The Shadow Roads were the property of the Cait Sidhe, who used them to move from place to place without being seen. Even changeling Cait Sidhe could access them, which explained how some cats could appear and disappear at will. So far as I knew, I was one of very few non-feline individuals to have spent much time in the freezing dark behind the shadows the Cait Sidhe used for transport. Distance was shortened on the Shadow Roads, but not always in a straight line. We ran through Arden's knowe, choosing speed to keep ourselves from freezing. It was a brief trip, thankfully; after no more than ten steps Tybalt was pulling us back into the light, emerging into a broad redwood-and-glass hallway, in front of a pair of double doors guarded by Tylwyth Teg in the royal colors of the Westlands.

The guards blinked at us. I hunched forward, hands on my knees, shivering, and put up a hand to signal them to wait. Tybalt, meanwhile, leaned against the wall, looking like he'd just been out for a stroll. I knew better—it didn't take as much out of him to pull me through the shadows as it had before I learned to run there without resisting, but it was still an effort. He no longer pretended to be untouchable when we were alone. It was probably hurting him to pretend that he was fine, but he would never willingly show weakness among the Divided Courts.

It was a gift that he would show weakness to me.

"Just give us a second," I said, directing my words toward the floor, since the floor didn't require me to lift my head. "Are the High King and High Queen up?"

"What is your business here?" demanded one of the guards.

Okay. *That* required lifting my head. "My name is October Daye, Knight of Lost Words, hero of the realm, tasked by your bosses to find out what the hell is going on at this conclave. We were polite in appearing in the hall, rather than inside the royal quarters, which I'm pretty sure I have permission to do, what with the whole 'please fix this' command they gave me. So are they up, or am I going to tell them I couldn't provide the update they asked for because you weren't paying attention during the conclave yesterday?"

The guards exchanged an uneasy look, and I realized two things. First, that they didn't look familiar: they had probably been guarding this door *during* the conclave, and wouldn't have seen me speaking to the group. Second, that if they were that much older than Quentin, I would eat my shoe. This was probably their first "real" assignment.

"Hey, I'm sorry," I said, straightening up. "It's been a long day, and it's going to be a longer night. Are they up?"

"Yes," said one of the guards. "Please wait here."

The guard who'd spoken opened the door and slipped inside, leaving the other to watch me and Tybalt uneasily. Tybalt pushed away from the wall and moved to stand behind me, putting one hand on the curve of my hip as he fell into position. It was a small, reassuring weight, and I stood a little straighter, knowing that no matter what, he had my back.

The remaining guard watched us for a moment more before asking, in a careful tone, "Pardon me, Sir Daye, but your companion, is he . . . ?"

"Tybalt, King of the Court of Dreaming Cats, and betrothed to Sir Daye," said Tybalt. He couldn't have sounded smugger if he'd been trying—and I'd known him long enough to know that sometimes, he tried. He was a cat, after all. "Don't look so surprised. Cats may have their lapses in judgment, just like everyone else."

"Maybe don't say these things when my elbows are so close to your kidneys," I suggested genially.

Tybalt laughed.

The door opened and the second guard emerged, pulling the door wider in the process. "Her Majesty, High Queen Maida of the Westlands, welcomes you."

"Excellent," I said. I walked forward, Tybalt following, and stepped into the largest receiving room I'd ever seen in anything short of a knowe's main hall. If the Luidaeg's suite was bigger than my old apartment, this one was bigger than my entire house. The décor matched the redwood-and-stained-glass theme of the rest of the estate. Unlike the Luidaeg's suite, the walls were solid, preventing the morning light from waking the occupants. The ceiling continued upward into a belled dome; while it was stained glass, it was all shades of dark blue, spangled with colored moons and constellations, like a grander version of the hallway.

"Whoa," I said.

"That's what I said," said Maida, rising from the chaise longue where she'd been eating her breakfast. She was wearing a long silver dressing gown that almost matched her hair, and her brief smile faded as she moved toward me. "What news?"

"First, a question, since I was sort of busy. Did Arden tell you about Duchess Dianda Lorden?"

Maida nodded. "The Duchess Lorden was elf-shot in her quarters yesterday, after the conclave had concluded. We were notified both due to the attack, and due to the request that we open the walls long enough to allow a healer to come inside."

"Good. Just checking. I was able to enter her dreams, with the assistance of Karen Brown and the Luidaeg, and speak with Dianda—who is *not* happy, by the way. Like, I recommend whoever wakes her be wearing protective clothing, because she's likely to wake up swinging."

"We can't wake her," said Maida. Her face smoothed into neutrality, and for the first time, I felt like I was having a private audience with the High Queen. "We must be seen to show no favor for those who are our allies, and while Saltmist is not allied with the Westlands, it has worked in alliance with the Mists. We regret what has happened to the Duchess Lorden, but—"

"But because whoever shot her could stand up and use this to prove it doesn't matter what the conclave decides, since anyone who's an ally of the Mists will always have access to the cure, she needs to stay asleep for now," I said. "I got that part. What I'm getting at is that we *know* who shot her. Dianda saw them. It was Duke Michel of Starfall."

"Do you have proof?"

"I do," I said. "It's called 'you're the High Queen, and your husband is the High King, and either of you can command Duke Michel to give you three drops of blood to verify a claim against him.' Which, by the way, I am happy to make, and Patrick Lorden will be happy to support."

"Her husband? Won't that seem a bit, well, biased?"

"Blood has no bias. Tell Duke Michel you need to clear the charges before the conclave can continue, and he doesn't get to say that it's unfair, because you're in charge of the continent." I shook my head. "If we don't do this, we run the risk of it continuing to happen."

"But why? Duchess Lorden was in favor of sharing the cure, as was Duke Michel."

I paused. "That's what he said. People can lie. Blood can't lie, but people can. Maybe he doesn't want the cure getting out at all, and so he did this, because he wins either way. If we wake her, he can call the conclave a sham. I'm assuming if there were a mass exodus of offended nobles, the cure would be suppressed?"

Maida nodded slowly. "For at least another year, while it was discussed behind closed doors. We don't *need* the support of the people to release it, but it would go easier if we had it. People get funny ideas about democracy these days."

"So there's a guaranteed delay. And if we don't wake her, now Michel knows he can erode the vote by shooting people. Faerie isn't a democracy, but most of us are used to having our opinions matter at least a little, and I'm betting that goes double for kings and queens."

"As it happens, we're very fond of our opinions being heard," said Tybalt mildly. "We tend to become incensed when ignored."

Maida sighed. "What would you have us do?"

I took a breath. "I would have you ride Duke Michel's blood and confirm what I've told you. Confirm he did it to sway the conclave. And then wake Dianda up, not because she's an ally of the Mists, but because Michel was trying to use the rules against you, and he doesn't get to *do* that. She wouldn't have been elf-shot if he wasn't trying to be a manipulative dick. Make it clear that the High Crown is not up for manipulation."

"I could easily point out that *you* are now trying to

manipulate the High Crown," said Maida, lips twitching with amusement.

"Yeah, but I'm upfront about it." I turned toward the half-open door on the other side of the room, raising my voice a bit as I called, "Isn't that right, Your Highness?"

The door swung open. Aethlin stepped out. "How did you know?"

"I live with your son. He likes to lurk. He's a lurky, lurky boy. He had to get that from somewhere, and he actually didn't get it from me." I shrugged. "I figured there was no way you were sleeping when people were getting murdered—no progress on that front, by the way, since Duke Michel decided to complicate my life by shooting my friend—and there's nowhere else in the knowe you have particular reason to be, which meant you were somewhere in this room, listening to us. I made an educated guess."

"It was a good one," said Aethlin. "Yes, I'll ride his blood to determine his guilt, and yes, if what you say is true, we will wake the Duchess Lorden regardless of what the conclave decides—but we'll do it *after* the conclave is finished, and her vote will go to her consort."

I frowned. "Why?"

"Because Patrick Lorden was once Patrick Twycross of Tremont, and I know how he'll vote, especially when his lady love lies sleeping. Hate me for it if you like, but I want this cure to have the support of my vassals, and I would rather deal with an angry man whose opinion is predictable and fixed than an angry Merrow whose thoughts will be more of revenge than what is good for Faerie as a whole."

There was nothing I could say to that. I shook my head slowly, trying to absorb his words, and finally settled for: "That's cold. Sire."

"It may be, but that's kingship," he replied. "I know you understand how important this cure is. We can change the world, but we need the vote to go the correct way."

"Forgive me for intruding on a matter that impacts the Divided Courts in so complicated a manner, but within the Court of Cats, my word is law," said Tybalt. "Why is it you can't simply wave your hand, declare, 'This is how things will be done,' and smack anyone who challenges you?"

"Well, first, I don't really, ah, smack my vassals all that often," said Aethlin. "It's sort of frowned upon. And second, you're the absolute authority within your own Court. Can you make rules for other Kings? Other Queens? Can you tell them how to do things?"

"Of course not," said Tybalt. "A King is sacrosanct within his own territory; the same of a Queen."

"So why do you assume I can?"

Tybalt paused before saying, more carefully, "The Divided Courts have always presented themselves to the Court of Cats as an authority unimpeachable, because they were founded at the request of the Queens. Maeve to stand for darkness; Titania to stand for light. We were granted our independence at the word of Oberon, but he has never stood for us as the Queens agreed to stand for you."

"And maybe if the Queens were still here to support us and back up our decisions, that's how it would work," said Maida. "Or maybe we'd be back to the old ways, with a different King for each half of the year, and half our children slaughtered out of fear that they'd challenge for the crown. Some aspects of absolute power have to be forgotten if you want to live a peaceful life. Call me strange, but I like knowing that the place I hold today is likely to be the place I hold tomorrow. Predictability is an odd obsession of mine."

I said nothing. I was thinking.

Back when Oberon and his Queens were still here—when they were people, not stories—the title "Divided Courts" *meant* something. Seelie and Unseelie, dark and light, beautiful and terrible, all those factors played into where someone belonged ... but what *really* mattered was which of the Queens had claimed your bloodline. Apart from them, we had the children of Oberon, the heroes, who were rarer, since Oberon has always been more reluctant to claim descendant lines as his own, and whose role was less rulership, and more "keeping everyone else from killing each other." The Tuatha de Dannan were Oberon's by birthright. None of the stories I'd heard about Faerie before the King and Queens vanished placed a Tuatha on a throne. It was always Daoine Sidhe and Tylwyth Teg before that, Titania's and Maeve's respectively, playing out the age-old conflict of our Queens over and over again in microcosm.

Sometimes I wondered whether our forebearers did us a favor when they disappeared. Maybe it was the only way we could ever have learned to stop slaughtering each other.

"Before we go too far down the political rabbit hole here, which hey, you boys can do all day if that's what floats your boat, but I have things to do and a murderer to find, so I want to be absolutely sure I understand how this is going to go," I said. "We're going to return to the conclave. You're going to open with the announcement that Dianda has been elf-shot, and with the statement that Duke Michel was responsible. After you ride his blood and confirm what I've said, you're going to do what? Kick him out?"

"No," said Maida, before Aethlin could speak. A slow smile spread across her face. "We're going to have him elf-shot."

I blinked. "I thought we were discussing the merits of getting *rid* of elf-shot."

"We were, and we are, and this will be an interesting conversation starter," said Maida. "If he objects too strenuously, then he's admitting he views elf-shot as an unfair punishment—one he was all too happy to inflict on someone from another Kingdom, and all because he thought he could do so safely. If he goes willingly and without objection, then he's saying the status quo is absolutely fine by him, and he, and the people he represents, would be happier if nothing changed."

"Oh, oak and goddamn ash," I said, putting a hand against the side of my head. "That's it. I'm going to go find a murderer before you make my head explode."

"No, you're not," said Aethlin.

"What?" I lowered your hand. "Begging your pardon and all, but it's my job."

"So is this. Go, change your clothes, and bring Quentin to the conclave. You can leave after Duke Michel is dealt with." He raised an eyebrow. "Unless you want to argue with me?"

"Uh, no." I laughed bitterly. "The last time I argued with somebody who had a crown, I wound up ambassador to Silences. I'm not making that mistake again. Tybalt?"

"How finely you pack an entire request into a single word of two syllables. Would that my name were shorter, that I might encourage you to even greater acts of brevity." He offered a quick, not quite mocking bow to the High King and Queen. "My lady needs a chariot, and I will serve her as well as any horse. I shall see you anon." With that, he slung an arm around my waist and stepped backward into the shadow.

The last thing I saw before the darkness blocked out the world was High King Aethlin's puzzled gaze, and High Queen Maida covering her mouth to hide her smile. Then everything was dark and cold, and they were blessedly the least of my worries. I didn't need to think about politics or playing fair; all I had to do was run. And so I ran.

FIFTEEN

WE FELL OUT OF the shadows, into the light of my temporary quarters. Tybalt let go, virtually shoving me away as he stumbled to the bed, grabbing the bedpost and holding on for dear life. I staggered to my feet, watching him long enough to be sure he was breathing without obvious distress. He liked to make a show of how invincible he was, how untouchable and eternal, but the truth of the matter was that he'd exhausted himself to the point of death twice while carrying me through the shadows—and while a short run inside Arden's knowe was nothing compared to some of the jaunts we'd taken, part of me would always be waiting for the day he collapsed and didn't get better.

It was almost ironic, in a terrible way. I was the one with mortal blood. *He* should have been the one worrying himself sick over *me*. But I was also the unbreakable one, thanks to the gifts I'd inherited from my mother; I was the one who'd live no matter what I did to myself. I'm pretty sure we're tied for deaths these days, although I'll never tell him if I can help it. Call me paranoid, but I don't feel like "I got stabbed in the heart and I think there's a good chance that I died" is the sort of conversation we can have without it devolving into a screaming fight.

"You do have a shorter name," I said, forcing my voice to stay as light as possible. I moved toward the suitcase I had packed for the occasion. If the High King wanted me to change my clothes, I needed to do it. "I just don't think you'd be thrilled if I started calling you 'Rand' all the time."

Tybalt shivered, still clinging to the bedpost. "The sound of that name upon your tongue is sweet torture. Would that you could have known him, the man who would not be King."

"Okay, now you're starting to freak me out." I turned back to the bed, leaving my suitcase unopened. I moved to stand behind him, placing my hand flat against his arm. He didn't lift his head. "Tybalt. Hey. You don't get this Shakespearean unless something is really wrong. What's going on?"

"There was a time when I could have said 'a man was murdered' or 'a woman lies dreaming for a century's time,' and had that be enough, you know." He finally lifted his head and turned to look at me. "There was a time when those words would have unlocked an ocean of sympathy, not a shrug and the words 'today is Thursday.'"

"It's not Thursday," I said automatically, before I winced and asked, "So what, is this about me being too flippant?"

"No. No, love, no." He let go of the bedpost and turned. He grasped my upper arms, holding them tightly enough that I could feel each of his fingers individually. It wasn't tight enough to bruise, but it came close. "This is about the fact that once we leave this room, I have to go back to holding myself apart from you. When the false queen was setting herself up as your enemy and opponent, I had the luxury of pretending to be an enemy. Anything I did would be taken as humorous, because it would antagonize you. Now ... I shed the mask that allowed me to protect you when I allied myself with you in the public sphere."

"So you're afraid I'm going to get myself hurt . . . ?" I ventured, watching him intently. This side of Tybalt—the side that had buried his first wife, the side that had held him away from me for years, out of the fear that any mortal woman he dared to love would suffer the same fate as Anne—was still new to me. It was no less endearing than the arrogant face he showed the world. The fact that I was allowed to see it at all made it precious to me. But sometimes it was still surprising, the places where his actual insecurities were buried.

He nodded. There was a gravity bordering on pain in his eyes. His pupils had expanded to soak up every bit of the available light; in someone less feline, the resulting effect would have looked drugged. On him, it just made me want to hold him fast and never let go.

Too bad that sort of mercy wasn't in my job description. "I might," I said. "I can't promise anything beyond 'I'll do my best to be careful,' and even that goes out the window if it's me or Karen, or Quentin, or Arden. I'd take a bullet for my kids because I love them, and I'd take a bullet for my Queen because my oaths say I have to. That's who I am. I don't get to change it just because the waters are too deep."

To my surprise, he chuckled, letting go of one arm and running the knuckles of his right hand down the curve of my cheek. "I love you because of who you are," he said. "I wouldn't change a thing, even if it were possible to do so. I hate that we've spent so much time among the Courts of your people of late, where I'm as much a hindrance as I am a help."

"Yeah, well, maybe after this one, we can have a nice, normal missing persons case," I said, as lightly as I could. "Or hey, I could take a vacation. Disneyland. We have to go to Southern California anyway, so I can tell King Antonio's heir what happened to him. I've always wanted to go to Disneyland. Mom wasn't interested, and I never had the money while I was living with Devin."

"That could be nice," he said. I must have looked baffled by that reply, because he burst out laughing. "Honestly, October, I've been in California since before the Park's construction. Do you think there's any possible way I missed the many, many, hundreds of billboards that have been erected and removed since then? I have no idea what one *does* at Disneyland, but I'm aware of its existence."

"You didn't know how to ride in a car," I said defensively.

He pulled himself up a little straighter. "I'm a King of Cats, with full and open access to the Shadow Roads. Why would I *need* to know how to ride in a car?"

Now it was my turn to laugh. I started to lean in for a kiss.

There was a sound behind me, like metal being torn, and a scent so faint that it was on the edge of existence, too thin and attenuated to identify. Tybalt blinked, giving me an inexplicably baffled look. I didn't think; I just acted on instinct, shifting my body a few inches to the side, as if I could shield him from the source of that sound.

The pain followed immediately on the motion, sharp and piercing and somehow new, a pain I had never felt before. It seemed like every time I reached the limits of my body's experience, someone went out of their way to hurt me in a whole new way.

I knew enough about my body and the way it worked to be certain that there wasn't time to turn and fight before I succumbed to my injuries. Maybe it was cowardly of me, but I didn't want Tybalt to attack my attacker only to find that I'd bled out while he was distracted.

"*Run*," I hissed, feeling bloody froth burst at the corners of my mouth as I pitched forward into Tybalt, knocking him back in the process. I caught a glimpse of his eyes, now wide and round with shock, before we fell into darkness. He'd clearly seen the blood; he knew I was hurt; he knew I wouldn't be telling him to flee unless I was also scared. So he fled.

I had never loved him more.

Tybalt carried me through the dark, my lungs aching and the blood freezing on my lips. I hadn't been able to catch a proper breath before we fell. That, combined with the pain in the left side of my chest, told me that whatever had hit me had probably punctured my lung. Definitely a new one on me, and when combined with the cold and the lack of air, it made it hard to stay awake. I clung to consciousness the same way I was clinging to Tybalt's shoulders, refusing to allow the deeper dark to claim me. I needed him calm, rational, and not stalking the halls of Arden's knowe searching for my killer.

We tumbled out of the darkness and into the bright, pancake-scented confines of the Luidaeg's chambers. She was seated at a large round table with Karen and Quentin, all of them turning toward the sound of our arrival. Karen went pale. Quentin jumped to his feet. And the Luidaeg, bless her, cleared the breakfast dishes to the floor with a sweep of her arm, creating a great clatter of crockery.

"Get her on the table!" she commanded. "Quentin, warm, damp towels, now. Karen, go to my room. Bring me the brown case." She paused for barely a second, looking between the two of them. "Well? *Move*."

"Shouldn't we get Jin . . . ?" asked Quentin.

"*Move!*" the Luidaeg howled.

They moved.

Tybalt carried me to the table, lowering me onto my side. Sheets of frozen blood cracked and fell away with every motion, freeing more to seep into my clothing. The Luidaeg grabbed one of the blood crystals before it could hit the floor and pressed it to my lips, like a nurse offering an ice chip to a wounded soldier.

"Suck on this," she said. "It'll make you feel better."

I managed to muster a nod and open my mouth, letting her place the blood on my tongue. It began to warm and soften, and she was right; it *did* make me feel better. The taste of blood always did. My blood was the best choice in some ways, because it didn't come with any unwanted, potentially uncomfortable memories: it was mine. I already knew all the secrets it had to tell me.

It was getting increasingly difficult to breathe. I closed my eyes, focusing on the soothing taste of the blood. I was in good hands.

"What happened?" the Luidaeg demanded.

"I don't *know*!" Tybalt sounded frustrated—and more, he sounded scared, like this was outside his frame of reference. "We were in her room, and there was a sound, like unoiled hinges creaking. She froze. Then she was falling into me, telling me to run. I never saw what struck her. Can you get it *out*?"

I knew whatever it was had to be still embedded in my back; the pressure on my lung wasn't getting any better. If anything, it was getting worse, making it harder and harder to pull in a full breath. *If I suffocate, will I still heal?* I thought, dazedly. I'd drowned once, I was pretty sure—maybe more than once. Something Connor had said to me on the beach, right after I'd returned from the pond . . . I had recovered from those short deaths. What was one more?

One more was one too many. It was a relief when the Luidaeg said, "Yes, but you're not gonna like it." Her hand touched my shoulder, skin cool against my own. "Honey, I know you can hear me, and that's important. The stake that hit you is like a harpoon. There are hooks. The cleanest way to get it out—forgive me, October—the cleanest way is to push it through. It's going to hurt. It's going to hurt *bad*. But it has to be done. Nod if you understand."

I nodded. It took everything I had left, but I nodded. The Luidaeg took her hand away.

"Good girl. Tybalt, you may want to look elsewhere. Quentin, get ready with those towels."

That was all the warning I received before she gripped the stake, twisting it and sending bolts of agony through my back and shoulder. Then she shoved, driving it deeper into my flesh. I think I screamed. I think I vomited. All I know for sure is that consciousness slipped away, replaced by blessed black nothingness. True nothingness: there was no pain, no awareness that time was passing, only absence. It was pleasant.

The pain returned, bright and blazing, and accompanied by the feeling of fingers inside my chest, poking through the ruined tissue that had been my lung. I screamed, or tried to, anyway; screaming was difficult without air, and my body was refusing to do anything that might have reinflated the collapsed organ.

"Towel!" snarled the Luidaeg, withdrawing her hand. There was a clattering sound as she dropped something on the table, and pressure was suddenly applied to my chest. It hurt, but in a different way. "Dammit. She's lost a *lot* of blood. I need a knife."

"Why?" Tybalt's voice. He sounded panicked, and I couldn't blame him; when the Luidaeg started asking for knives, someone was about to bleed. She wasn't always careful about her cuts, either, although I liked to think she was careless with me because she knew I'd heal.

I wanted to reassure him. I couldn't find the air.

"Because I'm going to bleed for her." Some of the pressure was removed from the towel at my breast. "Come on, kitty-cat. Scratch me, and let me bring her back to you. She'd do the same for me."

I did do the same for you, I thought. I still couldn't speak. I wasn't dead, but I wasn't getting any air. Everything was turning fuzzy and hard to focus on. My eyelids didn't want to respond. That wasn't fair. If I was going to die here, I wanted to see them before I went. I wanted them to know I was saying good-bye.

There was a ripping sound. The Luidaeg hissed, sounding pained. Then something was being shoved against my lips, and the smell of blood was invading my nostrils, so delicious I couldn't have resisted it if I tried. My mouth opened almost without my bidding, and I was drinking deeply, greedily, pulling at the Luidaeg's wrist like it was a lifeline. I needed the blood so much that I didn't think about the consequences until the world was washed in red, and everything changed.

My mother is wearing a gown of thorns and autumn leaves, and there are roses in her hair, and she is beautiful, and she is not listening to me. Her eyes are far away, fixed on the horizon; she would rather hear the wind than my voice. It isn't fair. *I love her so, I suffer for her so, and still she will not hear me, because she is too kind. She has always been too kind. Titania's children change their songs when she walks in the forest. The monsters come to sit at her feet and adore her, and she does not have to face the reasons that their claws are bloody, that their teeth are sharp. She doesn't have to* see.

"Please," I say—and the word was jarring enough to knock me back into my own mind, my own present, if only for a moment; the language the Luidaeg spoke wasn't English, and I shouldn't have been able to understand it. She said she'd forgotten the first language of Faerie, and she hadn't lied, because she couldn't lie, but somewhere deep down, below conscious thought, her blood remembered.

You remember, I thought. Then the blood overwhelmed me again, dragging me back down into memory.

"Mother, please," I say. "This is foolishness. You know the ritual has been compromised. You have to change it. You have to find another way."

"Tradition may not seem important to you, my Annie, who saw Tradition born, but it's not just you we Ride for," says Maeve. *Her voice is summer wind and autumn berries, and I want her to talk to me forever, and I want her*

to be quiet and listen. *"We Ride for our grandchildren, and our great-grandchildren, all the way down to the generations that have never known anything but this. We Ride to consolidate a legend, that someday, when we are gone, you can Ride without us."*

She doesn't see. She doesn't understand. She's as far above me as I am above the fae who swarm around their Firstborn parents, forever limited in comparison, eternally unable to grasp the full consequence of what they do. "Tonight is Hallow's Eve, Mother. Please. Send someone else to Ride for you. Take the true route elsewhere, or all is lost."

"My darling girl," she says, and steps closer to me. Her palm is soft against my cheek. She smells like wild roses and southernwood, like moss and loam and the first day of the fall. I will never love anything the way I love her, not as long as I may live. "The fae folk must Ride."

I sat up with a gasp, opening my eyes on the room where my friends were waiting. The pain was gone; my mouth tasted of blood, and inexplicably, of roses. I looked wildly around. There was Tybalt, reaching out to steady me, and there was Karen, clutching a brown leather case to her chest, her eyes wide and round as saucers. I turned my head. Quentin and the Luidaeg were standing on my other side. He had an armful of bloody towels, and she was stained red to the elbow with her own blood and with mine. Out of the four of them, only she looked anything other than terrified. She just looked tired.

"How are you feeling?" she asked.

"Like I licked a light socket," I said. Tybalt was still right there. I allowed myself to lean over until my head was resting against his chest. I didn't look down at my clothes. To be honest, I didn't want to know. "What did you give me? What happened?"

"What happened is whoever killed Antonio decided what was good for the gander was good for the goose, and rammed a rosewood spike into your back," said the Luidaeg. "Pretty good shot, too. They managed to get it more than halfway through. It would have gone farther on its own, but the tip of the thing broke off inside your lung."

That explained the probing fingers, and the reason they hadn't been able to wait for me to wake up. With the way I healed, a delay would have allowed my body to close up around the foreign object. Not too bad, if we were talking about a bullet or a bone or something else blunt and easily ignored. The tip of a harpoon, inside my lung? That was something else entirely.

"Wait," I said. "How did you get in there? Weren't my ribs in the way?"

"I went under the rib cage," said the Luidaeg blandly. Quentin made a face. I decided I was glad to have been unconscious when that decision was made. "I got all the bits out, but you'd lost a lot of blood. I had to feed you some of mine to give you the strength to recover."

"So that woman I saw—"

"Yes, that was my mother, and no, I don't want to talk about it. Whatever you saw, that is between you and the blood. I won't answer any questions." Something in her eyes . . .

"Won't, or can't?" I asked.

She threw her bloody hands up in the air. "Is there no end to your questions? Can't, October, can't, and won't, and we're sort of getting away from the point here, which is that you could have died."

"Maybe," I said, and closed my eyes, feeling Tybalt's chest rise and fall beneath my cheek, reassuringly solid and alive. Then I opened them again, and asked, "How long was I out?"

"Half an hour, end to end," said the Luidaeg. "The conclave hasn't started yet, if that's what you're worried about."

"I just got stabbed. I have so many better things to

worry about." I pushed myself upright. The motion forced me to touch the table, and my hands skidded in the jellied blood. The smell of it made me hungry and turned my stomach at the same time. "There was a sound like tearing metal. Everything jumped. I don't think it's a teleporter."

"No?" The Luidaeg raised an eyebrow. "How's that?"

"Whoever it was can't have been in the room before they attacked, or Tybalt would have smelled them. Unless they were Folletti, and then they wouldn't be using rosewood." Folletti were sky-fae, and used swords of hardened wind, as invisible as they were. Rosewood was too easy to see to be a Folletti weapon. "There was no lingering magic smell, which means any spells were cast *outside* the room. I think whoever it is, they're somehow pausing things. Making everything stop for a few seconds, and using the time to get into position." I looked at the Luidaeg expectantly.

She raised her other eyebrow. Then, firmly, she shook her head. "I know what you're asking, and no. There's no race in Faerie with that ability. Either you're wrong, or someone is using some sort of alchemy or a mixed spell to do this."

"So we don't even know where to start," I said. "Fun. Fine." I swung my feet around to point them at the floor. More blood squished beneath me. I winced. "I need clothes."

"Yes, you do. What's more, you need a shower."

"I don't have time for a — wait. There's a solution." I turned to Tybalt — blood-soaked and still unsettled, judging by the faint stripes on the sides of his face. He was having trouble holding to the more human aspects of his current form. That was a sign of either relaxation or stress in the Cait Sidhe, and given the situation, and the amount of blood on his clothes, I wasn't betting on the former. "Elliott is here. Go to Arden, find out where he's staying, and get him."

Tybalt blinked. "Why am I doing this exactly?"

"Because we don't have time to shower before we need to go back to the conclave, and I'm not ready to go back to the room where someone tried to murder me." The scene of King Antonio's death, and the absence of a magical signature in the room right after I'd been stabbed, told me that going back wasn't going to help us: not enough to put off cleaning up and reporting the attack to the High King. "Elliott's a Bannick. He can have all this blood gone in a flash."

"I don't want to go," said Tybalt. "I will, but I want you to understand how unkind it is for you to ask this of me."

"I do," I said solemnly.

He looked to the Luidaeg. "If you allow her to come to further harm . . ."

"Don't threaten me, kitty, I'm outside your weight class," said the Luidaeg. "Go."

Tybalt pulled his lips back, showing her his teeth. Then he turned and ran for the shadows in the corner of the room, leaping into them and disappearing. I looked longingly at the place where he'd been. With everything that was going on, I didn't like *anyone* going off alone. Not even Tybalt.

"Toby."

I turned toward the sound of the Luidaeg's voice. "Yes?"

"You could have died. You know that, don't you? You're not invincible. Hard to kill, yes, but unbreakable? No." She looked at me gravely. "You need to be more careful."

"All I did was go to my room to change my clothes," I protested. "I shouldn't have needed to be careful."

"Yet here you are, doused in blood again, with the memory of my fingers pressed into your lung," she said, and shook her head. "You have to take care of yourself. Replacing you would take a long time, and frankly, I don't want to go to the trouble."

I frowned. "Replacing me? For what?"

"I don't want to talk about it, and besides, your suitor is incoming," said the Luidaeg. Sure enough, the smell of musk and pennyroyal wafted through the room not a second later. I turned to see Tybalt standing there, empty-handed. I blinked.

"Tybalt?" I asked uncertainly. "Is everything all right . . . ?"

"No. You're covered in blood again. No day which includes you covered in blood can be termed 'all right.'" He shook his head. "I simply put to your Queen that perhaps it was better if she fetch the Bannick, as otherwise, a King of Cats dressed in crimson would be stalking her halls, and that might concern her guests. She agreed discretion was the better part of valor, and will be here shortly with your cleaner."

He had a point. He wasn't as bloody as I was—abattoirs weren't as bloody as I was—but he had more than a few streaks of dried and drying blood smeared on his arms, shirt, and even the line of his jaw. He'd been holding me while I was bleeding out, and there were consequences for that. There were always consequences for that.

I finished the process of standing, leaving the blood-drenched table behind, and walked the few steps to where Tybalt was waiting. Then I put my arms around him, and held him fast, letting him breathe in the scent of me. The muscles in his back and shoulders began to unknot. He wasn't the only one here in need of comfort; Karen almost certainly needed a hug, and Quentin was never going to get used to seeing me this way. But both of them were still clean, and even with Elliot incoming, I didn't want to cover them in blood if I could help it. Tybalt was already a mess. He needed me enough that he didn't care.

There was a faint rushing sound, and the scent of blackberry flowers and redwood bark. I looked over my shoulder. There was Arden, dressed in a white velvet gown with a chain of silver blackberries wrapped around her waist, forming a low belt. Elliot was next to her, gazing at the blood-splattered room with an expression somewhere between horror and delight. And Li Qin was next to *him*, wearing a black dress stitched with green-and-silver circuitry. She looked thoughtful.

"You brought company," I said, letting go of Tybalt and shifting so my back was to his chest. He put his arms around my waist, holding me there. I didn't bow. Under the circumstances, it didn't seem important.

"My daughter, Elliot's liege, insisted I promise to keep an eye on her people while she could not," said Li Qin. "I accompanied him because things have a tendency to become unnecessarily exciting in your presence."

"And because you wanted to see what the big deal was," I said.

Li Qin shrugged, expression unrepentant. "I'm curious. What can I say?"

"Nothing. I'd be curious, too." I looked to Elliot. "Can you clean this up? I'm supposed to be coming to the conclave with the rest of you, and I can't do it looking like an extra from *Carrie*."

"Wow," he said. "I thought there was a lot of blood the last time I saw you, but this is . . . wow. Do you *bathe* in the stuff? How often do you have to buy new clothes?"

"Not intentionally, and way too often, although in this case, the hole in the back of my bodice is going to be a much bigger problem than the blood," I said. "Can you clean it up? Please? It's drying, and that feels exactly as gross as you'd think."

"I try not to think about how that sort of thing feels," said Elliot. "Close your eyes and hold your breath."

I closed my eyes. Taking a deep breath was easy, and I reveled in it, enjoying the feeling of my lungs inflating without any foreign bodies getting in the way. Then I braced myself, flashing Elliot a thumbs-up.

The smell of lye rose in the air a heartbeat before a hot, soapy wave hit me, washing over me like some sort of bizarre waterpark attraction. The pressure of it knocked me back against Tybalt, who was making a thin, angry noise deep in his chest. He didn't mind showers, especially when I agreed to share them with him, but he was still a cat, and like most cats, he wasn't a big fan of being doused. Then the wave broke, leaving us as dry as if it had never existed. I opened my eyes.

The room, which had always seemed clean, was now spotless. The glass glittered, the hardwood floors gleamed, and the blood was gone, leaving no trace that it had ever been there in the first place. I pushed myself back to my own feet, glancing back to check on Tybalt before I turned to Elliot, preparing to tell him what a good job he'd done. Then I stopped.

He was staring at the Luidaeg, eyes very wide and filled with tears. She was looking back at him, an expression of profound regret on her face. She looked so genuinely sad that it hurt to see her that way.

"I don't . . ." he began. He stopped, took a breath, started again. "I don't know the forms for this, but I know you're a daughter of Maeve. Are you . . . ?"

"I'm sorry, but no," she said. "You're not mine."

"Oh," said Elliot, in a hushed voice.

"His name was Dobrinya. I haven't seen him in centuries. I don't even know if he's still alive. I hope he is. He was among the sweetest of my brothers. But you're not mine."

"Apologies, First," said Elliot, turning his face resolutely away. He reached up to wipe his eyes, trying to make the motion seem unobtrusive. He failed, but it was a valiant attempt. "I just never expected to stand so close to you. To any one of you."

"I know," she said. "You did good."

Elliot visibly swelled with pride, finally looking at me. "You need to stop doing this sort of thing," he said.

I shook off my surprise. It had been so long since I'd seen someone dealing with their first Firstborn encounter that I'd almost forgotten what it looked like. "Why should I stop? You do such a good job of fixing it." I glanced down at myself. The blood was gone. So were the holes in my clothing. Even my bodice had been relaced, although the laces weren't pulled tight; that would have knocked the air out of me, and that's never good when you're surrounded by a giant wave of magical water. I looked up again. "The High King told me to change my clothes. You think he'll be cool with me having them magically steam-cleaned instead?"

"No," said Arden immediately. "You need to wear something they haven't seen before. It's the only way you'll be taken seriously."

"Oberon save me from the purebloods and their rules," I muttered. "All right: I'm going to need an escort back to the room I'm supposed to be sleeping in, since all my clothes are there."

"Actually, no—you won't," said the Luidaeg. She turned and took the brown case from Karen, who had observed everything in silence, eyes wide and face drawn. She looked like she couldn't decide whether she wanted to be terrified or amazed. That was a combination I was very well-acquainted with.

Setting the case on the table, the Luidaeg opened it and began rooting through a welter of scraps. Finally, she pulled out a piece of coppery spider-silk. The edges were ragged, but the lightning jag remains of the embroidery that must have covered the entire piece of fabric were still visible. She walked over and held it out to me.

"Here," she said. "Now strip."

"Uh." I glanced at Quentin. As I had expected, his cheeks were so red that he could have replaced Rudolph as the lead reindeer for Santa's sleigh. "I'm going to go with 'no.'"

The Luidaeg rolled her eyes. "When you people

learned all this modesty shit from the humans, I may never figure out. There's a screen in the bathroom. Go get it, stand behind it, and strip."

"Why am I stripping?" I asked. Quentin was blushing harder all the time. I was starting to wonder if the Luidaeg missed the sight of blood all over everything, and was trying to make my squire explode.

"Because you need to change your clothes." She narrowed her eyes. "Unless you want to argue with the sea witch?"

I groaned, throwing my hands up in the air. "Sure, *now* you get all dire and terrifying, because you want something. Why can't you be dire and terrifying when people are stabbing me? That's when I need you to be dire and terrifying."

"The bathroom's over there," she said, pointing.

I stopped complaining and went.

The bathroom, as she called it, was bigger than my living room, and contained a recessed tub that would have given me nightmares if it had been full. If the Luidaeg hadn't been attending the conclave, this would probably have been the room assigned to Patrick and Dianda; she could have gone swimming in that tub. The promised screen was propped against the wall next to a large rack of soaps, bath oils, and baskets full of bath salts. I grabbed it, hoisted it up onto my shoulder, and returned to the main room, where the others were waiting.

"That is the biggest bathtub I've ever seen," I said, putting the screen down.

"So glad to know that your pedestrian concerns continue to take priority," said the Luidaeg. "Now strip."

Arguing with her wasn't going to get me anywhere. I unfolded the screen, stepped behind it, and began removing my clothes, trying to pretend I wasn't sharing the room with my regent, my squire, a sea witch from the dawn of time, and an easily amused Duchess with a penchant for rewriting the luck of others. Tybalt, Elliot, and Karen were almost irrelevant; none of them made me that nervous, at least where nudity was concerned. Finally, I stepped out of my trousers, and called, "Done!"

"Great. Hold the cloth in front of you, hold your breath, and close your eyes."

I did as I was told. I'd come this far. What was a little more ridiculousness?

The Luidaeg said something else, more softly this time. That was the only warning I received before a wall of hot, soapy water cascaded over me, leaving me gasping. Then I realized I could feel corset stays pressing against my sides. I looked down. The copper scrap had become a strapless, corseted gown. The skirt was loose enough for me to run in, cut mid-calf in the front and extending to the floor in the back. The whole thing was covered in that delicate forked lightning embroidery, giving the impression that I'd just walked out of the heart of a storm. There were even shoes, flats, made of leather that was the same beaten-gold color as the lightning.

"Well?" said the Luidaeg. "Come out."

I came out. "How?" I asked, gesturing to the dress.

"Bannick magic repairs what it cleans," she said. "Normally, that means patching and mending, but if you set up the right conditions—like, say, a piece of spider-silk cut from the gown of a dignitary at a conclave similar to this one, several centuries ago—you can sometimes convince the magic it should recreate the clothing out of whole cloth. You can keep the dress, by the way, assuming you don't manage to bleed all over it. I have no use for that sort of thing."

"And the shoes?"

"No outfit is complete without shoes, earrings, and, if necessary, gloves."

I looked down. The gloves were tucked into the top of my bodice. I pulled them out and pulled them on, managing not to grimace at the feeling of the silk wrapping tight around my fingers. "Happy now, Fairy Godmother?"

"Ecstatic," she said, somehow drawing the word out until it was four syllables long and packed with bitterness. "I won't tell you to be home before midnight. Just try not to get stabbed again."

"I'd prefer she try not to get stabbed in the first place," muttered Tybalt darkly.

The Luidaeg turned on him. "You, get out," she said—not unkindly, which was a nice change. "You need to get to the conclave without the rest of us if you don't want to damage that independence you cats prize so much. They can't start without Arden, but they'll start without you. Hurry along."

Tybalt cast me one last, pained look. Then he was gone, stepping back into the shadows and pulling them around him like a curtain, becoming nothing but the memory of a man.

The Luidaeg wasn't done. She turned to Arden, and said, "Now's your turn to play taxi. Get us to the conclave."

Arden blinked, raising her eyebrows. "I'm the Queen here."

"And I am clearly coming around too often and putting up with too much of your monarchist bullshit, because you seem to have forgotten the essential fact that I. Will. Fuck. You. Up." The Luidaeg took a step toward Arden. Her eyes were suddenly black, and while her features hadn't shifted, there was an element of menace to them that hadn't been there a second ago. She didn't need to change her form to be as brutal and mercurial as the sea. "Familiarity may breed contempt, *Your Highness*, but I recommend you find a way to shake off that tendency, because you have no power over me, no authority to command my actions, and no reason to expect my good will. Now, are you going to be a smart girl and open a door for us, or am I going to remind you why even the rulers of the Divided Courts listen when the Firstborn decide to speak?"

Arden had gone white. She didn't say anything, simply sketched an archway in the air with her hand. It opened, smelling of blackberry flowers, to reveal the stage in the arcade. Then she curtsied to the Luidaeg. Curtsied deeply, until her forehead was almost pressed against her knee, revealing the swan's-wing slope of her back, graceful and vulnerable in her white gown. The Luidaeg stepped forward, resting her fingertips against Arden's spine. Arden shivered.

"Don't mistake me for a friend because I sometimes choose to be friendly," said the Luidaeg. "Don't pretend you have some sort of control over what I do. I'm Firstborn. That means something. Even here, even now, in this washed-out mockery of Faerie, that means something. If you forget again, I'll have to leave you with something to remember me by. So please, Arden. Because I loved your father, in my own way, in my own time, don't make me remind you."

She stepped through the portal, onto the stage, leaving the rest of us to stare, silently, after her. For a long moment, no one could find anything to say. Then Karen, of all people, cleared her throat.

"I want to go home," she said.

Li Qin snorted. "Don't we all," she said, and followed the Luidaeg's trail.

SIXTEEN

OUR GROUP WAS THE only one in the gallery when we arrived. Arden was the last one through. A door opened at the back of the stage as the portal closed behind her. Maida and Aethlin entered, followed by their guards. Maida cheated a glance at Quentin as she walked to her throne. He offered her a thin, heavily shuttered smile that made my heart hurt. What was the value of a throne if this was what it meant for the relationship between parent and child?

Tybalt settled in the third row from the stage. Either they hadn't offered him a throne, or he'd declined it; both options made sense. He was watching Maida intently, and I wondered whether his thoughts and mine had been following similar paths. Probably not. Children were a concern for later, when he was no longer King and I was no longer getting stabbed on a regular basis. Which probably meant children were a concern for never, no matter how much I might quietly wish otherwise.

Siwan entered from the right side of the stage, moving to settle on her throne. Maida and Aethlin took their seats, looking to Arden. In turn, she looked to the Luidaeg. The Luidaeg nodded.

Arden turned her attention to the front of the gallery. "Open the doors," she commanded.

Two previously unseen courtiers pulled the doors open, and the gathered nobles, household staffers, and assorted onlookers poured through, looking suspiciously at one another as they settled. There were no introductions or other niceties today. The murder of King Antonio had successfully turned the conclave into a prison, and had removed any convivial atmosphere that might have otherwise arisen.

Patrick walked in alone, head held high, a loop of pearls tied around his upper arm like a lady's favor. He nodded and met my eyes as he sat. I nodded back. He wasn't going to be happy about the fact that Dianda was set to stay asleep for a day, much less for the duration of the conclave. He would also, probably, understand. He'd been doing this long enough to know how things worked. That didn't make the thought of telling him any easier.

The doors closed. The High King and High Queen rose, suddenly regal, suddenly untouchable. "Before we resume the business of this conclave, a new matter has been brought to our attention," said Aethlin. He didn't raise his voice. He didn't need to. The spells were active again, the air crackling with the faint scent of hot oil and ramps. "Will Duke Patrick Lorden of Saltmist please rise and approach?"

Patrick stood. A murmur spread through the crowd as he walked to the stairs and mounted them, slowly moving to the spot on the stage reserved for presenters.

"Please tell this conclave what happened."

"After yesterday's session, while I was retrieving refreshments for my wife, an intruder entered our quarters uninvited and struck her down," said Patrick. His voice never broke; his gaze never wavered from Duke Michel. "She was elf-shot by a coward who knew the Undersea would see this as an act of war, and did not fletch the arrow in the colors of their demesne."

"How can you be sure she didn't elf-shoot herself, to influence this conclave's decision?" The question came from Maida, which may have been the only reason it wasn't immediately followed by Patrick launching himself at the person who asked it. He'd been living in the Undersea for a *long* time. As it was, I saw the tension in his shoulders, and the way his fingers struggled not to ball into fists. He wanted to hurt her for even asking. I couldn't blame him, even as I silently thanked him for his patience.

"Elf-shot is not a weapon of the Undersea, Your Highness," he said. His voice was calm and clear. "We're here because we wish to know what is decided, and because our son is a Count sworn to service of this crown, not because the ban will impact our daily lives. Elf-shot is a coward's weapon. Even were my wife a liar and a manipulator of men, she would never use elf-shot on herself. She wouldn't know where to begin."

Maida nodded before looking to me. That was my cue, then. I stood, offering quick bows to the thrones and to Patrick, who wasn't technically my superior, but who sure needed the support, before walking up the steps to stand beside him.

"The arrow entered Duchess Lorden's shoulder from the front, passing through several layers of muscle before coming to a stop," I said. "Even if she'd wanted to stab herself, the shaft of the arrow was too thin. It would have broken. It needed to be fired from a bow, and as there was no bow found with the Duchess' body, she didn't do that."

"Sir Daye," said Maida. "Do you know who shot the Duchess?"

"Yes."

"How do you know this?"

"Karen Brown, the oneiromancer, who has been accepted by this conclave and vouched for by the sea witch, led me into Duchess Lorden's dreams. Duchess Lorden saw the man who shot her." I watched the crowd as I spoke. Duke Michel had gone very still, and was staring straight ahead, trying to look like none of this was bothering him. Poor thing. He'd been expecting to get away with it.

"Who was that man?" asked Maida.

"Duke Michel of Starfall."

"I object to this . . . this mockery!" shouted Duke Michel, jumping to his feet. Apparently, he was going on the offensive. Good. That would make him easier to knock down. "You'd take the word of a changeling who claims to have walked in a mermaid's dreams? What next — we listen to the testimony of pixies?"

"I would, if the pixies had something important to say," said Maida. "There is an easy solution to the question of whether Sir Daye is telling lies."

"I am not a liar," I said. "I would be happy to accept my punishment, if I were."

"Excellent," said Aethlin, sitting forward while Maida sat back, her part in this little shadow show complete. "The fastest, most honorable way for us to resolve this is, as always, through the blood. Duke Michel, will you approach the stage?"

Duke Michel went white. He'd always been a pale man, but now he looked like a wax dummy, bloodless and trapped. "I would prefer not to bleed for the amusement of the masses," he said stiffly.

"And I would prefer not to have a dignitary from the Undersea lying elf-shot in a private room, but if there's one thing I've learned since assuming my throne, it's that none of us is guaranteed our heart's desire," said Aethlin. There was a warning beneath his words, mild as they were: this was the High King. Refusing him could have negative consequences, not only for the unfortunate Duke Michel, but for the entire Kingdom of Starfall.

Duke Michel recognized that, or at least recognized that he didn't have a way out of this situation. He approached the stage, keeping his eyes on High King Aethlin the whole time. He either didn't see or didn't acknowledge Patrick's narrow-eyed glare, or the way people leaned away from him as he passed, making sure he didn't taint them by association.

When he reached the stage, he walked up the three shallow steps and knelt in front of the High King's throne. "This is an insult," he said, in a tone that was probably meant to sound humble, but came off as snide, like he was too good to be accused by a changeling and a man who'd given up his political aspirations to go and swim with the fishes.

"Perhaps, but since you've already offered insult to Duke Torquill, it could be said that we're merely evening the scales," said Aethlin. He removed the ring from his left index finger and pressed his thumb against the stone, which clicked and swung open, revealing a compartment on the other side. He shook the ring above his palm. A silver-coated rose thorn fell out. Grasping the thorn between thumb and forefinger, he looked at Duke Michel. "Your hand, Duke."

"This is an insult and a sham."

"Again, perhaps," said Aethlin. "Your *hand*."

Duke Michel grudgingly held out his hand, managing not to wince when Aethlin drove the thorn into the meaty pad of his pointer finger. They remained like that for a moment, the king pressing the thorn into the flesh of the duke. Then Aethlin sat back, pulling the thorn free, and moved it deftly to his mouth, allowing the Duke's blood to trickle onto his tongue.

It was theater. It was smoke and mirrors and unnecessary drama, and it was very important, because the blood wasn't a truth detector: the blood was the truth, and the truth was a big, messy thing. If Duke Michel had been thinking about what he'd had for breakfast that morning, the High King would have gotten the memory of eggs and bacon and brambleberry jam. If Duke

Michel had been thinking about his laundry, the High King would have learned far too much about how bright he wanted his whites. No: the Duke's thoughts had to be fixed on what he'd done. Public humiliation was the surest way to bring those memories to the surface.

High King Aethlin's eyes went unfocused for a moment before he looked at Duke Michel, sorrow etched into his features. "Why?" he asked. "I can see you drawing the bow, I can see the arrow fly, but what I can't see is *why*."

"Because the Undersea has no reason to be here; they should have no say in this matter," said Duke Michel. All signs of humility, false or otherwise, were gone. He'd been caught, and there was no more reason for him to pretend. "You're acting like this is a *conversation*, and not some sort of circus intended to blind the rest of us to the fact that you would withhold a shield against our greatest weapon. Are we truly to believe that Silences would refrain from using the tincture that returned their entire royal family to the throne? That the Mists would be willing to leave a tool shaped by one of their own unused? No. This is not a conversation. This is you pretending there's any chance the rest of us will have access to something that should belong to all or none."

"You shot my wife to make a point?" Patrick sounded quietly puzzled. I'd known him long enough to know how dangerous that tone was. Fleetingly, I wondered whether he was really the calm one, or whether it was just a matter of Dianda losing her temper faster than her husband did.

"I shot your wife because I knew they would wake her up," said Duke Michel.

High King Aethlin stood. All the little whispers and rustles that had spread through the gallery stopped. When the High King rose, it was best to be beneath notice.

"This conclave will continue," he said, in a soft voice.

"Should we vote to release the cure, Duchess Dianda Lorden of Saltmist will be the first to awaken. Should we decide the needs of Faerie are better served by keeping the cure under lock and key, she will sleep for a hundred years, in the knowe where she was felled, that we might remember what our failure has meant for an innocent woman and her family. The hospitality of this kingdom will be extended to her husband and youngest son for that entire time, by order of the High Crown—should Queen Windermere step down before century's end, her successor will be bound to grant the Lordens all the gifts and graces of an honored guest. You have done this, Duke. You have spent the coin of another kingdom as if you had the right, and for that, you must be punished."

Duke Michel's eyes widened. There were no rules against the use of elf-shot, which had been invented, after all, as a means of cutting each other down without killing. There were, however, a lot of rules about things like "abusing the hospitality of another kingdom." With one simple sentence, Aethlin had changed the game.

"Your Highness, I never—" the Duke began. Aethlin silenced him with a glare.

"Whatever your intent, this is what you have done," he said. "I apologize to Duke Torquill that he will be unable to duel you for a time, but you are needed elsewhere. You will be elf-shot. You will be held here until you wake, whenever that may be. And then, the Duchess Lorden will be asked what penalty the Undersea would lay against one who raised a hand against one of their diplomats. If she wakes soon, that penalty may be slight. If she sleeps a hundred years . . . you had best hope she understands the meaning of 'mercy.'"

"She doesn't," said Patrick.

Duke Michel's head dropped until his chin was almost level with his chest. It was done; he was beaten. All he could do now was stand silently as the High King's guards came and led him away.

High King Aethlin remained on his feet. He looked out on the arcade, and asked, "Well? Is there any further business to be conducted before we resume discussion of the matter that has brought us here?"

"Yes, Highness," I said. He shot me a startled glance. I shrugged, trying to look casual, like I interrupted this sort of thing every day. Which ... wasn't too far off, in general, even if the specifics were somewhat unique. "I've been granted permission to investigate the matter of Duke Antonio's murder, remember? I need to be working right now, not sitting here and listening to a conversation that I can't join or influence. Anything I need to know, someone can bring me up to speed on later."

"I see," said Aethlin. "Was there anything else you needed?"

"I was also given permission to remove people from this conclave as I saw fit. I'd like to speak to whomever accompanied King Antonio out of Angels."

"Very well." High King Aethlin turned to the audience. "Will the delegation from Angels please rise and follow Sir Daye to wherever she leads? I promise you, there will be no final votes taken in your absence."

Two Candela and a Glastig rose from where they'd been sitting on the shadowy side of the room. The Candela were unfamiliar. The Glastig ...

"Hello, Bucer," I said.

Bucer O'Malley, late of Home, currently of Angels, winced. "Toby," he said.

I offered a quick bow toward the gathered thrones before hopping down from the stage and heading toward the back door. As I'd hoped, the emissaries from Angels followed me, the two Candela walking almost as silently as one of the Cait Sidhe, Bucer tapping along on sharply pointed hooves that couldn't be muffled by anything short of being wrapped in pillows. I knew that from experience. He and I had done our share of breaking and entering back when we'd been street rats in Devin's service, stealing what we were told to steal, shanking who we were told to shank. Since Home had been a changeling domain, there'd been no one to stop us from hurting each other—it didn't break the Law, and so no one had particularly cared. The last I'd heard of Bucer, he'd been running for Angels, getting the hell out of town before he could be arrested for his part in the kidnapping of the Lorden boys. Looked like he'd managed to fall on his feet.

That was the thing about men like him. They almost always did.

I led my motley little gang down the hall and past the kitchens, stopping at a cold pantry that the household staff had shown me once, proud of how much ground they'd been able to recover from the cobwebs and decay. Opening the door freed a burst of cool air, and the distant, earthy smell of potatoes. "Inside," I said.

The two Candela, who were used to dust and shadowy spaces, went willingly. Only Bucer hung back, giving me an uncertain look. "Do I have to?" he asked.

"I'm coming in with you," I said. "It's not like I'm going to shut the door and lock you in there to die. Even if I did, you'd have two Candela with you."

"We're not carrying him through the web," said one of the Candela, sounding affronted. Her hair was pale gray, the color of volcanic ash, and cut in a shoulder-length bob. The other Candela, male, with darker hair, nodded his agreement.

"You wouldn't have to," I said. "You could just pop out of the room and open the door. Now come on, unless you want me asking for your King's dirty secrets while we're all standing around in the hall."

Bucer slowly walked past me into the room, glancing over his shoulder several times. I followed, closing the door behind me before yanking off my gloves and dropping them on the nearest shelf. The glow from the two Candela was more than bright enough to allow me to see their faces. They looked calm. Bucer didn't. Unfortunately, because of our history, I had no way of knowing whether that was because he'd done something wrong, or because he was waiting for me to kick the crap out of him again.

"Your King is dead," I said, without preamble. "The person who killed him attacked me earlier today, presumably because they were afraid I was going to learn something they didn't want me to know. Who would have wanted to kill King Antonio, and why?"

"Half the purebloods in Angels wanted him dead, for refusing to support their claims to this and that," said one of the Candela. "All the changelings wanted him dead, for refusing to order the purebloods to leave them alone. Angels is where dreams come true, after all."

A surprising number of film and television stars were changelings. Fae blood made them beautiful and sturdy enough to survive doing their own stunts; human blood made them resistant to the iron in camera rigs and muscle cars. And the nature of the industry was such that if you were careful, you could keep a career going for decades, writing off your apparent inability to age as clean living, drinking lots of water, and keeping a plastic surgeon on speed-dial. "Swell," I said. "Who *didn't* want him dead?"

"We didn't," said the male Candela. "He didn't make a lot of rules. He didn't interfere with people doing what they wanted to do. That's harder to find than you'd think."

"He brought me because I knew the Mists, and because I knew you," said Bucer. "He wanted to be able to predict what was gonna happen at this stupid thing. Said I'd be forgiven for a few little things if I came."

"Little things?" I asked.

"He stole the crown jewels," said the female Candela.

I had to swallow a smile. "Some things never change, I guess," I said. "Whoever killed him snuck up on him, yes, but they also disoriented him. I thought at first that it was a teleporter. Now, I'm not so sure."

The male Candela frowned. "Why are you speaking so openly to us?"

"Because you didn't do it," I said, very calmly. "When King Antonio was killed, his Merry Dancers shattered. Fragments, all over the floor."

The four Merry Dancers that shared our space swirled madly around their respective Candela, outward manifestations of their distress. Bucer flinched, but said nothing.

"If either of you had killed him, I'm reasonably sure you would have done it someplace where the Merry Dancers wouldn't have broken when they fell," I said. "Also, the magic doesn't match up. I know what Candela teleportation looks like, and this wasn't it. As for you, Bucer, you didn't do it. I know your magic, I know your methods, and I know you're too much of a coward to have tried to stab me while Tybalt was in the room."

There was always the chance that whoever stabbed me had been aiming for *Tybalt*—the stake had hit me in the back, but King Antonio had been stabbed in the chest. If I hadn't jumped in the way, the stake would have struck Tybalt in the same place. More than anything, that reinforced my conviction that Bucer hadn't been the one doing the stabbing. He would have been a fool to attack me in front of Tybalt. He would have been a *suicidal* fool to attack Tybalt in front of me—and if there was one thing Bucer had taken away from our time together at Home, it was a healthy respect for how much damage I could, and would, do if I was pissed off.

"So why are you talking to us if you know we didn't do it?" asked Bucer warily. "We're supposed to be in the audience, paying attention to the political bullshit."

"Why?" I asked. "You don't have a King anymore. Does any of you have a title?"

"I'm a Viscount," said the male Candela.

"Which means none of you have enough of a title to make a difference when the vote comes around, unless you expect the High King to go for a show of hands," I said. "He's not going to do that. The Court of Cats would carry the day. Even with the wards locked, you can't keep the Cait Sidhe out, and since they're cats, it's not like anyone would be able to prove they hadn't been here the whole time." The redwood paths in the high trees could be covered with sunbathing and mouse-hunting cats, and no one would know. It was a charming image. It was a terrifying image. The Divided Courts thought they were powerful, but cats could walk through anything, because Oberon had given them permission.

Bucer and the two Candela—who hadn't volunteered their names; it didn't seem important under the circumstances—looked at me, waiting to hear what I'd say next. I sighed.

"Nobody liked King Antonio. Fine. Can you think of anyone who would have wanted to *kill* him?"

"His wife," said the male Candela.

"Frequently," added the female, and they both laughed, small, near-silent exhalations of air. Then the female sobered, and said, "He was a poor king, but a poor king was the best thing for Angels. If you're wondering whether there had been threats against him, dangers we ignored to bring him here, the answer is no. No, there were not. He left his seneschal to run the kingdom in his absence. Not the act of a king who feared for his life. Antonio was a braggart and a bully and a foolish, foolish man. He was also a friend. Capable of great compassion. A person, like any of us, and like any of us, he was disinclined toward pointless risks."

What she was saying matched up with what Antonio had told me himself, although of course, that would be difficult to explain. The ridiculousness of the situation was starting to get to me. I'd spoken to a dead man, to a sleeping woman ... all that was left was for me to find a way to have a philosophical debate with the pixies, and I would have covered all my bases. "Before he died, the world stuttered," I said. "Before I was attacked, the world did the same thing. It wasn't teleportation—I didn't move—but the world moved *around* me. Can you think of anything that would have done that? Anything at all?"

"No," said the male Candela. His companions shook their heads.

I swallowed the urge to sigh. This was going to be an uphill battle after all.

SEVENTEEN

MY NEXT SEVERAL INTERVIEWS followed similar lines. No one outside of Angels had known King Antonio very well, although the kingdoms that shared borders with Angels generally thought of him as a good neighbor. He'd been so busy minding his own business and not telling people what to do that he'd never even threatened war, much less openly declared it. The kingdoms of Copper and Painted Sands both spoke fondly of him, mostly in the sense of "and nobody ever died because he was bored." No one volunteered to let me ride their blood, even when I hinted about how much easier that would make things. No one had heard anything about a new kind of teleportation — or quasi-teleportation — magic, or time magic, and no matter how hard I tried, I couldn't pick up any scents that would lead me back to the sound of tearing metal. Locking people in the pantry with me, one by one, meant I was learning magical signatures almost as fast as my mind could file them away, but none of them matched.

That wasn't quite true. None of them was exactly right, but I'd barely smelled anything at all when the sound had happened. I might be looking my attacker in the eye, and still not be able to recognize them. That was just swell. I have *one* freak talent, and suddenly even that wasn't dependable.

By the time I escorted the representatives from Evergreens back to the gallery, I was running out of both patience and ideas. High King Aethlin was on the stage talking about the importance of a unified continent, and why it mattered that we make choices that were good for everyone, and not only for the chosen few. I did my best to tune him out as I made my way down the aisle toward where Theron and Chrysanthe were seated. They turned toward the motion. Theron raised his eyebrows. I nodded, beckoning for them to follow me out.

They didn't look thrilled. They still stood, and their hooves clacked against the floor as we walked back up the aisle—not as loudly as Bucer's, but loudly enough that people turned to watch us go. I forced myself to keep walking, not making eye contact. I was going to have to talk with each of these people before the night was out, and I was running out of ideas.

I became a detective not because I'm any *good* at it, but because I was willing to try. That means a lot in Faerie, where sometimes "turning everyone into a statue to show them the error of their ways" is treated as a valid, even reasonable solution. I've gotten better over the years, but still, the majority of my cases involve following cheating spouses and recovering lost items, not questioning an entire knowe full of nobles who thought they were too good to talk to someone like me, hero of the realm or no.

We walked to the pantry in silence. Theron and Chrysanthe held their peace while I opened the door, gestured for them to step inside, and closed it behind myself. Theron sat in one of the chairs I'd scavenged from the kitchen. Chrysanthe lounged against the wall behind him, draping her arms comfortably over baskets of potatoes and onions. It was a nice gambit. Unless you were a courtier or a guard, standing while a king sat was generally considered rude. So was sitting while a queen stood. No matter what I did, I was insulting someone. In fact . . .

"You did that on purpose," I said, sinking into my own seat and crossing my ankles in front of me. "Am I supposed to be so flustered by trying to decide what I'm supposed to do that I freeze up and let you leave without questioning you? Because I've been flustered by the best. You're going to need to try harder." Back before Tybalt and I became allies—not even friends, just allies— he practically specialized in throwing me off-balance. After being the primary target of a bored Cait Sidhe for several years, there isn't much in this world that can genuinely shake me.

Theron and Chrysanthe exchanged a look. Finally, Chrysanthe spoke. "We could play at being offended, demand to know what gave you the right to suspect us, much less question us, but to be honest, we've been looking forward to the opportunity to speak with you," she said. "Why in the world are you working for these people?"

Well. That wasn't what I'd been expecting. I blinked, trying to conceal my bewilderment, before asking, "What do you mean?"

"You're a changeling. You may have given up much of your human birthright for power, but you've been mortal: you know what it is to be looked down upon for reasons you didn't choose and can't control," she said. "Why would you stay in the Mists, where you'll never be considered a full citizen of Faerie, when we're just down the coast? You would be welcome on the Golden Shore."

I gaped at her. Then, recovering my senses, I shook my head and said, "Because I was born in San Francisco. My liege is here. My friends and family are here. I wasn't going to give any of that up for politics. I'm still not going to do it. The Mists are my home."

"That may be so, but your choices might be broader down the coast," said Theron. "You should consider it."

I wanted to laugh. Here I was, trying to figure out who'd killed King Antonio and attacked me, and these people were attempting to recruit me? It was ridiculous, and that was what made it so understandable. Faerie had a lot of rules and manners, but it didn't always understand how to prioritize them for people who actually paid attention to *time*. When eternity was a given, there was really no good reason to treat anything with urgency.

Theron and Chrysanthe ran a kingdom of changelings, but they were still purebloods. No matter how much that statement might have offended them, offense wasn't enough to make it untrue. "I am sworn in service to Duke Sylvester Torquill of Shadowed Hills, whose Duchy has always been kind to changelings, and through him to Queen Arden Windermere in the Mists," I said. "I'm pretty cool with both of those things. And I'm getting married soon, and the man I'm marrying isn't exactly in the position to pack up and move. So while I appreciate the offer, I'm happy where I am. I just want to do my job and find out who murdered one of your peers. Do you think you could help me with that?"

"I don't see how you can be happy in a place that's made you give up so much of your heritage," said Theron solicitously.

I stopped. The urge to yell at him was strong. The urge not to get in trouble for insulting yet another monarch was stronger. Swallowing my rage, I said, "I wasn't forced to give up my humanity to prove I was as good as the purebloods. I did it to save myself, to save the people who cared about me, and to cure a goblin fruit addiction. Those might not be doors that are open to most changelings, but part of growing up in this world was learning that I can't refuse to do something just because it might be hard or inconvenient or impossible. Now *please*. Let me do my job."

"Are you in favor of this cure?" asked Chrysanthe.

The urge to start screaming was getting stronger. It

was like talking to a couple of missionaries, who wanted to bring things back to Jesus no matter how much I wanted directions to the nearest gas station. "Yes," I said, through gritted teeth. "I was there when it was developed. I would have died or turned myself completely fae without it. So I'm pretty sure this cure is a good thing, and that the purebloods aren't going to get more careless just because it exists."

"Would Duchess Lorden agree with you?"

That stopped me. *Would* Duke Michel have been so willing to shoot her, even knowing that his kingdom was landlocked and hence safe from Undersea reprisals, if he hadn't known she could be woken up at a moment's notice? The cure might already be changing how people thought about elf-shot. I just wasn't sure that was a bad thing.

"Nothing we say here is going to impact the conclave," I said slowly, feeling my way through the sentence. "I'm not running some secret poll where I find out how everyone really feels about the idea of the cure and then go and tell the High King how he should resolve the situation. You know that, right? I'm trying to solve a murder. Someone is dead. A *king* is dead. I need to find out who killed him."

"King Antonio sent us citizens from time to time," said Chrysanthe. "People who didn't want to stay in Angels anymore. He'd buy them bus tickets, if you can believe it."

"I can," I said. It wasn't even a surprise. Human cities did that all the time, bussing their homeless to San Francisco, where the milder weather was supposed to make up for the inhumanity of shipping people away from their communities.

"They were never mistreated, per se, or at least not by the Crown," said Theron. "Most had stories about ill-treatment at the hands of other purebloods, lesser nobles who felt their household staff didn't need to be protected. He'd send us the addicts, the ones already so far gone on goblin fruit that they could no longer manage whatever menial jobs they'd held before."

"What did you do?"

"Do?" Chrysanthe's laugh was small and bitter. "We gave them clean beds and brooms to hold, and fed them toast and jam until they were beyond even that. We buried them in safe places, surrounded by the graves of their own kind. Don't look so stunned, Sir Daye. We might have found a cure for elf-shot, but a cure for goblin fruit? That's a thing that will never be, unless we count the cure you've made for yourself—give up humanity, give up the addiction. Not a route that's open to most people."

The accusation in her voice was hard to miss. I fought the urge to squirm. She was right: my route out of addiction wasn't open to anyone who didn't share my bloodline or have access to something that could change theirs. Something like a hope chest, or my mother . . . or me. I had given that choice to the changelings of Silences, after we'd dethroned the puppet king who'd been tormenting them. That didn't mean I could travel the world, offering it to everyone.

"So Golden Shore was well-inclined toward King Antonio?" I asked, trying to get the conversation back under my control.

"As well-inclined as we are toward any of our neighbors," said Theron. "Angels buys our produce, sends us their broken, and refuses to change. The same can be said of any of the Kingdoms in this half of the continent. Maybe someday things will improve for the changelings. Maybe someday we can stop being so angry all the time. But that day is a long way from now."

"Why?" The question burst out before I could stop it. "You're purebloods. You could have whatever you wanted. Why are you so focused on the treatment of changelings?"

"I suppose this is where we're intended to say 'I had a changeling child' or 'I had a changeling sister,' or something of the like," said Chrysanthe. "That would be easy, wouldn't it? It's always easy to admit to someone's right to live when you have a personal tie to them. We don't have that. What we have is the memory that, before humans and fae met so often, before changelings were common, it was people like us—people who showed how close our King and Queens once were to the natural world—who bore the brunt of those prejudices. There was a time when 'animals in the court' was as bad as 'changelings.' So, yes, we're interested in knowing things are going to get better for the changelings, even if we have to fight for it. Not because we have a personal stake. Because it's the right thing to do."

I took a breath. "That's a good thing, honestly. We need all the help we can get." Most changelings didn't have stories like mine, where they got titles and responsibilities and respect. Most changelings had things much, much worse. And yet . . . "Now please, for right now, can we focus on the murder?"

"We didn't kill him," said Theron, without hesitation. "If you accuse us, we'll give the High King our blood, and you'll be revealed as a fraud."

"Would you even be suggesting that I would make false accusations if I were a pureblood, or do you have some particular reason to think that I'm too incompetent to know who to accuse? Because if not, this seems a little hypocritical of you, given the whole 'we speak for the changelings' position you claim to take. And I'm better at reading blood than High King Aethlin. Just so you know. Look: I don't think you killed him. For one thing, you're too obvious as suspects. For another, killing him doesn't stop the conclave. If you were going to break the Law, you'd have broken it in a way that would bury the cure for a few hundred years, and give you what you both seem to want so badly." The pair looked uncomfortable, Chrysanthe shifting her weight from hoof to hoof while Theron twisted in his chair. "What I need to know is this:

can you think of anything that would mess with time, which could be done easily, by someone who didn't necessarily have a natural gift for it?"

"A fairy ring," said Chrysanthe.

I raised an eyebrow. "Excuse me?"

"A fairy ring," she repeated. "You've heard the stories about humans who wandered into the woods and spent a night dancing, only to go home the next morning and find a hundred years had passed? That was the work of the fairy rings. They were commonly used in wartime, before the development of elf-shot. Instead of sleeping out your sentence, you'd simply go . . . forward. The spell would keep you frozen until you reached a time when the fight was over, and you could no longer serve your liege on the field."

"How hard are they to make? Are they portable?"

She shrugged, looking to Theron. He shook his head. "I don't know. Neither of us has the skill for crafting them. But they were a weapon once, and they could be again, if there was the need for them."

I opened my mouth to ask if they knew anything more. The tolling of the dinner bell stopped me. It was a light, chiming sound that nonetheless scythed through walls, making sure that everyone within the confines of the knowe was aware that their presence was required.

"With that, I believe this audience is over, Sir Daye," said Theron. He rose more easily than I would have thought possible for someone with the lower body of a stag, offering his arm to Chrysanthe, who took it with a smile. "We've enjoyed this chance to know you better."

The two of them walked to the door and let themselves out, leaving me to stare after them in frustration. The bells continued to ring. I slumped backward in my chair, putting a hand over my face. This was getting me nowhere. This was getting me nowhere *fast*. We couldn't let the nobility leave without losing the killer — but if we kept them here, we were keeping ourselves captive with the killer, and that could only end poorly. My wounds were healed, but there was a phantom ache in my shoulder that was happy to remind me of how badly things could go. I was hard to kill. That didn't make it impossible, and it didn't make the people I cared about any more equipped for survival.

Survival. I lowered my hand, staring up at the strings of garlic and pearl onions that obscured the ceiling. Whoever had attacked me couldn't have been expecting me to survive. Sure, I was sturdy, but *how* sturdy was still under discussion, and many people who knew and loved me had no idea how difficult I really was to kill. I'd been attacked—or Tybalt had—by someone who was expecting to have another body on their hands. So who hadn't been expecting to see me in the gallery? Who had been surprised by my appearance?

Blood contained all memory, and I'd been looking at the audience. I raised my thumb to my lips and started gnawing at my cuticles, trying to bite through the skin fast enough to draw blood. It wasn't working. I healed too fast, and my natural reluctance to hurt myself was a problem. I stood, scanning the shelves. There were no knives in here. There was a trowel in with the potatoes, but it was blunt and filthy, and I had enough common sense that I didn't want to drive it into myself.

The dinner bell was still ringing. There was my answer. Gathering my skirts in one hand, so as not to trip myself, I left the pantry and followed the sound down the hall. Most of the guests were already there, judging by how empty the place was; a few servants passed me, harried and laboring under the weight of their trays. They didn't look upset or ill-used; they were doing their jobs, and they had the focused looks of people who liked what they did and who they did it for. That was nice. I liked to hope Arden was going to be one of the better ones, a treasure instead of a tyrant, since her place on the throne was at least partially my fault.

I'd been friends with the household staff at Shadowed
Hills for years, and I knew that for some fae—the Hobs
and the Brownies and the Bannicks—service really was
their only joy. That didn't mean they didn't deserve to be
treated well when they were at work. Or that everyone
treated their servants with kindness. The Barrow Wight
from Highmountain walked by, despondent as always, a
heavy tray in her arms. I did a double-take: a *very* heavy
tray. It looked like she was carrying an entire roast suck-
ling pig.

The hall ended at a pair of redwood doors with
stained glass inserts, propped open to let the moonlight
slant through the colored panes and dance along the
hallway walls. Outside was a pavilion of black mesh, letting the starlight shine through while preventing leaves
or insects from falling to the deck below. Round tables
covered by white cloths studded the area, like something
out of a mortal awards banquet. It was a comparison that
would have been lost on most of the people here, and
laughed at by the rest. The servants I'd seen before
swirled through the scene like dancers, pausing to de-
posit trays and pitchers in front of people as they passed
them by. There was even music, courtesy of a string quar-
tet in the far corner. The cello player was a Huldra, and
held a second bow in her tail, using it to coax impossible
double stops from her instrument.

Arden, Aethlin, Siwan, and Maida were seated at a
table on a raised platform at the far end of the deck.
Tybalt was at a table nearby, keeping company with the
Luidaeg, Karen, Quentin, and Patrick Lorden. I started
in toward them, weaving around tables and dodging
passing servers. It was like a bizarre obstacle course, and
it was a relief when I reached the wide open space in the
middle of the dining area, although it took me a moment
to realize *why* that space was open.

It was a dance floor. Of course it was. Because nothing
said "let's pause for a quick waltz" like a political

convocation where people were getting elf-shot and murdered.

Conversation at the table stopped when I dropped myself into the chair between Tybalt and Patrick. "I thought you needed to avoid being seen with us too much," I said. "Shouldn't you be sitting at the high table?"

"I needed to avoid arriving with you, or having my status overtly twined with yours," said Tybalt mildly. He began buttering a roll. "I will not be the last to hold my position, and did not wish to unduly handicap my successor by implying that the Court of Dreaming Cats owed some debt of fealty to the throne of the Mists. Now that everyone understands that I'm not domestic, I will do as cats have always done, and sit where I like. Besides, the conversation among Kings and Queens is dull as dishwater. Hence all the common men in Will's plays."

"He's a fucking dumbass, but his heart's in the right place," said the Luidaeg. "So, Toby, how goes the systematic alienation of every noble on the West Coast? Get yourself banned from any new kingdoms yet? I understand the Kingdom of Copper is a great place to never go."

"They won't be sending me invitations to tea anytime soon, but I think I've mostly managed not to get myself banned from entry," I said. I looked around, frowning. "Where's Walther?"

"Things got a little shouty at the conclave," said Quentin. "Then they got a lot shouty. Then they got screamy, with a side order of shrieky. Walther and Marlis are having dinner up in the room with the sleepers, supposedly so they can help Jin check on everyone's condition, but really, I think, because Walther was afraid somebody would dump something on him."

"Oh," I said. The rolls looked good. My stomach rumbled, reminding me that with one thing after another, I hadn't eaten nearly as much as I'd bled since getting out of bed. I snagged one, taking the butter knife out of Tybalt's hand, and focused on the Luidaeg again. "So when

I get out of here, I'm going to be checking my own blood memories for anything that seemed out of place when we first got to the conclave this evening, but this seems like a good time to ask: what can you tell me about fairy rings?"

The Luidaeg sat up straighter, blinking in surprise. Her eyes changed color with each blink, going from driftglass green to foam white, then to solid black, and finally back to their original shade. "Fairy rings? Why are you asking me about those?"

"The monarchs from Golden Shores brought them up during their questioning. Supposedly, fairy rings can move stuff through time?"

"Sort of," said the Luidaeg. She was still looking thoughtful. "Subjectively. It's . . . not that simple."

"So how simple is it?"

"A fairy ring is a stepping stone. A fairy ring takes someone or something and freezes them for however long they need to be kept still. It's not time travel. It's not jumping from one era to another. It's just . . . a pause, before things continue on their normal course. It feels like moving forward in time to the people who've been affected, because they were paused."

There was a clink. I turned to Tybalt. He had dropped his fork and was staring at the Luidaeg, pupils reduced to slits and cheeks gone pale. I reached over and touched his arm. He jumped, gaze flicking to me for a moment before his attention returned to her.

"Would it look . . . to someone on the outside of the ring, would it look like the person had just stopped for some reason?"

"Yes," said the Luidaeg. "That's part of why they were never as popular as elf-shot. With elf-shot, you put the person to sleep for a hundred years. You can move them, hide them, do whatever you need to with them. With a fairy ring, they're stuck in the circle. As soon as the magic powering the spell is exhausted, time will start moving for them again. Until then, unless you want to break the ring, you have to keep an eye on them to make sure nothing disturbs the spell. Any time a human wandered into the woods and wandered out a hundred years later, some poor sap had been punished with watching a mortal spend a century standing perfectly still. You can't even draw mustaches on the people, for fear that you'll knock them out of alignment and start the clock again."

"The way Antonio described the shadows shifting," I said. "It wasn't someone teleporting him. Time was passing outside the ring, and when the ring was broken—for whatever reason—the shadows looked like they had moved."

"It happened to you, too," said Tybalt. I turned to blink at him. He was still watching the Luidaeg, but he was speaking to me; that much was very clear. "We were in your chambers. You were about to kiss me. Do you remember?"

"I got stabbed right before I could," I said. "That sort of thing is pretty hard to forget."

"You stopped." He finally turned to look at me. "You were leaning in, and then you *stopped*. Not long—only a few seconds—but long enough for me to notice."

"Oh." *Oh.* I remembered the confused look on his face, the way he'd suddenly been staring at me. It couldn't have been a long pause without him becoming alarmed, but any pause at all would have been strange, given the situation. "Did you see anything? Smell anything?"

"I saw you go still, and I was focused on that," said Tybalt. "I think I would have noticed someone standing behind you."

"Not if they were in a chained fairy ring, under a don't-look-here," said the Luidaeg. We both turned to her. She shrugged. "Set up two rings. One for your target, one for yourself. Tie them together. Set the spell so that the first ring will break when the second ring is activated, and cast the don't-look-here just before you step into the first ring."

"So as soon as *I* stepped into the second ring, the first ring broke, and they could start moving again," I said. "They'd know where I was, because they were the one who set the trap, and they'd still be hidden by the don't-look-here. They were never aiming for Tybalt at all. They were aiming for me."

"Or for me," said Quentin. "I'm your squire. I could have been going to the room to fetch something for you. That's a lot of what normal squires do for their knights."

"Good thing we've never been normal," I said, a cold thread of fear winding through my veins. If Quentin had been killed . . . it would have ended my usefulness right then and there, at least for a time. The need for vengeance would have come eventually, but would it have been fast enough for me to find anything? Or would the trail have gone completely cold? I sadly suspected the latter. I had my weak points, and Quentin was well known to be one of them. Take him out, and you took me out just through proximity. "Why would you need a second ring if you had a don't-look-here?"

"Because fairy rings freeze *everything*. Otherwise, people would have used them for some nasty forms of biological warfare—find a strain of flu that affects purebloods, shove a carrier into a fairy ring, cast a spell to hide them, and then bring all your enemies to get breathed on. Once inside the ring, the person who was trying to harm you couldn't be smelled, not even by a Cu Sidhe, or otherwise detected. It would even hide the scent of their magic." The Luidaeg shook her head. "Nasty things, fairy rings."

"And the second ring? What broke it?"

"It wasn't meant to hold you. It was just meant to slow you down, and to break the first ring when it was activated. I'm guessing whoever cast it knew that stabbing you would break the ring, and didn't want to waste their time crafting something genuinely secure."

I looked at her. "How hard is it to make a fairy ring?"

"Just this side of impossible, if you don't know how it's done, but if you do? It's so easy a child could do it, or a changeling. Merlins used to use them as snares to catch their pureblood relatives, once upon a time. Everything we can use against humanity, humanity can also use against us. That's something to keep in mind when you're making a tool, or a weapon. Everything cuts both ways."

"Why didn't you bring this up before?"

She looked flustered. "To be honest—and I can't be anything but honest—I forgot. It's been so long since anyone has used them for anything, and they were always such a *small* magic. They didn't seem worth remembering."

That was sadly easy to believe. "What would I need?"

"To make the ring, intent, the right materials, and a small amount of power—a trickle, really. The ring itself is the key. The ring is what magnifies and intensifies the ritual. That's how a simple spell could hold someone captive for a hundred years. Look." The Luidaeg leaned over and plucked four spears of asparagus off the platter, holding them up like they were the most important thing in the world. "Plants work well, although fungus works better. Toadstools were traditional, but daisy chains were almost as common, at least for a while. Take the material you're planning to use, plait it together ..." Her fingers were quick and clever as they twisted the asparagus into a rough crown. She dropped it onto the table.

"Once your ring is done, you can activate it whenever you like." Pressing a forefinger against the ring of asparagus, the Luidaeg murmured a string of hissing, rolling syllables that didn't sound like anything else I'd ever heard. The air around us chilled, dropping in temperature until it felt like we were standing on the shore just as the tide rolled in.

Karen shivered. The Luidaeg raised her eyes.

"Patrick, if you would?"

Patrick nodded, picking up a piece of potato from his

own plate. He weighed it briefly in his hand before lob-bing it across the circle. Rather than flying straight into the Luidaeg's lap, it stopped in midair, frozen above the asparagus. The Luidaeg looked pleased with herself.

"It'll stay there until the spell wears off—ten, maybe fifteen minutes, since I didn't put much power into it—or until something disrupts the ring. Like so." She picked up her fork, leaned forward, and stabbed the asparagus. The piece of potato promptly fell to the table, where it rolled to a stop against her water glass. "As temporary prisons go, you won't find any finer. As useless things in this modern world go, well, they're tops at that, too."

"Except that someone has apparently been able to set at least three, maybe more, and use them to catch people unawares. It's like marshwater charms."

Tybalt frowned at me. Patrick asked, "What?"

"I used to use a lot of marshwater charms—mixtures of herbs and intent that would help me see through illu-sions, or keep an eye on a target even when someone was actively trying to counteract my tracking spells." I shook my head. "I didn't understand my own magic that well, and I was a lot weaker. I needed every advantage I could get. I always thought the purebloods were stupid for not using the little tools—I'd keep a spray bottle full of mint and pond scum in my glove compartment and think it made me so much smarter than them, and I still started forgetting about those things as soon as I, personally, didn't need them anymore. Don't you see? Something that small won't hold much magic, so even if the spell was cast by someone powerful, they won't leave enough of a trace for me to track. It's perfect if you're a murder-ous bastard who needs to be stopped."

"Your priorities are, as always, genuinely unique to you," said Tybalt.

I elbowed him lightly; he took the blow with good grace. "I'm serious. Whoever's doing this has already at-tacked us—whether I was the target or not, they knew harming anyone who was likely to be in that room would make me stop investigating. And it wasn't Duke Michel."

That got Patrick's attention. "How are you so sure?" he asked.

"For one thing, Dianda's not dead," I said. "People like him don't start with murder and back off to misdemeanor. It's either one or the other, or misdemeanor turning into manslaughter by mistake. For another thing, he was way too willing to let the High King ride his blood. Sure, he wasn't thrilled about it, but if he'd broken the Law, he would have fought more, because there's no way he wouldn't have been thinking about the murder when his blood was drawn. It's the old 'don't think about pink elephants' problem. If you have something you desperately don't want people to know, that's all you're going to be able to think about when the time comes."

"So we have two separate miscreants," said Tybalt. "We know the Duke was trying to suppress the elf-shot cure. What does this second assailant want? October and King Antonio have little to nothing in common with one another."

"Could be the same thing," said the Luidaeg. "This changes the status quo a lot."

I frowned. "The status quo . . ."

Quentin's frown mirrored mine. "What are you thinking?"

"I'm thinking that sometimes we make things too complicated," I said. "King Antonio was all about power, right? Not necessarily using it for anything; just having it." But he *had* been using it for something. He'd been using it to protect his family, for all the good that had done him. "This wouldn't be the first time someone assumed I do the things I do because I want to support the monarchy blindly as a concept, rather than because I think they're actually what's right. Me, Quentin, Tybalt — any of the three targets you could reasonably hit by setting a trap in my room would undermine the local status

quo." That was before taking into account Quentin's position as Crown Prince. If someone knew about *that* . . .

"Dianda doesn't affect the status quo on the land,"
said Patrick. "She's well-inclined, because she married
me, but she has few standing alliances, apart from Goldengreen."

"And being allied with a County doesn't do much if
you're not also allied with the Kingdom it's in," I said. It
was tempting to view the attack on Dianda as related,
especially given that Quentin and Dean were dating—
but I didn't think that was common knowledge yet, and
again, for Quentin to be the common factor would require people to know about his heritage. We weren't seeing any sign of that. Quentin was vulnerable while he
was with me; none of the attacks had directly targeted
him. "So, yeah, we're definitely looking at two different
people here. But have all the attacks been about opportunity, or was the attack on King Antonio planned?"

"I don't know," said Quentin.

"Neither do I," I said. "On the plus side, I might have
a way of finding out who does. Dinner can wait. Can you
pass your steak knife?"

Quentin handed me his knife. Tybalt narrowed his
eyes.

"If you're about to do what I'm certain you're about
to do, can you please do me the immense favor of *not*
slicing your palm through the center?" he asked plain-
tively. "I know you heal with ridiculous speed—although
you did not, I should remind you, the first time you decided slicing your hand open was an expedient way of
getting what you wanted—but it still makes my teeth
hurt to see you treat yourself so."

"I'll skip the palm this time, I promise," I said, and
pressed the knife against the top of my wrist, pushing
down until the edge bit into the soft skin. I gritted my
teeth. "You'd think healing fast would come with reduced pain sensitivity."

"Nope," said the Luidaeg. Her voice was soft. I glanced up. She looked at me with sad, driftglass-colored eyes, and said, "Those who heal the fastest have always had to hurt the worst. It's the cost of being able to handle so much trauma. The pain will always be eager to remind you that it has a claim."

"Swell," I muttered, and yanked the knife toward myself, angling my wrist so I wouldn't bleed on my dress. The skin parted and blood welled to the surface, bright and coppery and smelling of secrets. I wanted it. The sight of it revolted me, but I wanted it all the same—a paradox that had been becoming increasingly common since my heritage had been shifted more toward the fae. Quentin stiffened. So did Patrick. Daoine Sidhe were blood-workers too, even if their talents didn't quite match my own. I offered the two of them an encouraging smile, lowered my mouth to my wrist, and drank.

The taste of blood filled my mouth and chased away everything else. As always, it made me feel stronger, more prepared to face the world around me. It was *my* blood: it should have had no strength to offer me that I didn't already possess, and yet somehow, it did. Magic is weird. Magic has always been weird.

The smell of cut-grass and copper began to rise in the air around me, the copper trending, as always, more and more toward the bloody. One day I was going to lose the metallic aspect entirely, and just smell like a pastoral crime scene. I knew people were stopping to stare. I closed my eyes to shut them out, drinking deeper, looking for the place where the present would drop away and I would fall into the red haze of my own blood memories.

You're trying too hard, I thought. *This should be easy.* I'd done this . . . well, not hundreds of times, because there wasn't that much call for my specific skill set, but quite a few times. Often enough that it had started becoming easier. Never easy. Easier was a matter of degrees: it was no longer like clawing my way uphill through an avalanche, no longer like drowning, no longer a matter of risking my life every time I tasted blood. It was still difficult.

You're trying too hard, I thought again, and let go, falling down into the red. The sounds of the tables around us went away, replaced by the sounds of the gallery from earlier. This was my memory, not someone else's: it was crystal clear, with none of the confusion or disassociation that I was accustomed to encountering when I rode the blood.

High King Aethlin was speaking. I ignored him in favor of looking at the crowd, trying to find some hint of tension or surprise. I couldn't do anything I hadn't done the first time—this was a memory, not a dream—but I had looked at the crowd the first time. I just hadn't known what I was seeing.

Several of the gathered nobles looked confused by what was going on. Confusion seemed to be the order of the day. But the King and Queen of Highmountain looked angry. Actively, furiously mad, like something had disrupted their plans. And their handmaiden, that sad-eyed, downcast Barrow Wight, looked openly terrified. She was staring at me, her eyes wide and her jaw slack. How had I not noticed her the first time?

The answer followed the question without pause. I hadn't noticed her because she was just a servant, and I'd been focusing on the purebloods as the important ones. I'd done to her exactly what so many of them had done to me. I had ignored her.

I'd known I was losing my humanity, but that was the moment when I realized I was never going to get it back.

I broke out of the blood memories with a gasp, pulling my mouth away from my wrist. The wound there had long since healed, leaving only a smear of drying blood to mark where it had been. I looked wildly around, searching the nearby tables for the King and Queen of

Highmountain. Someone pushed a napkin into my hand. I wiped my mouth, and kept looking.

"What did you see?" asked Tybalt.

"Not sure yet," I said. My table contained a Firstborn and a Duke on a hair-trigger. The last thing I wanted to do was trigger an international incident if I could avoid it. I kept scanning the room. "Is anyone missing? Do you see any holes?"

"Someone's always missing," said the Luidaeg. "That's the nature of the beast."

"Where's the King of Highmountain?" asked Quentin.

"Show me where you're looking," I said. He pointed. I followed the angle of his finger to a table on the other side of the room, where the Queen of Highmountain sat surrounded by a group of minor nobles. She was laughing, a goblet in her hand and an expression of studious unconcern on her face. She looked like every other carefree monarch in the place. It was amazing how many of them were smiling and clearly content, despite the seriousness of the situation. They wanted to be released from their captivity, but apart from that, this was exactly the sort of world that they expected to be waiting for them. Fancy meals, beautiful rooms, and every need met without their being required to lift a finger.

There was an open seat next to her. The King wasn't there. Neither was the sad-eyed handmaiden.

"What do you know about them?" I asked, without taking my eyes off of her.

"Verona and Kabos," said Quentin. He didn't hesitate. This was the sort of thing he didn't have to think about. "He founded the Kingdom, she became Queen when she married him. They're traditionalists. Highmountain predates most of the demesnes around it, because they'd been trying to get away from the 'decadent' coastal kingdoms."

"Fae puritans, got it," I said. "No surnames?"

"They've never needed one. No heirs, either. They've been married for three hundred years with no kids. Daoine Sidhe, both of them, and supposedly Kabos was in consideration for the throne of North America before it was given to Viveka Sollys, mother of Aethlin Sollys, third in line for the High Crown of Albany."

It took me a moment to puzzle through that. Then: "You're saying they've been in charge in Highmountain since before the United States was founded, and they don't like change."

"Yes," said Quentin.

This conclave was the ultimate expression of change. Changelings and the untitled were being allowed to speak as if they were equal to monarchs. The fact that we were speaking about something that would impact us all didn't matter as much as the fact that we were opening our mouths. King Antonio had been an asshole according to the people who knew him, but he hadn't enforced the classic lines of status and standing: he'd allowed people to be whoever they wanted to be, providing they were able to fight for and maintain their positions. He'd been a populist, in a lot of ways. If no one knew he had an heir waiting to claim the throne—if the assumption was that when he died, someone else would be able to take Angels and run it as a more traditional monarchy—

I stood so fast that the legs of my chair scraped against the floor. Antonio had been an excellent target because he'd been alone, but the attack had happened at mealtime. If I was right, this was the same setting, and another attack could be imminent. If I was wrong, the King of Highmountain was alone somewhere, and could be in danger. We had a wealth of potential targets, and either way, he was a person of great concern.

"Quentin, Patrick, find King Kabos," I said, scanning the ballroom again, this time trying to think like a bigoted pureblood who hated change. Who were the best targets? Chrysanthe and Theron seemed obvious, but in a weird way, that was what would keep them safe. They isolated changelings by removing them to Golden Shore and keeping them out of the way of the purebloods of the world. What they were doing was good and valuable and necessary, and yet it was almost the expression of a pureblood dream—sending all the changelings away to live on a farm and not bother anyone.

Arden was sitting on the dais with the High King, High Queen, and Queen Siwan. She'd been able to ascend to her throne because of a changeling and a King of Cats, and her upbringing hadn't prepared her to enforce the sort of rules most nobles found to be second nature. She thought more like a changeling than like a queen. But attacking her would mean risking the High King and High Queen. Maybe this would go that far. Maybe it wouldn't. I just didn't think she'd be the third target. Not when they still thought they could get away without being caught. Siwan was protected by the same logic.

I heard a sound like tearing metal, close enough that it seemed to fill the world. Once again there was a faint, distant scent I couldn't quite identify: attenuated magic, so bleached and thin it was like a ghost of itself. I whipped around. Karen was behind me, wide-eyed and pale, with little red dots on the white fabric of her dress. Little red spots, as if from arterial spray. She wasn't hurt; the blood wasn't hers. It wasn't mine, either. I would have noticed.

The world seemed to slow down. I knew I wasn't malingering, no matter how much I didn't want to see, but it felt like it took forever for me to turn and look at Tybalt, who was staring down at the stake protruding from his chest with wide-eyed shock. His gaze moved to me, pupils thinning to slits, before he collapsed.

Someone screamed as he hit the floor.

It may even have been me.

EIGHTEEN

"*J*IN!" THE NAME was ripped out of me, unthinking. A second name followed it: "*Siwan!*" Tybalt was bleeding; Tybalt was *dying*. Being a King of Cats made him sturdier than he had any right to be, but he wasn't me. He couldn't walk to the edge of death and come back none the worse for wear.

If his heart stopped beating, it might not start again. I could lose him.

I should have been screaming for him, not for the Queen of Silences, but it was her name I howled again and again as I fell to my knees and gathered my wounded lover in my arms, trying to stop the bleeding with the heels of my hands. It was hurting him, I knew it was hurting him, but that didn't matter, because he didn't have enough blood to keep on losing it. He needed to keep what little he had left.

Blood . . . it frothed at the corners of his mouth, a clear sign that the spike had pierced his lung, just like the last one had pierced mine. His breathing was labored and he was struggling to keep his eyes focused. They were fixed on my face, never wavering, like he was greedy for the sight of me.

"I need a fucking *medic!*" I shrieked. My throat felt like it had been stripped bare, like I wasn't giving it time to heal between screams. Tough.

There was a popping sound, and the smell of blackberry flowers and redwood sap. I looked up. Arden was in front of me, her dress disheveled, her hands locked around the upper arms of Queen Siwan Yates of Silences. Siwan's eyes widened as she realized what she was looking at. She'd been on the other side of the ballroom only an instant before. She must have heard the commotion, but she hadn't understood what it meant.

"Oh, oak and ash . . ." she breathed.

"Fix him," I commanded. "You fixed Holger's arm. Fix *him*." Jin would have been better. Where was Jin? Probably in the damn tower room with Walther and Marlis, avoiding the conclave. Curse her eyes.

Thank Oberon for intelligent people. Siwan's expression changed as she realized what I was asking. Offering a quick nod, she knelt and said, "I need flame. Flame, a knife, and as much blood as you're willing to give to me."

"Take it all, I don't care," I said, and held up my hand. A knife was slapped into it. I glanced up. The Luidaeg was standing there.

"Flame I can give you, but it will cost," she said, speaking fast. She knew as well as I did that we had no time to waste. "Will you pay?"

The Luidaeg did nothing for free. It wasn't in her nature, and more, it wasn't in the rules of her position as the sea witch. I nodded, not bothering to ask her price. Anything she wanted, I would pay. I would pay twice over, if that was what was required to save Tybalt.

She looked oddly sad as she returned my nod and held out her hands, suddenly full of green marshfire that burned and crackled with a chilly heat. I looked to Siwan.

"You need to be bleeding now," she said, voice tight. "I need marigolds, rosemary, love-lies-bleeding, and a handful of fishbones."

Arden stepped backward into a portal that opened in the air just in time to accommodate her. Karen took off running, presumably to scavenge supplies from the nearest table. And I did exactly what Tybalt had asked me not to do, and drove the knife through the center of my palm. The pain was excruciating. Watching him struggle to breathe was worse. The pain gave me something to focus on, something I could *hate* without worrying about whether my emotions were getting in the way of my actions.

"Keep bleeding," snapped Siwan, cupping her hands under mine. She began chanting in quick, fluid syllables. The smell of yarrow and sweet cinquefoil rose between us, sketched over the blood.

"Toby."

My name was barely a whisper. I glanced down. Tybalt's eyes were fixed on me, his jaw trembling with the effort of speech. He smiled when he saw me looking at him. In some ways, that was the worst thing that had happened since all this had started. He *smiled*, like there was no way this could be my fault; like I shouldn't have figured it all out sooner, like I wasn't supposed to save him.

"I . . . very much . . . wanted to marry you," he whispered, and closed his eyes.

My own eyes widened until it felt like the skin around them would tear, put under too much strain by the effort of keeping myself from breaking apart. "No," I said, and gathered him closer with my free arm, still bleeding for Siwan, the knife jutting from my hand. "No, Tybalt, no, you don't get to do this. Just because you're a cat, that doesn't mean you get to do this. You need to stay. You need to stay with *me*."

Siwan continued chanting. Arden had returned, and she and Karen were throwing things into the flame the Luidaeg held, following the instructions Siwan muttered between phrases. Jin was nowhere to be seen. All I could do was bleed. That's something I've always excelled at.

It didn't feel like it was enough, and so I bent and kissed him, hoping that something in the fairy tales Amandine had read me when I was a child would finally turn out to be true: hoping a kiss might convince him to stay.

His lips tasted like blood. A red veil slipped over the world, and I saw myself looking down at him, terror and compassion in my eyes. I was so beautiful when he was looking at me. I had never felt like I was that beautiful before.

This is always how I see you, little fish. The thought was in the blood, amused and pained and quietly furious. He thought he was seeing me for the last time. He was taking as much of me with him as he could, as he left me for the night-haunts.

I had never been so angry in my life. I raised my head, glancing toward Siwan. The blood in her hands had hardened into balls of what looked like red-frosted glass, all different sizes, none bigger than a cherry. She stopped chanting and looked at me.

"Get it out of him, now," she said, and dumped the glass into the flame.

"Not the way we got it out of you," said the Luidaeg, before I could move. "Shoving it through will kill him."

When did everyone around me get so *fragile*? I turned my attention to the spike in Tybalt's chest, moving to wrap my hands around it. The knife jutting from my palm made the motion impossible to finish. With a snarl, I ripped it loose and tossed it aside, not even waiting for the wound to close before I grabbed the rosewood stake and began to haul. Splinters bit into my palms, drawing more blood. I let them. Anything that could help me now was welcome; anything that could make this a little bit easier, a little more possible, was something to be absolutely desired.

The hooks on the harpoon caught and tore at his flesh as I pulled. I would have done anything to take that pain away from him. Anything.

Tybalt still wasn't moving. I couldn't be sure, as I wrested the stake loose and dropped it to the floor beside me, that he was breathing. I also couldn't allow myself to dwell on that thought. If I decided he was lost—if I let myself lose hope—then I was going to be finished, and this time, I wasn't sure I'd be able to find the strength to start over. My heart had been broken too many times. It no longer had the capacity to heal the way it once had. The rest of me might be immortal at this point, but my heart? No. That was wearing out.

The stake left a hole in Tybalt's chest that seemed deep as a well, at least for the split-second that it was empty. Then blood rushed in to fill the space I'd created, flooding everything in red.

And Tybalt stopped breathing.

I didn't think. I didn't pause. I just moved, taking a deep breath and clamping my mouth down over his. The taste of blood filled the world, almost choking me. I pulled back and pushed down on the side of his chest that didn't have a hole in it, trying to keep his heart beating as I forced air into his lungs and then pushed down on his chest again and again, doing everything I could to make him stay. Sweet Titania, let him stay.

Every time our lips touched, the memories were there, rushing over me, overwhelming me. Not all of them held my face—that would have been too much to bear—but there were so many of them. I saw Raj as a little boy, kitten-gangly and unsure, and was stunned by the depth of the love Tybalt had felt for that child, even when he'd known that Raj's father, Samson, hungered for his throne. I saw a red-haired woman with golden Torquill eyes, heard Tybalt's voice whispering *September* like a prayer, and knew her for his first love; I saw a dark-haired woman with nothing fae about her, and knew her for his first wife. His entire life was there, written in the blood drying on his lips, and I kept on breathing for him, for both of us, because I couldn't let him go. I couldn't. I *couldn't*.

.

Siwan was chanting again. Breathe in, breathe out. The taste of blood, and the laughter of a girl with calico hair.

The smell of my own magic rose around us, cut-grass and copper and an overlay of iced yarrow, like a frozen field. Breathe in, breathe out. The taste of blood, and a flash of my face, weary and bruised with iron poisoning, accompanied by a sudden, crushing terror that added even more weight to the terror I was already feeling.

Breathe in, breathe out.

Tybalt coughed.

I pulled back, heart hammering in my chest, and watched wide-eyed as he coughed again, before taking a deep, half-choked breath. The pit in his chest seemed to be getting shallower by the second, displacing the blood pooled there. Siwan was still chanting, her hands pressed to the base of his ribs — as close as she'd been able to get to the wound before without actually reaching *inside* of him. He was healing. He was getting better.

He was healing. I stiffened. My body was designed for that sort of magically accelerated recovery, and it still left me dazed and dizzy from the calories it burned. I looked frantically at the circle of people that had formed around us, seizing on Arden as the one who would need the least explanation.

"I need a gallon of cream and a bowl of raw salmon," I called, struggling to keep my words clear and concise enough that she would be able to understand them. Then I gave up, and shrieked "*Now!*" so loudly that the effort hurt my throat again, if only for a moment.

Arden looked surprised. Then she raised her hand and swept a circle in the air, disappearing through it. The scent of redwood sap attempted to overwhelm the smell of blood, but failed, disappearing completely into the red.

That brief distraction had been long enough for the hole in Tybalt's chest to become a shallow divot. New skin was forming over the wound, healing by the second. It was going slower now. The magic Siwan had been able to coax from my blood was running out fast—maybe too fast. There was internal damage as well, and I wasn't sure there had been time for all of it to heal before the surface started closing. I turned to her, pleading mutely.

She shook her head. "Our bodies aren't like yours. We're not made to do this. I can't treat him twice in quick succession; he wouldn't survive."

"Arden is bringing meat, cream—"

"And that would be the answer, if he were like you. He'd be able to rebuild what he's lost, and keep healing. He's *not you*. He needs to recover on his own."

I turned back to Tybalt. He was still breathing, but he seemed to be having trouble; his breath kept catching, and the pain in his expression was obvious. I reached out with one shaking, blood-smeared hand, smoothing the hair back from his face. He opened his eyes. Not all the way, but enough that I could see him looking at me. I forced myself to smile.

"Hey," I said. "How are you feeling?"

"'Tis not as deep as a well or as wide as a church door, but it will do," he whispered, voice rasping.

I wrinkled my nose. "Don't do that. Don't quote Shakespeare at me when you think you're going to die."

"He was a lovely man. You would have liked him." Tybalt winced, but didn't close his eyes. "Little fish, what did you do?"

I would normally have objected to him using that name for me twice in quick succession, but he hadn't used it the first time: the memories stored in his blood had done that. It was a name born of aggravation and affection, and I'd never been so glad to hear it. "Just a little blood," I said, letting my bloody fingers rest against his cheek. "You were hurt. We helped."

"I hate to disillusion you, but I'm still hurt." He grimaced. "Quite badly. I feel as if some things have been knocked askew. I am . . . afraid I won't be able to make it to the wedding."

"Over my dead body." The smell of blackberry flowers intruded. I looked up. Arden was pushing through the crowd, a tray in her hands. I shifted so I could prop Tybalt's head up on my leg. "I need you to try and drink as much of this milk as you can. If you can eat, do that too, but you're going to drink."

"October—"

"*Drink it.*" I shook my head. I was shivering uncontrollably. Finding a way to make it stop would have been too much trouble. Instead, I waited for Arden to come closer, and reached up to take the bowl of milk from her tray. It was unpasteurized, thick, with cream hanging heavy at the top. I lowered it to Tybalt's lips.

He gave me a dubious look. Breathing was clearly getting harder for him.

"Please."

He drank.

He drank all the milk, and when I took the plate, he managed to force down a few mouthfuls of fatty salmon, chewing thoroughly before he swallowed. Finally, he sagged against me.

"As last meals go, I could have been offered worse, but I beg you, no more," he whispered. "Something is broken. Toby . . ."

"You need time to heal. We need access to better magic. We need to find Jin and get her to put you back together." I looked up at Arden, the plate of salmon still clutched in my hand. It should have seemed comic, but under the circumstances, it was just sad. "Arden. He needs time."

She blinked at me, clearly not understanding. Tybalt took a sharp breath. He clearly did.

"Please," I said. "He needs *time.*"

"He needs time that won't kill him," said the Luidaeg, and pushed past Arden to kneel at Tybalt's other side.

She moved her hand in the air in a quick but complicated movement. When she was done, an arrow rested in her palm. It was short, no more than five inches in length, with a shaft of black wood too warped and riddled with thorns to have ever flown. The fletching was owl feather and dried leaves, and the tip was obsidian black, gleaming with oily rainbows.

Looking at Tybalt solemnly, the Luidaeg said, "I promise this is of my own making, and that it carries nothing more than the sleeping spell it was intended to spread. No poison, no tricks, no lies. You'll wake when your time is done, and we'll have had the time to heal you."

"What if they find against the cure?" asked Tybalt, his eyes darting to me.

In that instant, I knew why he was worried. I forced myself to smile. "I'll be here," I said. "I'll burn the mortality out of myself if I have to, and I'll be immortal, and I'll be here. For you, forever. Just don't leave me now."

"You know I've never wanted—"

"*Don't tell me what to do,*" I hissed, my smile dying. "Stay with me. Whatever it costs, stay with me."

Tybalt nodded fractionally. "Then yes. Let it be done; let me rest."

I leaned down to kiss him. He kissed me back, and I could have stayed that way forever, threats of violence and the taste of blood be damned. He wasn't going to leave me. I was home.

The tension went out of him, his lips going dead beneath mine. I gasped and pulled back. His eyes were closed; he was limp and motionless, and the Luidaeg's arrow protruded from his shoulder, the tip buried just deep enough to break the skin. I turned to look at her. She looked solemnly back.

"You would have fucked around and kept on promising to wait for him and all that bullshit, and you wouldn't have been able to get anything done," she said. There was no accusation or blame in her tone. Everyone around us was silent, too stunned to speak. She shook her head. "I need you moving. There was an attack. Find out who. Find out why. Stop this."

Stop this: yes. It needed to be stopped. I paused to kiss Tybalt one last time—his forehead, and not his distressingly slack lips—before standing. The knife I'd used to cut my palm was gone, lost somewhere in the blood slick covering most of the floor. I turned to Arden.

"I need a sword. Mine's in the trunk of my car, and I can't go outside like this." Even if I hadn't been covered in blood, I couldn't afford to waste the time.

"Take mine." The voice was Sylvester's. I turned. He had unstrapped the scabbard from around his waist, and was offering it to me. I raised my eyebrows, and he said, "You couldn't come armed because the nobility might take offense. The outside nobles couldn't come armed because it would have been a declaration of war. I live here. This is my home. I'll die here. No one, not even my queen, can tell me not to carry my father's sword."

"Fine," I said, and reached out to snatch the scabbard from him. It was difficult to get the belt to fasten around my waist. Not only was I substantially thinner than he was, but my hands were so thick with blood that my fingers kept slipping and sticking as I fumbled with the buckle. It didn't matter. Nothing mattered except finding the person who'd hurt Tybalt, and making them understand that they'd made a mistake. A huge mistake. Maybe the last mistake they would ever make.

I looked to Arden. Aethlin and Maida flanked her, one on either side, like they could catch their newest vassal if she fell. Maida's cheeks were flushed, and Aethlin kept stealing glances at the blood covering the floor. They looked like alcoholics trying to choose between an AA meeting and a bender. I was willing to bet I could find the same look on every Daoine Sidhe in the room. Blood held power, and secrets, and the blood of a King of Cats was a rare treat.

"Don't let anyone touch his blood," I said, voice cold and angry. "He has a right to his privacy." I'd seen too much, and I was probably closer to him than anyone else in the world. No, not probably: I'd seen his ghosts. I was the last one he loved enough to share them with.

"I won't," said Aethlin. "He'll be looked after."

"Good." I let my eyes shift to Tybalt. They would move him soon, clean him up, and consign him to that quiet attic room where the sleepers lay, waiting for their wakeup calls to come. A day or a hundred years, it wouldn't matter; he'd sleep through them all the same, not dying, but not getting any better, either, not without outside help. Jin would know what to do, how to put him back together. She would make sure that he lived, and when he woke up, I would be here waiting for him. Whether that wait was at the expense of my thinning humanity would be determined by what the gathered kings and queens of North America decided about the cure. If they decided not to use it . . .

Raj was going to be very surprised to learn that he was King now.

This stake wasn't quite like the one that had hit me: it was more like a thick spear, designed for throwing. It had hit Tybalt in the chest while he was seated, and it had gone in squarely, not at an angle. That implied a hard throw from nearby. I moved to stand behind his seat, crouching and narrowing my eyes. There was no table behind us; it was a clear walkway, intended to leave room for the servants who were working the dinner. I straightened and walked around the table, stopping when I was on the opposite side from Tybalt's place. I looked back once, aligning myself, before beginning slowly forward, my eyes trained firmly on the ground.

Here was where the Luidaeg had walked to her own

seat. Here was where the servants had passed. And here . . . I crouched down.

There wasn't much to see. If not for the perfectly polished wood of the floor, there wouldn't have been anything. But Arden's staff had cleaned this place so well that I could have eaten off any surface that struck my fancy, and that made the thin streaks where someone had drawn a circle of marshwater and mold all too visible. Those marks would have been scuffed away by feet or washed away by a charmaid if everything had gone as planned, leaving the spell unremarked.

I dropped to my knees, getting my nose as close to the floor as I could and breathing in deep. There was nothing there for me to latch onto, no trace of magic to follow back to its source. Despair flooded over me. I was never going to find the attacker. Tybalt was asleep, and we were all still in danger, and there was nothing I could do about it.

"Oak and ash, October, *think*," I muttered, still staring at the streaks on the floor. This wasn't a time for self-pity. This was a time for solutions. How did I usually solve something that seemed impossible?

With blood, or by asking for help. Well, blood had already done everything it could. That meant it was time to try another way. I sat up straighter, looking over my shoulder to the crowd. "Quentin, find Madden," I said. "I need him."

Quentin nodded and disappeared into the crowd. I turned back to the circle on the floor, trying to tease what information I could out of it. The streaky lines were thin, and the circle itself was no more than a foot and a half in diameter; it couldn't have held someone much larger than I was, and I wasn't sure it could have held *me* comfortably. We were looking for someone small but strong, capable of slinging a rosewood spear hard enough to pierce bone. There were races in Faerie who had that sort of intrinsic strength. They were dangerous as all hell.

That eliminated about half the conclave, though. The centaur King of Copper couldn't have fit inside the circle. The Candela from Angels who remained couldn't have thrown the spear. There were answers to be found, if I took the time, and looked for them.

Trolls were that strong. Trolls, and Goblins, and Huldra, and Barrow Wights. Barrow Wights . . .

The sound of footsteps demanded my attention. I raised my head to find Madden and Quentin next to me, carefully out of arm's reach. I straightened, pointing to the circle.

"Madden, I need you to find the person who drew this. Please." I was starting to have suspicions. I needed them confirmed.

The burly Cu Sidhe looked surprised for only a second. Then he nodded and folded in on himself, the air shimmering for an instant before the man was gone, replaced by a white-furred, red-eared dog. Madden pressed his nose against the floor, sniffing. His ears pricked forward. He barked once, sharply, raising his head and looking to me.

"Good," I said softly. "Fetch."

Madden took off running. I followed close behind.

NINETEEN

MADDEN AND I WERE out of the dining room and running down the hall before I realized that Quentin was running next to me. I couldn't glare at him without stopping or losing my step, so I contented myself with shooting him a sharp sidelong look.

"What are you doing here?" I demanded.

"Being a good squire," he said. There was a stubborn note in his voice that seemed first incongruous, and then so familiar that I could have laughed, if it wouldn't have made me start crying. He sounded like me. He sounded exactly like me.

"Just don't get yourself killed," I said, and kept running, following Madden's lead.

The halls weren't empty. Members of Arden's staff were moving here and there, carrying linens or trays from one room to another. Maintenance was always a challenge in a knowe this size, and having this many people in residence, however temporarily, made the job harder. Some of these people probably hadn't slept in days, and wouldn't until the conclave ended. They moved aside when they saw Madden coming, and stayed pressed against the walls as we passed. Madden paid them no real mind, and so I didn't either. We were trusting in his nose right now, and if I started to question it, we would have nothing. Better to follow this lead than to harass some poor, confused kitchen staffer who just wanted to get the dishes put away.

We ran until we reached a closed door. Madden stopped there, barking. I stepped past him and tugged on the handle, revealing the stairs on the other side. Madden took off immediately, rushing past me, onward and upward. I followed him, and Quentin followed me, and there was nothing in the world but running. It was almost nice. While we were in pursuit, I didn't have to think about the past or the future, what had happened or what was to come. I only needed to think about where I was going, about making sure my feet hit the steps and not the empty air. If I fell, I'd get back up again, but we would lose time, and time was something we didn't have to spare.

The stairs ended in another door. Here, Madden stopped, but didn't bark; instead, he pawed at the landing, blunt claws making a faint scraping noise. He followed the motion with an expectant look from me to the door and back again. I didn't have to be a genius to know what he wanted. I turned to Quentin, making a wholly unnecessary shushing motion, and reached for the door handle.

It wasn't locked. I pushed the door gently open, revealing a guest parlor. It looked similar to the main room of Patrick and Dianda's suite, save for the absence of a pond in the middle of the floor. Which made sense: a pond was the sort of feature most people would find more inconvenient and perplexing than anything else. The furniture was all redwood and purple velvet, and the open windows looked out on the high forest. There were no people in evidence.

Madden drew back his lips, showing his teeth, while his throat vibrated in an almost silent snarl. I placed a hand on his head, letting him know I understood, before drawing Sylvester's sword and starting into the room. If anyone came at me, I would be prepared. More importantly, I would be between them and Quentin.

Would it be murder if I killed the people who'd hurt Tybalt, who'd killed King Antonio? Or would it be punishment for their own violations of the Law? I'd been forgiven by the High King once before, when I'd killed Blind Michael. He could forgive me again if it came to that, and in the end, it didn't matter. If I killed them, it would be because they needed to die. Because they'd done too much damage. Because they'd come into a situation that could have been bloodless, even peaceful, and turned it into something terrible. Would Duke Michel have attacked Dianda if there hadn't already been a murder, giving him a convenient scapegoat for the crime? We had never needed to fight this way.

And that was all just pretty words. If I killed them, it was going to be because they'd hurt Tybalt. They had tried to take him away from me. They might even have succeeded, at least for a century. A century! I was a changeling. No one had the right to make me wait that long for anything. I wanted them to hurt.

We crept across the parlor, Madden in the lead, until we reached a half-closed door in an ornate frame that looked like pile upon pile of evergreen branches. We stopped there, Quentin behind me, Madden still slightly ahead, although he was crouching until his belly brushed the carpet. Someone on the other side of the door was weeping.

"Stop your caterwauling and lay out my dress," snapped a voice. "The cat's dead by now. There's no way he survived a shaft to the lung. The High King will call the conclave back to order at any moment, and we need to be in our seats looking properly contrite when the lecturing begins. As if that foolish populist knows the first thing about ruling, or how it's meant to be done."

The crying continued. Another voice, this one male, said, "Be glad we haven't punished you for missing the first time. You should have killed him before, not wounded the other one. She would have been off the scent if you'd killed the cat. Everyone knows the little Torquill bitch is besotted with the cat-king. She'll never be able to serve with him gone."

It was nice to have some of my suspicions confirmed. I tensed, motioning for Quentin to stay behind me, and stepped forward. It was a simple matter to kick the door open, slamming it against the wall and revealing the dressing room on the other side. The King and Queen of Highmountain turned to gape at me. Their silent, shivering handmaiden was standing between them, her hands pressed over her face. She was pale, seeming to have less substance than she should have, even though she took up space like anyone else. I breathed in almost unconsciously, looking for the scent of her magic. I couldn't find it, but I didn't need to.

The Barrow Wight had been the attacker, at the orders of her lieges. Her heritage explained the strength behind the attacks. Barrow Wights are surprisingly strong for their size, probably because they need to be able to move heavy stones in order to access the burial mounds where they traditionally make their homes.

"You can't *be* here," snapped Verona.

"Is that blood? Is it yours?" asked Kabos, sounding fascinated and horrified at the same time. He was Daoine Sidhe; of course he wanted to know whose blood I carried with me, whose secrets could be teased from the stains on my clothing and skin.

I moved Sylvester's sword between us, aiming the point at his chest. In that moment, I wished for a gun, a bow and arrow, for anything that would have allowed me to end his pitiful existence without having to depend on my paltry skills with a blade. Sylvester had done his best to teach me, but my lessons had been more than a year ago, and I wasn't sure what I was going to do if they fought back.

"In the name of High King Aethlin and High Queen Maida Sollys of the Westlands, you are under arrest for the death of King Antonio Robertson of Angels," I said, voice tight and angry in my throat. There was nothing I could do to keep my fury from showing, so I didn't even try.

Verona looked momentarily surprised. Then, slowly, she smiled. "One death," she said. "You're accusing us of one death. Is your beast-man lover still breathing, then? That's a pity. It would have been nice if the world could have been that much cleaner. Whoever hurt him was trying to do you a favor, darling. Imagine the children."

I snarled and started to step forward. A hand on my arm stopped me. I glanced to the side. Quentin had hold of me and was shaking his head, expression grim.

"Don't," he said. "She's not worth it."

"I am a Queen, child," snapped Verona. "You're what, a squire? The second son of some noble too minor to keep their spare offspring from being given into a changeling's care? You have no right to judge my worth."

I'd been there when people said similar things to Quentin, but that had been before I knew his true identity. This time, I could see the struggle in his eyes. He outranked this woman, even as a Prince; it would have been well within his parents' power to strip the regents of Highmountain of their thrones and give them to whomever Quentin chose. And instead, for the sake of his blind fosterage, Quentin had to let them say whatever they wanted to him, and just take it. He'd been living with this ever since he'd arrived in the Bay Area, and it was a miracle he'd borne it as well as he had.

"I suppose I don't," he said. "But I'm not a murderer, so there's that."

"But neither are we," said Kabos, sounding offended, like he couldn't understand why we were still talking about this when it was so clearly unnecessary. "I never hurt anyone. Neither did my dear Verona. We can't be held responsible for the actions of our servants."

The handmaiden was still covering her face with her hands, narrow shoulders shaking with the effort of keeping herself together. I gaped at the rulers of Highmountain, the extent of what they'd done—if not why—finally beginning to make itself clear.

Oberon's Law was simple, to prevent misinterpretation. Killing a pureblood outside of a formally declared war was a crime punishable by death. Forgiveness for breaking the Law was possible only under the most extremely extenuating circumstances, such as when I had killed Blind Michael—and even then, there would always be people who thought the punishments laid down by Oberon should have trumped any forgiveness the world chose to offer. Nowhere in the Law did it say "but it's okay if someone else made you do it." Nowhere did it say "if the people who control your life order you to take someone else's, we will find a way to forgive you."

"Arrest her," said Verona, flapping a hand in the direction of her handmaid. "Take her away. She was never a very good servant, anyway. Always wrinkled my gowns and pulled my hair. Her little sister will be a much better ladies' maid, I'm sure, now that she understands what the job entails."

The handmaid's shoulders stopped shaking. It was a small change, but a palpable one. Before, we'd been in the company of a living, if terrified, person. Now we were standing next to a statue.

"We did nothing," said Kabos. "The High King can ride our blood, and all he'll find is the truth: that we never laid a hand on anyone. We are innocent."

"I wouldn't go that far," I spat.

"No?" Verona raised an eyebrow. "We can't be held responsible for our thoughts, surely. That would be unjust and wrong. You, of all people, who has fought so hard for the rights of the deposed, must want us to be judged on what we've done, and not what we may have thought of doing."

The handmaid lowered her hands from her face. She was pretty, if pale, in the way of Barrow Wights; most of them stayed in their mounds, avoiding the company of the living, who moved too fast and wanted too much. Stacy's ancestors, whoever they may have been, would have been considered strange by their pureblood kin for loving another of the fae, even if it had only been for a night. Barrow Wights kept to themselves.

"Don't touch my sister," she said, in a voice like wind through a graveyard, thin and cold and filled with ghosts. "She isn't yours. That wasn't what you promised me."

"We never promised you anything," said Verona.

"I'm the one with the sword here, so maybe you could stop arguing and just agree that I'm arresting you all, okay?" I straightened the arm holding Sylvester's sword, trying to look like I wasn't confused and covered in blood. *Tybalt's* blood. The thought made it easier to lock my shoulders and glare. "The High King can sort this out." I could ask him to be merciful, if he found that the Barrow Wight girl really hadn't been given a choice in what she'd done.

I didn't want him to be merciful. I wanted her to burn. I wanted them all to burn. But that was why it was so important that someone else be involved in this. She'd hurt Tybalt. Whether she'd done it because someone else had forced her to or not, she had hurt him. That didn't mean the people who'd turned her into a weapon and aimed her at their targets deserved to get off without punishment. If anything, it meant exactly the opposite. They needed to be punished. They needed to *understand* that what they had done was wrong. And under the Law, they just might get away with it.

"You said that if I did as you ordered, you would leave my family alone," said the Barrow Wight doggedly. "You *promised*."

"Promises don't count when they're made to the lower classes," said Kabos.

Madden crouched suddenly, snarling in the back of his throat. I glanced down at him, taking my eyes off the scene for a moment.

It was long enough.

There was a cracking sound, followed by Verona, screaming. I whipped around. The King of Highmountain was sprawled on the floor, eyes open, neck bent at an unnatural angle. The Barrow Wight handmaid was next to him, breathing heavily, her features distorted into something more gargoyle than human, her mouth bristling with teeth. I stared. I'd heard stories of the Barrow Wights and their true faces, but Stacy's Barrow heritage was distant enough that she had no second face to hide— only the one she wore on the outside. This was what they were, down in the dark, where passing for human had never been a concern.

"Never touch her!" she snarled, and leaped for the screaming Verona.

I lunged forward, intending to put myself between them. There was a sound like ripping metal, and the world stopped—

—only for me to stumble into an empty room. The body of the king was still there, sprawled on the floor. The night-haunts hadn't come yet. Verona and the handmaid were gone. So were Quentin and Madden. I was alone.

Panic surged through my veins, followed by a cold, implacable fury. These people had turned a subject into a sword. From the things she'd said—and more, the way she'd said them—they had done it by holding her sister's safety hostage. It was a good technique, if you wanted to keep your hands technically clean while accomplishing the unthinkable. It was a technique that didn't leave much question about how far you would go to accomplish your goals. These people would go all the way, if that was what they considered necessary.

Only the plural was wrong now, wasn't it? Queen Verona of Highmountain was alone, and like any widow, she was going to be grieving. She was going to be looking for someone to blame. The people who had caused her to goad her handmaiden into lashing out were going to seem like excellent targets. I dropped to my knees beside the body of the king, not quite realizing what I was about to do until the sword was pressed against the unbroken skin of his arm, and I was slicing through his flesh, looking for the cooling blood beneath. Not cooling; cooled. It bubbled slowly to the surface, thick and deoxygenated after the amount of time it had spent sitting in the dead man's veins.

I ran my fingers through the clotted mass, bringing them to my lips and sucking them clean. Images flashed into focus at the back of my eyes: Kabos dancing with Verona on a balcony looking down on the city of Denver; Verona proposing they take advantage of this conclave to make things better for themselves in the Westlands; the handmaiden, whose name was Minna, weeping in the back of the coach that had carried them from Colorado to California. They were more impressions than full memories, perhaps due to the age of the blood, but they were enough for me to be sure of where the guilt in this terrible situation truly lay.

That wasn't going to save the handmaiden. She had killed at least two people, both of them kings. No matter how good her reasons had been, no matter how much duress she had been under, she was going to be punished. If Tybalt died, or if she had hurt Quentin . . .

I couldn't be sure that I wasn't going to kill her myself.

Kabos had been dead before the world froze. I looked back at where I'd been standing, and was unsurprised to see the crushed remains of a red-spotted toadstool ground into the carpet. Another fairy ring, and I'd leaped straight into it. I had no way of detecting them or knowing how long they'd last—or how long that one had lasted before it let me go. Long enough for King Kabos' body to cool. Not long enough for the night-haunts to come.

Too long.

Neither Barrow Wights nor Daoine Sidhe could teleport, which meant that wherever Verona, her handmaid, and the boys had gone, they had gone there on foot. I looked over my shoulder to the open door before looking back to the room. I paused. The floor was polished hardwood. Like all the floors in the knowe, it was impeccably clean. So where had that length of daffodil-colored thread come from, if not the lining of Quentin's vest?

"Clever boy," I murmured. Holding Sylvester's sword unsheathed and low against my hip, I rose and started deeper into the chambers assigned to this particular pair of visiting monarchs.

I wanted to shout for help: I wanted to bring down the roof, if that was what I had to do in order to get Quentin and Madden back. I knew it wouldn't do me any good. The knowe couldn't answer in words, assuming it was even interested in helping me, and the only person I would have trusted to hear her name no matter where it was spoken—April—wasn't here. I was on my own, at least temporarily.

There was a time when I'd only ever been on my own. It hadn't been so long ago that I didn't remember how it worked. I walked from the receiving room into a short hallway, which seemed extravagant even for housing intended for royalty, and paused. There were three doors, all closed. None of them looked any more or less likely than the others; all three looked like they would lead, one way or the other, to the outside wall of the knowe. Arden was fond of giving her guests sweeping views to remind them of the majesty of her kingdom, like a tour guide with some very specific goals in mind. I hesitated, looking from one door to the next, trying to decide which one made the most sense.

As I waited, I breathed. And as I breathed, the scent of blood tickled my nose. It wasn't mine, or Tybalt's, or King Kabos'. It was almost buried beneath all those other layers of bloodshed, faint enough that I would have missed it if I hadn't been forced to take my time and decide which way to go. It was coming from behind the central door. Still, I hesitated, looking toward the door on my right. This might be a trap, or it might be Quentin leaving me a clue.

My dress didn't have pockets. It did have hems, and I was carrying a sword. I sawed off a chunk of heavy, blood-soaked fabric, wadding it into a ball, and lobbed it in a gentle underhand arc toward the right-hand door. The fabric stopped in midair, hanging suspended for an instant before vanishing. A fairy ring. They had closed the doors they didn't use with fairy rings. It was a logical, effective choice, and I wished to Oberon that they hadn't thought to make it, because this was going to make an already difficult process unbearably hard.

But Quentin—and the more I breathed, the more I knew that it was him; the blood was whispering tales, even if it was too far away for me to taste it and be absolutely certain—had been smart enough to anticipate this problem, and had left me a trail to follow. I stepped cautiously forward. Time didn't stop. I reached for the doorknob, waiting for the world to freeze around me. When it didn't happen, I turned the knob and pushed the door open, revealing the elegant, mostly empty bedchamber on the other side. As in the Luidaeg's rooms, one wall had been replaced by glass panes, looking out on the redwoods.

Unlike in the Luidaeg's room, one of those panes had been smashed. No shards littered the polished redwood floor; the glass had been smashed outward, not inward. The smell of blood was stronger here. Quentin had cut himself on the glass. There: as I got closer, I spotted a small triangle of glass jutting from the frame, the edge of it outlined in red. There wasn't much blood. Verona probably hadn't even noticed it happen. As a Daoine Sidhe, she was attuned to blood, but experience had taught me that the normal Daoine Sidhe attunement was nothing compared to the appeal blood held for one of the Dóchas Sidhe.

I plucked the piece of glass from the frame, tucking it into the bodice of my gown. It didn't matter if it cut me; I'd heal. There was no way I was leaving Quentin's blood lying around for anyone to find. Not given who he was, and the secrets he was trying to keep. I took one more step forward, to the very edge of the broken glass, and blanched, feeling my stomach do a slow tuck-and-roll.

This room might not have been one of the highest points in the knowe, but it was more than high enough. The window wall looked out on an endless sea of redwoods, and the drop between me and the ground was easily fifty feet, maybe more. We were in the Summerlands, after all, where the laws of nature were superseded by the laws of Faerie, which were much more forgiving in certain ways.

None of the people I was looking for could fly. I closed my eyes, taking a deep breath, and looked again.

Far below me in the gloom—at least fifteen feet straight down—one of the wooden paths that Arden's people used to move through the trees wound its way into the darkness. Verona was a pureblooded Daoine Sidhe, and could possibly have some sort of spell in her arsenal to allow them to make the drop in safety. Fifty feet was too much, but fifteen? That wasn't out of the question. They could be down there.

If they were, and I was hesitating here, then I was allowing them to get even more of a head start on me—not good, since I had no idea how long I'd been trapped in that fairy ring. If they weren't, and I jumped down to follow them, I'd have to find a way back up in order to resume my pursuit. That could be the last straw. Quentin needed me following him, not running off on some wild goose chase.

Carefully, I leaned far enough out the open window to look to either side, searching for another way out of here. There wasn't one: the room ended in a sheer drop, an artificial redwood cliff face descending down into the misty dark. They hadn't gone back, I was sure of that; Quentin didn't heal the way I did, and would have still been bleeding if he'd been dragged out to the hall. There would have been some sort of sign, a trace for me to follow. They must have gone down. There was no other option.

"Oh, this is gonna suck," I muttered, and took three long steps back before I broke into a run, hit the edge of the room, and leaped out into the air.

Falling is easy. Anyone can fall. Landing without breaking multiple bones is a harder problem. I plummeted through the redwood-scented green, branches whipping at my face and arms. It was all I could do to keep one arm in front of my face, preventing the branches from hitting me in the eye. With my luck, I'd blind myself before I landed, and have to wait for *that* to heal before I could start moving again.

The path rushed up at me faster than I would have thought was possible, and I braced myself for impact as well as I could. I hit hard, and felt my ankle shatter under the pressure. The pain was sudden and immense, blocking out the rest of the world. I bit my lip hard enough to draw blood, rolling to bleed off my momentum. I thought I was rolling with the curve of the path until it dropped away, and I was falling again.

Years of struggling not to die when the entire world seemed determined to make it happen had honed my reflexes to an amazing degree. My hands shot out before I'd fully realized what was happening, grabbing the edge of the path and stopping my descent. I hung there, clinging to the wood, panting, with waves of pain rushing outward from my ankle and filling my entire body. Every time I thought the worst of it was past, another wave would hit, and I'd black out for a second. Not ideal for someone who was dangling above a seemingly infinite drop.

I whimpered. I couldn't help it. I fall off things with dismaying frequency. That doesn't mean I enjoy it, and the thought of how much more it would hurt if I broke every bone in my entire body was terrifying. At least the path had been treated with some sort of water-repellent; the wood was dry under my fingers, and I wasn't slipping. That would have been a step too far.

Quentin needed me. Madden needed me. Arden and the others were still back in the dining hall, or nearby, and had no idea who was behind this; they wouldn't be prepared if Verona and Minna came back in, claiming to have been attacked. I couldn't be sure that Minna would still willingly work with Verona, but Verona had Minna's sister, and Minna had . . . what? She'd killed the King of Highmountain. Verona would want revenge for that. Maybe not now. Maybe not yet. I needed to pull myself up.

"I hate everything," I muttered, through gritted teeth, and began slowly, laboriously hauling myself up onto the path. Every time I pulled, my ankle throbbed again. It was no longer the shooting, violent pain of a fresh break, but that was a problem in its own way: the bone was starting to set, and I didn't know whether the leg was straight. The thought of rebreaking my own ankle before I could walk was not an appealing one.

Sometimes healing faster than anything natural is not as good as it sounds. I kept hauling, and my ankle throbbed with every motion. I couldn't really get a grip on the wood; in the end, I had to ram my fingers between the planks and pull hard enough that the skin shredded, healed, and shredded again. I was almost there. I could topple back down, or I could pull myself up. I took a breath, tensed my shoulders as tight as they would go, and hauled, boosting myself over the edge and onto the planking.

I collapsed as soon as I was safely on the path, lying flat with my face pressed to the wood and the wind howling around me. My ankle wasn't throbbing anymore. I didn't have the necessary materials to rebreak the bone if it hadn't set right, and so I didn't look at it; I just pushed myself back to my feet, wobbling as I went, and pressed down on my formerly injured foot, waiting to see what it would do.

It held my weight. Something felt wrong about the way the bones fit together, something in the interaction between joint and muscle, but it didn't hurt, and I could handle a little limp if it didn't slow me down. I stopped, closed my eyes, and breathed in as deeply as I could, looking for the blood that I knew was there.

The wind wasn't helping. I crouched down a bit, getting closer to the wood. Quentin would have tried to bleed somewhere that wouldn't be noticed or wiped away by the passage of feet. The path was a poor choice, which left . . . I turned to look at the trees around me, moving slowly, sniffing the whole time. Some of the redwoods had branches that overhung the path, making walking more difficult than it might otherwise have been. One of them slapped me in the face as I turned, and I stopped.

I smelled blood.

The branch would have been shoulder height if I'd been standing upright, which put it slightly lower for Quentin, who had been taller than I was for a while. It would have been easy for him to run his fingers over the fronds as they walked. I ran my own fingers through them, stopping when I hit stickiness that couldn't be attributed to sap. They came away red. I hesitated for barely a second before I brought them to my mouth. Quentin would forgive me for violating his privacy, considering the circumstances.

The world washed in red. My perspective shifted, becoming higher, looking down on things that should have been at eye level. I closed my own eyes, giving myself over to the memory.

Verona is smiling. That's the worst part of this whole thing. Toby's frozen in a fairy ring and maybe Tybalt is going to die, and Verona won't stop smiling. Maybe she can't. Maybe this is the way she breaks.

"Keep moving," she says. The Barrow Wight girl has been good since Verona shouted her sister's name. She's holding Madden in her arms, his legs pinned and her hand clasped around his muzzle. I don't think he can turn himself human when she's holding him that way. I've never seen Tybalt transform when Toby was holding onto him. I'll have to ask later, if we get through this.

I don't want to die. As we head down the path toward the tower, I run my fingers over the nearest leaves. Toby will come. Toby will find us. Toby will know what to d—

The memory shattered, leaving me gasping for breath. I opened my eyes, turning until my view of the trees matched Quentin's. Then I started walking, wobbling as I compensated for my ankle, and gathering speed as I figured out my current limits. Finally, I broke into a run, feet pounding on the redwood slats, chasing my ghosts into the night.

Pixies flittered through the trees above me, their wings casting panes of candy-colored light onto the redwood at my feet. I kept running but glanced up, calling, "If you know which way I'm supposed to be going, this would be a great time to help."

Most people don't think pixies are very smart, and maybe they're not, as big, slow creatures measure intelligence. We have the time to stop and think about things, while pixies lead fast, violent lives. Like all fae, they're technically immortal. Unlike most of us, they have a tendency to wind up splattered across car windshields or be eaten by birds, and so have the high birthrate and bad attitude of creatures with much shorter lives. So maybe they're not intelligent, but they can be *smart*, and they can hold a grudge.

Pixies swooped down from above, swirling around me like a wave of living leaves, their thin, translucent wings beating a maddened tattoo that only served to underscore their chiming. Then they surged forward, lighting the path ahead, showing me the way I needed to go. Verona had offended them somehow, maybe just by breaking that window: pixies could be very territorial, and protective of the places that were good to them. Whatever the reason, they were willing to help me now, and so I trusted them, and I ran, praying with every step that I wasn't too late.

TWENTY

THE PATH WOUND THROUGH the redwoods like a river, looping and doubling back on itself several times, until I was grateful for the pixies keeping me on the right heading. Without them, I would have drifted off-course and fallen, and there was no easy way to get back up. Occasional stairways sprouted off the main path, ascending and descending to other levels in the tangle, but that wasn't the same as finding my way from the ground, which seemed even farther down than it had been before. Maybe it was. Geography could be dramatic and odd in the Summerlands; it wouldn't be out of the question for a canyon to be hidden somewhere below me, in the trees.

I ran, and the pixies flew, until we reached a curving stairway cut from a living redwood bough. They landed there, clustering on the bannisters and lighting up the area like a Candyland dream, chiming in a constant, dissonant wave. The stairs led up to another redwood, this one big enough around to qualify as a tower. The door was standing slightly ajar. Not enough that I would have seen it from the path; without the pixies, I would have run right on by.

"I owe you," I said. The pixies rang even louder, startled expressions on their Barbie-sized faces. It occurred to me belatedly that I might have just pledged fealty to the local flock. I decided not to argue with it. They wouldn't be any worse than the actual nobility, and I could probably buy them off with a bag of cheeseburgers and some open cans of Pepsi.

The smell of blood lingered near the top of the stairs. I paused long enough to find the smear on the left-hand banister, wiped it away with my finger, and pushed the door open, putting one hand on the hilt of my borrowed sword as I stepped through. The antechamber was dimly lit, and empty. A staircase wound itself in a tight upward spiral, beginning to my right and ascending up into the dark. I took a breath, steadied myself, and began to climb.

Midway up, the smell of blood began getting stronger. Not all of it was Quentin's. Most of it wasn't. I climbed faster.

After another ten feet, I found the body. Not a human's body: a dog's, white fur stained with blood, head lolling. *He's past helping,* whispered a small, shameful voice. *Keep going.* If I stopped to help him, I might be too late to help Quentin. I might not be able to save my squire.

And if I didn't stop to help him, I would never be able to live with myself. I dropped to my knees on the step below the one where he was sprawled, reaching for him. The fur on his neck was thick and tacky with strings of slowly drying gore, but most of the blood, I realized, wasn't his: it had run down from the red stains around his mouth. The only actual injury seemed to be in his belly. It would still be enough to kill him if it wasn't cleaned and bandaged—the fur there was practically black—but it wasn't enough to have killed him *yet.*

I dug my fingers into his fur until I found his pulse. It would have been too fast in a human, or a Daoine Sidhe.

I didn't know what was usual in a dog. Were they faster than their bipedal companions? Slower? I just had to hope that this was normal. His breathing was shallow but steady.

"Madden," I whispered, leaning closer. "Can you hear me?"

His eye opened and he whined, low and shrill in the back of his throat.

I hadn't realized how tense I was until my shoulders unlocked. I forced myself to smile, running my hand along the curve of his neck. "Hey," I said. "Can you shift? I can help bandage that hole in your stomach, if you can shift."

He rolled his eye, which I took as an indication that he was willing to try. I moved back, watching as he shivered, a small motion that gradually spread to his entire body, becoming a shudder, and finally becoming a shift in the world. The dog disappeared, replaced by a burly man with red-and-white hair, wearing a white ruffled shirt and a pair of blue linen trousers. The front of the shirt had turned almost completely black. There was no hole in the fabric. That seemed odd for a moment, before I realized the shirt hadn't existed when he was stabbed: the knife had gone through fur and skin, not fabric. Magic was strange, and its inconsistent rules were sometimes unforgiving.

"Hey," he whispered.

"Hey," I replied, and moved to help him into a sitting position. He grimaced, but didn't make a sound. "I need you to take your shirt off."

That was enough to coax a pained smile from him. "I don't swing that way, and Tybalt would murder me. He doesn't like dogs to begin with."

"Tybalt will understand battlefield necessity," I said, beginning to undo Madden's buttons. "I need to bind your wound. I don't expect you to walk, but if we can stop the bleeding, you'll be okay long enough for me to deal with the Queen of Highmountain, get back to Arden, and find Jin."

Madden grimaced again, rolling his shoulders to help me with the undressing. "I don't mean to be a pessimist, but maybe you're expecting too much of yourself? I can't stand. I don't think she's going to get here in time."

"Hope can be cruel, but giving up is worse," I said. Revealed, the wound in his stomach looked about as good as it was possible for that sort of thing to be. It was high and off to the side, where it might have sliced into the fat and muscle of his abdomen, avoiding his internal organs. If we were only dealing with blood loss and not sepsis, I might not be being overly optimistic after all.

His shirt was linen, sturdy enough that it refused to rip when I pulled on it. That was good. I used Sylvester's sword to slice it into strips and wrapped them around Madden's middle, doing my best to stop the bleeding without tying them tight enough to do additional damage. He was panting and pale by the time I was done, but still sitting upright; he hadn't blacked out even once. Under the circumstances, I was willing to call that a win.

"I have to go," I said quietly. "Did she say *anything* about what she was hoping to accomplish?"

"She told her handmaiden her hands were too dirty; she'd burn for what she did," said Madden. He frowned. It was impossible to tell whether the pain in his expression was physical, or due to remembering Verona's words. "She said if she was willing to finish this—the queen said that if the handmaiden was willing to finish this—her sister would be taken care of. The handmaiden's sister, I mean."

"I understand," I said. Blood loss was making him loopy. I wasn't going to get much more out of him. Still, I paused, and asked, "Madden, what's at the top of this tower?"

He blinked, seeming perplexed. "The sleepers," he said. "I thought you knew."

"Oh, root and *branch*," I muttered. "No. I didn't. I'll be back." I pushed myself to my feet and started up the stairs, faster now that I knew what I was racing toward — and what I was racing against.

The tower where the elf-shot sleepers were kept was an interesting target, tactically speaking. Nolan, Prince in the Mists was definitely there; Dianda Lorden might or might not be. Either way, they'd make excellent hostages. The thought that Tybalt might have already been moved up there crossed my mind, and was promptly dismissed. Arden's people couldn't have moved that fast. If they had, they would have been in the room when Verona and Minna arrived.

Or would they? I didn't know how long I'd been trapped in that fairy ring. *I didn't know*, and now two of the people I loved could be in that tower, alone with a woman who thought nothing of killing as long as her own hands remained technically, dishonestly clean. My ankle was damaged enough to make the stairs difficult. I ran through the pain, feeling things shift and straighten within the confines of my skin as my body adjusted.

Sometimes I think the true power of what I inherited from my mother is the ability to keep running, no matter how badly it hurts.

The stairs ended at another door. This one was closed. I tried the knob. It was also locked. Verona had anticipated someone following her. Not enough to have set a fairy ring on the threshold, which is what I would have done: I would have made sure anyone who thought they could interfere with my plans wound up a frozen, helpless bystander. Either she was cocky or she was scared. Either way, I needed to get into that room.

Swords are not good lock picks. My earrings were silver; too soft to work the tumblers in a door this size, even if I could twist them into the right shape. I cast around for something else I could use, pausing when I saw the banister. Like everything else in the knowe that wasn't made of stone, it was polished redwood, enchanted to remain smooth and snag free.

"We'll see about that," I muttered, and retreated a few steps down the stairs, trying to put some distance between me and the door. It was a foolish to hope that I might be able to go unheard, but it was all I had at this point, and I was going to hold on to it.

The banister was sturdy. My first blow with the sword didn't even scratch the wood, and the recoil was enough to send me staggering back a step. Not the safest thing ever, with me near the top of a long stairway. I didn't want to climb back up, and so I kept my second swing more controlled, hitting the banister harder. This time, the blade bit in, just a little. So I swung again and again, chipping away at the wood until it gave way, shattering along the cut I had made. I kicked the broken spot, and kept kicking, breaking off a chunk of banister about the length of my forearm.

"Arden needs to give me a damn skeleton key," I muttered, and settled to breaking down the chunk still further, until I had a handful of skewers. Wooden lock picks aren't my favorite, but they're better than nothing. I shoved the sword into its scabbard and walked back up the stairs. The door was still closed. That was actually a bit of a relief. Maybe Verona hadn't heard me after all.

She'd hear me soon. I crouched in front of the door, inserting the tips of two of my skewers into the lock and beginning to work. Everything else fell away, replaced by the calm simplicity of the tumblers and the way they interacted with my makeshift lock picks. Devin had always called me a natural where breaking and entering was concerned, and while I might not be proud of my roots, that didn't mean I was going to reject the skills they'd given me. Better to be a respectable detective who could pick a lock than one who stood helplessly outside a locked door, refusing to do something I was fully capable of.

Morality, like everything else, is often a matter of which side of the situation you're standing on.

The tumblers clicked open. I left my skewers in place as I drew my sword. Then I reached up, grasped the knob, and turned it. There was no point in hiding the evidence that I'd been here when I was about to show up in person.

Verona was standing near the window shouting at Minna. Minna was shouting back. They were too wrapped up in their private drama to have noticed me, and so I risked a glance around the room, trying to get a feel for what had gone on in here.

Too many of the biers were occupied. I blinked, bringing them into focus, and swallowed a gasp. Quentin and Walther were both there, the one crumpled like a discarded rag, the other stretched out like a king in state. They were asleep, their chests rising and falling with drugged slowness. Elf-shot. They'd been elf-shot. They wouldn't rejoin the land of the living for a hundred years, or until the cure was administered—and Walther was the one who knew how to make the cure.

I had a moment of sickening terror before I remembered that Siwan could almost certainly recreate Walther's work, even if he wasn't awake to help her with the potion. Assuming the conclave went well, they'd be awake sooner rather than later.

Nolan and Duke Michel were on their biers, where I'd expected them to be. Dianda's bier had been replaced by a shallow trough of water, with her lying at the bottom like a drowned maiden. It was a disappointment but not a real shock to see Tybalt lying on Dianda's other side. The fairy ring had kept me in place long enough for Arden to move him to a place of supposed safety, and now here we were, all in danger together, one more time.

Jin wasn't here. Either she'd been somewhere else, or she'd managed to get away. That gave me a small amount of hope. We might be able to survive this. I turned back to Verona and Minna. They still hadn't noticed me. That was about to change.

"In the name of Queen Arden Windermere in the Mists, High King Aethlin Sollys, High Queen Maida Sollys, and a bunch more nobles who'd like you to cut this shit out, you are under arrest," I said, as clearly and coherently as I could. The urge to charge in and start swinging was strong. Surely I couldn't be charged with violation of the Law if the decapitation was accidental.

Verona and Minna stopped shouting at each other and turned to stare at me in wide-eyed disbelief, briefly united by their surprise. Verona found her voice first. "You," she said. "How are you *here*? We left you prisoned in a circle. You can't have followed us."

"Turns out the circle was pretty half-assed," I said. "It broke, I followed. You have nowhere left to run. Come quietly and maybe the High King will be gentle with you." That wasn't going to happen. Whether she realized it or not, Queen Verona had signed her own conviction when she jammed an arrow into Quentin's arm. The Sollys family might have been able to forgive her treason and insurrection, but they weren't going to forgive a direct attack on their only son.

"I told you," said Minna. "I didn't have time to set the traps in that room, not with you moving around and refusing to let me mark them. The fairy rings I scattered were weak, to prevent you being snared and stuck until someone came to free you."

"That didn't stop you from killing my husband, you washed-out, death-born bitch," snarled Verona. Her attention swung back to me. "You can't arrest me. I've done nothing wrong."

"The Law may be the only crime that can carry a death sentence, but I'm willing to bet that between Arden and the High King and Queen, they'll come up with something to punish you for," I said. "That's the trouble with having a justice system built on royal whims. Sometimes they work against you."

Verona turned to Minna. "Kill her," she said calmly.

I blinked. "Excuse me?"

"No," said Minna.

"Kill her or I'll kill your sister," said Verona.

"I'm right here," I said. "I have a sword."

"You can't threaten her anymore," said Minna. "I know you won't hurt her. Not as long as you want to control me. Leave my sister alone, and maybe I'll be willing to listen to you."

"Didn't you just, you know, kill her husband? King Kabos of Highmountain? Remember him? He's dead. Maybe you should move away from her, and stop letting her tell you what to do." I've been attacked and I've been belittled. I'd never been ignored while people argued about what to do with me. Especially not when I was heavily armed and already covered in blood.

Covered in blood . . . "Minna," I said, causing the Barrow Wight to look at me in surprise. She'd never told me her name. Kabos had done that, bleeding out his secrets under my hand. "Who stabbed Madden?"

"She did," said Minna, indicating Verona. "He wouldn't stop barking."

"There's no crime in killing a *dog*," said Verona dismissively.

"There's certainly a crime in killing the Queen's Seneschal," I said. Verona turned to stare at me. I smiled. "Madden is Arden's best friend and closest confidant. More importantly, he's Cu Sidhe. You're not innocent anymore."

Verona took a step backward. "Don't touch me!"

"Now you'd run? Now you'd flee? Because your hands aren't clean?" Minna reached out and grabbed Verona's arm, digging in her fingers until the other woman yelped and squirmed, trying to get away. "My hands were clean! My sister's hands were clean!" Her face was starting to distort, becoming the monstrous mask she had worn when she killed the king.

Verona wailed.

I lowered my sword. "Let her go," I said, softly. "She deserves justice. So do you. Let her go, and I'll take you both to Arden to stand trial. If there's any way to go gently on you, she'll find it." There wasn't. Minna was going to die. But maybe she would be the last.

"My sister's name is Avebury," said Minna. "She's only fifteen. She doesn't know what the world will do to you. She doesn't know what the world demands. Get her out of Highmountain. Don't let them hurt her."

"Please, let her go." I took a step forward. "You know that an easy death is more than she deserves. Let her stand trial."

"Did the dog live?"

Minna's question was so abrupt that it took me a moment to realize what she was asking. I nodded. "Yes, but—"

"Then so will she. What's a hundred years, to a monster? That's what she made of me. She could only do that because of what she was." Minna's face softened a bit. "She came to me after my mother died and said 'do what I say and your sister will have the best of everything; refuse me, and she will have the worst.' My mother died as her assassin. This ends only with an ending, not with a pause."

"Please, she's mad, please," moaned Verona.

"This ends," said Minna, and ran for the nearest window, dragging Verona by the arm.

I realized what was about to happen as soon as she began to move. "Minna, *no*!" I shouted, dropping my sword and lunging for her.

Her shoulder hit the glass. It shattered, and she fell through, dragging Verona with her. I grabbed Verona's arm, hoping to pull them back. Minna turned to look at me, briefly arrested in her descent. There was sorrow in her eyes, deep and profound and utterly resigned.

"I'm sorry," she said, and jerked me forward with all of her Barrow Wight's strength. There was no time to catch myself before we were falling, all three of us, caught in the unyielding grasp of gravity.

That was all we were caught in. Minna let us both go and fell with her eyes closed and a beatific smile on her face. Verona screamed, grabbing first at the Barrow Wight and then at me, like we could somehow stop her fall. I pushed her away. I couldn't save her, not now, not with the skills I possessed; all I could do was hope that she wouldn't suffer overly much.

I tried to go limp as I fell, hoping it would minimize the pain of my impact with the ground, which was rushing up on me faster and faster, becoming a black sheet that blanketed my vision and blocked out everything else.

This is gonna suck, I thought.

Then I hit the ground, and everything disappeared.

TWENTY-ONE

CONSCIOUSNESS CAME ON LIKE a flipped switch: one moment I wasn't in the world, and the next moment I was. There was no pain. That was probably a good sign. While I was pretty sure that it was possible for me to experience such profound trauma that I lost the ability to feel pain, one little fall from an impossible height wasn't going to be enough to do it.

I opened my eyes.

The ceiling was redwood, spangled with the cutout shapes of stained-glass stars in blackberry purple and deep sea blue. Matching shades covered the lights, keeping them from becoming too bright. I blinked twice, and decided to skip the whole process of testing my body to see whether it still worked. Either it did, or it didn't. There were no other options.

I sat up. A wave of dizziness swept over me, forcing me to throw my hand to the side to brace myself. It hit a softly padded surface. I looked down. I was sitting on a bed, sheets beneath me and patchwork quilt atop me. I was also clean. There was no blood on my clothing, which had been changed while I was asleep, replaced by a simple white cotton shift with a drawstring neck. Tiny blackberry flowers had been embroidered around the neck, white on white, virtually invisible save for the tiny pops of yellow at their centers. I was still in Muir Woods, then. Arden seemed to have an almost compulsive need to spatter blackberry symbolism on everything she owned, just to make sure people knew it was hers. I couldn't blame her for that, considering how long she'd been exiled from her family's throne. Sure, I would have done the claiming with a label-maker, but to each their own.

"What the *hell* do you think you're doing?" I turned toward the voice and found a slim, short woman with pale skin and sharp features standing in the doorway, arms crossed and dragonfly wings beating a mad tattoo in the air behind her. A sleek, short-cropped pageboy haircut framed her face in black silk, making her look like the poster girl for medical responsibility. "You need to lie back down, now."

"Hi, Jin," I said, pushing the quilt back. My legs were bare, although my shift extended to mid-thigh—long enough for decency. I rotated my left ankle experimentally. It moved smoothly and without that little catch that it had been showing before. "Did I rebreak my ankle? Where were you before?"

"I went out the window when they came in. Unlike some people, I can fly. Toby, I need you to look at me." There was something wrong with her voice. I had heard her in distress before; had heard her struggling to save a patient who she thought was not going to willingly stay. I had never heard her sound so *serious*. Startled, I looked back at her.

Jin wasn't frowning, exactly. Her expression was one of profound and absolute sorrow. I felt myself go cold. "Toby—"

"When did he die?" The question came out surprisingly even. My voice didn't shake. My voice didn't do anything. The words fell between us like stones in a wall, and part of me knew that this had always been the way things had to be. I didn't get the happy ending, the man who loved me and the bouquet of roses in my hand. The world has never, never been that kind. Not where I'm concerned.

Jin blinked, sorrow fading into confusion. "When did who die?"

"Tybalt. That's why I was screaming for you before, remember? So you could try to save him?" He'd lost so much blood. It was easy to forget that for other people, blood loss was a dangerous problem, not just an inconvenience to be fixed with Pop Tarts and protein. I'd become so accustomed to being invulnerable that I'd allowed myself to believe everyone I cared about was, too.

Maybe if Verona hadn't interrupted her. Maybe if she'd been allowed to work. Maybe if we'd gotten the elf-shot into his arm a little sooner.

You can hang the stars on maybe, but they won't light up the sky.

"Oh, sweet Titania, Toby, no." Jin's face relaxed as she understood. "Tybalt is *fine*. I was able to patch up his remaining injuries and give him a potion to help regenerate the blood he lost. He may be sore when he wakes up, but he's alive. He's going to be perfectly healthy. There won't even be a scar."

I stared at her. "What?"

"Tybalt is recovering. He's still asleep because the conclave isn't over, and we don't have permission from the High King to wake anyone, but he isn't going to die."

None of this made sense. "Then why—"

"*You* died."

I froze.

Jin kept talking. "I saw you fall. I was hiding on the roof of the tower, trying to decide whether it was safe to go for help, and when you came out of the window, I went after you. You landed at the base of the tower, and you were . . . you were *broken*, October. I don't have the words for what I saw when I looked at you, except to say that I never want to see anything like that again. I didn't rebreak your ankle. *You* did, when you fell. You broke . . . I think you broke every bone in your body, and even a few that shouldn't have been breakable. You *shattered* yourself."

"Oh."

"Yours wasn't the only body there, but you were the only one still breathing. I don't know *how* you were still breathing. You should have been dead before I could reach you. I was trying to figure out how to move you when Queen Windermere appeared. The pixies had gone to find her." Jin shook her head. "I gave you an anesthetic, and we carried you back into the knowe. It took me three hours to set your bones, Toby. Three *hours*. It was like doing a jigsaw puzzle."

"I guess it was a longer fall than I thought." The words sounded weak even to my own ears.

Jin glared at me. "You think? As soon as your bones were set, the Luidaeg brought me a decanter filled with blood. She said she owed it to you. I've been feeding you the blood of a Firstborn for the last two days, watching your body put itself back together after a fall you should never have been able to walk away from. You died, I'm sure of it. I don't know how you can be talking to me now."

"I don't think it was the first time."

Jin's eyes narrowed. "Explain?"

Haltingly, I did. How the false Queen of the Mists had stabbed me through the heart; how Evening Winterrose's wards had swatted me out of the sky and into the unforgiving sea. All the other near misses and narrow escapes that maybe hadn't been misses after all. Finally, I said, "I still think I can die. Everything that lives can die. But I think . . . unless my body is so broken it can't heal, I think there's a really good chance I'll come back."

"That explains why the Luidaeg assumed you would live," said Jin. "I'm sure that also explains why I need you to lie still and recover. You've been unconscious. You need to rest."

"If I've been unconscious, all I've been *doing* is resting," I said. "I need to find out what's going on. I need to tell High King Aethlin what happened." They must have found Quentin by now, sleeping peacefully in the high tower. I needed them to understand.

Jin shook her head. "He already knows. He took a sample of your blood as soon as we were sure you would live. It told him the whole story."

I stared at her. It was hard not to feel like my privacy had been invaded, even though what she was talking about Aethlin doing was exactly what I did every time I rode someone's blood without their consent. I would have said he could go ahead if I'd been awake, not because I wanted to, but because I knew that refusing would have been seen as suspicious. I would also have been able to focus my thoughts on Verona and her crimes, rather than allowing him to roam at will through my memories.

At least it had been him. He already knew most of the secrets I was tasked with keeping, although he might not have been quite so aware of Arden's insecurities. I pushed the sleeves of my shift up to my elbows, trying to cover my discomfort with a question: "How's Madden?"

"The knife missed all the major organs, and you did a pretty decent job with the field dressing for someone who has no medical background."

Jin probably hadn't gone to a human medical school. Ellyllon were natural healers, and their knowledge of the body and its ailments was mostly instinctual. I decided not to point that out. I was already pissing her off enough by refusing to get back under the covers, and I had once seen her knock Sylvester out with a touch of her fingers and a gentle command to go to sleep. "Good. Arden needs him, and he didn't deserve to die that way. Where are we in the knowe?"

"Oh, no." Jin narrowed her eyes. "Get back in the bed. I am not going to be responsible for you running off and hurting yourself again."

"No, you won't," I agreed, and stood. "But I'm awake now, and I need to tell High King Aethlin that I'm his to command. I can't just lie around here waiting until you feel like I'm well enough to deal with my daily existence." Especially with the conclave still going; especially with Tybalt still sleeping. I needed the High King to remember that I was here.

Quentin was probably going to be a sufficient reminder of the urgency of the matter at hand. I couldn't imagine any parent would want to leave their eldest child to sleep for a hundred years if there was any way around it.

Jin took a breath, looking like she was going to object again. Then she stopped, and sighed, and said, "I never win this fight. Just once, I'd like to win. You know that, right?"

"I do," I said solemnly. "Next time I'm at Shadowed Hills, I'll stub my toe and let you put me to bed for a week, okay?" The idea was appealing. Peace, quiet, access to the kitchen ... I could deal with that sort of break.

"It's a promise," said Jin.

"Great," I said. "Now where are my clothes?"

Her smile was slow, and more than a little sadistic. "Oh, I'm sorry, did you want me to do you a favor beyond saving your worthless life? That's not on the books for today."

"Don't think I'm going to stay in here just because you refuse to give back my shoes," I said.

"I don't think even you will go streaking around a royal knowe."

"You call this streaking?" I held out my arms. "I'm

more covered than a tent. Don't think I won't walk out that door."

"You won't."

"Watch me." I walked past her, choking a little on the cloud of pixie dust thrown up by her frantically buzzing wings, and out the door into the hallway on the other side, where my dignified escape was promptly thwarted by Sylvester Torquill.

"October!" he cried, rising from the lion-footed chair where he'd been sitting, nervous as a father waiting for news from the delivery room. He swept me into a tight hug before I could react, lifting my feet off the ground. I made a small sound of protest. He didn't appear to notice, occupied as he was with swinging me around and exclaiming, "Jin said you were recovering, but I never expected to see you up and about so soon! And looking so well! My darling girl, can you ever forgive me?"

"Not dead," I managed to wheeze. "That means I need to breathe."

"Sorry! Sorry." He set me gingerly to my feet and took an exaggerated step backward, giving me my space. "Are you all right?"

"I'm still in one piece, despite the best efforts of gravity and the ground," I said. I felt light-headed with relief. This was the closest thing to an intimate moment Sylvester and I had shared since the night I'd learned that he had lied to me for my entire life. He'd done it out of loyalty to my mother and love for me, but he had still hurt me, and that had damaged my trust in him. I hadn't realized how much I'd missed feeling like I could turn to him in times of crisis.

"Please don't do that again. My heart can't handle it."

"I'm pretty sure you're not the only person who's going to say that to me," I said. "Did you get your sword back?"

"I did," he said. Then he smirked. "Even dropping yourself from a great height is not enough to defeat the art of a good blacksmith."

"I'll try harder next time." I took a deep breath. Let it out. And said, "I'm still mad at you. If you ever keep secrets from me for my own good again, we're done. I will ask you to release me from my oaths, I will find a new liege, and I will be *gone*. But I miss you. I miss my friend. I miss my liege. Please, can we make up now?"

Sylvester nodded. He looked tired. Daoine Sidhe don't age after they reach maturity, staying young and vital forever, but there were still shadows around his eyes, and he looked older than he had before Evening Winterrose came back, before I learned that he could lie to me. "I'm so sorry," he said. "I will do my best never to break your trust again."

This time, I was the one who hugged him, wrapping my arms around his waist and breathing in the reassuring dogwood and daffodil scent of him, letting it fill my lungs. Sylvester put his arms around my shoulders, and I allowed myself to take a moment and just exist.

But only a moment. I had work to do. "I need to get to the conclave," I said, letting go and stepping away. "I need to find out what's going on."

Sylvester blinked. "Forgive me if this is indelicate, but ... were you planning to go in what you're wearing?"

"First Jin, now you, I swear, it's like you think this is a bikini or something." I crossed my arms. "I don't have clean clothes here, and I'm not going to my room to change. I can't lace myself into half those outfits without help." Quentin usually helped me, or Tybalt, and both of them were asleep in a high tower, waiting for the people who held the final say to tell me whether or not I was going to get them back.

Fae don't age, but humans do. If I wanted my boys returned to me, I was going to have to burn away the last of my humanity, and I was never going to forgive the gathered Kings and Queens of the Westlands for demanding that of me. Never.

"I could spin you an illusion—"

"No. I got hurt in their service. They can take me as I am." Still mortal. Still breakable. Still longing to go home.

"At least take my coat." Sylvester shrugged out of his greatcoat, which hung to his knees and would fall almost to my ankles. It was soft blue wool, embroidered with abstract yellow daffodils and white dogwood flowers, and it felt like he was still hugging me when I pulled it on. I had to belt it tight around my waist to keep it from slipping off my shoulders, but when I was done, it looked almost like an overdress rather than a coat stolen from someone bigger than me.

"Cool," I said, and smiled. Sylvester smiled back, offering me his arm. I slipped my hand into the crook of his elbow, and together we walked down the hall, his shoes clicking with each step, my bare feet slapping softly against the redwood.

My recovery room was located in a part of the knowe I wasn't familiar with. Sylvester led and I followed, down a long hall and two flights of stairs, until we came to those old, familiar receiving doors. They were flanked by guards. Lowri stood on the left-hand side, and her eyes widened when she saw me.

"October," she said. "You're alive."

"Alive, awake, and in sort of a hurry to get back to work, hence the lack of shoes," I said. "Can I go inside?"

"The conclave is already in session," said Lowri.

"We were invited," said Sylvester. His tone was mild. His expression was steel.

Lowri hesitated for a bare second before she looked to me, said, "Welcome back," and opened the door, revealing the arcade. I offered her a quick smile, and stepped through.

There had been deaths and political intrigue, but we'd started with a large enough group that the absences were only noticeable if you took the time to look at them. As I walked down the aisle in my borrowed shift and coat, I took the time to look. To find the holes. Some of the missing would be back—Dianda, Quentin, Tybalt—but others were gone forever, and they were owed the small acknowledgment of my attention. As for the rest, they were dressed in their court finery, as always, listening with impatient attention as the Centaur King of Copper explained, in a droning voice, why distributing the elf-shot cure would endanger his community, and thus could not be borne.

We walked down the aisle, and as we passed, people began to whisper and point. Arden, who had been slumped in her throne like she was dreaming of finding an excuse to go for her phone, sat up straighter. Maida stiffened, tapping Aethlin's arm. The High King turned his head, saw me, and stood, cutting off the King of Copper mid-sentence. The Centaur stared at him for a moment before turning to scowl at whatever was causing this disruption. Then he went very still, only his tail swishing.

Sylvester let go of my arm when we reached the row where Luna was seated. I offered him a smile. He nodded in reply, and walked away, leaving me standing alone in the center of the aisle. No use in putting this off any longer. I turned to face the dais, and curtsied deeply before I rose and said, "Sorry for the disruption. I figured if I was awake, I should probably get over here."

"Sir Daye," said Aethlin. "You're . . . surprisingly mobile, considering."

"I heal fast," I said, with a quick, one-shouldered shrug. "Jin told me you'd taken my blood to determine what happened. Did you have any questions for me, or are you content with the order of events?"

"I doubt I'll ever be content with a choice that left three of my vassals dead, an abused woman equally so, and a brave knight on the verge of following them into the dark." The fact that he was willing to say "dead," rather than something flowery and useless like "has stopped dancing" did more to drive home the gravity of his words than anything else could have done. They were gone. They were dead, and they had died in a way that forced this collection of fae royalty to admit it, to actually *see* it. There was something incredible about that. Mostly, though, it was just sad.

High King Aethlin took a breath, steadying himself, and continued, "But I'm content that you took all measures within your power to try to prevent this tragedy; you did not act out of anger or the need for revenge, however justified you might have been; and you did not break Oberon's Law. You have not committed murder."

Hearing him say that should have felt good. I wasn't going to stand trial, again, for something that I didn't do. All I felt was tired. "Cool," I said. "We still talking about the whole 'should we distribute the cure for elf-shot' thing?"

"Yes," said Maida.

"Cool," I said again. I looked toward the King of Copper. "I'm really sorry to ask for this, but I'm still wobbly, and my fiancé and my squire have both been elf-shot. I'd like to go and sit with them for a while. Do you mind yielding the floor for a moment?"

He minded; I could see it in his eyes. He just had no way of saying so without coming off as insulting, and possibly winding up challenged to a duel for my honor. Under the circumstances, I was okay with that. "Please," he said.

"Come to the stage," said Arden. "Given what you've done for us, you should be heard."

Walking the last ten feet to the stairs that would take me to the stage seemed to take almost as long as walking from the back of the gallery. Karen and the Luidaeg were seated in the short row of chairs that had previously held us all; they looked very alone there, even when the Luidaeg offered me a quick, almost solemn smile and an equally hasty thumbs-up. I nodded to them, trying to keep my nerves under control, and took up the spot where I had stood to explain how the cure was formulated in the first place. It seemed like such a long time ago. It was definitely several ruined dresses and a lot of bloodshed ago.

I didn't want to do this. I had no right to do this.

I had to do this.

"My name is October Daye," I said, looking toward the audience. "Knight of Lost Words, sworn in service to Duke Sylvester Torquill of Shadowed Hills, daughter of Amandine the Liar." When did I start thinking of my mother using the title the other Firstborn gave to her? Probably when I found out how much of my life she'd spent lying to me. "I, uh, have spoken to you before, so I guess you knew all of that. And I know the High King has told you what he learned from my blood, how Queen Verona and King Kabos decided to take this conclave as an opportunity to get rid of some people they didn't find politically convenient. But what I really want to talk to you about is how they did it. See, they were royalty. Nobility, just like most of you, and they knew the Law. So they didn't kill anyone. They threatened the sister of one of their vassals, and used that vassal as a weapon to keep their own hands clean. Technically, Kabos died innocent of all wrongdoing under our laws.

"How is that fair? He orchestrated the death of King Antonio Robertson of Angels. He was complicit in the attacks on me, and on King Tybalt of the Court of Dreaming Cats. He gave the orders, and he pulled the strings, and had he been brought before this court, he would have been innocent, because we put too much focus on the wrong things. We look at the letter of the Law. Oberon was a pretty cool guy, according to all the stories I've heard. He made the Law so we'd stop killing each other. How is it any different to stand behind a throne and give orders that can't be refused? How is that *better*?" I paused, trying to read the room. Most of the faces looking back at me were impassive, giving nothing away.

I wanted to turn and look at the Luidaeg. I didn't dare. "Elf-shot was created to get around the Law, but it still kills. I've encountered elf-shot modified to carry a slow poison, for use against purebloods. When it's used against changelings, it doesn't even need that to be deadly. It's a killing weapon. Changelings . . . we probably outnumber purebloods in today's world, because the humans are so close, and the human world is so tempting. We're part of Faerie, too. We're part of this community, too. And continuing to use a weapon that's a guaranteed violation of the Law in spirit, if not in the way it's written, is wrong. It's as wrong as what Verona and Kabos did. It's as wrong as murder.

"But I also want to talk to you about theft. The theft of time. I'm standing in front of you today, wearing this face, wearing these clothes," I plucked at my borrowed jacket, "because my stepfather, a pureblood, transformed me into a fish to save my life. I'm not saying he was wrong to do it—I like being alive, and at the time, he didn't see another option—but when he made that choice, when he made that very *pureblooded* choice, he destroyed my life. I lost my child. I lost the man I was planning to marry. Everything I'd worked for was over in an instant, because someone who thought of time like it was air forgot I had a shorter supply than he did. That I lived in a faster world. Well, we *all* live in that faster world now. If you have a cell phone, if you drive a car, hell, if you watch soap operas, you're living in the fast lane. Elf-shot doesn't take away fourteen years, like Simon did. It takes away a century. It kills changelings, and it steals time from the people who survive it. Imagine trying to catch up with the last twenty years of mortal innovations. Now imagine trying to catch up with a *hundred.*"

The arcade was silent, everyone watching me, some of them barely seeming to breathe. I thought Liz, the Selkie clan leader, was nodding, but I couldn't be sure; she was too far away, and my vision was blurry with unshed tears. I wanted to wipe them away. I wasn't willing to show that kind of weakness. Not here, not now, not with all these people listening for a change.

"Duke Michel used elf-shot to remove Duchess Lorden from the conclave because he didn't want things to be different. He wanted to disrupt this meeting and take your choices away. Queen Verona and King Kabos used their vassal as a weapon to remove the people whose politics and policies they didn't like from the world, because they didn't want to live in a world where a crown was anything other than an absolute pass to do whatever they liked. All three of the people who've disrupted this gathering did it because they want to keep living in the past. They want to steal our time. Don't let them." I turned to the three people seated behind me, Arden and Aethlin and Maida. "That was all. May I be excused now?"

"Yes, you may," said Arden.

I couldn't find the words. I had said too much, and my tongue no longer wanted to obey me. So I curtsied, as deeply and formally as I could manage, and turned to walk back down the stairs and along the aisle, through the silent arcade to the door.

I had done all that I could do, and there were people who needed me. Whether they woke up tomorrow or in a hundred years, I was going to honor that.

TWENTY-TWO

GUARDS FLANKED THE DOOR to the tower. More guards stood at the door two floors up. That was a welcome change. Maybe if there'd been guards stationed here before, Minna and Verona wouldn't have been able to get inside. Maybe Quentin and Walther would have been awake. Maybe Minna and Verona would have been alive.

And if wishes were fishes, then beggars would ride. I didn't recognize either of the guards at the door, but they clearly knew me; when I nodded, they nodded back, and the one on the left opened the door for me. I stepped through, still barefoot in my borrowed coat. The door closed behind me, leaving me alone with the sleeping.

Five of the spaces were filled now. Nolan, in his Gatsby-era finery, was the closest to the door. I wondered whether he would have been a good Prince, if he'd been given the opportunity; whether he would have made Arden a better Queen. I touched the bier beneath him and walked on. I paused when I came to Walther, who was still wearing his alchemy gear, leather apron and sturdy canvas shirt with burns on the hem. He'd never wanted to get involved with this sort of nonsense. That had all been me.

"Sorry," I whispered, and walked on.

Dianda looked angry, even in her sleep, the surface of the water and the glistening sweep of her tail throwing back the room's lights like a prism. They'd probably need to change the water periodically, to keep her from getting moldy. Keeping a mermaid on land was never going to be an easy task. Maybe that was why she and Patrick had chosen to live in the Undersea after their marriage: easier to keep her healthy down beneath the waves.

The next bier stopped me in my tracks.

Quentin was lying there with his eyes closed and his arms straight at his sides. He looked so small that for a moment, I couldn't breathe. I looked at him and saw the gawky teenager with the dandelion fluff hair, the boy who'd refused to listen when I told him "no," who'd argued and challenged and demanded his way into my life. Our relationship had been one long process of me telling him to go away and him cleaving ever closer to my side. He was the same age as my daughter, but unlike her, he was never going to turn human and leave me. That alone would have been sufficient reason for me to burn the mortality out of my blood. If he was going to sleep, I was going to wait for him.

"Damn your eyes for making me care about you," I said. My words were too loud. I kept talking anyway. "You could have backed off, you know? All you had to do was tell Sylvester I was a weird recluse who didn't want to let you do your job. He would never have forced you to have anything else to do with me. You could have been fine. You could have been free. Not yoked to a loser like me."

Quentin didn't say anything. He just slept. Maybe that was for the best. I took a shuddering breath and moved on to the last, and hardest, bier.

Tybalt was still too pale. Whatever Jin had done to convince his body that it wasn't on the verge of death, she hadn't been able to restore all the blood that he'd lost. She said he was going to live, and I believed her. Maybe he'd recover immediately upon waking, and maybe he'd need time to recover, but I'd never known her to be wrong about someone's chances of survival. Thank Oberon for that. I wasn't some frail, fainting flower, to wither away to nothing because my lover died. That didn't mean I was ready to grieve for another lover, not with Connor still flying among the night-haunts.

"Hi," I said softly, and sat on the edge of the bier, reaching out to take one of his hands and lace my fingers through his. I could feel the edges of the claws beneath his skin, and somehow, that was reassuring; somewhere in the last year, that had become the way a hand was supposed to feel. "Jin told me you're going to be okay. Just in case you were wondering. Not that you can hear me, which I guess means this is a good time to tell you this."

I took a breath. It shook, and felt like it was burning my throat. I forced myself to keep going. "The conclave is going to be over soon. They're going to vote, or . . . whatever it is they do at something like this, and then the High King and High Queen are going to pass a verdict they think their vassals will be willing to live with. The vote doesn't matter, but I figure they'll at least consider it, because they don't want to start a war. And maybe they'll say the cure can be used, and everything will be fine, but maybe they won't. I think we have to be braced for the idea that too many of the monarchs will be set against it, and the cure will be buried for another seventy years, or whatever seems reasonable to immortal people. They have time."

Time. That was the problem. I paused before I said, more softly, "I know you've always said you love me like I am. I know you'd never ask me to change. But I meant what I said before. If the cure is buried, I'll take the humanity out of my veins. I'll learn to live as a pureblood, whatever that means. And I *will* be here when you wake up."

What would I look like, with the last of my father's influence sliced away? Would my hair turn golden, like Amandine's, or would it just keep getting lighter? Would my skin bleach to bitter paleness, my eyes lose all claim to color, and leave me as an outline of a woman, looking for the artist who could fill me in? The copper in my magic would leave me completely, I was sure of that; it was already turning bloody. I'd smell like a slaughter every time I cast a spell or spun an illusion. I would see a stranger in my mirror, and iron would burn me so badly that I'd have to avoid it like the poison it was, and *I didn't care*.

Maybe it was unhealthy to consider making a change that big for the sake of a man, but this wasn't just about the man. This was about the boy on the next bier, the one I'd promised to usher into knighthood. This was about the mermaid who would have wanted me to look out for her family, and the alchemist who should never have been involved in this bullshit. Tybalt was my lover, yes, but this wasn't about love. This was about *family*. This was about keeping my word to all of them. If I had to become a little less human to hold on to my humanity, then there was no question of what I needed to do.

I just had to be strong enough to do it.

The tears finally started falling as I curled up next to Tybalt, resting my head on his chest and tucking my hands under my cheek. I closed my eyes. "I don't think you can hear me, but if you can," I whispered, "if you can, please. Remember that I love you. I love you, and I am not sorry. No matter what it costs me. I am not sorry."

His chest rose and fell beneath my hands, and for the moment, I could almost believe he was honestly sleeping, not enchanted to stay that way for a century.

Healing, even magically aided, always put a strain on my body. Sometimes I didn't even realize it was happening until the collapse came later. My eyes stayed closed, and eventually the tears stopped, and I fell asleep.

A hand touched my shoulder. "Toby." The voice was soft, almost gentle, but it left no room for argument: I was going to listen. "You need to wake up now."

I didn't want to. I was warm, and I was comfortable, and since I hadn't been elf-shot, I wasn't going to get the questionable luxury of sleeping for a century. I just wanted to rest for a little while longer.

"You can be just like your mother sometimes, you know that?" The exasperation in the statement gave the identity of the voice's owner away: the Luidaeg, sometimes called Antigone, my mother's eldest sister.

Insults weren't going to be enough to make me open my eyes. I nestled tighter against Tybalt.

The Luidaeg touched my shoulder again. This time, she left her hand there. "Toby, the conclave is over. They've voted, and the High King has given his decision."

I opened my eyes but didn't roll over. Instead, I stared at the slope of Tybalt's cheek, and waited to hear the shape that my life was going to take.

"You want to know something funny? I think my jackass sister decided the vote, at least a little. No one wanted to side with her. She's evil. You never want to side with the forces of evil, at least not where anyone can see you." She paused. "But I think you decided it a lot more. You shouldn't have been allowed to speak, and that meant that when you did, they listened. They *heard* you. And none of those assholes wanted to think about how confused they'd be if they missed a hundred years of Internet memes."

I rolled over, staring at her. My heart felt like it was going to explode. "Do you mean . . . ?"

The Luidaeg smiled. Openly, honestly smiled. Her

eyes were green as driftglass, and her features had settled in the broad, acne-scarred teenage face that I was
most familiar with. "They're going to allow the cure for
elf-shot to be used."

I was on my feet before I knew it, throwing my arms
around her shoulders and squeezing her as tightly as Sylvester had squeezed me back in the hall. It was a full
second before I thought to question the wisdom of hugging the sea witch without consent, and by that point, she
was hugging me back, which made the question, if not
moot, at least a little easier to answer.

"Not everyone's going to get it," she said. "People
who were sentenced to sleep for their crimes will still
need to wait and wake up the usual way, and we're sure
as shit not going to go onto Mom's old Road to wake my
sister. I'll find a way to ward her away from Karen. Kid
deserves a break. But the innocent and the targeted and
the accidental, them, we can wake up."

"When?" I let her go, taking a step back. "When are
we waking them up?"

"Arden is trying to decide how they're going to wake
the Prince. Guess he's sort of a big deal." The Luidaeg
nodded toward Nolan, making sure I knew which of the
available princes she meant. "And I'm pretty sure they're
planning to buy all the sushi in San Francisco and wake
Dianda up as part of a formal apology to the Undersea.
Siwan is figuring out the materials they'll need, and she's
coming up here to wake her nephew in a little bit. Says
she wants him to help her get everything in order."

I nodded slowly. "And Quentin and Tybalt . . . ?"

"That's why I'm here." She held up her empty hand.
"Nothing up my sleeves." She closed her hand. When she
opened it again, a glass potion bottle on a long silver
chain dropped to dangle near her elbow. At my shocked
look, she smirked, and asked, "You really thought some
wet-behind-the-ears alchemist would come up with an
elf-shot cure and I *wouldn't* demand samples? Walther

will be able to help his aunt brew a fresh batch, but I didn't figure you'd be big on patience. You've got three doses there. Enough for all three of the boys."

"I can't . . . I don't . . . I mean . . ." I stammered to a stop, took a deep breath, and said the only thing that seemed even halfway sufficient: "Thank you."

"Yeah." She seemed almost sad as she held the pendant out to me. "I guess you'd have to."

I wanted to ask what she meant by that. I didn't want to know. I held the potion bottle in my hand, feeling the cool glass getting warmer where it pressed against my skin, and looked from one bier to another. I needed to wake one of them before the other. But which one?

The Luidaeg rolled her eyes. "Oh, for Mom's sake. Feed it to your kitty, and give the rest to me. I'll wake up the kid and the alchemist. They don't want to see you sucking face first thing out of their coma anyway."

Thanking her again would have been excessive and potentially dangerous. I bobbed my head in silent understanding and turned back to Tybalt. His lips were parted. That seemed like a prompt. I pulled the glass stopper out of the potion bottle and leaned forward, pressing the rim to his lips. Then, keeping my movements slow and easy, I tipped the bottle upward until a third of the liquid trickled into his mouth.

He wasn't choking. That was a good sign. I turned to hand the bottle to the Luidaeg.

When I looked back to Tybalt, his eyes were open. He seized immediately on my face, eyes widening as his hand scrabbled on the bier, looking for mine. I gave it to him, and he clutched my fingers tight. The color was already starting to come back into his cheeks, slow but steady, as Jin's magic woke and finished its healing.

"October?" he asked, and his voice was raspy, and the sound of it mended something in my heart that I had thought was broken forever.

"Hi," I whispered.

"Your hair. It's still brown." He reached up with his free hand, running his fingers through my hair before bringing them to rest against the tapering curve of my ear. Then he smiled. "You didn't have to change for me."

I knew instantly what he meant, and nodded, raising my hand to curl over his, keeping him in place. "The conclave just ended. They voted to wake up everybody who isn't asleep for good reason." I could hear Quentin stirring behind me—his squawk of indignation, and the Luidaeg's pained exhale as he threw his arms around her neck. Everything was normal, then. Playing out exactly like it was supposed to.

Tybalt nodded slowly. "I feel . . . better."

"Jin was here."

"Ah. That explains it."

I was going to have to tell him about what had happened with Verona and Kabos, how they'd manipulated Minna and used her as their murder weapon. He needed to understand why all this had happened, and how it was that I'd found myself hauled out of a tower window and plummeting to my death. He wasn't going to like that. Hell, *I* didn't like it. But he was awake for me to tell, and right here and now, that was more than enough for me.

I bent to kiss him, quick and glancing, and left our hands joined as I twisted to cast a smile at my newly reawakened squire.

Things were getting back to normal.

TWENTY-THREE

THINGS WERE *NOT* GETTING BACK to normal. There was no version of normal I could envision where I would save the day—nearly getting killed in the process—awaken my lover, my squire, and my friend, and find myself not eight hours later standing in front of the High King and High Queen of the Westlands, the Queen in the Mists, and Duke Sylvester Torquill, listening to them deciding my fate.

Some days it's not worth crawling out of the shallow woodland grave, I swear.

"Be that as it may," Aethlin was saying, "she has now been present for the deaths of two monarchs, responsible for the replacement of two others, and directly responsible for the death of one of the Firstborn. These are issues we must consider."

"I don't see why," said Sylvester. "October is a hero of the realm. It's her *job* to become involved with awkward situations."

"How many crowns did you redistribute, exactly, before your retirement?" asked Maida. Her question was mild, but Sylvester flushed red and turned his face away. "My husband is right. While October may be innocent of any wrongdoing, our vassals are starting to become concerned. One cannot simply leave a king-breaker unattended."

"She's not unattended," protested Arden. "She's a willing member of a noble household, and is here on a regular basis."

"She has allegiances among the Undersea, she socializes with Firstborn, she's set to unite the Divided Court with the Court of Cats, and our son thinks she hung the moon and stars," said Aethlin. "Again, we know that she's innocent, but to the outside eye, it certainly *looks* as if she's gathering power for a political coup."

I had been told to stay silent unless addressed directly, but I couldn't help myself: I burst out laughing, causing all four of the people acting as my judge and jury to turn and stare at me.

Sylvester was the first to recover. He had spent the most time with me, after all. "Is something funny, October?"

"The idea of me even attempting a political coup, much less pulling it off," I said. "I mean, come *on*, really? I don't want power. I've given up power every time it's been given to me. I've done my best to be responsible for as little as possible, because sometimes I don't even trust my ability to take care of *myself*. I'm not a king-breaker. I'm not a scheming vizier waiting for my chance to seize the throne. I'm just trying to get by. That's all. No big secret plan, no hidden agenda. Survival."

"You've isolated yourself from your liege," said Aethlin.

I glared at him. "I don't care if you're Quentin's father or not, how Sylvester and I handle our personal conflicts is none of your damn business."

He raised an eyebrow. "I would have thought my position as High King of the continent where you live might have been more important than the identity of my son."

"Which just proves that you don't know me very

well," I shot back. "Yes, Sylvester and I have had our problems, mostly relating to the part where he lied to me for my mother's sake. I don't like being lied to by anyone, least of all the people who are supposed to be looking out for me. We're working things out. Don't get in the middle."

"You can see where it would look like you were trying to act independent of his control."

"I never do anything heroic or stupid unless I'm under *someone* else's control," I said. "I'd be a lot happier if everyone would just leave me alone to eat pizza and watch television, but you people seem to constantly need saving, so here I am."

Maida looked amused. Aethlin looked unconvinced.

"She had the opportunity to take the throne of the Mists, you know," said Arden. Everyone turned to her. She looked coolly back. "Once the pretender Queen had been proven false, if October hadn't forced me to come forward, she could have claimed the throne on the grounds that there was no legitimate heir, and she was the daughter of a Firstborn. No one would have contested her. Probably not even you."

"That's true enough," allowed Aethlin. "It doesn't change the rest."

"It changes everything," said Arden. "If she wanted power, she would have it. She went to Silences on my order. The King and Queen of Highmountain came here on your invitation. She may be a nexus for chaos and disorder, but she's not a political genius. She can barely dress herself half the time."

"You're too kind," I said dryly, suddenly very aware that I was still wearing a borrowed coat over a shift, and no shoes. "What do you need me to say? Because while I get that this is politically necessary, my fiancé and my squire just woke up, and they probably want me in shouting distance."

"We need you to say that you have no intent to

destabilize the political structure of the Westlands," said Aethlin.

I shrugged. "Easy. I have no intent to destabilize the political structure of the Westlands. I may do it anyway, but if I do, it'll be a mistake."

"October—" began Sylvester.

"No, don't," I said. "Look, Your Highnesses, I'm not going to promise never to do something I'm already not planning to do, because I can't see the future. But I've never gone out of my way to hurt anyone who didn't deserve it. From what I can see, you don't deserve it. I like you okay, and Quentin loves you. Honestly, I just want to go home, and maybe start planning my wedding." It no longer seemed quite so abstract. It was something that needed to happen.

"Will you have the wedding in Toronto?" The question came from Maida.

It knocked the wind out of me. I stared at her, my mouth working soundlessly, like the fish I used to be. Finally, I managed to stammer, "W-*what*?"

"Will you and the King of Cats marry in Toronto, at our knowe?" Maida shrugged. "It would show there was no bad blood between us; that you had the support of the High Throne, and that the High Throne was not set to be a target of your accidental wrath; and it would be nice to host a wedding. It's been too long."

Again, I stared at her. My mind was racing. Tybalt's objection to getting married at Shadowed Hills was two-fold: he didn't like Sylvester, and he needed to avoid looking like he was swearing fealty to the Divided Courts. Getting married in Muir Woods shared the second problem, if not the first. Arden was his equal, not his superior.

But there was no High King of Cats. Getting married in Toronto could solve a lot of things. "I can't agree without talking to Tybalt, but I'm not opposed to the idea," I said carefully.

"In that case, I believe we can agree that your actions were necessary and proportionate, and do not represent a pattern of hostility against the nobility of the Westlands." Maida gave her husband a challenging look. He nodded, and she smiled. "We appreciate your time."

"Uh, sure," I said. "Look, about time . . . when are you planning to wake the others? I feel like I should be here for that."

"Queen Siwan expects to have the potion ready by morning," said Arden, sounding confident now that she was back on comfortable ground. "They'll wake Dianda first, so that we can focus our apologies on her, and let her decide what's to be done with Duke Michel. I'll wait to wake my brother until after all the guests have gone. He'll have enough to adjust to without adding in a hundred new faces that he won't need to remember right away."

I nodded. "Smart."

"Yes." Arden looked down the line to Sylvester.

"Luna is already agitating to have Rayseline woken," he said gravely. "I would appreciate it if you could be there."

"Of course," I said. "Whenever you need me."

He inclined his head.

"The others who sleep will be dealt with one by one, until all are either awake or sleeping off a sentence that shouldn't be commuted," said Aethlin. "It may take years, but by the time we're done, no one will slumber who doesn't deserve it."

I thought of all the people who might be woken, and what they might be deserving of—especially Simon Torquill. But that was Sylvester's problem, not mine, and all of this was a problem for another day. "That's good," I said. "May I go?"

"You may," said the High King. I curtsied deeply to the four of them—my liege, my Queen, the parents of my squire, the people who had called this conclave and

changed our world forever—and turned as I straightened, moving toward the door. There were people waiting for me out there, people who I had thought were
going to be lost for a long, long time, who were magically,
gloriously still with me. So I was going to go and be with
them.

Out of everything in the world, that was the only
thing that really mattered. Everything else was just stage
dressing. They were the show.

Read on for
a brand-new Arden Windermere novella
by Seanan McGuire:

DREAMS AND SLUMBERS

You are for dream and slumbers, brother.
                    —William Shakespeare, *Troilus and Cressida*

ONE

June 10th, 2013

"I'M SCARED."

The words were simple: their meaning was complex. My entire life is like that these days. It got complicated almost a year ago, when a wild-eyed woman crashed into the bookstore where I worked and ordered me to take back my father's throne. Like it was a little thing to ask for, or an easy thing to do, and not just a complicated way of committing suicide.

A year ago, if something sounded simple, it probably *was*. "Yes, we have that book in stock," or "no, we only carry science fiction and fantasy," or "let me ask Alan if he knows." There were days when I'd been bored, restless, convinced I was meant for something better . . . and on those days, I'd slip into the basement, past the bounds of the illusion I used to keep everyone—even Alan, who owned the place—from realizing I lived there. I'd go into the tiny sanctuary I had carved from the flesh of the mortal world, and I'd wipe the dust from my brother's lips, and I'd remind myself that boredom was a blessing.

Boredom meant the nameless Queen's agents hadn't found us. Boredom meant I wasn't faced with the choice between running and leaving my sleeping brother alone and defenseless, or staying and risking us both. Boredom was *everything*. Until October Daye, Knight of Lost Words, daughter of Amandine, bane of my peace of mind, smashed her way in and ruined it all.

I'm going to fuck up the tenses here, because past and present get blurred when you're talking about more than a century, but I'll do my best. Here it is:

My father was a King, which made me a Princess born and an orphan before I turned sixteen. It made my brother Nolan a Prince, but there was never any question of who would take the throne; I was the elder by two full years. My magic came in earlier and stronger than his. And when we were children, I was fearless. I treated the world like a game that could be won, and I was going to be Queen someday.

Not that anyone knew. My father was unmarried; my mother, his mistress, hid in plain sight as a servant in his Court. Nolan and I lived in a house by the sea with our nursemaid, Marianne. She disguised us as changelings when she brought us to see our parents, and it was the best of all the wonderful games we played. I was a princess in hiding, ready to dazzle the world by bursting forth fully-formed and ready to rule. Someday. After decades and decades and decades of watching how my father did it, learning from his experiences, and preparing.

No one could have been prepared for the earthquake. It came out of nowhere, shattering the Summerlands and

San Francisco in the same blow. When it ended, my brother and I were orphans. It was just the two of us and Marianne, who was old and tired and hadn't signed up to be our replacement mother. She did the best she could. She taught us to run, and hide, and keep our heads down. She honed our illusions until we reached the limits of what our blood allowed.

It wasn't enough. There were people who remembered her from my father's Court, people who'd heard the rumors about Gilad having children and were starting to put two and two together. She had to go. Staying would have gotten us all killed. I knew that, and still I cried the night she said good-bye. Nolan was even worse. He'd been so *young* when the world fell down. Ten years old when we were orphaned; fourteen when Marianne walked away. He cried until she had to charm him into sleep, because otherwise he would have betrayed our position.

He hit the ground like a sack of potatoes, like he was dead, and I was going to throw myself after him when Marianne grabbed my arm and said, "Wait."

She'd been my keeper and companion since I was nursing. One of my first memories is her smiling down at me, a rag soaked in milk and honey in her hand. I stopped moving and looked at her, letting the habit of obedience guide what happened next.

Marianne smiled sadly. She was Coblynau; I never knew how old she was, but her face was a maze of wrinkles, and her sorrow showed all the way down to her bones. "Here," she said, reaching into her pocket and pulling out a handful of driftglass beads strung on a braid of unicorn hair. "I got these from the Luidaeg when you were a baby; they've kept you safe until now, and they'll keep you safe hereafter."

I gasped. I couldn't help myself. The Luidaeg's gifts were never things to take lightly, or to request without dire need. "But Marianne, the cost—"

"Was paid long ago, and I never begrudged it. Here."

She pressed them into my hand. "This is all I have. This is all you have. Be careful, Arden, and never forget that I love you as much as I love my own children. Never forget to stay safe, for my sake, for your sake, for the sake of the Mists."

Then she was gone, and I was alone with my brother, too young to be a woman, too young to be a surrogate mother to a confused boy still getting the hang of his own teenage years. The Princess who would never be a Queen. My father taught me about ruling, and my mother taught me about hiding, and my nursemaid taught me about running away, and of the three of them, Marianne's lessons were the ones that served me the best for years, and years, and years. Her lessons got me through the time I spent alone, after Nolan was elf-shot by the false Queen's forces. She kept me safe.

Until October. Until the challenge, and the crown, and this great barn of a knowe, where the air still sometimes tastes like my mother's perfume when we let the ghosts out of rooms that have been sealed for more than a century. Until I left my mortal life the same way I left my fae one: not walking away but running, fleeing into a different future. I was born a Princess in hiding. Technically, I grew up the same way. But the way I hid as a child was a glorious game, and the way I hid as an adult was a constant threat, and they are *not* the same.

The girl I should have grown up to be is never going to sit on the throne of the Mists. That girl died with our mutual mother, in the 1906 earthquake, when palaces that should never have shifted tried to shake themselves to the ground. That girl has neither grave nor night-haunt mannequin to remember her. She only has me, and I hate her sometimes, because she would have been so much *better* at this than I am. She would have had tutors and secret allies and an army preparing her for the pressures of queenship. She would have been a committee.

I didn't get any of that. I got good at disposable identities and confusion charms, at lying until potential employers believed me, at moving my elf-shot brother under the cover of night, going place to place in pursuit of the lie of a safe haven. I got a bookstore and a best friend and barely time to catch my breath before October barged in like a changeling battering ram and took it all away.

I'm sure there are people who'd say it was worth it to lose everything and gain a throne, but since I stopped wanting the throne decades ago, I'm not one of them. I want to make my parents proud. I want to keep my brother safe. I can do those things better from the throne of the Mists than I could from the basement of Borderlands.

But some days, most days, that basement felt more like home than this knowe did.

The conclave—my first major political event—had been a success, and they'd left me alone, all of them after it was over and we'd finished waking the majority of the sleepers. October had walked away clinging to her squire and her alchemist and her Cait Sidhe fiancé, checking every five minutes to be sure they were all awake. It would have been funny if I hadn't been on some level fiercely glad to see it. Sometimes it feels like she doesn't know how to lose. Maybe it's small and petty and human of me to want her to understand what it's like for the rest of us, but I've spent more time with humans than I've spent with my own kind. I guess a little had to work its way in.

Waking Duchess Lorden had been a more involved process, and had involved finding a way to restrain her without hurting her. We couldn't afford to offend her any more than she already was—I mean, being elf-shot is pretty damn offensive—but she was likely to wake up swinging, and that woman can *hit*. In the end, we'd resorted to binding spells to hold her down while Queen

Siwan of Silences administered the cure and Dianda's husband, Patrick Lorden, stood in full view at the foot of the bed. As we'd hoped, the sight of him stopped her from either hurting herself or figuring out how to break the bonds and hurting the rest of us.

The fact that her attacker had been elf-shot for hurting her helped. The fact that he was being left that way until she decided on his punishment helped more. She and Patrick will be enjoying the hospitality of my household for another three days while they decide what to do.

Many of the land nobles are hoping she'll show mercy, if only so they won't have to explain why they'd stood idly by as one of their own was dragged away to the Undersea to sleep out his sentence. Personally, I hope she'll go for the worst punishment she can think of. I don't want people thinking they can attack each other willy-nilly under my roof.

When did this become *my* roof? It's supposed to be my father's roof. It's supposed to have been his for the last hundred years. I groaned and dropped my head into my hands.

"I swear, Nolan, I'm scared out of my mind here, and I don't know what to do."

The last remaining sleeper didn't say anything. Hadn't said anything, in fact, since August fifteenth, nineteen thirty-two. But who's counting, right? Who measures the days a brother spends in an enchanted sleep, unable to comfort the sister who loves him?

I guess I do.

It doesn't help that, hello cliché, the last things we said to each other weren't particularly kind. He hated the false Queen sitting on our father's throne. He wanted to raise an army and depose her and take our lives back. Maybe it was because I was older and more aware of what we had left to lose, but I wanted to stay safely under the radar, avoiding her attention. He kept saying that if I *really* wanted to pass unnoticed, I'd move us out of the Kingdom, to someplace where our resemblance to our lost father wouldn't draw stares on the street, and he wasn't wrong, and I kept not moving. I was frozen. Like a rabbit that sees the hunter coming, I was frozen.

I should have listened. I should have gotten us the hell out of the Mists. But I was afraid that anywhere we went, we'd be seized on and used as the figureheads of a revolution. Faerie loves nothing like it loves to go to war. Putting the daughter of a dead King back on the throne where she belonged? That was a *lovely* excuse for a slaughter. If it was going to happen no matter where we were, why should we leave the only place we'd ever called home? I was a coward, and Nolan was burning to prove himself, and it was a combination destined to end in tragedy.

These were the last words he said to me: "I don't know why you bothered surviving if you weren't going to live."

I'd been on my way out the door, heading for the job that was keeping a roof over our heads and food in our mouths. I was serving as the nanny of a local mortal family, using the skills I'd copied from Marianne to support us. She was still saving us, after all those years. I'd thought it was an ordinary day. Nolan was impossible when he got into one of his moods: I hadn't even tried to talk to him. I'd just left. I hadn't told him I loved him. I hadn't said I was proud of him.

I'd just left, and when I came home from work, he'd been gone.

I hadn't worried right away. Nolan was a young man, headstrong and angry and looking for an outlet. I couldn't keep him with me all the time, no matter how much I wanted to. But hours had gone by, and he hadn't returned, until fear had driven me into the night to look for him. I'd gone to his favorite haunts, the places he went when he was angry with me, and I'd searched and searched and searched until I found him. The arrow had

still been in his chest, pinning the message from the false
Queen to his shirt.

'Little Princess;

I hope you enjoy my gift. Take it for the opportunity it is, and walk away. I will not be so kind
again, to either of you.'

It hadn't been signed. It hadn't needed to be. Nolan
never hurt anyone in his life. The only person with a reason to attack him or threaten me was the woman holding
my father's throne. Unless I decided to raise an army
against her, she couldn't have me killed without breaking
the Law. Threats and intimidation were her best tools.
And oh, she used them well. So well that I dragged Nolan home to the boarding house without a word to anyone. We needed to disappear again.

And that's exactly what we did.

Now here we were, eighty years later, and he was still
asleep and I was finally the Queen he'd always wanted
me to be. But the things I'd learned as a child were fuzzy
and distant; I was making all this up as I went along, and
I was terrified of letting him down.

If I wanted to, I could leave Nolan to sleep out the rest of
his time. What was another twenty years? I'd been frantic to
wake him when I thought I only had a little while before the
cure was banned, but now that the cure was being openly
distributed, I could afford to wait. I could give myself the
time to figure things out. I could establish myself as a Queen
to be feared and respected, not some untrained stranger
whose butt had barely hit the throne. I could mature without him ... and we'd wind up even farther apart than we
already were. I'd turned into a different person while he
slept. If I left him asleep while I turned myself into a ruler,
he might not even recognize me when he finally woke up.

But at least he'd be proud of me. If I was going to be

a stranger, why shouldn't I be a stranger he could respect, and not just a girl with a PhD in running away?

"I wish you could hear me." I turned the bottle containing the cure—*his* cure, the potion that would wake him up immediately, instead of in another twenty years—in my hand, watching the way the liquid lapped against the glass. It was pink with streaks of purple and gold, like a sunset, like a future.

"I wish you could tell me what to do."

Nolan, saying nothing, slept on. After a long pause, I stretched out on the bier next to him, the bottle still held tightly in my hand, and closed my own eyes. Maybe everything would be clearer on the other side of a nap.

TWO

Everything was not, in fact, clearer on the other side of a nap. I opened my eyes, and for one dizzying moment, I had no idea where I was. The room was round, ringed with windows to let the fresh air in. It smelled like redwood sap and rain. I don't know how the bedding around me stayed so dry; with the fog the way it was in the trees, everything should have been damp all the time. The ceiling was a mural of blackberry vines twining around several small, sleeping animals. A fawn, a rabbit, a unicorn, a bear. The usual menagerie.

I sat up. The bottle was no longer in my hand. My breath sped up and my chest grew tight as I looked around me. It was gone. It was gone. I'd failed him again, I'd lost it somehow, and now he was going to sleep for another twenty years whether I wanted him to or not—

Light glinted off bias-cut glass. I leaned over the edge of the bed. The bottle was on the floor, nestled against the bedpost. I leaned farther down, snatching it off the floor, feeling its reassuring weight settle in my palm. The sky outside the windows hadn't changed; it was still twilight, the sky painted purple and rose, like a darker version of the liquid that would wake my brother. It's almost always twilight in the Summerlands.

Carefully, I slid off the bed and walked to the nearest window, pushing the curtains aside. The sky was cloudy, but there were patches where the stars shone through, gleaming bright. Once, this sky was all I knew. These days, I sometimes think I'd trade it all for the light-polluted mortal stars of San Francisco. At least they'd be familiar.

"I'm scared," I whispered. Nothing answered me, not even the distant jingle of pixie wings. That was probably for the best. Queens aren't supposed to be scared. Queens are supposed to be calm and steady and prepared for anything. They make the choices. My choice should have been simple. Give the potion to my brother. Open his eyes twenty years early. Let him see how far we'd come, that we didn't have to run anymore; that we were safe. It would be simple. It would be *easy*.

So why couldn't I do it?

I turned away from the window and toward the bed where Nolan slept, silently waiting for me to make my decision. He looked like he'd looked for the past eighty years: peaceful. He had our father's dark hair, same as me, black in shadow and glinting purple in the light. If he opened his eyes, they'd be mismatched: one the almost-golden color of pyrite, one metallic gray, like liquid mercury. He hadn't seen the sun in decades, but his skin was still tan, with olive undertones. No one who met me could look at him and not see him for my brother. There had never been any chance of us repudiating each other.

"Would you have been better off without me?" I

asked. He could have run, if I hadn't been there counseling caution and holding him back. He could have made a home for himself in some far-away kingdom, one where no one knew what King Gilad Windermere looked like, one where he could start again. Two children with a dead king's bone structure and coloration were a target. One was a curiosity. One could disappear where two couldn't.

And I was the one who'd been old enough to scar instead of healing. I was the one who'd found our mother's body with a canyon where her throat should have been. Nolan had been with Marianne. He'd always *known* how Mother ended, but he'd never *seen* it. It was a little thing in the grander scheme, and yet. He'd never been forced to go to sleep with our mother's murdered face watching him from behind his eyelids. He'd never walked through the world understanding what would happen to us if we put one foot wrong. He'd known, because I'd told him—over and over and over again—but knowing and understanding aren't the same thing. Maybe they never can be.

Nolan didn't answer. Nolan couldn't answer. Nolan had passed beyond answering decades ago, and if he was going to start answering again, it would either be because I'd dithered for twenty years, or because I'd forced him to drink a potion I couldn't make and didn't fully understand.

"I could wait, you know." My words fell into the silence, filling it, softening its edges. I wanted to open the door and call for Madden, or for Lowri, or for any other member of my court. I wanted someone to tell me what to do. I wanted someone to tell me whether waking my brother was right or wrong.

And that was why I couldn't ask. I was the Queen now. I had to make these decisions on my own. I walked back to Nolan's bed, perching on the edge.

"Eighty years is a long time. Twenty more on top of that is nothing. I haven't even been Queen for a full year, you know? Nine months. That's not long enough to know what I'm doing. I keep waiting for Jude to call and say my vacation's over and I need to come back to the store." Not that she could. I've changed phone numbers, addresses, and names. No one from my old life could find me if they wanted to.

I held up the bottle. "So what if I let you sleep for another year, or another five, or whatever, while I get my feet under me? I'll be a better sister if I'm not busy trying to learn how to queen while I teach you about the Internet. It would be better for both of us if I waited."

Nolan didn't answer. Sometimes I wasn't even sure I remembered what his voice sounded like. Elf-shot is supposed to be the kinder option during wartime, and I guess it is, since it just takes our loved ones away for a century, instead of forever. But a hundred years was long enough to make us into strangers to one another. I'd been less than thirty when he'd gone to sleep. Sometimes I felt like he was more of an idea than an individual.

Sometimes I wonder whether it's like that for the older ones, too. My father was over three hundred years old when he died. Would he have forgotten us eventually, if he'd been able to live and stay King in the Mists until Nolan and I grew up? It might explain a few things. Memory is a funny thing. It can be worn away if it's revisited too often, smudged and warped and winnowed down to symbols when it used to be about people, real people, living real lives. If the older fae don't remember what happened to them when they were young, it makes sense for them to be distant and cold. They have no emotional connections to the world.

I don't want to be like that. I still don't know *what* I want to be, except for maybe a bookstore clerk, and that door is closed to me now. But I was going to find out.

The cork came free of the bottle with a soft popping sound. The smell of roses wafted out, making me want to sneeze. It was almost like the smell of Countess

Winterrose's magic, but not quite right; it was too warm, too comforting, too *friendly*. This wasn't a charm that had been designed to hurt people. It only wanted to help.

"I hope you're okay with this," I said. "I guess eighty years isn't as bad as a hundred. I guess I'm not being selfish by waking you up now. I guess . . . I guess I'm lonely, Nolan. I've been talking to you for eighty years, and you've never answered. I'd like that to change. I'd like you to answer."

Last chance. I could put the stopper back in, put the bottle in my pocket, and walk away. No one would question me deciding to let my brother sleep out the rest of his enchantment. Well, maybe Toby would. She doesn't really have a lot of respect for the fact that I'm the Queen and thus technically the boss of her. I'd be upset by that, if not for the part where she doesn't have a lot of respect for anyone, including the Luidaeg. So it's not like I'm *special*. She treats me the way she treats everyone else.

After a decade or two of queening, that will probably offend me. Right now, it's a relief. No matter how far I rise, there will always be someone standing there to laugh at me.

It didn't have to be just one person.

"I've been so lonely," I said, and lifted the bottle to Nolan's lips, pushing down until his mouth opened enough to let me start dripping the cure through, one drop at a time. I didn't want him to choke.

He swallowed. It was the first time I'd seen him move in decades. I pulled the bottle away and stepped back. The cure worked, I knew that—I had *seen* it work repeatedly, from Madden to Dianda. Nolan was special to me, but that didn't make him special to the rules of magic that governed Faerie. If the cure worked for one, it would work for all. He was going to wake up. He was. But with every second that passed without him opening his eyes, I became a little more convinced that something had gone wrong.

Finally, I couldn't take it anymore. I tucked the bottle into my skirt before reaching out and touching his shoulder as gently as I could, like I was afraid of waking him. But that was silly, wasn't it? I *wanted* to wake him. I wanted to wake him more than I'd wanted anything in years.

"Nolan," I said. "Hey. Can you hear me? It's your sister. Wake up."

He made a small noise deep in his throat; a sound of protest, a sound of displeasure. Hearing it woke a hundred "just one more minute" memories, images of a younger Nolan begging me to let him stay in bed when it was time to get up and get the night started. I smiled as tears rose in my eyes. Memory wasn't as complicated as I'd feared. It was still there. It was all still there. It just needed to be woken up. Like my brother, it just needed to be woken up.

"Come on, Nolan. You've been asleep long enough. It's time to open your eyes."

"Ardy?"

His voice was the creak of a rusty gate, ragged and shallow and worn. I could have mistaken it for a dream, something I wanted so much that I was imagining it, if it hadn't been followed by his lashes fluttering against his cheeks before finally—finally!—his eyes opened and he was squinting up at me.

He blinked, and frowned. "Ardy?" he whispered again. "When did you get so *old*?"

Laughing through my tears, I fell upon my brother and gathered him in my arms, and for the first time since our parents died, I felt like I was on my way home.

THREE

The only person left in the sleeper's tower was Duke Michel, who had been elf-shot for committing a crime: for the first time in a hundred years, there were no innocent victims of elf-shot in the Kingdom in the Mists. We were free of Eira Rosynhwyr's poisonous gifts—and more, I was free of the injunction not to use magic in proximity of the cure, which was somewhat unstable, according to the alchemist who'd created it. He was still tinkering, and he promised to have something more reliable by the end of the year, but that was later, and this was now. Nolan's head resting on my left shoulder, I used my right hand to inscribe a wide arc in the air, opening a portal.

As always, using my magic openly sent a little thrill through me, like I was getting away with something. My powers had never been suppressed, although I'd considered it a few times. There were always underground alchemists working in San Francisco—lean, hungry fae who thought they were going to rival the sea witch one day. They would have been delighted to sell me blocking potions, keeping me from accessing the powers I got from my parents and hence potentially giving myself away. And they would have remembered my face, filed away the scent of my magic, maybe even gone to the Library of Stars to compare it to the census.

The fae world is an easier place to be anonymous than the human world. There's no question of that. But that doesn't mean it's *safe*.

Nolan lifted his head, blinking at me in confusion. He

only seemed to have two expressions at the moment—confused and bewildered, which were subtly different. I couldn't have distinguished them on anyone else, but he was my brother, and his face was so much like mine that it was like looking into a mirror.

"Ardy?" he said blankly.

"Hey," I said, smiling to cover my increasing distress. Madden had been back to normal within seconds of waking. Dianda had come to swinging and ready to murder people—which, for her, was also back to normal. So why was Nolan taking so long to recover?

He'd been asleep so much longer than they had. This was probably perfectly normal. Master Davies had just forgotten to warn me, that was all.

"Where are we?"

My smile froze, turning rigid. "Nolan, we're home. This is home. We got it back."

His confusion wasn't going away. If anything, it was getting deeper. "Home?"

"Come on." I stood, pulling him with me. He stumbled in the process of getting his feet under him, but in the end, he did it. I had to take that as a good sign. It *was* a good sign, wasn't it? Wasn't it?

Nolan let me pull him through the portal, which closed behind us with a faint pop. He looked around the new room, eyes skipping over the bed, wardrobe, and writing desk without recognition. He turned to me, and in the same blank tone, asked, "Where are we?"

"Home," I repeated. His tone might be staying the same, but mine wasn't: the desperation was creeping in around the edges, coloring everything I said. Something was really wrong. "This was your room when we came to visit Mother at Court, remember? That's your bed." Like all Coblynau furniture, it was enchanted to grow with its owner; the bed he'd slept in as a child was still long and wide enough to cradle him now that he was an adult.

"Bed," Nolan breathed, showing his first sign of

recognition since he said my name. He pulled away from me, less walking under his own power than staggering drunkenly to the bed.

I watched in horror as he collapsed onto it, falling facedown into the pillows. "Nolan?"

He didn't respond.

"Nolan!" I ran to his side, rolling him over, so his face was turned toward the ceiling and he wouldn't suffocate. His chest was rising and falling like a normal sleeper's, without the slow, drugged tempo of the elf-shot. I shook him. He didn't open his eyes. I shook him harder, and still, he didn't open his eyes.

"Nolan?" My voice cracked, becoming young and shrill in my throat. I felt like the girl I'd been when I found him in the bushes, the arrow in his chest and blank serenity on his face. I hadn't felt like her in years. She'd been so innocent. She'd truly believed, deep down, that we'd suffered enough; that the world would start being kinder. The world still wasn't being kinder.

I took a step backward, my hand sculpting an arch in the air behind me and opening a portal to the veranda. Madden was there, going over the household records and trying to figure out what we had too much of versus what we didn't have enough of. It was one of his tasks as Seneschal, at least until I hired a Chamberlain— something I'd been in no hurry to do. Madden knew me. Madden *understood* me, and that was something I couldn't put a price on.

Madden wouldn't judge me.

Taking one last look at my slumbering brother, I whirled and fled through the portal, stumbling from the sweet-scented air of the bedroom into the cool Summerlands night. Globes of witch-light lit the veranda, bobbing a few inches below the living, mossy canopy that kept the area dry even during heavy rainfall. Madden sat at the largest of the three round tables, a pair of comically small spectacles balanced on the tip of his nose. His head snapped up when my foot hit the floor; by the time I had reached the table, he was on his feet, arms up to catch me.

"Ardy, what's wrong?" he demanded.

Hearing my nickname from one of the two people in the world allowed to use it brought tears to my eyes, where they hung, stinging and hot, refusing to fall. "Something's wrong with Nolan," I said, burrowing into Madden's arms, allowing myself a split-second where I wasn't a queen; I was just Arden Windermere, the girl without a kingdom, without a crown, without a brother to comfort her. "I woke him up, but he's not awake. He barely knows me. He barely knows where he *is*."

"Where is he now?"

"In his room." Madden knew where that was: he'd helped me prepare it once we knew it was both possible and permissible for me to wake my brother. We'd wiped away dust and cleared away cobwebs, and—for a little while—I'd allowed myself to dream of a future where things started going right for me. My lips twisted into a bitter line as I continued, "Asleep. Again. He was awake less than five minutes before he passed out. What did I do *wrong*?"

"I don't know." Madden didn't do anything to soften his words. He didn't need to. He was my best friend and my seneschal and the only person who'd known who I was before October came along and ruined everything. He'd never cared that I was a princess, and now he didn't care that I was a queen. He just cared that I was his Ardy, and I was in pain.

There are people in my Court who think he's disrespectful, and maybe I'd agree with them if I'd grown up as the girl they want me to be. But I didn't, and I find his willingness to be my friend before he's my subject more refreshing than anything else in the world.

I pulled away from him, wiping my eyes with the back of my hand. "I need to talk to the alchemist," I said. "Where is he?"

"Uh." Madden looked at his wrist. His watch—a cheerful, brightly-colored thing with Mickey Mouse printed on the strap—was charmed eight ways from Sunday to keep mortal time even when we were in the Summerlands. It's a necessary affectation. He still works at the Borderlands Café, slinging mochas and looking sad when Jude asks whether he's heard from me. He doesn't like lying to her any more than I liked disappearing from the face of the world, but his position leaves him with time to interact with the human world, and mine doesn't. Even when I'm not doing anything, I'm being a queen, and being a queen means staying where my people can find me.

"It's almost midnight," said Madden. "I'm pretty sure there aren't any classes at midnight, but I don't know. I did all my college stuff online."

"He's not in the knowe?"

"No." Madden looked deeply regretful. "He went back to work this morning while you were asleep. You had the potion, you had your brother, and you'd said you didn't want any of us there while you woke him up."

"Do you know where his office is?"

"Yes, but—"

"Where is it?"

Madden frowned. "Ardy, I don't think this is the best idea. You should send someone. Send me. Send Lowri. She has a car."

"She has a rusty piece of junk that needs about twenty thousand dollars' worth of work before it'll be shitty enough to sell for scrap," I said. "I'm going. Where's his office?"

"He's in the UC Berkeley Chemistry Building. I *really* don't like this."

"Something is wrong with my brother." I grabbed a fistful of air. It writhed against my fingers, protesting my intentions. Tough. I twisted it into a human disguise, throwing the features of the woman I'd spent so many decades pretending to be over my own. The weight of her was comforting. I'd been Ardith Heydt for years; longer, really, than I'd been Arden Windermere. I was better at being a bookstore clerk than I was at being a queen.

The one thing we'd always had in common was our brother. Nolan, who'd been the focus of my life since his birth, regardless of which version of me—lost princess, retail worker, or newfound queen—I was allowing myself to be. I straightened, forcing myself to breathe.

"Madden, you have the knowe until I return. If anyone needs me, try to fix whatever their problem is, and if you can't, tell them to come back tomorrow. I'm busy for tonight."

He sighed. "All right. Just be careful, Ardy. I don't want you to get hurt."

"Too late for that," I said. "Years and years too late for that."

A sweep of my hand opened a window between the balcony and a copse of trees on the UC Berkeley campus. I touched the tip of my ear, verifying that my illusion was solid, and stepped through.

FOUR

The air in the mortal world was thicker, flavored with gas fumes and pesticides and pollution. I breathed in deeply, filling my lungs. This was what home was supposed to smell like. This was where I belonged.

Stupid duty. Stupid bloodline. Stupid inheritance.

It was late enough that the campus was virtually deserted. Somewhere in the trees an owl hooted, protesting my sudden appearance; something rustled in the bushes, too small and quick to be human. That was a relief. Somehow I didn't think High King Aethlin would be too thrilled if his newest and least-prepared queen was the one who betrayed the existence of Faerie to the human world. We'd managed to stay under the radar for centuries. I wasn't going to be the one who gave us away.

When nothing else moved, I started walking. My skirt wasn't the smartest choice for the tree-peppered UC Berkeley grounds, but my illusion was cosmetic only; it hadn't changed the structure or length of my clothes. Transforming them would have taken too much out of me, especially when I was transporting myself—and hopefully, soon, Master Davies—between Berkeley and Muir Woods. My range is average for one of the Tuatha de Dannan. I can manage a hundred miles on a good day, if I'm aiming for a target that isn't super precise, like "somewhere in the trees on campus" or "in Muir Woods," as opposed to "this exact square foot of clover." I can do three or four jumps a night if they're that distance, and a lot more if they're not. But my power is as limited as anyone else's, and there was no sense frittering it away on unnecessary tactile transformations.

The campus was like a midnight dream, quiet and verdant and intermittently lit by flickering energy-efficient streetlights. Pixies darted overhead, not many, but enough to make it clear that I wasn't alone. As always, I wondered if they recognized me, or if they cared. Pixies aren't smart enough to know who's in charge—or maybe they're smart enough to realize it doesn't matter. As long as they have wings, they can get away, and they don't have to get sucked into the bullshit we mire ourselves in. Maybe the pixies are secretly the smartest things in Faerie, and the rest of us will never know.

I hadn't been to UC Berkeley in years. My last visit had been during the early nineties, when Madden had lured me away from the used bookstore where I was working long enough to come to a place named the Bear's Lair and hear a scrappy young mortal band called the Counting Crows play a set. They'd been out of tune; the lead singer had been so drunk that he'd barely been able to stay on his feet for the last three songs; it had been one of the best nights of my life. We'd laughed and cheered and sung along, even though we didn't know half the lyrics, and it had been perfect. I'd been avoiding campus ever since.

When you live a life like mine, you learn that it's best to leave the good things alone. If you give the world a chance to ruin them, it'll take it. Every single fucking time. Case in point: I was alone, and there was no music, and no beer, and no beautiful mortal men to watch admiringly with my best friend. There was just me, and the silence, and the knowledge that this night was going to overwrite the one I'd treasured for so long. That was just the way it was going to be. Again. Always.

The chemistry building was locked. That wasn't a problem. I peered through the glass, confirming that no one was inside before I waved my hand in the air and opened a portal. I stepped through and the door was behind me, glass unbroken, lock unpicked. It was an elegant, impossible solution to a very mortal problem. Even if I'd been here to rob the place—which I wasn't—and even if they'd decided to spring for cameras, no security guard would have believed the footage. The illusion I was wearing would keep them from tracking me down to ask how I'd done it, and Faerie was not going to be revealed by what looked like a glitch on the tape.

I didn't know which office belonged to Master Davies. I didn't need to. Most of them were dark, their doors locked against the night; of all the doors along the hall, only one was cracked enough to let a sliver of light escape. It showed the scuffs and muddy footprints on the linoleum. The janitorial staff probably didn't come until closer to morning.

As I drew closer, I heard voices from inside.

"—tried to explain that actually, I *do* need to show up for classes once in a while if I want a shot at tenure, but you know Toby." The alchemist: Master Davies. Tylwyth Teg, originally from the Kingdom of Silences, currently living in the Mists and hence subject to my laws.

Wry laughter followed his words. "Oh, man, do I know Toby." The voice was unfamiliar: the subject material was not. I sometimes thought half of my reign was going to be spent trying to explain October to people who didn't have any context on her, and hence assumed we were all screwing with them.

"Did you know she elf-shot herself *on purpose*?"

"See, and here I was thinking there was something stupid left that she hadn't done. Stop disillusioning me."

"Sorry."

I felt like I was intruding. But my brother was unwell, and I was Queen in the Mists, and it was time for me to make my presence known. I stepped into the sliver of light, reaching for the partially-open door at the same time.

It opened to reveal Master Davies sitting at his desk, and a woman sitting *on* his desk. They were both wearing human disguises—only sensible, if they were going to hang around with the door unlocked—and I didn't recognize her at all. Sadly, that didn't necessarily make her a newcomer to the Mists. My kingdom was large, and I'd spent more time avoiding it than I had going door to door and meeting the people whose fealty was technically mine to command.

The woman blinked at me. So did Master Davies. Then, in a tone that was pleasantly polite without being friendly, he said, "I'm sorry, but office hours happen before the campus is closed for the night. Is there something else I can help you with?"

It was the first time he'd spoken to me like I was a person, instead of just a crown. My illusions aren't strong enough to change my voice, and so I hesitated, enjoying the feeling of being part of the scene, instead of holding myself above it.

The girl slid off the desk, landing lightly on her feet. Her hair was brown-blonde, darkening to black at the tips, and somehow didn't look dyed. She was softly rounded, wearing cut-off denim shorts and a tank top that left her belly bare. Not the sort of clothes one wears to visit a professor at midnight—not unless the visit is a lot more social than professional. And she'd admitted to knowing October. I took a breath, and took a guess.

"I need you to return to Muir Woods with me," I said. Master Davies's expression went blank. I felt bad about that, I genuinely did, but I couldn't *stop*. Not when Nolan needed me. "Something's wrong with the elf-shot cure. My brother woke, but he didn't stay that way."

"Your Highness." Master Davies stood and bowed, looking at the floor as he continued, "You do me too much honor by coming to me here on campus. I would have gladly come had you called."

"It would have taken longer," I said.

The woman looked between us, her eyes getting wider and wider. They were an unprepossessing shade of blue, the sort of thing no one would choose for an illusion unless they were natural. She was dressing up, but only in the most textile of senses. She wanted him to see her for herself, or as close as was possible under the circumstances.

"Wait," she said. "Is this—I mean, are you—I mean—oh, shit." Her cheeks flared red. "I just swore in front of the new Queen, didn't I?"

"You did," I said, unable to smother my amusement completely. It was sort of a relief. Humor makes the bad times easier to bear, even if it never lasts long enough to make a real difference. "Don't worry. We don't have any rules against that. I think because my father probably didn't realize that humans *had* profanity. He was sheltered like that. Also, that's exactly what October said when she met the High Queen. Clearly, you know her."

"Ah," said Master Davies. "Queen Windermere in the Mists, I'd like you to meet my friend Cassandra Brown. Cassandra is a student here."

"Not one of his," she hastened to clarify. "Nothing inappropriate is going on. We were just catching up."

"Brown," I said. "Are you related to Karen?"

Cassandra looked startled. "She's my sister. How did you . . . ?"

"She came to my conclave. She seemed nice. A little shy, but I'd be shy, too, if I had one of the First accompanying my every move. Are you an oneiromancer?" Karen Brown's powers were the kind that appeared only rarely, and even more rarely in changelings.

"No, ma'am. I mean, Highness. I mean . . ." She stopped, a frustrated look crossing her face. "I have no idea how to do this. I'm just a changeling. I'm not *supposed* to know how to do this. If I leave right now, will you pretend this never happened?"

I paused. Something about her tone told me she was holding something back. It might be nothing. So many things were really nothing, when looked at in the light of day. But if there was a chance she was withholding information that the alchemist had shared with her . . .

"I'm afraid not," I said. "I need you both to come with me."

"Cassandra's not part of this," protested Master Davies.

"My brother is unwell," I said. "That means my heir is unwell. The security of the kingdom requires you both to come with me now."

"Toby's not even here," muttered Cassandra. "How the hell am I in trouble when Toby's not even here?"

I ignored her and swept my hand in an arc through the air, opening a portal to the upstairs hallway of my knowe. I didn't want to drop us in the receiving room, where my servants might see. Most of the household staff was on loan from the local nobles, and that meant if I wanted to keep Nolan's condition a secret, I needed to keep them from suspecting anything. The alchemist reappearing after I'd dismissed him would certainly be suspicious enough to make people start talking.

Master Davies looked at the portal with dismay. Like Cassandra, he couldn't believe this was happening to him. Unlike Cassandra, he'd been raised in a royal household, and knew better than to express his displeasure aloud.

Belatedly, I realized I didn't remember his first name. I was already falling into the habits of queenship. And if it got me my brother back, I didn't care.

"After you," I said.

Master Davies paused to pick up the valise containing his alchemical supplies before stepping through the portal. Cassandra exhaled when she saw him appear on the other side, casting one last, anxious glance at my face before following him through. I went after her, and the portal closed behind me.

The servants had been here recently. The hallway smelled of wood polish and fresh blackberry flowers. Master Davies shoved his hands into his pockets and released his human disguise, adding the scents of ice and yarrow to the mixture. Mostly yarrow. He didn't remove his glasses. I knew they were cosmetic, but they seemed to be making him feel better, and I didn't want to push it. I was already pushing him hard enough.

Cassandra, in contrast, was looking around with open-mouthed amazement. She reached up to push her hair behind her ears, releasing her illusions in the same gesture; they dissolved in a wash of grapefruit and turpentine, revealing the tufts of black-and-brown fur crowning her dully pointed ears. I frowned. I'd never seen ears like that anywhere in Faerie, and while I might have forgotten many of the points of queenly etiquette, I'll never forget the nights I spent with Marianne, her calm, steady voice drilling me on the things I'd need to know to recognize all the denizens of our vast and varied land. Whatever her heritage was, I didn't know it.

Master Davies cleared his throat. "Your Highness? Where is your brother?"

"This way," I said, and pulled my regard away from Cassandra's ears as I turned.

The room where Nolan slept was a short distance down the hall. The lock was open; the knob turned easily under my hand. I pushed the door open and stepped aside, letting Master Davies get a look at his patient.

Nolan was exactly where I'd left him. His chest rose and fell with more vigor than was normal for a victim of elf-shot, but that was the only indication that the cure had been administered; from the way he was lying there, he might as well have still been under the original spell.

"Your Highness." Master Davies' voice snapped me out of my contemplation of my brother. I turned to him. He looked at me gravely. "I need a sample of your brother's blood to determine what's happening. Is this going to distress you? Do I need to ask you to leave the room? I will."

He had that authority. Alchemists and healers could command monarchs in the course of treating their patients. It was a small twist in the archaic rules that bound us all, intended to protect our healers from the wrath of people like me. I stared at him, not sure whether I should be grateful that he was worried about my delicate sensibilities, or whether I should start screaming and never stop.

I settled for neither. "I worked in retail during the holiday season, and I've met October more than once," I said, barely managing to keep myself from snarling. "I can handle a little blood."

"Even when it's your brother's? I don't want to fight

with you, Highness, or find myself banished because you don't like what I have to do in order to do my job."

I took a deep breath. That didn't do much to make me feel better. I took another one. Finally feeling calm enough to speak without yelling, I said, "I'm staying. You have my word that nothing you do in the course of helping my brother will be held against you."

"Heard and witnessed," said Cassandra. I glanced at her, surprised. She shrugged. "You pick things up."

"I guess you do," I said.

Master Davies moved toward the head of Nolan's bed, pausing to put his valise down on the bedside table and begin rummaging through it. His hands seemed to dip deeper than the bottom of the bag. That was an easy charm, for some fae; treat the leather, spell the stitches, and produce something that was bigger on the inside than it was on the outside. Like a TARDIS doing double-duty as a book bag.

He produced an antique silver scalpel and a glass bowl barely larger than the tip of his thumb. After glancing nervously in my direction, he bent and nicked the side of Nolan's jaw. It was a clever place to conceal a cut; if not for the fact that Nolan hadn't needed to shave in eighty years, it could have passed for part of his normal morning routine.

The cut wasn't deep, but it was enough. A few drops of blood welled up. Master Davies used the blunt side of the scalpel to direct them into the dish. Straightening, he put the scalpel down next to his valise and waved his hand over the blood, chanting something quick and sharp in a language I thought was probably Welsh. The smell of his magic rose again, stronger than before, chilling the room by several degrees. I shivered. Cassandra didn't. She was staring at the air above the blood, eyes slightly unfocused, like she was looking at something I couldn't see.

I frowned. Something was wrong here. Something was—

"Oh, oak and ash." Master Davies' voice was hushed. My head snapped around, attention going back to him. He was pinching the bridge of his nose with his free hand, the smell of ice and yarrow hanging heavy in the air. He looked like a man defeated.

And Nolan was still asleep.

"Master Davies?" I had to fight to keep my tone level. I nearly lost the battle. "What is it?"

"The elf-shot—" he began, and stopped, thinking better of whatever he'd been about to say. Carefully, he put the dish containing my brother's blood down next to the scalpel and turned to face me, folding his hands behind his back. "Your Highness, the cure I developed was intended to treat elf-shot. Do you understand what that means?"

Irritation washed through me like acid. "It means my brother is supposed to wake *up*."

"Yes, it does. But more, it means that I was able, with the assistance of Sir Daye, to brew a tincture specifically designed to counter a sleeping charm developed by Eira Rosynhwyr."

"I *know* that," I snapped. "You tested Nolan's blood before, to make sure he'd been hit with a variation of the charm that your cure could fight."

"And he was, and it did," said Master Davies. "The problem is . . . people have been tinkering with the recipe for elf-shot since it was created. Some of them were trying to make it kinder. Others were trying to make it worse. Do you know who brewed the elf-shot that felled your brother?"

"I wasn't exactly in a position to ask when it happened," I said.

"Yes, of course. My apologies." He took a deep breath. "The elf-shot itself was a standard recipe. As close to generic as you can get without changing the way it works. But it was hiding a secondary charm, something related, yet not the same."

"A second sleeping spell?" I asked, aghast. "Can you *do* that?"

"Could I do that? Absolutely. It would be child's play. Elf-shot is so dominant in the blood while it's active that it can be used to hide all manner of things. The alchemist who brewed this spell tucked it behind the elf-shot, and keyed it to consciousness. The second spell might as well not have existed until your brother woke."

This time, despair washed through me, chasing away the irritation. "So he's going to sleep for another hundred years, or until you find another cure?"

"I'm afraid not," said Master Davies. "This isn't elf-shot, which—cruel as it is—comes with certain protections. Someone who's been elf-shot doesn't need to eat or drink. They don't even really need to breathe. Elf-shot in its purest form was designed *not* to break the Law."

"So what are you trying to say?" I wanted to go to my brother, grab his hands, and hold onto him so tightly that there was no possible chance he could slip away. I was failing him again. I was a queen now. I had our father's crown and our father's knowe, and I was going to have our father's failures, too, because I wasn't going to save Nolan.

I had never been able to save Nolan.

"This is a more traditional sleeping spell, the sort of thing people used to cast on each other before we had elf-shot." Master Davies grimaced. "Remember that elf-shot was a kindness once. It was a slumber people could wake up from. This is just . . . it's just sleep."

"He'll die," said Cassandra. She sounded horrified. The emotion was so simple, so pure, that I had to blink back tears. She was as young as she looked. She was still capable of being shocked by how cruel Faerie could be. "Dehydration, starvation . . . you can't sleep forever."

Master Davies glanced at her. Then he looked at me, and his expression hardened. "Maybe not," he said. "But you can sleep for a while before you have medical consequences, and we don't need much more than that. The charm isn't dangerous in and of itself. It's what it does that's bad. Your Highness, how do you feel about larceny?"

I blinked at him. Then, as hope dawned, I smiled.

FIVE

One convenient thing about spending so much time living in the human world: I not only knew the location of all the local urgent care centers, but I knew which ones were in good enough financial shape to handle a few losses. Better yet, I knew where the security cameras were. Street fae and changelings—the sort of people I was likely to be dealing with, the ones who thought I was like them, who'd never had enough interaction with the Courts to figure out that maybe I looked a little too much like our dear lost King Gilad—didn't usually have much disposable income, much less health insurance, and sometimes they needed to be able to manage their own long-term care. I'd lifted my share of antibiotics, IV bags, and syringes over the years.

One gate and we were inside an urgent care clinic halfway down the Bay, one where the clientele could afford discretion and the nurses could afford coffee breaks. They weren't understaffed and overworked like the people at County. It was easier to steal certain supplies from the big hospitals for exactly that reason—chaos forgives a lot of ineptitude—but I didn't like doing it, also for that reason. A facility that was already stretched thin couldn't afford to lose things.

But this was for Nolan. If Master Davies had directed me to the smallest, most underfunded clinic in the Bay Area and told me to steal every drop of morphine they had, I would have done it. My brother mattered more to me than all the strangers in California.

As soon as we were inside, Master Davies dropped a don't-look-here on the three of us and murmured something in Cassandra's ear. She nodded, and they took off in different directions. There wasn't time to wonder what they were up to. I had my own shopping list to fill. Bags of saline solution; needles; tubing. I filled my arms with my brother's salvation, hoping either Master Davies or Cassandra had some medical training. I've done my share of petty theft, but I'd never been the one trying to keep body and soul together until a healer could be called.

A healer. The thought was like a bulb coming on in a dark room. I stiffened, nearly dropping my stolen goods. Jin. She worked for Sylvester; he'd loaned her to me during the conclave, and I was sure he'd loan her to me again if I asked. I could bring her to Muir Woods and have her monitor Nolan's condition. I could—

I could ask her to sit there and cure his dehydration, over and over again, saturating the area with magic, while Master Davies tried to mix a countercharm to something he couldn't identify yet. She wouldn't make things better. She could make things worse. It was amazing how fast I was falling back into the habit of thinking of magic as a cure-all, and it never had been.

"Damn," I muttered, and grabbed another bag of saline.

Master Davies and Cassandra were waiting when I returned to the hall. Cassandra had an IV stand and a bag of first aid supplies. Master Davies had a brown canvas satchel that he must have pilfered from somewhere, packed full of small bottles. I frowned. He didn't meet my eyes.

"We should go," he said.

Right. If my new court alchemist—and there was really no question whether I'd be offering him the job after this; I was virtually obligated to do so—wanted to have a painkiller addiction, that was on him. It was better than goblin fruit, at least. I waved my hand through the air. The portal opened again, and we were gone, stepping back into Muir Woods.

My head began to ache as soon as the portal closed behind us. I hadn't overexerted myself yet, but I was on the cusp of it. "I can make one more jump tonight, and that's assuming you don't mind taking the bus back," I cautioned. "I haven't got the sort of range I had when I was younger."

"You'll get it back," said Master Davies, releasing his don't-look-here. We were in the hall again, outside my brother's room. That hadn't been intentional on my part; I'd been trying to get us back to Nolan as quickly as possible. Exhaustion was messing with my aim.

He opened the bedroom door. Cassandra and I followed him inside. For a few moments, everything was simple. Master Davies told us what to set up and where to put it; we did as we were told, hanging bags of saline, helping him run tubes from the equipment to my brother. He seemed to know what he was doing. That was reassuring. If it had been entirely up to me, things would have gotten ugly.

"Thank Oberon for gravity," he said, turning Nolan's arm over and rolling up his sleeve. "If we needed electricity to operate an IV, we'd have bigger problems."

"I still have the generator you brought in to power the lights up in the tower," I said. "We could use that."

"I don't like using generators in the Summerlands when I have a choice." The needle in his hand slid under the skin of my brother's arm, so quickly that it was like a magician's trick. Different from real magic, but reassuring all the same. "The smell upsets me. It's like I'm profaning something holy."

"You're a nerd," said Cassandra. There was a deep fondness in her tone. He didn't seem to notice.

For her sake—for his sake—I hoped he'd notice it soon. Immortality is hard enough without spending it alone. "Nerd or not, whatever you need, you've got it. I want my brother back. You have the resources of my kingdom at your disposal."

Master Davies turned to look solemnly at me. "I'm not going to insult you by asking whether you mean that. Instead, I'm going to ask you to leave."

I stared at him. "What? No."

"Yes. I need to analyze his blood. I need to figure out the roots of this spell, and I need peace and quiet while I do it. So I need you to go. Take Cassie with you. She can help with anything you need that isn't this."

"Yeah," said Cassandra. Her eyes were on the air above Nolan's arm, unfocused again, like she didn't know what she was looking at. She was frowning. That was what really stood out. She had good reasons to be nervous—she was locked in a small room with the Queen in the Mists and the Crown Prince, even if it was sometimes difficult for me to remember that those august personages were me and my brother—but she didn't have reason to frown like that.

"What are you looking at?" I asked.

Cassandra jumped, flinching away from me. "Nothing," she said.

She was lying. I *knew* she was lying, and sadly being queen didn't come with magical truth-sensing abilities, so there was no way for me to prove it. "You keep looking at something," I insisted. "If you know something . . ."

"I don't know anything," she said. "I'm not an alchemist, and I'm not pre-med. I'm a physics major. A tired, hungry physics major who wasn't planning to be in the royal knowe tonight, so I'm a bit freaked out right now, your, um, splendidness."

"Not a standard form of address, but we'll roll with it," I said, and sighed, running a hand through my hair. "Master Davies, we'll be in the kitchen if you need us. Cassandra, if you'll come with me, I can help with the 'hungry' part of your problem."

She cast an anxious glance at Master Davies before turning back to me. "Lead the way," she said.

There was no more reason to stay, and quite a few reasons to go. I led her to the door, and out into the hall. The last thing I saw before the door swung shut was Master Davies leaning over my brother, the scalpel once more in his hand. Then the wood blocked my view, and I was grateful.

A hand touched my arm. I turned to find Cassandra looking at me with the sort of honest, uncalculated concern that I hadn't seen since the last time I'd talked to Jude. "He'll figure it out," she said. "If there's anyone who can do it, it's Walther. The man works miracles in his spare time."

"Walther," I echoed. She looked at me quizzically, and I shrugged, feeling sheepish. "I couldn't remember his first name, and it seemed rude to ask when I was already asking for his help."

Cassandra's laugh was bright and surprised. "Oh, that's awesome. No, really. You're just a normal person with a crown, not some sort of, like, mystical fairy superhero."

"See, that's what I keep trying to tell people, but they keep bowing anyway." I started down the hall, beckoning for her to follow me. "The kitchen's this way."

"Great." Cassandra trotted to catch up, rubbernecking shamelessly as we walked. I took a moment to look where she was looking, trying to see the knowe through her eyes.

October thought—and had explained to me, at great

length—that knowes were alive, capable of changing and rearranging themselves on a whim. I didn't think she was wrong, exactly, but I thought she was discounting the work of the many craftsmen and artisans who had poured their hearts and souls into the very walls.

If the knowe is alive, it's because so many people bled and dreamt and spent their magic like water to wake it up. I liked to think it knew that, on some level; that it remembered my father, and my grandparents, who had done everything they could to make it grander, and more worthy of being the seat of the Mists, which had been the largest, grandest Kingdom in the West for so long.

The hall was sparsely decorated, leaving the focus on the carved redwood walls. Panels set at eye level told the story of my family's time in the Mists, carved in a style that was half-representative, half-symbolic. I didn't think my grandmother had actually coaxed the moon down from the sky to light her way when she was courting my grandfather, for example, but I was sure it had felt that way, at least to her.

They died long before I was born, victims of the long, slow dance of regicide. It was because of them that my father chose to hide the fact that he had children of his own. He knew what happened to kings and queens. I sometimes thought that they had saved my life by dying. There's no amount of gratitude that makes up for that. But I still wish I'd had the chance to meet them.

"You don't do your own dusting, right?" asked Cassandra. "Because if you do, you should quit."

"I'm not allowed to quit," I said.

"Who says?"

"October."

Cassandra snorted. "Naturally. Aunt Birdie is great at telling other people to step up and do their duty, but did she hold onto her County? Nope. Passed it off to the first out-of-town noble she could find."

"Aunt Birdie?" I asked blankly.

"Toby," she said, and laughed at my expression. "My mom's her oldest friend. They were kids together. She'd be my godmother if we did that sort of thing. As it is, she's the first adult I remember who wasn't my mom or dad. When I was little, I couldn't pronounce 'October,' so I called her 'Birdie,' and it stuck inside the family. Sometimes I forget anybody calls her anything else."

"Ah," I said. "Your family lives . . . ?"

"In Colma. We're not sworn to any specific demesne, if that's what you're not asking. Mom's thin-blooded, Dad's half and half, and no one ever wanted us. Not until Karen started walking in dreams." She grimaced. "A Firstborn asshole kidnaps half my siblings and half the Courts in the Bay Area start banging on the front door offering to save my sister from a life of useless peasant-hood. They sort of forget that we're not serfs anymore. We have jobs. We do stuff. We've been politely turning them down for years. Now that Karen's started hanging out with the Luidaeg, maybe they'll listen."

"The sea witch does seem to have taken an interest," I said, as neutrally as I could. "I don't know whether that's a good thing or not."

"Karen doesn't seem to mind."

We had reached the first stairway. I started down, Cassandra trailing behind. "You're studying physics?"

"Yeah. Do you, uh . . . shit. There's no way to say this that isn't super rude, so I'm going to go with it. Do you know what that means?"

I smiled a little, wryly. "I may be a pureblood, but I've spent the last hundred years in the mortal world. I know about physics. I watched the moon landing on TV along with everyone else on my block. I even know how to program a VCR."

Cassandra looked at me blankly. I rolled my eyes.

"I promise you, references used to stay topical for longer. I know how a cell phone works, okay? Does that prove I'm down with the modern world?"

"What did you do for a hundred years among the mortals?"

I shrugged. The stairs ended in a narrower, less extravagant hallway. The walls were still carved redwood, but the ceiling was straight, not domed, and there were no flowers. "A lot of things. I was a seamstress for years, before it got hard to make a living that way. I worked as a nanny for wealthy mortal families for a while, until they started wanting references and proof of identity. A few odd jobs, and then, in the 1950s, I discovered I liked selling books. So I've been a bookseller for the last sixty years. I'm good at figuring out what a person might like to read, and convincing them to give it a chance."

"Huh," said Cassandra. "You know, when Aunt Birdie said she'd found the lost princess, I was expecting something more, I guess . . ."

"Disney on Ice?" I smiled faintly. "I can do my best, but I'll never be the kind of girl who willingly stands in front of the glitter cannon."

"Boom," said Cassandra, deadpan.

I laughed. It was a relief. Nolan was asleep, but Master Davies—Walther—was going to find a way to wake him up, and everything was going to be okay. It had to be. I'd already lost more than I could stand to lose. One more thing would be too much.

We arrived to find the kitchen occupied by two Hobs, one standing on a stepstool at the sink with her arms buried in soapy water, the other sitting on a box and peeling potatoes. They froze at the sight of me and Cassandra standing in the doorway. I forced a smile.

"Hi," I said. "Pretend we're not here."

The two Hobs continued to stare. Finally, the seated Hob lowered her knife and said, "I'm not sure we can do that, Highness."

"Why not?"

The question came from Cassandra, and it was enough to make all three of us turn to look at her. She shrugged.

"This is the kitchen," she said. "This is your space, right? I mean, a queen's a queen even when she's peeling potatoes, but you have to have a certain amount of authority here, or what would stop princes and princesses and the like from just rampaging through the place sticking their fingers in scalding water and ruining soufflés? If Queen Windermere wants to sit and have a sandwich or something, that's proof that you're doing your jobs *awesomely*."

"Really?" asked the potato peeler, looking dubious.

"Really," said Cassandra. "She feels safe here, being incognito and feeding her guests. By which I mean me. I'm starving."

The two Hobs exchanged a look. The dishwasher focused on me.

"You would truly not be offended, Highness?" she asked.

"As long as you don't mind me making myself a sandwich while you keep working, I'd be overjoyed," I said. They were starting to look uncomfortable again, so I added, "Remember, I grew up here. I know where everything is. I like making my own sandwiches."

"If you say so, Highness," said the dishwasher.

Neither of them looked happy, but they weren't arguing, and they went back to their respective tasks as I led Cassandra to the kitchen table, only pausing occasionally to shoot uncomfortable glances in our direction, like they were expecting me to start yelling about dereliction of duty.

"Wow," said Cassandra, voice pitched low. "Is it always like that?"

"Oh, this was mild," I said. "They're kitchen staff. They don't expect to have to deal with me on a daily basis, and so they don't really have a script to follow. Watch me try to talk to the guards if you want a laugh. They're so busy bowing that they don't hear half of what I say."

"Putting the fun back in feudalism."

"Something like that." I looked at the rest of the kitchen. The shelves were well-stocked; preservation spells meant pastries and pies could be baked days before they were needed. Roast meat could be frozen at the perfect level of doneness and kept that way indefinitely. "What did you want to eat?"

"I don't know," said Cassandra. "I really would be happy with a sandwich."

"Got it," I said. "Be right back."

My childhood raids on the kitchen had been hasty things, Nolan giggling at my side while Marianne watched tolerantly from the door, ready to sound the alarm if it looked like we were going to be caught. Mostly they'd been focused on cookies and cakes, the sort of easily-snatched sweets that defined a child's world. That had still necessitated a certain understanding of where things were kept. Since the knowe had been sealed for a century, it wasn't like the place had been remodeled.

I found a dish of sliced beef and carried it back to the table, dropping it in front of her. "Hang on," I said, while she was still blinking in bewilderment at the massive amount of meat. My second pass garnered bread, cheese, mustard, and something purple and spicy-smelling that I suspected of being beetroot ketchup. Fae cooking can get odd sometimes.

I spread the rest of my pilfered wares in front of her with a deadpan, "Ta-da."

"I'm not going to eat all this," said Cassandra.

"I wouldn't expect you to." I settled across from her. The thought of eating made me feel sick. The slowly-growing ache in my temples told me I didn't actually have a choice. Food is one of the only things that helps combat magic-burn. Food, and rest, and if Walther needed me, I was going to be there for him. Rest wasn't going to be an option for me until my brother was awake.

Slowly, I began assembling a sandwich, starting with a

healthy smear of the beetroot ketchup. Fortune favors the bold.

"I am coming here for lunch from now on," said Cassandra, shaking off her shock and starting to put her own sandwich together. She was a healthy eater, judging by the amount of meat she piled on her bread. "If this is how your pantry is always stocked, I may move *in*."

"We'd be happy to have you, as long as you didn't mind being put to work," I said. Cheese went onto the beetroot; meat went onto the cheese. It was an automatic process, but it made me feel better. Human or fae, queen or commoner, a sandwich went together in the same order. "I'm so understaffed that I keep wishing there were a temp agency that served noble households."

"I don't know that there's anything I could do here."

"You might be surprised. Most of these jobs, no one actually *knows* how they're done. They just sort of happen. Half the households around here have conflated their Seneschal and their Chamberlain, which is great if you can get away with it, but when you're talking about a knowe as big as this one ... it's not gonna work forever."

Cassandra raised an eyebrow. "Because the difference is ... ?"

"Seneschal runs the non-household side of the knowe. My schedule, organizing balls, keeping our records accurate, updating the local Library whenever we have a chance so the record never falls out of true, all that fun bullshit. The Chamberlain runs the household. Kitchen, cleaning staff, laundry. The positions are frequently combined at the County level and below. Ducal houses can go either way. Royal houses? You need both. There's too much for one person to do."

"So if I ever need a job, you'll have a place for me."

"Exactly." I took a bite of my sandwich. The beetroot wasn't bad. Strange, but not bad. Swallowing, I asked, "How did you and Walther meet?"

Cassandra raised her eyebrow again. "Small talk now?"

"I'm trying to distract myself. Humor me. It's this or I pace back and forth in front of my brother's room until I wear a hole in the carpet, and I don't think that would be good for anyone."

"Right," she said. "Well, we met on campus. I'm not in any of his classes, but we tend to be in the same buildings. We're both disguised as humans, of course, so it's possible I would have missed him entirely if not for his grad student, Jack."

"What did the grad student do?"

"He's a friend of one of the girls from my study group. Apparently, Aunt Birdie came by while Jack was on campus, and Jack thought she was dating Walther—as if. I mean, he's sweet and funny and cute and everything, but he's not her type."

"Too academic?"

"Insufficiently Tybalt." Cassandra smirked. "She's had a thing for kitty since she came back from the pond. Maybe not instantly, but I'd say within six months of her return. She'd come over on Friday night to have a drink with my folks and spend half the time complaining about what Tybalt had been doing during the week. I'm pretty sure Mom and Dad had a bet going about when she'd finally give in and start dating him."

"But you recognized her from Jack's description," I guessed.

"Exactly. I mean, how many grumpy, stressed-out brunettes named 'October' can there be in the world? I'm hoping the answer is 'one.' Any more than that would be too many. Jack said she was visiting his advisor, so I went to welcome said advisor to the 'October Daye Occasionally Ruins My Life' club, he asked if I wanted to grab a beer, and we've been hanging out ever since."

It was difficult not to look at her, look at him, and see the age difference as a problem. It would have been, in the human world—assuming it had even been *possible*. The word for humans as old as Walther is "dead." But Faerie has different rules, and she hadn't actually said her interest in him was romantic. She'd just chosen clothes that would draw attention to her figure and a human illusion that would call attention to her eyes. Both of those could have been coincidence. I didn't think so. And it was none of my damn business. I was Queen, not babysitter to the kingdom.

"He seems nice," I said neutrally. "He's a good alchemist. I don't think I've ever known someone who could accomplish what he's been able to do already."

"You mean despite things not working exactly as you want them to."

I glanced at the kitchen Hobs. They were still hard at work, but I knew they were listening. That was one thing Marianne had worked hard to drum into my skull, reinforced by years of working retail in the mortal world: the staff was always listening. Especially if it looked like they weren't. I would forget that at my own peril.

"Yes," I said, keeping my tone forcibly light as I turned back to Cassandra. "Even despite that, he's done amazing things. A cure for elf-shot is just ... I never thought I'd see it in my lifetime. And him living in the Mists means it reflects well on me that he accomplished it, even if he was in Silences at the time."

"Are we, like, friends with Silences now?"

"I probably shouldn't send October to visit any time soon, but I think we are." I took another bite of sandwich, and swallowed before saying, "We put the rightful ruling family back on the throne. We corrected a profound wrong. The whole coast is healthier now, and Queen Siwan is grateful for our help, even as she hopes that we don't need to do any more diplomacy in her presence for a long, long time."

Cassandra leaned closer, lowering her voice conspiratorially as she asked, "Did you do that on purpose?

Send Aunt Birdie because you knew she'd mess things up in the best way possible, I mean?"

"Honestly, I was just mad that she'd touched me without permission." I smiled wryly. "I guess I'm getting used to this queen thing after all."

"What?" Cassandra blinked. "What do you mean?"

"Oh, I know this is all 'poor little rich girl' of me, but . . . I gave up expecting to be Queen in the Mists a long time ago. I'd adjusted to the idea that I wasn't going to have the opportunity, and then I'd adjusted to the idea that I wasn't going to have the responsibility. I figured I'd spend the next few centuries selling books, or whatever comes after books, and not worrying about anything outside my immediate sphere. When October showed up at the bookstore where I was working, I hated her a little. She forced me to take a job I'd given up on wanting."

"That must have been hard," said Cassandra.

"You know what's funny? The hardest thing is remembering not to thank people."

She cocked her head to the side. "Come again?"

"I worked in retail. 'Thank you, have a nice day' is such an automatic thing for me that I might as well have a pull-string in my back. I thanked the staff something like a dozen times my first week here. They were all volunteers, half of them were from the old Queen's Court, none of them had any idea what kind of ruler I was going to be, and I was *thanking* them. Some left as soon as I said the words. I don't think they're ever coming back."

"I . . . wow." Cassandra began to laugh helplessly. "Please don't take this the wrong way, but holy *shit*, Toby actually did it. She went and got us a changeling queen."

I blinked. "Come again?"

"You don't sound totally pissed. That's a good sign. Look." She took a deep breath, getting her laughter under control. "You're a pureblood, absolutely. I mean, if you weren't, there's no way you'd be Queen now. It's a pretty simple logic problem. But you have the same problems interacting with fae society that I do. It's not natural to you. You're not really a changeling. That doesn't mean you're one of *them*."

This time, my blink was slower, and accompanied by another bite of my sandwich. Chewing gave me time to think. "Huh," I said finally. "I . . . that makes a lot of sense. Maybe if I think about it that way, I won't feel so damn out of place all the time."

"I live to serve."

"Good, because I want you to come work here."

Cassandra's eyes went wide. "I didn't mean it *literally*."

"You need to learn to watch your mouth around royalty, then."

"I can't imagine why I wouldn't have picked that lesson up in elementary school." She shook her head. "I can't come work for you. I have college, I have a job—"

"What do you do?"

"I'm a clerk at Rasputin Records on Telegraph."

"So that's what, slightly better than minimum wage?" I waited for her to nod before I said, "I can pay you thirty dollars an hour, and if you don't have a car, I can pick you up wherever you want."

"What, you mean the," she made a circling motion with her hand, "thing? And how are you going to pay me? My bank doesn't take fairy gold."

"Funny thing: neither did the BART system. I've been working mortal jobs for a *hundred years*, and I've been socking it all away against a time when I might actually want to buy something. If the imposter who stole my family's throne had ever thought to check with Wells Fargo, she would have found me a long time ago."

Cassandra raised her eyebrows. "So, what, you're loaded?"

"Let's just say that I never need to worry about money." I shrugged. "I can pay you. I can work around your school schedule. And I can give you a room here, if you were thinking it might be nice to get out of your parents' house. That maybe you're ready to start dating without worrying about them waiting up for you."

Her cheeks flared red. "Am I that obvious?"

"No, but I'm that observant, and he's cute. A little nerdy for my tastes, I'll admit. Still cute." I took one more bite of my sandwich before putting it down. "I'm not asking you to swear fealty on the spot. Just give me a try."

"What would I be doing? I'm twenty-two, studying for my physics degree, and have basically no skills applicable to a noble household. Unless you wanted me to peel potatoes, and you already have someone for that."

"I want you to translate for me." Her shocked expression made smiling easier. "You *know* how purebloods are. Honestly, right now, you probably know better than I do. And you can explain to people that sometimes the Queen says the wrong thing out of habit without it coming off as condescending. I'll need you less as I learn more, and who knows? You might find that you like working for me. Having a scientist on the staff wouldn't be a bad thing."

"What happens when I get my degree and want to go off and, you know, do physics? I'm going to figure out what magic *is*. That means I'm going to need resources."

"First, again, rich. You get your degree and convince me this is a question worth answering—and I think it is—I can set you up with your own lab. A legit one, even. There's a computer company in the South Bay, Tamed Lightning, that's a part of my demesne. I can get them to help us make you look totally normal, and you can do your work on my dime. If we become the kingdom where all the big breakthroughs are made, I won't complain. Second, even if you don't want to feel beholden, do you really expect me to believe that a tenure-track position won't mysteriously open up the second you want it? Changeling or not, you're fae. Someone will make it happen for you. Don't try to convince me you'd refuse it because you want to earn it. You're a changeling, you're a woman, and you eat like someone who knows what it is to be hungry. You've already earned it by living this long."

"Huh," said Cassandra, after a long pause. "I'd ask whether you'd practiced that, but I just met you, so I'm assuming the answer is 'no.'"

"I had a lot of time to learn how people work," I said.

Cassandra laughed, and reached for her sandwich.

SIX

We finished eating, and then we finished drinking our mugs of tea, and then the kitchen staffers were looking at us with a mixture of dismay and confusion that made me think it was time to move along. They'd never *tell* us it was time to leave—I wasn't sure they were allowed to tell me to leave, since it was my kitchen, my knowe, and most of all, my kingdom—but they weren't comfortable having us here.

Cassandra moved to pick up her dishes as we stood. I raised a hand, signaling for her to stop. She looked at me, bewildered.

"We need to take our dishes to the sink," she said.

"If I didn't already know you lived at home, that would be enough to confirm it," I said. "We can't take our dishes to the sink. I mean, we *could*, but it would be a dire insult to my staff, and they'd either decide they'd done something wrong or that I was showing another place where I couldn't be a proper queen."

Cassandra blinked. "So we leave the dishes?" she ventured.

"We leave the dishes," I said.

We left the dishes. We walked past the relieved staff—who were at least trying not to look like they were happy we were finally getting out of their space—and into the hall, where Walther was waiting. I stopped. Cassandra stopped. An awkward silence fell.

Finally, Walther said, "I looked inside, but you seemed happy with your tea and your, you know, girl talk, and I didn't want to interrupt."

My heart sank. Good news would have had him interrupting us without hesitation. Good news would have had him trumpeting it from the rooftops, because good news would have meant he could go home. "What is it?"

"Do you want to talk about that here?"

No. I did not. I didn't want to talk about it anywhere. I wanted it to go away, to not exist. I wanted my brother back, and I—by Oberon—did not want to keep my composure any longer. "Let's go back to the room."

Walther nodded. He didn't look relieved. If anything, he looked sad. He *really* didn't want to tell me whatever he was going to say next.

We walked silently down the hall. Either the kitchen staff had sent out some alert or the knowe was between shifts, because we didn't see anyone as we made our way to the room where Nolan slept. Madden was responsible for organizing the household staff, with assistance from Lowri; there was no reason for me to know who was going to be where, or when they were going to be there. I still felt a little bad, like I was letting my people down on some profound level by not keeping track of them.

I was deflecting, trying to turn my anxiety on a target that was less personal and less painful, than my brother. And knowing that did nothing to make me feel better. Understanding my own mind doesn't stop it from hurting me.

Walther went into my brother's room. Cassandra and I followed. The table next to Nolan's bed had become a tiny alchemical laboratory, complete with a bubbling vial of pinkish liquid propped over a ball of lambent blue witch-light. It was the sort of scene that would have seemed like something out of a dream, once, but which was becoming more and more commonplace as I settled into my new life. It was the sort of scene that left little room for hope.

"What's wrong?" I asked, eyes on my brother as Walther shut the door behind us. "Why can't you wake him up?"

"Alchemy isn't the solution to every problem," said Walther. His voice was low, his words deliberate. He was trying not to upset me. Fat lot of good that was going to do him. I was already upset, and getting more upset by the second. "I can counteract most charms and potions, if I have a sample of the original potion or know the magical signature of the person who brewed it. I can ease certain spells. But I can't change the laws of magic."

"So?" I whirled to face Walther. "This was a charm, you said so yourself! Fix it!"

"It's in his blood," he said. "It spent almost a century masked by elf-shot, aging, maturing, *changing*. And now it's mixed into his body, and I can't separate it out enough to pick it apart. I don't know who brewed it. I don't know what I'm looking for. Give me a year and I might be able to make some headway. A night is not enough."

"A year will be too long," I snapped. "He'll die."

"Not necessarily; we can get someone in here who understands care for long-term coma patients," said Walther. "It's not perfect, but . . . I don't like telling you this any more than you like hearing it. There's nothing I can do."

"We could elf-shoot him again."

"I don't know how it would interact with the awakened sleeping charm. It could kill him."

I took a breath to answer, and stopped as I saw Cassandra's face. She was gazing at the air above his bubbling beaker, her eyes unfocused and her lips slightly parted, like she was focusing so hard on whatever it was she saw that she couldn't spend the energy to keep them closed. My eyes narrowed.

"Okay," I said. "This is what's going to happen. You're going to tell me whatever it is you're not telling me, and you're going to do it *right now*. In exchange, I will not have you both thrown in the dungeon until I forget about you."

Cassandra didn't react. She kept staring at the empty air.

Walther sighed before reaching over and touching her shoulder. "Hey," he said. "Come back. You need to come back now."

She jumped, giving a convulsive full-body shudder as she turned to face him. "What?"

"You zoned out for a second," said Walther, gaze darting toward me, like he was trying to assess my reaction. No, not like: that was exactly what he was doing. I'd seen that look before, usually from shoplifters who were hoping they could put one over on me.

I wasn't a retail employee anymore, allowed to back off and let my manager handle things. I was the goddamn Queen, and they were going to listen to me. "That's not what happened." Keeping my voice level was a fun challenge. I was not rising to meet it. "Something is going on. Tell me what is going on."

"Cassie," said Walther. His hand was still on her shoulder. "It's your call."

"Why do people say that kind of shit?" I planted my hands on my hips. "Now I know there's something going on. No one makes a call about saying nothing."

Cassandra sighed, looking from Walther to me and finally, almost longingly, back to the air above the beaker. Then she looked down at her feet and said, "I was telling the truth when I said I wasn't an oneiromancer. I can't move through other people's dreams or use them to tell the future."

"But . . . ?" I prompted.

"But I wasn't telling the whole truth." She glanced up, searching my face before she said, "I'm an aeromancer. I read air."

"Air," I said flatly.

"The motion of air. Yes."

"Air is invisible."

"Not to me." She turned to the beaker again. "Not when I look at it right. Light and dust and wind, they all move in the air, and they tell me the future. It's easiest by candlelight, but I can't light candles in my house anymore. Not after everything that happened with Blind Michael. It upsets my youngest sister too much."

"Wait." I dropped my hands. "I'm trying to understand. You're a Seer. You . . . See things. And where you See things is in the way air moves."

"Yes."

"Your sister is a Seer, too. She Sees things in dreams."

"Yes."

"But you're both changelings." My frustration was threatening to bubble over. "That doesn't make *sense*. Seers are—they're incredibly rare! My father didn't have a Court Seer, because he couldn't find one! *His* parents had a Shyi Shuai in their Court, but she didn't See the future as much as bend the luck to make it do what she wanted, and maybe that's what got them killed, since Shyi Shuai always get backlash. How the hell are you and Karen Seers? You can't be."

"Well, we are." Cassandra shrugged. "Karen was the one who showed me. She didn't know what she could do until Blind Michael took her. After that . . . it was like the dead bastard had woken her up by putting her to sleep. She watched the way I watched the air, and she started telling me how to interpret it. You want humbling? Try having your baby sister teaching you how do something that feels like it should be as natural as breathing, but somehow isn't. I See things. My sister Sees things."

"I . . . okay. Okay. I am going to stop arguing with reality, because it never gets me anywhere, and just beg you, please. Tell me what we need to do to wake my brother up. I need him. I need . . . I need my family back, and he's the only one left for me to save. Please."

Cassandra grimaced, reluctance written plainly across her features. "Can you get me a candle?"

"I have one in my bag," said Walther.

"Of course you do," said Cassandra, with the ghost of a smile. "Will someone turn out the lights?"

"I've got it," I said.

The knowe wasn't wired for electricity, but we knew how to mimic it. Most of the rooms were lit with a marsh-charm that looked a lot like witch-light without requiring each bulb to be lit independently. I turned the dial next to the door. The tubes feeding the charm into the room went cold, and the light dimmed before flickering out, so only Walther's witch-light provided any illumination. He handed Cassandra a candle before dousing that light as well. Everything was darkness. The starlight creeping in around the edges of the curtains cast the walls into vague relief, more an idea of architecture than anything clearly seen. That was all.

There was a brief flare as Cassandra lit a match and held it to the wick of her candle. She had sunk into a cross-legged position on the floor while I couldn't see her, and her hair fell around her face like a curtain as she bent over the flame. It would have been easy to assume that she was staring at the fire. I took a step closer, and saw that she was staring at the air above it, her eyes unfocused again, darting back and forth as she followed the motion of something only she could see.

"The first sword didn't come from the stone; it came from the sea," she said, voice hollow and distant. "They called it a lake, later, when they were trying to contain its power, but it was sea-forged and sea-drawn, and its blade knew brine before it knew blood. Sharp it was, and cold it was, and unforgiving, always."

"What?" I demanded.

A hand touched my shoulder. Walther. I tensed, ready to remind him that touching queens without permission was never a good idea. He caught my eye and shook his head.

"I'm sorry, Highness, but you need to let her work," he said, voice low—he was trying not to distract her. "She can use the wind to scry, and that's clear, just like Karen can walk in lucid dreams, but when you ask her to See, what you get is images and ideas. We'll interpret them when she's done." Unspoken: *This is what you asked for. This is what you wanted.*

I forced myself to calm. I nodded. He withdrew his hand.

"She gave the sword away. She gave so many things away. Some for good and some for ill, but oh, she gave them all away." Cassandra sighed. "So many things, and yet she can't forsake the water. She never set the sleepers sleeping, never plumped their pillows or made their beds. Still, people came to her and asked for clever trinkets, and she had to say them yea. She never had a choice. Not since she chose once, and all her choices were taken away."

Silence fell. Cassandra tilted her head to the side, like she was looking at something she didn't understand. Finally, she said, "They asked and she said 'yes.' She has to say 'yes.' That's why she hates us for asking. She gives and she gives and she gives, and we built a world on the idea that thanking her for what she's already given is against the rules. We built a world on never being grateful, because we were entitled to everything we got. She's the one who bottled the moon. She's the one who refined the stars. She's the one we have to talk to. But there will be costs. There are always costs. There have to be. It's the only way we ever thank her. With our tears."

She pitched forward, hands hitting the floor on either side of the candle. The motion was so swift that the wind it generated blew out the flame, casting us into total darkness. A wisp of smoke rose through her hair, paradoxically visible.

"Ow," muttered Cassandra.

I leaned over and turned the lights back on. They trickled into life, revealing Cassandra unmoving on the floor. Walther was watching her, lips thin, face drawn.

"You okay?" he asked.

"No," she said, and raised her head, offering him a shaky smile. "You know, I think I'd prefer to have been an oneiromancer. At least Karen gets to go to bed before she beats the crap out of herself."

"Do you remember what you said?"

She looked at me and nodded. "I do. I don't understand it, but I remember it."

"Sadly, I understood it," said Walther. "There's only one woman I can think of who has to help when she's asked, who resents basically everyone, and who always charges for her favors. She doesn't do anything for free. I'm not sure she *can*."

"Who?" I asked.

"The Luidaeg," he said.

Silence fell.

SEVEN

The Luidaeg. The sea witch. The terror of the fens. The woman who had, not a week ago, stood in my place, enjoying the hospitality of my home, and told me that while familiarity might breed contempt, I should never make the mistake of thinking she was a tame monster. She would end me if she was given half the chance.

And yet. And yet.

And yet it was because of her that I'd survived to reach adulthood. Without the charms Marianne had purchased from her, the false Queen would have tracked me down long ago and put me into the ground with my parents. Without the Lùidaeg supporting October, I would still have been in the bookstore—and when Nolan's elf-shot had worn off on its own, the secondary sleeping charm would have killed him for sure. It was only the fact that I'd woken him early that had allowed us to discover it existed, much less start looking for a cure.

The fact that according to Cassandra, the Luidaeg had also brewed the sleeping potion hidden under the elf-shot, was almost beside the point. I knew she hadn't had a choice. That was one of the things Marianne had been very clear about, back when I'd been a child and she'd been teaching me about the kingdom that would one day be mine.

"The Luidaeg is the oldest of Maeve's daughters, first-born among Firstborn," she'd said, Nolan asleep with his head on her knee and me sitting on the floor in front of her, her hands moving through my hair, braiding and binding, tying elf-knots in every lock. I could barely remember my mother's face, but I would always remember Marianne's hands, and the sound of her voice by firelight, when she meant safety, when she meant home.

"She was born so long ago that time has no meaning; it's a name and a number, and it barely matters, because she was happy then, my sweet girl, she was at peace. She and her sisters kept to the fens, to the places where land met sea, and they kept their own counsel, and they made their own peace. But time will have its due. She buried both her sisters, and she saw her powers bound by her father's other wife, turned to the cause of service. She does what she's asked, and she dies a little more inside with every gift she grants. That's why she asks for voices and for peace and for the sound of a baby's laughter. She charges dear not out of cruelty, but as a plea to be left alone."

"But why?" I had asked. I'd been so young back then, and those times with Marianne had been my favorites: when she sat behind me and braided my hair, and I could close my eyes and pretend that if I turned around, we'd look alike. That I would change, or she would change—it didn't matter—and she'd be my mother, and it wouldn't be just me and Nolan anymore. "If she can do anything, shouldn't she want to?"

"If she had a choice in the matter, she might want to, but that was the beauty of the binding lain upon her by Oberon's Summer Queen," had been Marianne's reply. She'd tied off my braid, and finished her story with her hands resting on my shoulders. "Go to her and ask her the price of her tongue, her heart, her bed, and she's bound to tell you. Ask her what it would cost to have your throne back, and she'll draw you up a bill of sale. She is the answer to all our problems, if we're willing to force them upon her. She charges dear, so dear, because she's done so many things she'd never want to do. She'll do so many more before that binding is undone, if ever it is. The Summer Queen wove her workings well."

The night had been warm and her hands had been soft and I had gone to sleep not long after that, leaving her to carry me to bed, the way she'd carried my brother. Marianne had been a Coblynau, and strong enough to shift the world in its foundations if she needed it to move.

I missed her so much. I probably always would.

My head exploded in a kaleidoscope of pain as I stepped through the latest—and last—of the gates I'd opened since the sun went down. This was it: I'd hit my limits. I staggered, and Madden caught me, shooting a venomous glare at Cassandra and Walther. They had been the first ones through, in part because I was afraid the gate would close before we could all use it, and they were better suited to being stranded in mortal-side San Francisco in the middle of the night than I was. I didn't even carry a wallet anymore, much less a working BART card.

"Ardy?" he asked. "You okay?" It probably shouldn't have been a surprise that he'd insisted on joining us when I'd gone to tell him what we were doing. I was sort of sorry he had. I appreciated the company, but a gate for four was just that much harder than a gate for three.

"Dandy," I said, and forced myself to stand upright, grimacing as the motion set up a raucous clanging in my head. "Ow."

"Magic-burn?" asked Walther sympathetically. His hand dipped into his pocket, coming up with a small white bottle, which he offered to me. "Here. This will help."

"Alchemy?" I asked. I took the bottle without waiting for his answer. Magic-burn is the worst. I would have taken just about anything to make it stop.

"Close," he said. "Aspirin."

I laughed. Then I winced as the laughter made my head hurt worse. "Ow," I said again, and dry-swallowed two aspirin.

Through all of this, Madden was keeping himself busy with glaring at Walther and Cassandra. "I still don't understand why you're here," he said. "You could have stayed home. Safe. Let your vassals do this for you."

"Can't," I said, giving him what I hoped would be a reassuring pat on the arm. "She's going to charge for this. You know she's going to charge for this. They're my subjects, not my vassals—although we're going to be talking about permanent positions after all this is finished—and I can't ask subjects to pay in my place."

"I would," said Madden.

"I know you would," I said. I smiled at him, as

earnestly as the pain in my head would allow. "That's why you don't get to. You're my best friend. I need us to stay as close to equal as we possibly can, under the circumstances, and that means you don't throw yourself on any grenades for me. You're here to make sure I get home after whatever happens. They're here because Walther needs to get the countercharm, and Cassandra's helping him."

And because I might need a Seer to find the Luidaeg's house. She was rumored to live in this part of the city, where the gentrification ran headlong into the urban decay, forming a strange band that could go from absolutely modern to crumbling and antique in the space of a single block. I liked the older parts of the City, the ones that didn't feel like they were changing so damn *fast*, but this neighborhood had always unnerved me. It didn't feel slow. It felt frozen, like time was standing still in this little slice of dockside real estate.

I looked to Cassandra. She winced. "I'm not Google Maps," she said.

"You're the closest thing we've got," I said. "Tell me which way to go."

"How should I know?"

"Ask the air."

Cassandra took a deep breath, looking like she was going to argue. Then she sighed, tilted her head back, and looked at the empty, foggy air for a long moment. "That way," she said, jabbing a finger at the nearest alley. "We need to go that way."

"And if you're wrong?" asked Madden.

"I guess we find out when the muggers appear," snapped Cassandra.

Walther put a hand over his mouth to smother his laughter. I rolled my eyes.

"This is going to be a fun night," I said.

"This has already been a fun night," said Cassandra.

I couldn't argue with that. We started walking.

The sidewalks here were interesting. I found myself staring at them, trying to puzzle out what about them was so off. The sound of our footsteps was the only thing breaking the silence.

The *only* thing. No one was tripping, or stubbing their foot on cracked pavement, or walking on broken glass. I stopped and gave a crack an experimental kick. It was there—I could feel its edges—but somehow it didn't catch my foot. It was like the sidewalks had been enchanted to make them safer.

They probably had been. The sea witch lived here. I'd known since my days with Marianne that she wasn't evil, just compelled to do things she didn't want to do; I'd known since starting to deal with October that she was protecting my city and my subjects, in her own occasionally brutal way. Things had gotten pretty bad under the custodianship of the woman who'd stolen my father's throne. Without the Luidaeg, things would have gotten even worse.

It was a sobering thought. I started walking again, catching up with the others. Cassandra hesitated from time to time, gazing off into the distance before choosing our next turn. Either we were going to get to the Luidaeg, or we were going to be attacked by mortal muggers who thought we were a bunch of foolish club kids wandering too far from the bright lights of downtown. We all had our human disguises on, and we made a motley bunch: Walther in his professor's clothes, Cassandra the coed, Madden the barista, and me, Queen in the Mists, in my blue jeans and Borderlands Books hoodie, with my hair tucked behind my rounded human ears. If not for the fact that my brother was in trouble, it would have been almost relaxing. We were just out, walking, enjoying a beautiful night, not running a Kingdom. Not wearing a crown. We were people.

The scholars who like to have accurate notes about such things think Oleander de Merelands was the one who killed my parents; that she slit my mother's throat and did some terrible thing to my father, using the earthquake as cover. The people who care about "who" and "why" have lots of notes, and some of them have shown up at my Court, trying to show them to me. The people who want history to make sense don't seem to understand that it doesn't matter who killed him; what matters is he died, and he took us all with him to the grave. The person I am now is not who I would have been, had my father lived. The person my brother would be when he woke—and he was *going* to wake—was not the person he would have been, either. Every death is a massacre.

"Here," said Cassandra, coming to a stop. I blinked. Somehow, the street had disappeared; we had wandered down the sort of narrow alley that every one of my city dweller's instincts normally worked double-time to keep me out of. We were in front of a wooden door painted in faded, peeling blue, set back into an old brick wall, like the architect had wanted the occupant to be able to stand on the stoop and smoke without getting wet when it rained.

It wasn't a welcoming door. It wasn't a menacing door, either. There was nothing arcane or significant about it. It was just a door.

"Here?" I echoed.

Cassandra nodded. "That's what the air says. We need to be here." She looked at me expectantly. Walther and Madden did the same. All of them were waiting to see what I would do; all of them were following my lead.

Taking a deep breath, I stepped forward, and knocked.

The door was *actually* made of wood. That was nice. Given who we were dealing with, I'd half-expected my hand to thump against illusion-wrapped kelp, or something even less pleasant. I took a step back, folding my hands behind my back, and waited.

Seconds slithered by before the deadbolt clicked and the door swung open, revealing a girl who didn't look like she could be more than eighteen years old. Maybe nineteen, if I assumed her attire—denim overalls over a white tank top, bare feet, and pigtails secured with black electrical tape—was making her look younger than she was. Her hair was thick, black, and curly; her eyes were pale green, like beer bottles, and her cheeks were round and pitted with shallow acne scars. Nothing about her looked even remotely fae.

The slice of apartment visible through the open door was like something out of an episode of *Hoarders*. Garbage spilled around her feet, and I was pretty sure I saw mold growing on the walls. No one should have been living there. The place needed to be condemned.

She didn't say anything. She just stood there, looking at me for a long moment. Finally, she sighed.

"I guess I should have been expecting assholes tonight," she said. "It's been too long without them. Hello, Your Highness." She smiled, and there were too many teeth in that expression, all serrated like a shark's. Her mouth shouldn't have been able to contain that many teeth.

Cassandra stepped forward. "I'm Karen's sister, Cassie," she said. "Karen told me you were kind to her. I'm glad there was someone in a position to be kind to her. I wish it could have been me."

Oh, sweet Oberon, the girl's eyes—the *Luidaeg's* eyes, and I was standing in front of the sea-witch, like some sort of fool, like some sort of *hero*—moved to Cassandra, looking her up and down, taking her measure. Her smile faded, taking those terrible teeth with it.

"Your sister is a brave girl, and she'll need to be, in the days ahead," she said. "So will you. Now." She clapped her hands, returning her attention to me. "I'm assuming that when the Queen in the Mists shows up on my porch, it's because she wants something, not just because Cassandra wanted to show her appreciation for me taking care of Karen. Normally, I'd expect you to send Toby. Let her rack up all the debts for keeping your kingdom in

one piece. I guess that means whatever brought you here
is important. Tell me, little queen, are you here to pay?"

I took a deep breath. "Yes," I said.

"Good girl." This time, the Luidaeg's smile was nota-
bly devoid of teeth. "Come on in."

I stepped onto the porch. Madden moved to follow.
The Luidaeg raised her hand.

"Oh, no," she said. "I can see why you might think
that, but you'd be wrong. The three of you will wait outside. What comes next is between Arden and me." She
waved for me to enter the apartment.

I looked over my shoulder. Madden was shaking his
head. Walther was standing frozen. Cassandra, though . . .

Cassandra was looking at the air above me. As I
watched, she nodded, fractionally.

I'd trusted her this far. I stepped through.

EIGHT

The smell inside the Luidaeg's apartment was like the
Bay at low tide: brackish and terrible and rotten and *natural*, necessary, even. This was what happened when the
sea rushed out. It left all its scum and debris behind.

She closed the door before turning to look at me. "You
had to know what you were doing when you came here."

"I did," I admitted.

"So why?"

"Because my brother won't wake up."

The Luidaeg snorted. "Didn't we just have an entire
conclave about this? Your brother's been elf-shot. Wake
him up or don't wake him up; it's no concern of mine."

I damped down my growing irritation. This was the Luidaeg, and I didn't want to spend the next hundred years as a lawn gnome. "I used the cure on him. It cleared the elf-shot from his system. He fell asleep again almost immediately. Walther found a sleeping potion in his blood, something old, that doesn't have elf-shot's protections on it. He's going to die if we don't wake him."

Realization flashed across her features, followed by a slow neutrality. "And I brewed it."

"Yes."

"I remember a few potions like that. The people who asked for them paid dearly, but they paid. I had to give them what they wanted."

"Yes."

"I'm not going to give you the antidote just because you're pissed that I helped someone hurt your precious brother."

"I know."

"It's unreasonable of you to—wait, what?" The Luidaeg turned to look at me, cocking her head to the side. "What did you say?"

"I said, I know." I shrugged. "I know you didn't have a choice. You have to do what people ask for, as long as they pay you."

Her eyes seemed to darken, bottle green shifting toward pine. "You know, do you? How do you know?"

"You sold some charms to my nursemaid, to keep me and Nolan hidden from the people who would hurt us. She said . . . she said it was worth what she'd paid if it meant we stayed safe. And they worked. They worked for a long, long time, until October asked you to help her find us. It's sort of funny, really. You hid us, and then you found us, and you didn't do it because you wanted to either time." I forced myself to smile. My head was still throbbing, and every nerve felt like it was on fire. If I tried to open a gate, I'd probably dump myself into the

Bay, and that didn't change the part where I desperately wanted to try. I wanted to get out of here.

I wanted to save my brother. I had to stay.

The Luidaeg's eyes had continued to darken. "Your nursemaid," she said. "What was her name?"

"Marianne."

"Marianne." She said the name like it tasted of the finest wine in Faerie. "She used me to hide you. Your brother didn't stay within the wards, and someone else used me to hurt him. Faerie might do better if all the Firstborn were gone, don't you think?"

"You're the only one I've actually met," I said. I paused before adding, "No, wait, that's not true. Amandine's Firstborn, right? And Evening Winterrose. How many of you *are* there?"

"Don't ask that." There was steel in her voice. She took a step toward me. "Here's what's going to happen. You're going to tell me what you want—exactly what you want—and I'm going to tell you what it costs. You'll pay, or not, as you see fit. If you pay, you get what you asked for, and I let you leave here unharmed. If you refuse, you get nothing, and you may not find it that easy to get away from me."

I stiffened. "I'm Tuatha de Dannan."

"Yes, and you stink of burnt magic and overexertion. You couldn't teleport to the corner store right now. You're trapped with me until I let you go, and I'm not letting you go until you do what you came for. What do you want?"

"I want my brother awake." The words came easily. Relief followed. Until I'd been speaking, I hadn't been certain I'd be able to. "I want him to open his eyes and look at me. I want him back in the world, unharmed, unchanged, ready to be my brother again. I want him *back*."

"Is that all?" The Luidaeg raised an eyebrow. "No bone for your puppy? No three wishes and a new toaster?"

"Madden finds his own bones, and I have kitchen staff. I don't need a toaster."

"I see." The Luidaeg looked at me, assessing. Finally, she said, "Wait here," and vanished down the hall, leaving me alone in the mess.

No, not quite alone: a cockroach the length of my index finger strolled along the wall, antennae waving, apparently unbothered by the fact that I was standing less than four feet away. I wrinkled my nose, but didn't smash the disgusting thing. It could be the Luidaeg's familiar or something. I didn't want to come all this way only to incur her wrath over a bug.

The smell of love-lies-bleeding and kelp drifted in from the direction the Luidaeg had gone, notable mostly because it was so much fresher than the scum around me. The Luidaeg herself appeared a few moments later, a small vial in her left hand. Its contents were pearl gray and glowing like a fallen star. She held it up, showing it to me.

"Feed this to him and any sleeping potions will be cleansed from his body," she said. "He'll go back to sleep. He'll sleep for eight hours. He'll sleep *restfully*, and when he wakes, he'll be fine. Eighty years out of time, but fine. That's what you want."

"Yes, it is," I said. I started to reach for the vial, catching myself and pulling back at the last moment. "What does it cost?"

"Clever girl." She smiled, ever so slightly. "I know why you sent Toby to Silences. I know she touched you without permission. I know she did it because she was chasing you, trying to make sure you didn't abandon your post. And that's what I want from you. If you take this from my hand, you take your throne as well. You will not be able to step down or step aside without my permission, ever."

I bristled. "I'm not going to be your puppet."

"Did I ask for that? I didn't ask for that. I don't care how you rule. I care about this kingdom having some stability. I have shit to do, and some of it includes Toby being clear-headed and focused enough to listen when I call for her. So I need you to stay on your damn throne." The Luidaeg's smile grew. The teeth were back. "No stepping down. No stepping aside. You die in the saddle, or you get my permission to leave."

"What's to stop me from breaking my word?" That might have been a bad question to ask someone like her, but I needed to know.

"You won't be able to," she said. "If you try to say the words, your tongue will stop in your mouth. If you try to give your crown away, your fingers won't let go. You'll die before you step down without my consent. But you'll have your brother back, and I'll never ask you to do me any favors. Not unless you ask me for something first."

The vial in her hand continued glowing. If I took it, I could save Nolan, but I'd never be free; I'd be queen until I died, or until the Luidaeg didn't need October's full attention anymore. That could be centuries. No more exits, no more escapes. If I didn't take it . . . Walther was an excellent alchemist. He might be able to find a way to save my brother. The future wasn't set yet. I could still have my freedom and my family. It would be a risk. It would be a gamble. It wasn't an impossibility.

It was more than I could afford to risk. Still . . . "Is there any chance you'll give me permission in the future, when the region is stable, when I have a named heir standing ready?"

Her smile told me she understood what she was asking of me; there was mercy in her eyes, and a kindness that reminded me of Marianne's hands moving through my hair. "Ask me in a hundred years," she said.

I nodded once and took the vial. It was surprisingly heavy, like it was filled with liquid mercury. Her smile turned from sympathy to pleasure.

"Do we have a deal, Queen Windermere in the Mists?" she asked.

"We do," I said.

The air turned electric around us, making the hairs on my arms and the back of my neck stand on end. The charge only lasted for a few seconds. When it passed, my headache was gone and the vial in my hand was no longer glowing. I looked at the Luidaeg, eyes wide.

Her smile continued to blossom, becoming a grin. "You did something I wanted you to do, and you didn't whine nearly as much as I expected," she said. "I'm allowed to do favors. Now get the fuck out of my house, and if I see you before a hundred years have passed, I reserve the right to stab you in some nonfatal spot."

"Why nonfatal?"

"Because guaranteeing myself a stable monarchy only works if I don't go killing the monarchs." She pointed to the door. "Get out."

I got out.

Madden was right outside the door. Walther and Cassandra were a short distance away, standing close together. I wasn't sure Walther realized *how* close, or that he'd positioned himself to protect her from anything that might come bursting from the apartment. I swallowed a smirk. Cassandra would be pleased when she figured out how well he was picking up her signals.

"Ardy!" Madden rushed to meet me as the door slammed shut. "Are you okay?"

"Better than okay." I held up the vial. "We have our solution, and the Luidaeg threw in a fix for my magic-burn. We're going home."

I started to sweep my hand through the air, and stopped when Madden grabbed my wrist. I turned. He was staring at me, clear concern in his wolfish eyes.

"Ardy, what did you pay?" he asked, voice low.

I didn't have to think about it before I smiled at him, and said, "Only what I deserved."

He looked confused. But he let me go and took a step back, allowing me to open the gate that would return us to Muir Woods. The smell of blackberry flowers and redwoods washed over us, and we stepped through, all four of us, leaving the shadows of San Francisco behind.

NINE

It was past sunrise by the time Walther was done verifying that Nolan was stable and feeding him the potion from the Luidaeg, one slow sip at a time. Both Walther and Cassandra availed themselves of the hospitality of my house for a few hours, sleeping until midafternoon, when they woke, showered, and left, both of them riding on a yarrow branch that Walther produced from inside his jacket. I excused myself from Nolan's bedside long enough to wave farewell.

Cassandra hugged me before leaving, surprising us both, and whispered, "I'll be back," in my ear.

I was still smiling about that when I returned to the room where my brother slept and sat down next to the bed. I had a book. The kingdom could get by without its queen for a few more hours. After all, it was never going to lose me again. Not for at least a hundred years.

Time passed, seconds blending into minutes into hours. Nolan stirred. I looked up from the page, trying not to let myself hope, trying not to let myself *want*.

His eyes were open. He was looking at me, confusion writ large across his features.

"What in the world," he asked, "have you done to your *hair*?"

I dropped the book as I fell upon him, laughing and crying in the same breath, and I gathered my brother in my arms, and we were finally, finally home.